I0635151

VIDEO GAME PLOTLINE TESTER

a novel
by Michael Atamanov

Wishing you safe travels on your fantasy journey,

Michael Atamanov

Dark herbalist
Book One

Magic Dome Books

Video Game Plotline Tester
Dark Herbalist, Book 1
Copyright © Michael Atamanov 2017
Cover Art © Vladimir Manyukhin 2017
English Translation Copyright ©
Andrew Schmitt 2017
Published by Magic Dome Books, 2017
All Rights Reserved
ISBN: 978-80-88231-20-2

All books by Michael Atamanov:

The Dark Herbalist LitRPG series
Video Game Plotline Tester
Stay on the Wing
A Trap for the Potentate
Finding a Body

Reality Benders LitRPG series
Countdown
External Threat
Game Changer
Web of Worlds
A Jump into the Unknown
Aces High

Perimeter Defense LitRPG series
Sector Eight
Beyond Death
New Contract
A Game with No Rules

League of Losers LitRPG Series
A Cat and His Human

You're in Game!
(LitRPG Stories from Bestselling Authors)

You're in Game-2!
(More LitRPG stories set in your favorite worlds)

Table of Contents:

"HAVE YOU EVER played *Boundless Realm* before?" the middle-aged HR employee asked me, starting off the interview with the question I was most dreading.

In the job posting, there had been a rather unambiguous requirement that I must have: "Never played the game before." I suspect that, if I had answered "yes," the interview would have ended as quickly as it had begun.

"And have you played any other popular online games, uh... Timothy?" he asked, having finally read my name from the screen in front of him. He was at the end of a long day. He must have been tired.

"Yes, of course. I've been a gamer for about six years now. I used to be pretty active in *Kingdoms of Sword and Magic*."

"Gamer..." he muttered back disdainfully.

The slang term, it seemed, was not to his taste. The man furrowed his brow in dismay. "And how did you do in our competitor's game? Were you able to achieve anything noteworthy, Timothy?"

Should I tell him the truth? Or was it dumb to expose such things to this total stranger? Despite my misgivings, I decided to risk it:

"For the last five years, it has been my only source of income. I didn't earn enough for a luxury yacht or a villa on a tropical island or anything, of course, but it was more than enough to survive on and pay my way through college."

"Why do you say, 'of course' there was no yacht?" He inquired. Much to my surprise, the man began laughing. "The top players from *Boundless Realm* easily make enough for a simple ocean-going vessel. But as far as I know, in *KSM*, withdrawing game money was against the rules. Would you care to tell me more about that, Timothy?"

I guess I chose wrong. I shouldn't have said anything. Was this the end? Would I be sent on my way? The man didn't insist on an answer, though. Instead, he asked a different question entirely:

"Then why did you leave *KSM?* Although, I guess we can skip that. The answer is obvious. The number of active players has been falling sharply. More and more people have been changing over to *Boundless Realm*. It's more entertaining and realistic, after all. The money must have simply dried up."

I just nodded in silence, as I really didn't have anything to add. Once upon a time, our clan could gather five or even seven thousand players for PvP raids into enemy territory or to take down superbosses. But those times were long gone now. Yesterday, we had barely been able to scrape together fifteen players for an assault on an enemy castle, and three of them were noobs who'd only been in the game for a week. And yet we... took the castle! The only defender from the enemy clan who remained actually seemed glad to be rid of the burden, wishing us the best of luck, and trying to unload his account onto us, as he was preparing to leave for *Boundless Realm.*

That was when I decided once and for all that the time had come to ditch that sinking ship before the competition put it on the bottom of the sea. It was a huge shame to see all the money I'd put into the game go down the drain, though. You see, I inherited the family apartment after the tragic death of my parents but I had to sell it to pay off my sister's medical bills. There was a decent chunk of change left over from that, though, and I decided to invest it in virtual property near one of *Kingdom*'s capital cities. At that time, *Kingdoms of Sword and Magic* was growing quickly, so the purchase had seemed a sound investment.

Who could have foreseen that, literally two

weeks after my risky acquisition, the previously unknown *Boundless Realm* corporation would launch their own game servers? And could anyone have predicted that they would then go on to become the largest and richest corporation on Earth in just three years, pulling hundreds of millions of gamers from all over the globe into their extremely realistic world? Now, the value of my virtual property in *Kingdoms* had fallen so severely that it couldn't even justify the time I had put into building it.

The HR employee spent a few minutes reading my resume more closely, then raised his eyes to me and said with a smile:

"A level-three-hundred-ten human paladin, a level-two-hundred-seventy drow bowman, a level-one-hundred-ninety half-elf mage... Not bad, not bad at all. So Timothy, have you been made aware that, in *Boundless Realm*, a player can only have one character, and changing or deleting it is not possible? It's the best way to make sure our players truly mesh and sympathize with their characters as we would like. Only then do they perceive the game world as true reality."

I just nodded in silence. How could I not have known...? That was the thing that had most worried me when I first saw an advertisement for *Boundless Realm* game tester positions online. The problem was that I *had* already tried to play *Boundless Realm*. That was over three years ago, though. At that time, it was still just an open beta, and it had seemed a bit "undercooked" for my tastes. There weren't any training scenarios, guides or in-game hints yet. In the place I started, everything just looked blocky and incomplete. There were no "glorious beckoning horizons," or "enchantingly real sunsets," as their ads now proclaimed. Back then, *Boundless Realm* had nothing of the sort.

And what was more, I had only played for seven minutes. I made myself a level-one barbarian, took a two-handed ax, left the starting area and, right next to the village, found myself face-to-face with a group of vampire bats around level-seventy. A second later, I was dead. The game told me I'd have to wait a whole hour to come back at the respawn point, so I just cursed at the half-baked imbalanced game and deleted it from my computer. But now, I was hoping very much that my abortive previous experience would not be hampering my attempt to find work as a "Video Game Plotline Tester," as the official job notice called the position I was now interviewing for.

"What can I say, Timothy? You really do have a lot of video-game experience, and no physical or mental health issues. I don't see any real obstacles to your employment with our corporation," said the man, smiling at me again and extending a computer tablet with a survey. He told me to find a seat in the small room next door and complete the questionnaire, then wait for the introductory meeting to begin.

I went into the room, got out my cell phone and, pretending to take a selfie with a sleek poster of a blue water dragon, sent a message:

"I passed the interview."

Almost instantly, my phone gave a slight vibration. It was the reply:

"No rush, but what did they offer? I'll run through the forums."

Then, I found a chair and started ticking boxes on the tablet. The survey covered many questions about my health, family life, criminal history and bad habits. The second half of the survey turned out to be of a totally different type, clearly aimed at determining the game character best suited to my personality.

Next to me, there were other job seekers mashing away at their tablets. Most of the men and women were around my age, though some were older, even including a few senior citizens. It didn't take me long to form an impression of my future work environment. I saw students, who had been expelled for truancy or failing grades, down-sized office workers, down-on-their-luck stock brokers, hopeless gaming addicts, and desperate retirees who hadn't managed to find more suitable employment... To generalize, the people sitting around me were losers, who hadn't found themselves a place in the real world.

I didn't consider myself a loser, but I could agree that I fit into the group very organically. I was already twenty-two years old, but I didn't have a job, a girlfriend, money, or even a place of my own. So, it wasn't really clear what separated me from them. I had a good head on my shoulders, I suppose. I graduated from college with a degree in Research Chemistry. I could hold down a conversation, wasn't especially ugly and had a reasonable talent for sports. Also, I had an easy enough time getting along with women but, for some reason, all my girlfriends had left me for other guys. Usually, when they found out I had to take care of my disabled sister, who couldn't walk, they would run for the hills. It was a shame, but I would never have agreed to trade in my baby sister for some shallow Barbie.

My sister, Valeria, was eleven at the time of the accident. My father was behind the wheel of the family flying car when it crashed full-speed into a thief trying to evade the police. The impact and resulting thirty-meter fall killed my mother and father instantly. My younger sister, though, lost both her legs and suffered many lacerations and broken bones. The police finding my father not at fault in the crash didn't make it any easier, either. I had to sell our apartment in the good part of town to pay for Val's treatment and other expenses.

For my sister's sake, I became her parent,

her friend, her shrink and replaced the whole world for her. It was hardest of all right after the accident. Valeria was in so much constant pain that she couldn't see a reason to exist. Many times, she asked me to give her a handful of sleeping pills so she would never have to wake up again. I did my best to comfort my sister and convince her not to commit suicide and, day by day, her will to live grew stronger. We tried many things to improve her mood, but the first thing that worked was taking walks. We used to live near a large park, and it was always pleasant there. Unfortunately, not long after that, we were forced to move from the center of the metropolis due to lack of funds, and took up residence in the outskirts of town. Soon after, the walks stopped on Val's own request. My sister just couldn't bear the jokes and laughter of the neighborhood kids. They called her a cripple, and even pelted her with rocks. It was just too much.

But then, she found a new way to forget about her physical handicap. Virtual computer-game worlds allowed her to blow off steam and enjoy beautiful surroundings once again. This new pastime didn't really bring us much money, though. In fact, it was more the other way around. The situation became especially dismal in the last few months, when the game world she'd chosen a few years earlier, *Kingdoms of Sword and Magic*, began to show obvious signs of giving out...

I shook my head, chasing away the sad thoughts, and returned to the survey. After breezing through the questions, I stopped at the very last point: "Desired method of payment." There were two options: fixed monthly income or the ability to withdraw game currency and exchange it for real money. In *Boundless Realm*, as in the majority of MMO's, it was normally only allowed to give money to the company. You could put real money into the game, but there was no way of taking it back out. An exception was made only for employees of the corporation. They were allowed to withdraw virtual currency from the game in lieu of a real salary, if they so chose.

As for me, that possibility was the very reason I was now so driven to find work at the *Boundless Realm* corporation. I mean, it was clear that no sane company would ever offer a stable salary to any of the pitiful losers in the room with me today. But with a legal method of turning game money into real money... There was no telling what could happen. My character could get rich in the game, for example. And that would immediately solve my financial problems in real life as well. That said, my sister and I had a perfect understanding that for every person that got lucky, there were thousands of people who made the wrong choice and would just be pouring their blood, sweat and tears into a job that would almost certainly end up giving them less than minimum wage. But we had made our choice, and it was a conscious, shared decision.

The chubby middle-aged accountant-type woman sitting next to me gave me a nudge. She got to a question about "charisma," and was whispering loudly to everyone around, asking what that word even meant. I couldn't make out what the guy sitting on the other side of her said, but he was clearly trying his best to maintain a serious facial expression. The woman grew a dark shade of crimson and began entering text on her tablet at the speed of a printer, covering what she wrote with her left hand. I shook my head. Well, if this was the caliber of my competition... I marked the option "Withdraw game currency" with determination.

Alright, decision made. There was no going back now. All the same, I tried to cast off the creeping sensation of dread coming from my empty bank account. And it wasn't just that I had no money. I also had a past-due loan with interest slowly accumulating on top of it. If I couldn't pay off at least part of that loan in the next few weeks, the bank might block my card. Beyond that, my sister and I hadn't paid rent for three months. Our landlady was already threatening to evict us. It would be very, very hard to get by without a stable salary.

But I still decided to take the risk, just as I had when buying in-game property in *Kingdoms of*

Sword and Magic. But this time, I wasn't just betting a two-bedroom apartment in a prestigious neighborhood, but everything my sister and I had left.

* * *

"Alright, everybody. Welcome!" An elegantly dressed swarthy man with dark curly hair walked out onto the small stage. "My name is Alexandro Lavrius. I am Director of Special Projects for the *Boundless Realm* corporation. And you all have been selected to work under me as videogame plotline testers. What's wrong with the microphone?"

The microphone was giving off a horrible screeching sound, making my ears ring. The director's young assistant, looking afraid, scurried nimbly out onto the stage, and adjusted the microphone attached to Alexandro's collar. The director cast a very unhappy gaze at his subordinate, promising the girl a chewing out, and continued:

"Alright, now that's out of the way. So then, first a short introduction. The virtual *Boundless Realm* you will come to occupy is in fact quite large. It's not actually boundless, as you might think from the name but, still, it is quite substantial in size. It is already larger than the actual earth, so you can travel around discovering new and interesting locations in a practically limitless way. At present, there are around two hundred forty million players in *Boundless Realm*, and that number continues to grow by two to three million each month. You'd think our corporation would be proud of that, and simply rest on our laurels and rake in the cash. But, no. Our management is constantly dreaming up newer and more grandiose plans, and the development of the game is still in full swing. However, the planning department saw certain risks in the medium-term future and our directors agreed the threat was real.

We see two main problems. The first is that, despite the abundance of different races in *Boundless Realm*, and their unique characteristics, seventy-eight percent of players choose to play as humans. That is a clear imbalance. And, if we consider the fact that another seventeen percent play as different types of elves and half-elves, while three percent are dwarves, then we see straight to the root of the problem. Those who chose one of the other selectable races, and there are over one hundred, account for just two percent of players.

The reasons for this disparity are many. Not least of all is that potential new players have practically no positive examples of gamers using the less popular races. And this is at the fact that the game forums are full of the most detailed guides on human paladins, wood-elf bowmen, drow mages and half-elf assassins. There's nothing surprising in the fact that new players are afraid to take an untested path. Since they can only have one character, they don't want to take any chances. The unfortunate result of this is that new players tend to create human paladins, elf bowmen or drow necromancers, and our world is already overflowing with them. Our existing users are justifiably losing their sense of uniqueness and interest in the game because, every day, they meet several exact copies of themselves.

The second problem is choosing a place to live. Before our players, there stretches out a truly *Boundless Realm*, which can be expanded even further whenever necessary. All the same, the currently existing map is hardly being used: ninety percent of players live in one of just a few huge megalopolises or in their immediate vicinity. The reasons for such overcrowding are also many, but above all, they are economic in nature. Resources are available in cities, money circulates in cities, and there are banks where players can safely store their property in cities. That is why, despite the high price of real estate and resources there, players still come in droves to live in these very cities. Millions of beautiful locations, created by talented designers and teeming with unique missions and local inhabitants are sitting around unused. And what is more, we are becoming aware of a growing dismay among players, who feel that 'there's nothing new to discover and it's starting to get boring.'

Why am I telling you all this? As you may have already guessed, none of you will be allowed to choose human or elf characters, and none of you will be becoming yet another knight or bowman. What's more, you will start the game in far-off wildernesses, and getting to densely populated locations from there will be very, very problematic. Also, such a move would be looked on with extreme disapproval by our company. You will all have an alternative start to the game, which will make encountering dangers and difficulties a near certainty, and that is no accident. Our test groups have shown that successfully overcoming trying situations is the very anchor that holds our players in the game world. With time, we hope that all newbies will start in such locations, so one of your missions will be checking if it is possible to survive and level up your character in these challenging conditions.

Your group is one of many chosen in the previous weeks to attempt new atypical race and class combinations, taking bumps and bruises along the way. But at that, you will make interesting guides that eloquently describe the virtues of your unusual races, classes and professions. I warn you now: few of you will pass the trial period and be hired on permanently, as our corporation only needs the personalities and stories that garner a keen response among existing and potential players. But, even if you don't pass the trial period, this will give you all invaluable experience in the video-game field, and be an excellent opportunity to immerse all your senses in *Boundless Realm* through the most modern technologies.

Now, you will be given your assigned character cards, which the system automatically chose for you based on today's test results. After that, you will have time to ask questions of my assistant. Then, you should go to the HR department before the end of the business day and sign your contracts, so you can start working tomorrow."

"Can we start playing today?" asked a chubby boy, whose pale face was abundantly smattered with the pimples of adolescence.

Alexandro Lavrius, looked over us at the clock on the wall, then quietly asked something to his young assistant, after which he answered:

"You can only start working after you've signed a contract. Also, don't forget that it is currently around four in the afternoon in *Boundless Realm*, and it gets dark at nine. After this meeting, you'll be going to the HR department, shown to your workstation and given instructions on how to use the virtual-reality capsule. You'll then have to create a character, start the training missions and get out into the main world... You won't have very much time to find a safe place to spend the night. Night in *Boundless Realm*, outside the cities and other safe locations, is very brutal and treacherous. It is highly likely that you will be eaten by monsters. If that does happen, you would lose some of the experience you gained and a whole hour for respawn. But, if you want to risk it and start work today, I don't see why not. If you can survive the first night, it will be a useful experience for you and will have a positive effect on your further career as a tester."

* * *

Goblin herbalist??? I stared at the card handed to me in incomprehension. I even took out my smartphone to look up information on goblins in *Boundless Realm*. The first link rewarded me with the following text, taken from a forum:

"Goblins are vile little bastards who play mean tricks, steal vegetables from gardens, and attack lone travelers. Thankfully, goblins are very weak, so even a total noob can handle them. Sometimes, you find whole villages of goblins. They're decent sources of experience, and an easy way for beginners to level themselves up. I don't know why, but the developers made this NPC race

available to players. I would personally find it hard to imagine someone dumb enough to choose this green abomination, especially considering the very restrictive penalties to intelligence and strength, which make it practically impossible for a goblin to be a decent mage or fighting class. From a purely theoretical standpoint, I could imagine a goblin player as a bowman or a crossbowman due to their bonuses to agility and perception, but I've never met someone disturbed enough to try, because all the kinds of elves have even stronger bonuses there. Oh yeah, these green freaks also have a serious penalty to relation with humans, so goblins won't be able to go to normal game locations by default."

Given that anyone about to create a character would see this text, if they were considering playing a goblin, how could the developers of *Boundless Realm* be surprised that no one wanted to be one?!

The person who wrote the text was called Overgrown Woodsman. According to his forum account, he played a level two-hundred-four human druid. For curiosity's sake, I read through the next seven links from the search engine as well, but everywhere I looked, I found the same unappealing information. I sent my sister a message about the character I'd been stuck with, and continued looking intensely into guides on goblins and Herbalism.

I was distracted from my reading by a

strange sound nearby. I raised my head. The director was long gone, and now the very same old accountant-looking lady who had earlier asked about charisma was arguing with his assistant.

"Is something the matter with your assigned character?" the employee asked in a calm, even boring tone.

"Is something the matter?! The fact that I'm a dryad dancer! I saw on the game forums that dryads don't wear clothes! I mean, just think about! I thought I was applying for an office job. I mean, I knew the schedule might be a bit wonky, but I didn't think I'd be working as a stripper!"

The director's assistant was already on edge after the incident with the microphone, so some annoyance started slipping through in her voice:

"The system determined that this combination of race and class would be optimal for you. If it isn't to your liking, I'm afraid I have to tell you that you did not pass the trial period and will be first to leave the group..."

I noticed a mocking grin pass over the face of the boy who had earlier told her the meaning of charisma. The system had probably made this bizarre choice because of his misleading hint. The assistant outstretched her hand demandingly, preparing to take the character card back from the lady's hand but, just then, a young woman's voice sounded out from the back rows:

"Wait! Could I trade characters with her?" A

pretty girl with a good figure and hair in a long dark chestnut braid down to her belt stood from her place and started toward the stage. "I took a look at the introductory information on dryads. Sure, their only equipment slots are for rings and bracelets, but all that is compensated by their racial bonuses. Also, the dancer class seems uniquely suited for dryads. *They have bonuses to* attractiveness, charm, and the reaction of any member of the opposite sex, after all."

The director's assistant agreed:

"That's exactly right. It's a good part to play, and an easy character to gain experience with. Also, the path of a dryad dancer is very unusual. There isn't a single guide out there, and leveling up a character like that successfully practically guarantees that you would pass the trial period."

The accountant-type woman cringed and muttered in dismay:

"Let's just see what kind of filth they tried to push on you... It could hardly be worse than an exotic dancer." She took the thick card from the girl's hand and read. "Oh! Yes! Yes! Gremlin banker! I've been dreaming of something like this my whole life!"

The middle-aged woman practically kissed the pretty girl she traded cards with. After that, I heard people all around me shouting:

"Would someone want to trade for a troll cannibal?"

"I'll trade a hobgoblin trickster for any other class!"

"Does anyone want an orc astrologer? I'll trade for any melee character!"

Not waiting for the end of the freak show, I stood up and headed for the HR department. Goblin herbalist didn't seem so bad anymore. I was totally fine with my lot.

* * *

Though I tried not to show my emotions, I was under a strong impression from the opulence and luxury the corporation had on display. The *Boundless Realm* corporation had a huge skyscraper, which seemed to have many underground floors as well. As the elevator went down, I noticed a few floors there was no button for on the panel. But, through the transparent glass elevator doors, I could see them. They were filled with well-equipped armed guards wearing body armor and gas masks. Arthur, the kindly technician leading me to my workstation, explained that these underground floors were off limits to us mere mortals. They housed the corporation's holiest of holies: the game servers. And it was harder to gain access to them than it was to get into a bank vault full of gold. These technical floors were crammed with an endless number of security systems and filled with poison gas to make sure no criminals would even think of trying to get inside.

After that, without stopping, we passed by the underground parking ramp. It was crammed full of luxury automobiles and flying cars. The elevator doors opened on the testing department's floor, and I saw IT: a huge room that stretched out to infinity with a great many high, raised walkways, lined with rows of small identical-looking cabins. Arthur and I walked down one of the long platforms and stopped before a translucent door. I stared blankly at the writing on it: "4-16A."

"Floor four, side A, cabin sixteen. This is where you'll be working. Go in, get your bearings and take off your jacket," he said, pointing me inside to a chair and a coat hanger on the wall, but not going inside himself. "Every cabin has a pullout desk and a built-in refrigerator, so you will be able to store food here and have snacks before work. There is one set of restrooms every fifty cabins, and at either end of the walkway, there are also shower rooms. But you should know that every row has three hundred cabins, so don't count on the showers being free, especially in the evening near the end of a shift. Alright then, I wish you the best of luck!"

As Arthur said the last sentence, his eyes were drawn away from me by a beautiful and I would even say glamorous lady with luxuriant red hair and a proud look who walked past my cabin. She was wearing a long, emerald green dress and high-heeled shoes, and a hat with a wide brim. Her fingers were adorned with gemstone rings, which glimmered up at me, catching the eye. The woman didn't stop to look at Arthur. It seemed she didn't even notice me. She walked another fifteen meters, then stopped before a standard door, just the same as mine. She beeped in with her electronic key, and the mystery girl ducked into her cabin.

"Who was that?" I asked the stick-straight technician at half voice.

Arthur jerked back to reality with a shudder.

"Who is she? How am I supposed to know? She works here. She comes around in the evening, and only leaves in the morning. She must play a night character. Clearly, she is a good player and makes good money. Once, I saw her parking in the underground garage. She drives a luxury sports car, which is so nice I'd never be able to afford it, even if I saved up for the rest of my life. But I have no idea who she is in the game. We cannot see your game avatars, we just help you set up the equipment. Generally, though, elite players get their own offices on the upper floors of the building, but she must prefer the convenience of coming right down here from the parking lot. Alright then, I'm getting off track. Get undressed, I'll size you for a sensor suit and helmet."

Just after the door closed behind Arthur, I got out my phone and told my sister I was ready.

"Call up the console and tell me the number of your virtual reality capsule and game session. I'll try to link in."

I typed a technical command into the keyboard and took a picture of it on my phone camera.

"Wait five minutes, so we can start at the same time."

I put on the suit, which was bristling with electrodes and laid down in the virtual reality capsule. Looking at the timer on the small monitor, I waited five minutes, then closed the lid of the virtual reality capsule, cutting myself off from the real world. The screen lit up before my eyes...

❋ ❋ ❋

Damage taken: 2757 (Bite from Cursed Bat)
You have died

❋ ❋ ❋

What the hell was that?! The message jumped in as soon as the screen loaded! The image slowly faded out and I found myself enshrouded in darkness. One minute went by, then another, and maybe a few more. Nothing was happening. Was this it then? There was no game interface, nor any other menu windows, just pitch black all around. Something must have gone wrong. Bats! That was right! They were the last thing I saw in my short game as a barbarian. That meant I would now be dragged from my capsule and fired for lying in the interview.

The world around me suddenly lit back up, and the character-creation window came onscreen. Yikes, I made it by the skin of my teeth. So, what was I seeing? A level-one goblin herbalist. I couldn't change race or class.

Character name: Amra.

Here I was again overcome by a cold sweat. When I made the barbarian, my first move had been to try and give him the name "Conan," in honor of the famous television barbarian, but it was taken. Then, I checked another name used by the famous hero, "Amra," and it was free. As far as I knew, the game rules had changed over the past three years and, now, all characters had to have two-word names: "Tony Blackheart," "Ahmed Slinking_Snake," "Ellie Very_Pretty." Things like that. But my name was only one word, and what was more, it was only four letters long...

A noob with one-word name? I guess it could help me hide the fact I worked for the company. I wasn't opposed in principle, either. It was nice to be a bit unique. Now, the time had come to deal with my appearance and stats.

I saw a green face staring back at me. It was defined by a huge set of eyes, and ears of a magnificent dimension. The system suggested I play around with the settings and turn this standard-issue goblin into something more personalized and suited to my taste, but I decided not to do that yet. A hint told me that I would be able to change my character's appearance for free all the way up to the end of level ten, so I decided I could skip this for now. I was much more worried by something else: Alexandro Lavrius had said that there wasn't much time left until nightfall, so I didn't have a second to waste.

First and foremost, I wanted to see the bonuses and penalties for the goblin race. Unfortunately, Overgrown Woodsman hadn't been lying about the penalties:

> *50% penalty to Intelligence increase rate*
> *50% penalty to Strength increase rate*
> *-20 penalty to relations with the following races: Humans, Elves, Dwarves, Gnomes, Dragons*
> *20% penalty to experience gain*

The penalties were a very hard pill to swallow. I was especially unhappy with the penalty to experience gain. The negative characteristics of the goblin race were hardly compensated by the bonuses, either:

30% bonus to Agility increase rate
30% bonus to Perception increase rate
+20 bonus to relations with the following races: Goblins, Orcs, Kobolds, Ogres, Giants
+30 bonus to the reaction of forest and swamp creatures
30% bonus to movement speed in forest and swamp tiles

Finally, I reached the main stats of my big-eared goblin. Every character in *Boundless Realm*, whether an NPC or a real person, had only six main statistics: Strength, Agility, Intelligence, Constitution, Perception and Charisma. Overall, it was very standard and easy to understand. Strength governed the damage you could do with hand-held weapons and the maximum weight you could carry. Agility was important for ranged weapons and dodging. Intelligence allowed you to understand the properties of objects, and defined the amount of mana a magical character had, as well as how effective their spells were. Constitution influenced the number of hitpoints and endurance points. And perception was for a character's eyesight, smell and sense of hearing, and also gave it a higher chance of discovering hidden objects. And finally, charisma: a stat that determined how those around your character would relate to it.

There were several ways to raise the base stats: you got to assign a certain number of new stat points every level, you could raise stats by leveling up primary skills, or you could raise them with magical objects.

Name	Amra
Race	Goblin
Class	Herbalist
Experience	0 of 100
Character level	1
Hitpoints	15/15
Endurance points	15/15
Statistics	
Strength (S)	2
Agility (A)	2
Intelligence (I)	2
Constitution (C)	2
Perception (P)	2
Charisma (Ch)	2
Unused points	3
Primary skills (2 of 4 chosen)	
Herbalism (P A)	1
Trading (Ch I)	1
Secondary skills (0 of 4 chosen)	

~ Video Game Plotline Tester ~

The developers had assigned my character two primary skills by default: Herbalism and Trading. And though I didn't have any questions on the first one (it was, of course, hard to imagine an herbalist who didn't have a good understanding of herbs), Trading was somewhat confusing. I couldn't delete Trading from my skills. Based on that, the developers had the notion that I was supposed to be a dainty little goblin trouncing through the forest collecting bunches of plants and selling them to local traders. So, I needed the Trading skill to make sure unscrupulous hucksters weren't taking me for a ride. My character's intelligence was about that of a stool, so if I didn't have a specific skill for negotiating, I'd be getting duped out of money constantly. I was also a bit confused by the letters in parenthesis next to the skill names, but I quickly realized that they were the statistics the character gradually built up by using it.

Three free stat points didn't seem like much! After playing around a bit with the parameters, and reading their descriptions, I discovered that hitpoints and endurance points depended only on constitution. Alright, I'd put one of the free points into that. My total hitpoints grew to 21, while endurance grew to 20.

Next, I stopped on agility. Based on the guide from Overgrown Woodsman, and what I could figure from my racial bonuses, it was agility precisely that would be the main determinant of my big-eared character's success. I put two points there, bringing it up to four. That seemed to be all. Although... At the very last moment, just before I started playing, I decided I couldn't bear how low my goblin's intelligence was. In the description of the stat, it was directly stated that an intelligence score lower than three would hamper my ability to speak properly or understand others. That meant, as it was, I wouldn't be able to talk to other players and NPC's nor understand missions and hints. I lowered charisma to the minimum (he already wasn't a beauty, but he became a downright monstrosity) and moved that point over to intelligence.

Now I really was done. Time to get going!

Orcish Galley

FEAR. COLD. PAIN. HUNGER. My beaten body ached and tingled. Through the pain and fatigue, I could also make out some loud noises. What I wanted to do was just ignore them and lose myself further in a soothing dream, but the sounds kept growing louder and louder. I could hear weapons clanging, cries of rage and the screams of the dying. My nostrils caught the smell of freshly spilled blood. I strained to peel back my eyelids and discovered myself lying on the rotten-straw-covered floor of a dark room. I tried to move and discovered that my left wrist was firmly secured in a heavy metal cuff, which was attached to a chain that led to a brace hammered into the wall. So, I was a prisoner?

At the edge of my vision, I saw a tall orc dressed in leather armor run by with a crooked saber. Then, literally a couple seconds later, I saw his bloodied body fall to the ground. The orc's killer, who turned out to be a huge armored human, walked up to the body on the floor and prudently finished the orc off, driving a short spear into his chest.

"Seems to be the last of them!" he shouted out to someone far behind and was answered in a creaky voice:

"Great! Free the prisoners and bring them out to our ship! This orcish galley will soon break on the cliffs!"

Now I was going to be freed! I didn't even have time to feel relieved by that, though, before the huge soldier turned to look at me, made a disgusted face and drove his spear right through me!

* * *

Darkness came over again. I was lying there fully dumbfounded and could not believe what had happened. That man had killed me, or at least seriously wounded me, even though he was clearly supposed to save me! Why?

An internal voice laughed and hinted mockingly that I should have been expecting this.

The goblin race already had a -20 penalty to human reaction, and I had completely stripped myself of charisma. So now, that was how every human, elf or dwarf I met would react.

The pain returned and I opened my eyes. I saw the world in dark and red tones. As before, I was lying on old putrid hay, but now that hay was also soaked with thick dark blood. My blood.

+1 HP from Regeneration

The spear wound to my stomach had almost totally healed, but my health bar was flashing alarmingly at 3 of 21. And it should be said that I didn't even know goblins *could* regenerate health. Why did none of the guides say anything about that? Perhaps regeneration had been put in recently to make the race more playable. In any case... the wound to my stomach hurt like hell! No matter what, I had to admit that dying was extremely unpleasant, even in a computer game.

I'm not sure what I would have thought up next, or what I might have done, because a rat suddenly scurried under the wooden bars of my cell.

Level-1 Rat

The little creature was following its nose inquisitively, bewitched by the intoxicating aroma of blood. I moved slightly, pulling my right leg in a bit. The rat instantly turned toward me, but didn't run away. Instead, it started looking at me. And what was more, it clearly had an ever-growing interest in my culinary properties. Probably, if I were in perfect health, killing such a creature would have been no problem. But now, I had just three pitiful hitpoints... It was gonna eat me right up!

Clearly, the creature also came to that conclusion and headed in my direction. What happened next, neither I nor the rat were expecting:

Damage dealt: 10 (Vampire Bite)
Health restored: +5 HP

Experience received: 8 Exp.
Object received: Rat meat (food)

Achievement unlocked: Taste Tester (1/1000)
Racial ability unlocked: Taste for Blood (Gives +1% to all damage dealt for each unique creature killed with Vampire Bite. Current bonus: 1%)

Parameter Unlocked: Quenching the Thirst (10/ 15)

I sat for a few long seconds, taking in the vile flavor of rat blood and digesting what had just happened in all senses of the word. Did this mean I was a vampire? I opened my character window to check, and it left me with no doubt on the matter:

Race: Goblin Vampire

Fortunately, the second part of my race could be hidden simply by placing a check in a special field reading "Hide from other players." I read the description of the vampire race, and thanked the heavens and developers of the game that I could hide it:

-50 penalty to reaction of all living races if revealed
Penalty: Legal target for murder by players and NPC's of living races if revealed
Penalty: Cannot hide true nature when in the state Thirst for Blood
Penalty: Instant death when hit by sunlight

This put me in quite the pickle... From this moment on, my biggest priority would be keeping this a secret. It did come with some advantages, though, too. At level one, for example, a vampire could get +1 HP Regeneration per minute and an additional type of attack (and unlike most, it was neither right nor left handed):

Vampire Bite
Cost: 10 EP (endurance points)
Damage: (1-6) * Strength
Attacker's health restored by 50% of damage done

When attacking sleeping, unconscious, or paralyzed targets, chance of success is 100%, and attacker may choose an effect: (Instant death/6-hour deep sleep/Infect with Vampirism)

I read the description of the attack again. So, this meant I could kill any creature, no matter the level? All I had to do was find it asleep, and even level-100 characters were done for. What a great source of experience for leveling myself up! And I could do it to players just as well as to NPC's... Hold up! I rebuffed myself. If I even once used this ability against a player, my secret would be revealed. I would be hounded for the rest of my days in the game, and killed over and over, just because the rules allowed it. And every time I died, it would hurt me physically, and I would lose experience. So then, I had to be sure to keep the secret of my vampirism.

"Who's there? I can hear you!" came a voice from outside my cell, bringing my fears to life.

I jumped up in surprise and quickly wiped my lips with the back of my hand. The last thing I needed was for this stranger to see blood on my face.

"Rat I beating. He attack. Smack-smack I beat," I answered.

What the hell?! That wasn't what I said, but the only thing that would come out of my character's mouth were these awkward broken phrases. It turned out that even three intelligence points was not enough, after all. I shuddered to think how my character would be talking if the number had been lower.

"Rat? Yes, I saw it. It looked at me for a long time, but it ran away. Have you figured out how to get your arm out of the chain yet? I'm not strong enough."

Mission received: Escape from the Slave-Traders' Galley
Mission class: Required, training
Reward: 80 Exp., access to main game world

"Chain I no know. Me hurt. Man stabbing with spear."

From behind the wall, I heard the other player's strange, gurgling laughter.

"I can only imagine what your charisma must be like if they decided to kill you instead of free you. But I'm surprised you didn't die. All the soldiers are level twenty-five. they should be able to send you to respawn in one hit. The soldiers simply didn't notice me. As soon as the massacre started in the hold, I used my Stealth skill and even managed to get it to level two before they left. But I wasn't really thinking. Maybe they would have freed me along with the other prisoners. Or just sent me to respawn. Then I wouldn't have to deal with this chain. I'd just come back at the respawn point, free and clear."

I froze in fear. The respawn point this creature was talking about couldn't be seen from where I was. But what if the only way to freedom for characters with such disarming appearances as mine was to die and come back? Come on, that was nonsense! There must have been other decent ways of getting out. I looked at the short, rusty, half-meter-long chain holding my arm. At first, I just tried to break it.

Your character doesn't have enough Strength to complete this action
Strength required to break chain: 7

Alright, I clearly didn't have enough strength. But what about breaking the shackle at my wrist?

Your character doesn't have enough Agility to complete this action.
Agility required to break chain: 7

.

Another fail. I looked closely at my left hand. I had a thin wrist. My hand was also thin, but I had a big thumb jutting out to the side stopping me from slipping out of the manacles. But what if... The idea of gnawing off my own thumb seemed utterly barbaric, but I didn't chase it off right away. I did have Regeneration, and the thumb would soon grow back. Would a real goblin seriously be above this? No, I decided. They would not.

I tore my teeth into my own flesh. The pain was overwhelming and my hitpoints started falling fast. I even had to quickly eat the rat meat to restore some health. But my idea worked! I pulled my bloodied hand from the rusty shackle. Freedom! The blood immediately stopped, leaving me just two hitpoints of my full twenty-one. But what did that matter? Regeneration would gradually restore my life to max. Just then, though, a debuff popped up...

Your left hand is injured
For the next two days, you will not be able to use any weapon in your left hand, nor swim or climb cliffs and trees
All other actions done with the left hand will be subject to a penalty of 30%

I didn't get any experience for taking off the chain. Either the developers didn't like my method, or the mission simply wasn't finished.

"What was that?" my acquaintance asked from behind the wall.

"Me chain off. Now go you."

I finally got up and looked into the neighboring cell. And the guy sitting there was a real freak! It was an exhausted, blue-colored half-human-half-fish with huge bulging eyes lying on the dirty floor and taking ravenous gasps of air.

Trong Diver
Naiad
Level-One Diver

"You look pretty hideous, Amra!" the fish man exclaimed. His reaction to my appearance was the same as the man's.

We both laughed, then he answered the question I was about to ask:

"When making the character, I had no idea what to name myself. I figured the second word should show my profession. So now, I'm Mr. Diver, the diver. But it's nothing. I'd rather you tell me how you got that chain off."

I did my best to explain in layman's terms my method and the two-day debuff I'd gotten as a result. The fish shook his head.

"Cripes... No, that's not for me. I need to be able to dive and swim underwater. But I won't be able to do that with my left hand broken. It's easier for me to simply die and be reborn in an hour, totally free and without any debuffs or missing body parts. How about this: I'll keep trying to think up a way out of this chain, but if nothing sensible comes to mind, you can just kill me, and I'll respawn. I need the hour away anyway. I've got mail to answer and a bunch of minor things to take care of. You can go off somewhere and eat or just take a walk, then we can keep playing together. It seems to me that it's way too hard to get out of this alone. Sound good?"

At first, his suggestion made me squirm. Trong Diver was talking so calmly about his own death. It was as if he wasn't at all worried about the pain it would cause. But afterwards, I realized that he was just a regular player without a virtual reality capsule. He was sitting at home in front of his monitor or wearing a virtual-reality helmet on his head and trying to get out of the boring training location and into the huge game world as quickly as possible, no matter what it took. That explained a lot, as any player that could feel everything their character did as I could would clearly have preferred other ways of getting free.

"Good. Agreement. I walk there, go for look," I said, answering the shackled naiad, and walked down the dark hallway.

The time had come to figure out the interface. First, I called up the location map, made it semitransparent and placed it in the upper right corner. The map, by the way, told me I was in the hold of a slavers' galley. Trong Diver, behind me, was shown on the map as a yellow triangle, while before me in the darkness, there were three red dots lying in wait. I looked at the information on the marker colors, and found out that red (as I could have guessed) indicated a hostile enemy. Yellow was for NPC's and players whose opinion of you was unknown.

I went carefully and slowly forward. It smelled of recently spilled blood, but the bodies of the prostrated soldiers hadn't disappeared, as happened after a certain amount of time in most games. I felt something with my foot, and a glass container rolled down the floor.

Empty vial
Used to store alchemical elixirs

I picked up the vessel. Maybe I'd need it. I stopped my gaze on it, trying to figure out how to make it close. A few seconds later, a message popped up:

Would you like to take Alchemy (I A) as a primary skill?

I was slightly taken aback. It was that easy to pick up a skill? No teachers or missions, no insanely expensive scrolls? Alchemy... It could, of course, be very useful to me. I would be finding a lot of herbs and roots in my profession, and this way I didn't have to sell them raw for little money. I would be able to prepare the plants into valuable elixirs, which would probably be worth more than normal herbs. I chose the option "Yes."

You have taken Alchemy as a primary skill

Skill level: 1

Primary skills taken: 3 of 4

Only then, after a long delay, did I realize what I had just done. I had filled one of the two remaining skill slots without giving it serious thought. Even worse, it increased intelligence, a stat that the goblin race leveled 50% slower than normal! That was a considerable thing. What a boneheaded move!!!

Instead of Alchemy, I should have chosen a skill that leveled up agility and perception, the goblin's strong points. If I increased the level of such a skill to, let's say level one hundred, I would get 130 agility points (100*1.3) plus 65 perception points (50*1.3). In the end, it would have added up to a whole 195 extra stat points! But with Alchemy at level one hundred, considering the 50% penalty to intelligence leveling, I would get just 50 points (100*0.5) of intelligence and 65 (50*1.3) Agility points, adding up to a total of 115 points for my character instead of the 195 I could have gotten, if

I'd been thinking with my head...

Feeling ashamed, I practically smashed the ill-fated vial on the wall, but still I tried to keep calm and took it with me. I don't know for sure where the objects went in the game's logic — I was wearing nothing but a dirty loincloth — but I was still able to store things in my inventory. In any case, it had just eight slots. That was very little. I wanted to find a bag to store my things in.

A few steps later, I found another such container, then four more. There must have been a raging battle here not too long ago, based on the abundance of drying blood and deep gouges in the wooden table. The fighters were probably using alchemical substances to increase their strength, or heal themselves. The six identical containers, fortunately, took up just one slot of the eight available in my inventory.

I was getting closer and closer to the red dots on the map. I couldn't see the enemies yet, but I started walking a bit more carefully. And literally at that exact time, another message popped up:

Would you like to take Stealth (A C) as a primary skill?

I didn't rush the decision this time. On the one hand, using Stealth would level up agility, which was useful. But on the other, I'd be filling up all four available primary skill slots before I'd even started playing... This might not be the best possible choice for my character's long-term progress. Also... I shouldn't forget that I was a vampire. Being able to conceal my primary skills from others was not something the game mechanics allowed for. It made sense that you could judge someone in a certain way when you met them, right? But if every character I came across saw that I had the Stealth skill, that would only lead to unnecessary questions. I was supposed to be a peaceable goblin herbalist, after all. With some measure of pity, I refused to make Stealth one of my primary skills, but I did make it a secondary. Though secondary skills didn't increase stat points, the very ability to move in hiding could be quite useful for a nocturnal vampire. And, critically, secondary skills were not shown to other players.

You have taken Stealth as a secondary skill
Skill level: 1

It was no challenge to enter Stealth mode. But it did make my character walk significantly slower. I wasn't in a hurry, though, so I just walked like that as long as I could. As I was still looking at my stats, I didn't miss the moment when the empty Stealth-skill bar suddenly began to slowly fill up. Look at that little bar go! Someone might see me if I started moving carelessly. With redoubled caution, I went on into the darkness of the ship's hold.

Level-1 Rat

I noticed it while still invisible.

Stealth skill increased to level 2!

Feeling happy, I looked at the message and carelessly tripped over a little step I hadn't noticed, laying myself out on the floor. At that very moment, the rat saw me. The aggressive animal threw itself at me in leaps and bounds, but I didn't even have any weapons!

Damage taken: 4 (Bite from Rat)
Health level: 6/21

Two more bites and I was done for! I then punched the rat twice. Once with my left hand and once with my right. No damage! I missed.

Damage taken: 4 (Bite from Rat)
Health level: 2/21

No longer hoping for my weak punches to do anything, I made a determined attempt to bite it.

Damage dealt: 8 (Vampire Bite)
Health restored: +4 HP
Health level: 6/21

Ha! Hot diggedy! What was some little rat against a terrifying creature of the night! The next bite came from the rat, cutting another 4 HP from my bar, but then it was my turn again...

Not enough endurance points to use the Vampire Bite skill

What a bad time to run out of endurance! I'll be devoured whole! In despair, I tried striking at the rat with my fists once again.

Damage dealt: 2 (Punch)
Experience received: 8 Exp.
Object received: Rat meat (food)

I dismissed the importune suggestion that I choose Fist-Fighting (S C) as a primary skill. Instead, I sat down on the damp straw-covered floor in exhaustion. My hitpoint bar was flashing ominously at 2/21 HP, while my endurance was at just 1/20. Hrmph... I had to honestly admit, at least to myself, that my big-eared goblin had escaped from the encounter with the rat only by a miracle. I shouldn't keep asking for trouble, that was for sure. So, before going after the other rats, I had to prepare myself. At the very least, I had to restore my health and endurance, and ideally, I would also find a weapon of some kind.

I sat for ten minutes, just breathing. In that time, my endurance rose to ten, while my health, due to regeneration and the meat I ate, was fully restored. So, I ventured onward and, almost immediately, discovered a knife lying forgotten on the floor.

Rusty Kitchen Knife
*Damage: (1-4) * Strength*

It was clearly better than punching with my bare fists at (1-2) * Strength! I had barely picked up the knife when the system suggested I choose Dagger (S A) as a primary skill. I snorted unhappily. Stop trying to get me to do things without thinking them through! If agility were the primary stat in that skill, I may have even considered it, but strength with its 50% penalty... No thank you. Alchemy, with its penalized intelligence stat, was quite enough for me! I also didn't want to choose Dagger as a secondary skill.

It was much easier to take down rats with the kitchen knife, though. I would be hit with a 4 HP bite, answer with a knife strike for 6 HP, then finish the creature off with a Vampire Bite. My endurance was again sagging down in the single digits, so I had to wait. And though there was another rat in front of me, and I had already seen it, the time had come to return to Trong Diver.

The fish-man was sitting in the same pose as before, fettered to the wall with metal shackles. I called Trong by name several times, but it took him a few minutes to come to and answer:

"Sorry, I was afk. As soon as you finish your business, kill me as we agreed. I'll run out to the store and get dinner. Just make sure to wait for me to respawn in an hour, alright? We'll make it further together!"

I raised the dagger over the naiad's chest and drove it deep in between his ribs. And though the strike roll was not bad, doing 8 HP of damage, Trong's life bar only drooped down by a quarter. Son of a gun! His life points were one and a half times higher than my big-eared goblin's! I had to hit him again and again. After my fourth stab, Trong's life indicator was flashing in the critical zone... I stopped and asked the fish-man if I should finish him off or not. No answer followed. The player had clearly already walked away from the monitor. So, I made up my mind!

I had read about this in the forums. I had come across some information saying that, for the professions assassin or thief, it was desirable to have the Veil skill to remove or modify game logs so you could hide criminal actions from your victims, reduce the amount of time the Criminal tag would last and, with time, erase the marker altogether. And that was just what I needed! I tried to edit the last game message about the knife strike.

Would you like to take Veil (I A) as a primary skill?

No, taking Veil as a primary skill was not the right move. There was no reason for my harmless goblin herbalist to advertise his dark inclinations. But as a secondary skill, the ability was useful and then some!

You have taken Veil as a secondary skill
Skill level: 1
Effect time: 1 minute, uses 5 EP

I clicked the Veil icon. Now I had a whole minute to do all of this in secret:
Damage dealt: 6 (Vampire Bite)
Health restored: +3 HP
Experience received: 80 Exp.

Level two!

Achievement unlocked: Taste Tester (2/1000)

Achievement unlocked: Player killer (1)

Racial ability unlocked: Night vision (lasts 12 hours, costs 15 EP)

Racial ability improved: Taste for Blood (Gives +1% to all damage dealt for each unique creature killed with Vampire Bite. Current bonus: 2%)

Attention! Your character is has gained the Criminal marker! For the next eight hours, you will be a legal target for attack!

Trong Diver's body started flashing and became translucent. No, I hadn't acted thoughtlessly. This time, I really had done everything in a calculated fashion. I had found a target to level up my very useful Taste for Blood ability, so I took my shot. Naiads were a very rare race, after all. When else would I get the chance to add one to the list of unique species I'd bitten? But I wasn't the only one who could see the game logs. What would Trong Diver's reaction be when he discovered the messages about his death and read that a vampire had killed him? I had to do something to keep my secret.

So, what could I do with the log? I managed to open the message Trong Diver would see in fifty seconds for editing:

Damage taken: 6 (Vampire Bite from player

Amra)

> *You have died*

I didn't delete it entirely, though I could have. Instead, I edited it, changing out "Vampire Bite" for "Rusty Knife strike." Much better!

Veil skill increased to level 2!

Not bad, not bad at all! Life was turning around! Now, I just had to assign the stat points I got when leveling up, and get back to new adventures! By the way... For some reason, two of the five points had been spent automatically. My strength had grown to three, while constitution had grown to four. Strange...

Digging around in the guides, I figured out that it was a peculiarity of the vampire race: like it or not, strength and constitution would grow every level. I'd have to make peace with that. There was nothing to be done. I had just three stat points left.

I decided I should put two straight into charisma. I didn't like the idea that every person I saw would kill me just because of how ugly I was! And my last stat point, after significant consideration, I placed in intelligence. It was time to become smarter than a stool!

* * *

The last rat was no problem, dying after just two stabs — clear evidence of my character's increased strength. After picking up a piece of rat meat, I headed further into the visible end of the dark hold where there was a stairwell leading to an upper deck. Just after getting on the first step, the map updated, now showing not the lower hold, but the oarsman deck.

On this level, there was a stench. It smelled of filth, dirty bodies and rotting blood, all mixed into a cocktail that practically knocked me off my feet. My goblin had to cover his nose with his crippled left hand. Alright, message received. *Boundless Realm* was praised for its hyperrealism, but did they really need to go into this much gory detail? And also, if I thought about it, how had the designers even managed to convey the horrible smells of this wretched place? Even the slight breeze couldn't carry the stench away as it wound its way through the deck.

Slightly coming to, I took a look around. Everything near me bore witness to a recent slaughter: drying blood on the floor, oarsmen's benches broken and splintered by blade strikes, pieces of chain, and tatters of dirty clothing. There were no corpses. They had already managed to disappear in the game world. Then, on the map, beyond the markers for a few far-off Rats, I saw a yellow triangle. A player?! I stole up closer, and caught a glimpse of him, or more accurately, her:

Valerianna Quickfoot
Wood Nymph
Level-2 Beast Master

My sister! I recognized her right away. Valeria always used the same name for her main character, no matter what game she was in. I didn't come up any closer, though. My sister and I had agreed that we wouldn't advertise our relationship, or even prior acquaintance. So, I crawled forward, watching with satisfaction as my Stealth bar crawled upward.

And meanwhile, the graceful nymph with her long blue-green hair was busy exterminating rats. She was doing it in a fairly unique way, too: trying to keep her distance from the vermin, she would use a spell to take one under her control and set it against the others. I read the information on Valerianna's primary skills:

Level-2 Animal Control
Level-1 Water Magic

Suddenly, the girl froze and turned sharply.

"Who are you?" she asked, sounding more curious, or even threatening than startled.

I had given away my presence somehow, and was discovered. It would have been dumb to keep hiding, so I stepped forward.

"You're a criminal! Stay away!" The frightened nymph placed her palms together and put them in front of her. When she split them apart, there was a little flickering blue flame between them.

"I no bad-hurt for you!" I hurried to reassure her, mentally cursing my tongue-tied character. "I just to start game. Chain to take off hand. Then other fish-player say he need help. I kill he, and he reborn without chain. This only way, he say. He no can take chain off."

The nymph, a well-built, very thin girl in a short green cape, couldn't hold back a smile.

"You're funny, goblin. But you clearly don't have a great mind. Are you saying there weren't enough strength, agility, intelligence, or perception points between the two of you to add up to seven? You could have worked together!"

I froze, surprised and embarrassed. The idea to have both of us try to pull Trong Diver's chain from the wall had truly not come to mind. It couldn't be that my goblin's chuckleheadedness had rubbed off on me, right? It was all so elementary! Valerianna thought for a couple seconds and said with worry in her voice:

"I think I figured out what happened between you. You seem to be describing a standard PvP con. You killed a player on his request, and now have the status Criminal for the next several hours. He knew that he could easily kill you, but didn't want to be marked as a criminal for so little reason. You wouldn't lose anything from dying, while he would get just one hundred experience points. That was why he gave you the chance to level up on rats and training missions, get a few levels, then kill you. I'm sure he asked you to wait for him, so you could go on together. Or am I wrong?"

I nodded, confirming my sister's theory.

"So you see, his character must have been specialized for PvP. He probably has a tendency toward a combat stat. Strength for example, and is preparing to use a melee weapon. I'm sure he also has constitution leveled up, so he'll have a large number of hitpoints, too. With you at level three, he will get three hundred experience points for killing you, not just one hundred. That makes quite a big difference at the beginning of the game, and is more than enough to get him up to level four. Also, some races and classes get extra experience for killing players or special bonuses and missions, so your new friend is sure to kill you. That way, when he gets out into the main world, he'll be a fairly high level, and will have a clean record to boot."

I realized Valeria must have taken off her virtual reality helmet, opened the *Boundless Realm* forum on the monitor, and was reading all this from there. This meant that Trong Diver's suggestion that I kill him was in fact a trap. He was letting his prey get a little exercise so it would taste better when he ate it. He must have been planning to kill me after he came back.

"If it's not a secret, what race was he?" asked the nymph, sending another rat into the distant herd of vermin.

"Naiad, diver," I answered, and my sister froze in contemplation.

While she stood motionless, the rat under her control continued fighting against its former buddies. I was surprised to see the body of the frozen nymph start glimmering in different colors. It must have been a skill leveling up. I looked at her visible stats. That was right! Valeria's Animal Control skill had gone up to level 3. By the time I'd checked that, my sister had come back into the game.

"Just so you know, naiad divers are their version of human warriors or dwarven berserkers. They get an extra ten life points for every constitution point, and double endurance points for doing various combo attacks as well as an additional bonus to strength."

"I running away?" I asked, but the nymph shook her head, and asked how long it would be for the naiad to respawn.

I looked at the time shown and answered that it would be forty minutes.

"Don't run, goblin. If he really does attack,

I'll help you. I don't like tricksters and con-artists. But I'll only get involved if he attacks you first. For now, I'll raise my water-magic skill to level two, then my intelligence will go up from primary skill bonuses to seventeen."

What she said didn't get through to me right away. Valerianna was already at level two, and had already leveled up her intelligence to seventeen. But how?! I myself didn't have any stats above four, which is where I had agility, intelligence and constitution.

The nymph explained eagerly:

"My race has a bonus to charisma and intelligence leveling, and I skewed my character toward intelligence above all else. Both of my predefined primary skills level intelligence first as well. I just took the shackles from my own wrists, as I immediately figured out how the latch lock worked and simply swung it open."

After these words, the nymph called over a rat under her control, and I noticed that the animal had grown slightly larger, having leveled up against its own compatriots to two. After that, Valerianna, ordering her pet to sit at attention, released an icy blue arrow into a far-off, barely visible hostile rat, killing it in one blow. She had the same success with two neighboring rats. Again, the nymph lit up in various colors. Her water-magic skill had raised to level two.

"Cool! Another fifty or so experience points,

and I'll be level three!" the nymph laughed happily. "Amra, I need to take a break for a bit and restore my mana. After that, I can cast up to nine ice arrows, each one doing an average of forty damage. No matter how much your naiad friend leveled up constitution, he won't be able to survive that. But it is important that you not let him get near me. I have only eleven HP, so he'd be able to kill me just by spitting. By the way, why are you not leveling up? There are a few more rats left. Take them for yourself."

I nodded obediently and walked out in front. And it should be said my thoughts were quite far from the rats as I did it. I could only think about the attack I was now expecting from Trong Diver. Valerianna promised to intervene if the naiad attacked. But in any case, I had to survive one or two blows from the fish-man. And, if his character really was specialized for PvP with all modifiers for dealing damage, then... I wonder how much damage he could do with one hit? It probably was no less than the nymph with her magic, and my sister had said something about forty hitpoints per ice arrow. If I took forty HP as a reference point, how could I possibly survive the attack, given that I had just twenty-seven myself?! Could I hope to dodge? It seemed that was the very way out I needed.

When the nearest level-1 rat threw itself at me, I didn't hit it right away, instead jumping back and to the side.

Would you like to take Dodge (A P) as a primary skill?

The skill leveled up agility and perception, my strongest stats! Just what I needed! I agreed right away.

You have taken Dodge as a primary skill
Skill level: 1
Primary skills taken: 4 of 4
You may take a fifth primary skill at level 10

Having already killed the rat, (it managed to bite me once, the pest, but it meant nothing. Regeneration would heal all wounds, after all.) I noticed that my Dodge skill had increased my agility to five and slightly increased my perception.

At that, of the four primary skills, only Dodge had been activated. The others were marked with an inactive gray and clearly had yet to have any impact on my stats. Was that because I hadn't used them yet? Perhaps that was exactly the reason.

I took an empty vial from my inventory and filled it with the blood of the dead rat.

Rat Blood (alchemy ingredient)

The Alchemy skill lit up. My intelligence and agility immediately increased, but just barely. So, that was how it worked! To activate a primary skill and have it start growing your stats, you just needed to use it once! What else did I have that wasn't "turned on" yet? Herbalism and Trading. I'd have to wait a bit to use Herbalism. We were on a galley. I wasn't gonna find any plants growing on board the ship. But Trading couldn't have been easier. I went back to my sister and tried to sell her the container of rat blood.

Valerianna began squirming in disgust and, of course, refused. But I didn't have to actually sell the object. After noticing with a satisfied look that Trading had already been activated as well, raising my charisma by a whole point and slightly bringing up my intelligence with it, I poured the blood out on the floor, as I had yet to locate any kind of stopper.

I spent ten minutes evading the last vermin, as I wanted to raise my Dodge skill to level three quickly. Covered in bites and impossibly happy with myself, I returned to my sister.

"Hey dumbo, have you got far to go until level three?" the nymph asked with a bored look as she sat on the oarsman's bench staring at her well-kept nails.

"Three hundred forty experience is. Five hundred want," I reported.

My sister frowned in dismay and seemingly

grew upset:

"Raise your intelligence to at least five. It's hard to understand you. But that's for later. For now, listen carefully, big-ears. We've just got to get up to the upper deck of the galley. I found a description of the location in the guides. There is an angry sea up there. The waves might crash through the broken ship. If you don't have enough agility, you'll be washed overboard, then you'll lose experience and have to wait an hour at the respawn point. Or can you swim, Amra?"

"No can. Agility is enough."

"Are you sure? Alright then. I have an underwater breathing spell, so I'll just sink to the bottom. Your naiad friend is a sea creature, so there's no way he'll drown. But you'll have to lower the boat with a crane, despite the waves and weather, then you'll have to row your way in to shore. That is a side quest, so you'll get a hundred experience points for it. That means, when you reach the shore, that quest will be completed as well as the main training mission, which gives you another one hundred experience points. So, as soon as you set foot on shore, you'll reach level three. But, once you get there, don't just kick your feet up. Either run as fast as you can from the shore, or prepare for combat. Your friend is sure to attack you, so stay on your guard. Got it? Let's go up, then. You should lower the boat without my help so all the experience will go to you. Otherwise, you won't reach level three and you'll be too weak to stand up to the naiad."

* * *

My sister was just sharp as a tack. Once above board, the only thing that kept me from going over the side was her warning. Because of it, I took hold of a taut rope as soon as I got up there, which helped me stay on the boat when a jet of water blasted me off my feet. The orcish galley smashed into the cliff and got wedged between the rocks. Huge waves rolled over the deck, taking with them all kinds of trash, barrels, broken oars and furniture.

The dingy, which had survived all this chaos only by a miracle, I spotted on the aft of the broken ship. To get to it, I had to run across the slippery, inclined deck, which had foamy breaks of water rolling over it constantly.

"I'll be waiting for you on shore!" My sister managed to shout before a wave pulled her down to the depths.

The level-2 rat my sister had been controlling swam past me. It had lost its link with its master, and was now aggressive to me again. But the rat didn't care about me at all. It was flailing its paws in desperation, trying to struggle against the raging elements. I then, after waiting for the wave to ebb, threw myself up the inclined deck toward the dingy.

Successful Agility check
Experience received: 8 Exp.

Before the next breaker slammed into the broken ship, I managed to overcome the open space and latch into the side of the canvas-covered boat.

Mission received: Use the Dingy
Mission class: Optional, training
Reward: 80 Exp., Small Bag

The dingy was tied to a set of ropes that led up to a crane on the side of the boat. I had to turn a crank on the crane to lower the fragile vessel into the water. As I was turning the mechanism, I totally forgot that I was in a game. The sensations I was feeling were just that realistic. The storm, the wind, the creak of the stretched-out ropes, the foamy waves, the cold wind and the smell of seaweed all combined to form something very close to reality. My wounded left hand burned as if on fire in the salty water. I strained to twirl the spinning device with my one good hand until, finally, the boat made it into the water.

"So then, there you are, goblin!" The satisfied voice of Trong Diver rang out from behind my back.

I turned. The naiad, smiling a toothy grin, took a seat on the side wall of the galley.

"This weather is just awesome for me! I love stormy seas. So then, you go on the boat, and I'll swim in underwater. We'll meet up onshore."

After these words, the fish-man made an agile jump overboard. I then saw that the naiad was holding a trident in his hands, but it wasn't clear where he'd gotten it from. He suddenly had a weapon. Bad news!

I let go of the rope and took hold of the oar. Damn! I couldn't row with my left hand, so I pulled the oar from the ring and grabbed it with both hands. This way was much easier. When rowing, I gradually lost endurance points, but I wasn't too worried. I had plenty of them left. Navigating around the jagged stones jutting up from the water, I pointed the boat at the lagoon. Beyond the reefs, which served as natural breakwaters, the sea grew much calmer. A few minutes later, I had reached a sandy point, wedging out into the sea in a thin band. My sister was already waiting for me on the shore and waving from afar. I had just touched foot on the wet sand when my body began to light up:

Mission completed: Use the Dingy
Experience received: 80 Exp.

Mission completed: Escape from the Slave-Traders' Galley
Experience received: 80 Exp.

Level three!

Racial ability unlocked: Apathy of the Undead (lasts 3 hours, costs 20 EP)

Alright then, so where was the bag it promised me? I looked under the rowing bench and found an over-the-shoulder canvas bag.

Small bag: +10 inventory slots

Before Trong had come ashore, I set about assigning the new stat points. Strength and constitution went up by default. From the three points that remained, I put another in constitution, and two in agility. I now had 39 hitpoints.

I had barely finished with the stats when Trong Diver emerged from the salty sea onto the sandy peninsula, cutting off my path to the shore. His body was also giving off a colorful glow. The naiad had hit level three, too. The fish-man shot me a malignant grin, demonstrating several rows of needle-like teeth, then suddenly extended his bright red back fins and screeched in dismay, having discovered another player not far from me.

"Hey! That's my trophy," Trong Diver shouted, pointing his trident at me. "I've been shepherding him along since the beginning of the game!"

The nymph didn't answer the insidious naiad in any way but, between her hands, the bright blue flame of a spell being cast appeared.

"Alright, we can split it down the middle," suggested Trong Diver, and that was when my sister attacked.

The ice arrow that tore itself from her fingers instantly overtook the distance between the two and broke into a hail of pieces on the naiad's scales, at which Trong Diver's health fell by about a quarter. The spell to take forty hitpoints had only reduced the naiad's health by a third?! How many hitpoints did he have?!

"Not expecting that, were you nymph?" the fish-man laughed. "I have a natural resistance to water magic!"

After these words, Trong Diver got a better grip on his trident and threw himself at my sister to stop her from casting another spell. I, without thinking it through, dashed off after him. The naiad was almost half way to her when his path was blocked by a level-1 crab crawling out of the sea onto the sandy shore.

The naiad slowed his pace and destroyed the unexpected obstacle with a flick of his trident. But even that second of delay was enough for me to catch up to him and work my knife into his back.

Damage dealt: 9 (11 Rusty Kitchen Knife strike — armor 2)

Trong Diver's life bar went down, but not very much at all, just ten percent. Hrmph, I should have taken the dagger skill. Perhaps then, I could have gotten a critical hit from my stab in the back. Now, probably feeling more surprised at my impudence than really feeling injured by the attack, Trong turned toward me.

"So, that's where you've gone off to, Amra! There's nowhere for you to run now!"

Another ice arrow flew into the fish-man's back, lowering the naiad's health to forty percent. His health bar changed color from green to yellow and Trong Diver winced in pain:

"It's nothing, I'll survive another icicle attack, and then I'll have two nice trophies, you and the nymph! Sixty experience points from the two of you is enough to get me straight to level five!"

At these words, the naiad made a sharp lunge forward and stabbed my chest with his trident. I tried to dodge the attack, but I didn't manage. Son of a bitch! That hurt like hell!!!

Damage taken: 34 (Trident strike from player Trong Diver)

~ Video Game Plotline Tester ~

Health level: 5/39

The shooting pain caused me to miss the chance to hit him back. The naiad jumped away from me, making it impossible to hit him with the knife again. But, fortunately, my sister didn't hesitate, and sent another magic icicle into my attacker's back. Trong Diver's health was flashing red, but the fish-man started smiling an eerie smile:

"Ha! I survived! Now, you're dead and I'll get all my health back after I level up!" With these words, Trong jumped toward me and jabbed with his trident.

In an incredible jump with simultaneous front flip, I craftily evaded the sharp points under his raised left hand. But doing so had made my endurance points fall severely. Because he was very close, I made an abrupt strike at his fine-scaled throat, helped by the fact that the naiad was no taller than I was.

Damage dealt: 16 (18 Rusty Kitchen Knife strike - 2 armor)

Experience received: 120 Exp.

Dodge skill increased to level 4!

Would you like to take Acrobatics (A S) as a

secondary skill?

So, that's what this was! In my attempt to elude the certain death flying toward my chest, I had used not only Dodge, but also Acrobatics! What could I say? It was a skill that was useful to my survival. I should take it. In the distance, the nymph lit up like a projector, having reached level four already.

After the technical matter, I took a look around. The body of Trong Diver was lying in the shallows giving off a slight glow. I bent down over it and tried to pick up the trident lying on the sand, but my fingers went straight through the object. It must have been that the laws of the game world didn't consider the weapon to have "dropped," so it was still in his inventory. Too bad. Bowing over my vanquished enemy, I tried to look at him. I didn't have to rummage through the body. The trophy window opened. My take was three silver coins, two empty vials and one with a cork, filled with a pale blue liquid.

Insufficient Intelligence to identify object

Alright, I'll figure that out later or show it to my sister. I headed to Valerianna. The wood nymph was peeved:

"All my pets die too fast, both rats and crabs. Some beast master I am. I can't even keep any beasts under my control! Also, I now have a red criminal marker over my head. I had to attack the naiad preemptively, which means I committed a crime. Now, my character won't leave the game world for eight hours, even if I leave the game. Also, have you looked at the map?"

I shook my head, then looked at the game map on my sister's advice. There was just a tiny circle lit-up, showing discovered area: the sea shore, the two of us, and a huge black mass representing undiscovered territory. I increased the scale, but no additional markers showed on the map. Our little circle just got smaller and smaller until it became a dot. The words on it didn't add any information, either:

Coordinates ??????????
Region ????????

"So, you see," the nymph agreed after seeing the look of dismayed confusion on my green face. "We're like in the middle of nowhere, and the only known respawn point is on the broken galley, which I really don't want to go back to. Unfortunately, the weather today is cloudy and it's quickly growing dark. Night will come before we can do anything. Soon, just being out here will be a threat to our lives. But there's no reason to wait on the shore. We need to go somewhere. Maybe we'll get lucky and find other respawn points. At least then it wouldn't be so bad to die. We wouldn't have to get out of that stinking galley again."

I agreed with Valerianna that staying where we were was stupid, and went onward. The wood nymph followed after me. We started walking down the sandy beach and, just after we got close to the dark bushes, before our eyes flashed a message:

Congratulations, you have passed the training mission!
Welcome to **Boundless Realm***!*

Surviving the Night

"IT'S YOUR CALL, big-ears. Should we stay together, or split up?"

My sister continued playing up our original conceit, putting on a show for potential observers that we didn't know one another and had met coincidentally. Good girl. She was acting out the role admirably. For a fourteen-year-old girl, I couldn't have asked for better. I agreed with her:

"Together good. We two be together night, no die," I answered the wood nymph and her face lit up.

"Great! Because I, to be honest, am afraid of the dark. I know it's stupid, all the more so in a computer game, but there's nothing I can do. Now is the exact time to determine how we can best complement one another. I'll take Cartography as a primary skill..."

Plant! The way I felt at that moment was probably exactly how a casino visitor feels after winning a jackpot. I forgot about everything on earth and threw myself at an inconspicuous bush with wide, lobed leaves and underripe greenish-red berries. My Herbalism skill finally activated, leveling my perception up to five, and agility to twelve.

Unlike the other bushes and trees nearby, this plant lit up green when I got near, indicating that it was possible to interact with. I ripped down a handful of the underripe berries.

Swamp Currant (alchemy ingredient)
Experience received: 4 Exp.

My Herbalism bar went up by ten percent. Cool! Nine more bunches of berries and I'd reach level two! But right after I ripped down one bunch, the bush stopped glowing. I couldn't take any of the other berries from it. I had to look for other usable plants.

"Dumbo, you need to stay on task!" my sister chided me, unhappy with the fact that I had gotten distracted by a berry bush.

But I didn't think myself at fault and tried to explain my actions:

"Plant, me getting-getting. Awareness jump on up. Good for looking nighttime. If I nine herb can find, then much better will be senses."

My visual radius really did grow noticeably as my perception increased to five, which also raised our chances of surviving the night in this forest, which was swarming with dangerous beasts. So, raising my Herbalism skill to level two and increasing my perception and visual radius in the process had become a priority mission.

Despite the confusing nature of my explanation, Valerianna understood me perfectly:

"Alright, Amra. Gather your herbs and level up perception. It's helpful to us both. I took Cartography as a primary skill. That's another one that levels intelligence. It also gives more light radius on the map, and could end up allowing us to discover many useful locations. But we need to worry about more than just seeing far; we also need to make sure no predators see us. That's why I'm taking Stealth as a secondary skill. On top of my racial bonus as a nymph of -50% to discovery radius, we shouldn't have any problems. You also chose Stealth. I realized that as soon as we met. Also, your agility will be higher than mine, so I'm not too worried about you. Just turn off the bright colors when you level up in the game settings. After all, what's the point of us being invisible if, at the worst possible moment, you level up some skill and light up like a firework?"

It was a very practical piece of advice. I called up the game settings menu and chose the visual effects window, then turned all the colorful illumination off. Of course, all these multi-colored little glowing lights looked pretty, but they were completely inappropriate for trying to walk secretly through the forest at night.

Beyond that, I hadn't forgotten about another useful tool I had: the night vision skill I had gotten when I became a level-2 vampire. I didn't say anything out loud, but activated it when it got dark, which cost 15 endurance points. The world became more contrasting in color, and I could clearly make out a bright silhouette far in the distance, which must have been a forest creature.

"Me seeing enemy. There. Skull above him," I whispered to the nymph, and she commented just as quietly:

"If there is a red skull marker over a beast, that means the difference in levels is more than twenty, so we'd better stay away. And if the skull is black, the difference is more than fifty levels, so we'd be goners for sure."

The skull was red. It could have been worse but, still we walked a wide arc around the enemy. As we walked, I watched with unhidden surprise how quickly my Stealth skill bar was filling up. I just needed a few more meager points for the skill to hit level three. I even wanted to stay there intentionally and wait a few minutes, but my sister dragged me forward:

"I assure you, Amra, that is not the only monster in this forest. And if we have to walk a big circle around every one, we'll never get anywhere. In just one minute, according to the rules of *Boundless Realm*, night will fall, so there will be even more dangerous beasts about."

I looked at the timer. There were a few seconds remaining before nine in the evening. Not long after that, a few messages jumped up on my screen:

Night is not a good time for walks outside the city

> **Mission received: Surviving the Night**
> **Mission class: One-time, personal**
> **Reward: 160 Exp., +2 stat points**

> **Additional mission received: Find Safe Shelter**
> **Mission class: Optional**
> **Reward: 80 Exp., one random piece of equipment**

Seeing that my sister had also frozen, I realized she must have just gotten the same messages. The nymph turned to me and whispered:

"If I can complete both missions, I'll get exactly enough experience to reach level five. But now, not a word. We'll walk the rest of the night in Stealth mode without talking. Most nocturnal predators don't need to see you to find you. They hunt with their ears."

* * *

The creators of *Boundless Realm* had managed to recreate the atmosphere of a spooky swampy forest perfectly. Everywhere around, I could hear predators howling and roaring. Sometimes, I would hear something hooting above me then laughing wickedly, every time making my heart freeze in fear. Several times, on the very edge of my vision, I noticed some ghastly silhouettes scurrying by. Every one of them had a red skull over their head. My sister and I were constantly forced to change the direction we were walking or hide among the gnarled roots of ancient trees, waiting out some nearby danger.

There were monsters everywhere. Only by some kind of miracle were we able to remain unnoticed. Freezing in fear, we were terrified of giving ourselves away with our footsteps, breathing or just heartbeats. Once, when Valerianna stepped on a dry branch and it snapped, I practically pissed myself in a very real sense.

But at that, I was clever enough to gather some plants on our journey: swamp currant, swamp blackberry, and swamp horsetail. When I had gotten Herbalism to level two, the variety of valuable herbs and berries I found immediately grew as well. By level three, bitter lily-of-the-valley, wild heather, bitter wormwood and wild clover had all become old hat. I was elated to have found a bag, otherwise I wouldn't have had enough slots in my inventory to store all the different herbs.

At a certain point, the wood nymph carefully touched my shoulder and pointed in the direction of a far-off looming black splotch. Danger? As it turned out, it was nothing of the sort. My sister was insisting that we turn in the direction of whatever it was. Soon, I could also see why she was interested. On the local map, there was a marker showing three interlocking gray rings. As the interactive hint told us, that symbol stood for a respawn point.

Then, hiding behind a shaggy lichen-covered tree, we hid from an overgrown wolf the size of a large calf that crossed our path. After that, we rushed to the marker on the map. As we approached, I felt the earth below our feet start to tremble. In that place, I could feel some kind of natural force. The center of the anomaly was a huge boulder dug into the earth on top of a small hill. The boulder was covered with worn-down carved runes in a language I didn't recognize.

"We can talk here no problem," my sister assured me. "NPC's don't come near respawn points. The game mechanics don't allow it. That is why the only people you need to worry about in these places are living players. Bad people commonly use a method where they provoke their victim to aggression or tempt them to steal, thus marking them as a criminal. After that, they can kill the unfortunate individual unpunished and wait at the same respawn point, killing them again and again, getting experience and dropped items as they do so. But you're not like that, are you Amra? Can I leave the game here? It's safe here, so I'll survive the night. Of course, I'd like to finish the side quest, but my eyes are starting to droop."

"Nymph sleeping. Amra no is evil. No bad goblin," I assured Valerianna, though I did get slightly upset that my sister would be leaving me temporarily.

From her perspective, I could easily understand. It was already after midnight, and the fourteen-year-old girl really should have been sleeping some time ago. Normally, I put her to bed at nine or ten, so today, she had stayed up quite a bit past her bed-time. The little nymph took a seat on an outcropping of warm stone and closed her eyes. I called out to her, but no reaction followed. My sister had signed off.

What should I do, then? Should I also just

be satisfied that I finished the primary mission and go to sleep? There was an internal voice telling me not to. The longer I played, after all, the happier my employer would be. What kind of game tester was I, if I was satisfied with the slightest bit of play, and would now just sit stupidly in one place for hours? Also, I only needed seventy experience points to reach level four, and I could easily get that by gathering forest plants.

Plus, if I thought about it, where would I go in the real world when I crawled out of the virtual reality capsule? It was the middle of the night outside. The metro and trolley-buses weren't running, and I wouldn't be able to convince a cabbie to bring me to the crime-ridden outskirts of the megalopolis. Even the police stayed away from that place at night. That meant it was decided. I would continue to play alone, even though it was twice as dangerous.

Do you really want to change your respawn point?

Yes, of course. I was totally sure I didn't want to start the game over on that far-off orcish galley, if I happened to get eaten by some monster. I sighed and walked off decisively into the dark night. Three minutes later, I had already found a fairly well trodden path. On my map, it was shown as a thin red line.

If there was a trail, that meant there must have also been someone walking on it, cutting down the vegetation and keeping it in order. But which way should I go, right or left? For some reason, I couldn't make up my mind. Both ways led into the dense, deadly forest. Should I flip a coin to let fate herself make the decision?

I took a heptagonal silver coin from my inventory. It had a round hole in the middle, so you could put it on a string and wear it as a necklace. So then, if the coin fell with the fortress tower up, I'd go right. If it fell with the... what was that, anyway? The coin was old and worn and the image could barely be made out. It was probably a dragon, or maybe it was an octopus. It didn't matter. If the weird creature fell up, I'd go left. I threw the coin and caught it gracefully in the air. I unclenched my fingers. The up-side was showing the dragon or octopus creature.

At that moment, I noticed that the interactive map was showing a red dot suspiciously close to me. Too close. There was a monster next to me. I turned in fear and, a step from me, saw an overgrown wolf looking like the one my sister and I had hidden from.

Level-27 Seasoned Forest Wolf

The red skull over the forest predator's head confirmed that the difference between us was more than twenty levels. Epically bad luck. That's what I got for walking around without my sister. At least the respawn point was very close. There was absolutely no point running, even less fighting...

Successful check for Seasoned Forest Wolf reaction
Experience received: 20 Exp.

The wolf's marker on the map unexpectedly changed from red to yellow. I suspect that was my goblin racial bonus of +30 to the reaction of all forest and swamp beasts. I never imagined that would actually come in handy. For some reason, the seasoned wolf didn't walk away, instead looking at me in curiosity and sniffing. What did it want from me?

I unbuttoned my side bag and took out some rat meat. The wolf's gnashing teeth practically ripped my fingers off. I even winced for a few seconds. The wolf swallowed the food, waved its tail lightly just like a dog, and began staring at me again with its unblinking yellow eyes. I dismissed the suggestion to take Animal Empathy (Ch I) as a secondary skill, then fed the wolf the remaining two pieces of rat meat I had on me.

"That all. Food no," I told the predator and showed it my empty hands.

The wolf sniffed around me incredulously, and even stuck its impudent snout into my bag to make sure it wasn't being tricked. Only after that did the toothy predator turn away from me and retreat. The animal's marker on the map acquired a green color. Friendship. Well, alright...

"Wait! Goblin house live where? Wolf is knowing?" I asked aloud.

The thought that an animal might understand my speech seemed nonsensical. On the other hand, it was no worse than my idea to gnaw off my own thumb, which had actually worked. The wolf turned to me, looked for a long time with an unblinking gaze, then unexpectedly laid down on its belly.

SYSTEM ERROR! You cannot change class from Herbalist to Wolf Rider

Would you like to take Riding (A Ch) as a secondary skill?

I refused the tempting suggestion, then climbed up on the animal's back. The wolf stood up and trotted toward the bushes. I had to duck so the branches wouldn't scratch my face. On the map, a whole group of red dots showed up. And as a matter of fact, we were going right in their direction.

Successful check for Seasoned Forest Wolf reaction

Experience received: 20 Exp.

Successful check for Seasoned Forest Wolf (female) reaction
Experience received: 16 Exp.

Successful check for Seasoned Forest Wolf reaction
Experience received: 20 Exp.

Level four!

Racial ability unlocked: Detect Life (lasts 3 hours, discovery radius: Perception * 2m, costs 20 EP)

I didn't manage to come back to my senses after the cascade of messages before the seasoned wolf took off at full speed, crossed a shallow stream and stopped unexpectedly before a long, dark barricade. I looked more carefully at it and recognized it as a stockade fence three times my height, thickly crisscrossed with thorny ivy and made of weathered logs driven into the earth. It was a well-made fortification. Its creators must have spared nothing in its construction. The wolf lowered down on its belly, showing me that the ride was over.

Just after I jumped onto the earth, the predator silently disappeared off into the forest, leaving me alone with the stockade. I walked the perimeter, cursing under my breath at the thick vegetation. Everything was overgrown with the horrible ivy, its flexible vines covered with sharp thorns ten centimeters in length. Soon, I came to the wooden gates. One side was ripped from the hinges and was lying on the ground, while another was coming off and just barely still standing. But both were covered in deep grooves from the claws of a gigantic predator. The fissures in the wood had grown dark with time. No matter what had happened here, it had happened quite a long time ago.

I walked carefully inside the barricade and saw a high dark blockhouse. It was constructed from huge logs nearly a meter in diameter. I could not say for sure what race this construction was made for, but it was more like a fortress than a simple residence. Its walls were incredibly thick, and it had very narrow arrowslit windows, that even a cat wouldn't be able to crawl through. And though the door of the building was sitting open welcomingly, I didn't rush inside.

First, I called up my Detect Life ability and walked a circle around the wooden opening. It was all clear. There were no creatures inside. Only then did I get up on the porch and enter the building. Once inside, I saw a heavy beam that could lock the door. I put it in its place.

Mission completed: Find safe shelter
Experience received: 80 Exp.

It was a dark room. The only source of light was the narrow arrowslits. The building had a small entryway, a stairway to the second floor and one other room on this floor, which must have been a kitchen based on the massive table and fire pit made of cement-bound stones. I got up to the second floor, scraping my way up the high steps as I went. This must have been where the original owners had slept. There was a crude low trestle bed heaped high with old, stinking animal pelts, a stool, a small table and an empty box. And in the very middle of the room, there was a huge dark spot, dirty fragments of clothing and a great many old, picked-clean bones. I squirmed in horror and disgust. Based on what I could see, the previous inhabitant of this building had been eaten in this very location, and the high stockade and thick gates had done nothing to save him.

Near the site of the bloody scene, next to the pelt bed, there was a pair of leather boots that looked about size thirty standing totally untouched. If I wanted to, I could have crawled into one with both legs, and it would have come up approximately to my belt. I judged that this was the "random piece of equipment," I had been promised for finishing the quest. Yes, game developers knew how to joke, too. They just had a very particular sense of humor...

Before my eyes there appeared a yellow, translucent image: a plate overlaid with a crossed fork and spoon. That must have meant that my big-eared goblin was getting hungry. I opened a page of more detailed information on my character. The hunger bar had fallen below twenty-five percent. The hint told me that I had just six hours left before I would suffer a penalty. But much worse was that, together with the hunger, I was also threatened by Thirst for Blood. My Quenching the Thirst bar was only at 5/15, which could bring lots of problems five hours down the line. And though I could overcome normal hunger by eating the berries I'd gathered during the night, I had no desire whatsoever to turn into a vampire who'd lost his mind from Thirst for Blood, unable to control his behavior.

So, I made myself a mission. I had to eat before dawn, and it had to be meat and raw at that. That meant I had to go on a night hunt. But what could I possibly kill, if the only thing around were the very high-level monsters I'd been seeing all night? And also, if I approached the problem from a purely technical perspective, how could I kill anything? Certainly not with this pitiful kitchen knife, right? I needed another weapon, and it had to do damage that depended on my main stat, agility. Bow, for example. But the Bow skill used both hands, and my left hand was still injured and wouldn't be able to hold a weapon for another day and a half. I needed a one-handed weapon with agility. There just had to be something like that!

Finding such information while inside the *Boundless Realm* world was very difficult, so I called up the game menu and pressed the option "Exit Game." I opened the virtual reality capsule and crawled out, taking off my helmet and suit immediately. Sitting in just my skivvies on a chair, I took out my smartphone and, before anything else, called my sister, wanting to tell her about finding shelter. Valeria answered, but it took her some time.

"Tim, it's one in the morning. I've been asleep for a while. What do you want?"

I told her about the blockhouse I'd found where she could finish the optional quest and told her what direction it was in, but I didn't hear any enthusiasm in her voice.

"One hundred exp. is not worth sacrificing my sleep and risking the experience I've already gotten. Without you, I'll be totally blind in the dark. I'll be eaten by wolves or something, so I not only won't finish the side mission, I'll also fail the main one. But I'll set my alarm for five in the morning, when it starts to get light again. If the nastier creatures are sleeping by that point, I'll come before sunup to your house and finish the side quest. Just make sure to send me a personal message about it in the game, otherwise there might be questions about how I

was able to get the information about the shelter. Also, when are you coming home?"

I answered that I would be coming back no earlier than morning when public transportation started running again, then hung up. After that, I went into the *Boundless Realm* forum and set about carefully studying the advice of authoritative players on weapon choice. There were a good number of one-handed weapons with the main stat agility in the game: one-handed crossbows, throwing knives, darts, all kinds of thrown pointed weapons, bolases and lots of other things.

I was most interested in the blowgun, which allowed you to shoot needles and thorns. The guide informed me that I could also use various kinds of poisons on the thorns, which would be able to cause negative effects to my victims including loss of orientation, stat reductions and even paralysis. Blowguns used the Exotic Weapons (A P) skill, and training in it allowed you to also use lassos and throwing nets as well, though they required two hands.

A great option for me! That was that. I had more than enough thorns near my shelter on the ivy wrapping around my stockade. And horsetail, which had a hollow stem, I had seen growing abundantly along the banks of the swamp. Not wasting time, I crawled back into the virtual reality capsule and headed off to get ready. I found a nearly meter-long tube and cut it right away. I cleaned it with a thin branch and was very satisfied with the result:

Hand-made Blowgun (weapon)

It was slightly harder to gather thorns, though. They were too hard to take off the ivy vines. I had to work for a long time with the knife to get twenty spines and fill one slot of my inventory. I returned to the building, cut a few small fur-covered pieces of skin from one of the old pelts and drove each one through with a long needle-like thorn.

Hand-made Blowgun Ammunition
*Damage: (1-3) * Agility*

And then finally, in my first test, I blew sharply and a thorn embedded itself deep into the wooden wall with a dull thump.
Would you like to take Exotic Weapons (A P) as a secondary skill?

Would I?! That was all. I'd taken the last of the possible skills. I would only be able to take another one at level ten. I trained by shooting at targets I scratched into the wall, and was left very satisfied with the result. Finally, I had an appropriate weapon for my big-eared goblin.

When I'd reached level four, some of my stat points had gone into strength and constitution by default, but I had yet to assign the others. I placed one each into intelligence, agility and perception. The detailed character information showed that, where I was, at level-one Exotic Weapons skill, considering the modifiers from agility (now 14.15) and taste for blood (1.02), I could now deal from 28 to 57 damage. I was simply a horror of the night! Beware of me!

It was already past three in the morning, so I didn't try to use the remaining time before sunup to prepare a powerful poison or anything. I understood that without a recipe, without the necessary equipment and without leveling up Alchemy a good deal, that wasn't very likely. I had to press on with normal, totally poison-free thorns for my weapon.

* * *

It was just a duck. A normal duck, all gray with little splotches of color, with one distinction: it was the size of a large turkey. The bird was sleeping on an island in the middle of the swamp.

Level-11 Swamp Duck

The words were red, meaning that the duck

was quite a fearsome enemy. Though on the other hand, it was the first time I had ever seen anything in this area without the skull symbol. The level-eleven duck must have been one of the weakest inhabitants of the whole region. Not counting me, of course. I was lying in the bushes near the water, seven meters from my potential victim and couldn't make up my mind to attack. The tempting idea to get up close and kill the duck with a Vampire Bite had to be thrown out. Right next to the shore, there was a squelching thick muck that I would never be able to walk through unnoticed.

Stealth skill increased to level 6!

After seeing the pleasant message, I decided to go on the attack. I raised my weapon very slowly, aimed it and gave a firm blow! The thorn went straight into the duck's neck, right where I was aiming.

Damage dealt: 31 (48 missile damage - 17 armor)

The duck's health bar went down by a slightly noticeable amount, just seven or eight percent. Jesus! It had more life than three Trong Divers! Now I'd stepped in it! The bird woke up and turned unflinchingly in my direction, flapping its wings loudly, quacking and basically expressing the strongest disapproval of its rude awakening. I jumped to my feet and reloaded the tube with another thorn.

Damage dealt: 12 (29 missile damage - 17 armor)

No luck. I got almost the minimum possible damage. In reply, the duck went silent, made a strange swallowing motion and, spit at me! I barely managed to jump away.

Acrobatics skill increased to level 2!

Right where I'd been standing, the pebbles by the shore gave off an eerie hiss and dissolved in acid. Hey, no fair! Was this really a duck, or a horror-movie alien?! The next two shots missed. The bird sharply tore off upward and set about spinning circles above me with an uncanny quacking, periodically spitting its acid down from above. I couldn't hit the tiny far-off spot, so I decided not to waste the ammo. On the plus side, it also took no effort on my part to jump away from the duck's spit.

Dodge skill increased to level 5!

Great! Perfect timing! I was happy with the growth of the useful skill all on its own. The parallel increase in agility, which also brought with it increased damage taking and aiming ability, was even better. After making an allowance for my target being in motion, I tried to shoot again.

Critical hit: 126 (63*2 missile damage - armor ignored)

Exotic Weapons skill increased to level 2!

The thorn hit the duck right in the eye. My enemy's life bar sagged down by half. The bird was also blinded in the left eye. The duck did a few awkward somersaults in midair, then spit a few times at random, apparently having lost me from view. But after that, it discovered me again, changed tactics and decided to come in for close combat. I flipped away, dodging the pecks it was aiming straight at me. I shot it on its way back up, but missed. And again, looking like a kite in midair, the swamp duck turned around and dived straight at me. But this time, I was expecting it:

Damage dealt: 42 (59 missile damage - 17 armor)

After that, I had to contort myself again to avoid being hit. After taking a shot to the chest, the bird was unable to change its flight trajectory and crashed into the dry swamp-shore pebbles. While the duck was on the ground, I attacked it again.

Damage dealt: 30 (47 missile damage - 17 armor)

The bird, flapping its wings and scrambling to its feet, threw itself at me, but I dodged toward its blind left eye. The duck stopped, having lost sight of me.

Damage dealt: 51 (68 missile damage - 17 armor)

The duck's life bar was down deep in the red and was barely visible at all any more. It had just a few life points left. I walked a semi-circle around the bird to get back on its blind side and hit it with a bite.

Damage dealt: 23 (Vampire Bite)

Experience received: 504 Exp.
*Objects received: Duck meat * 3 (food), Handmade blowgun ammunition * 6*

Level five!

Achievement unlocked: Taste Tester (3/1000)

Racial ability unlocked: 10% Resistance to Poison

Racial ability improved: Taste for Blood (Gives +1% to all damage dealt for each unique creature killed with Vampire Bite. Current bonus: 3%)

Now that's what I'm talking about! That battle with the duck had given me almost as much experience as the total I'd gotten up until that point! Also, my Thirst for Blood was totally sated (15/15). And, speaking of the thirst... I took the empty alchemy container and filled it with the bird's spilled blood. I walked up to the nearest tree and cut a piece of its bark out with my knife, whittled it down and made it into a cork for the vial.

Duck Blood (alchemy ingredient)

It was already starting to get light out. In just half an hour, the deadly sun was going to rise. But I was in no rush to seek shelter just yet. I needed just seven or eight more useful plants to level up my Herbalism skill. It wasn't very far to the building, so I calmly set about gathering plants.

Herbalism skill increased to level 3!

Alright, that was enough. I hurried back to the wooden blockhouse. With four minutes left until morning, I ran up onto the porch... but the door was locked from the inside! The map obligingly informed me that the player Valerianna Quickfoot was currently inside. My sister! She got here after all!

I started pounding on the door, but she wouldn't open up. Had Val gone back to sleep or something?! If she didn't open the door for me in the three minutes I had left, it would be the dumbest death a vampire had ever died in the history of this game. Not in some epic battle with a holy warrior, but right before the front door of his own home, which his own beloved sister had locked! That's what you call bad luck! Also, the respawn point was on an exposed stone square, and appearing there after the sun rose would have meant a guaranteed death...

I wrote a personal message to Valerianna to make her open the door right away, but I wasn't especially counting on being saved. Around the house, there was nowhere I could hide myself from the sun's rays. My only hope was getting inside the building. As the last minute was passing, I was in a true state of panic. Fifteen seconds. Ten...

I heard the heavy beam being moved off the door.

Nine. Eight. Seven. Six. The door peeked open a few centimeters.

"What's all the racket about, Amra?" the yawning wood nymph asked lazily from the doorway.

I flung open the door and pushed the girl from my path in one fluid motion, then dashed up the stairs. Here in the entryway, it was still too bright. The sun's rays might be able to come in through the windows. Five. Four. Three. In the two seconds before the sun came up, I threw myself on the bed and buried myself under a pile of animal pelts. I made it!

__Mission completed: Surviving the Night__
__Experience Received: 160 Exp.__
__Reward: +2 stat points__

__Level six!__

__Number of Thirst for Blood points increased: 15/20__

"Sorry, it's just time for me to get out. It was an emergency. I've got business waiting for me in the real world," I told the nymph, who was in a state of total confusion, then left the game without even assigning the stat points I'd accumulated.

* * *

After taking off the helmet and sensor suit, I sat powerless right on the floor. My hands were still shaking and my heart was pounding in my ribcage. The game had me so worried, it was as if the sun rising in the game really could have killed me torturously, not just made me lose a few hundred experience points. In the moment, the thought didn't even cross my mind that dying in the game really meant nothing. After all, I could get the experience back. No, I wanted to survive with all the cells in my body.

I calmed down a bit, got dressed and walked out of my cabin. I had an unbearable urge to use the bathroom. I rushed down to the end of the long walkway to the nearest bathroom. There were just two doors on the whole floor with a red light over them, mine and that of the redheaded lady I'd seen earlier. The other three hundred doors, as well as all the doors on the opposite walkway were showing green: free rooms. That meant just her and I were still here. So, I immediately noticed the sound of water coming out of the locked shower. At this early hour, there was someone taking a shower on the deserted floor.

Putting myself in order after freshening up, I walked up to the coffee machine. My eyes were sagging. I needed a pick-me-up. Here, at the end of the *Boundless Realm* tester floor, there was a break room with tables, couches, a television on the wall which was now off, and vending machines selling snacks and water. With a mug of hot coffee in my hand, I walked down the row of vending machines and looked over the selection. What I was looking for was a pack of gum drops for my sister. She loved that stuff. I tried paying with my card, but a fully predictable message came up on the screen: "Transaction denied. Insufficient funds." I had to go through my pockets to find coins. Cash had practically gone out of circulation in recent years, but snack machines still took coins. Just after fishing out all the money, I lowered the coins into the slit. What had I done to deserve this?! The baggy of gum drops got stuck on a piece of the internal machinery.

"Woah! I wasn't expecting to see anyone here so early!" A sonorous woman's voice rang out behind my back.

I turned around. Beyond all doubt, this was the very same mystery girl I had seen earlier in a chic emerald-green dress with a hat covering her fire-red hair. But now, she was standing before me with containers of shampoo and lotion in her hands, while the only thing covering her nakedness was a towel wrapped around her body.

"Excuse me, I didn't mean to startle you," I answered, but the woman laughed:

"You?! Startle me?! Believe me, I'm a pretty hard person to startle. It's just that, for the last half year, I've been the only person on this floor to work at night. I wasn't expecting to see anyone, which is why I came out looking like this," she said, pointing at the towel.

"Don't worry about it. I won't bother you. I just finished the quest 'Surviving the Night.' You know it, I'm sure. It's for beginners."

"Oh, you could say I know it," the mystery girl smiled. "I'm the one who designed it two years ago. It was the only way of getting people out of cities at night. So then, did you make it?"

"Yeah, I made it, but it wasn't easy," I answered, talking myself up.

"Good job. Lots of people try, but not many manage to survive all the way to morning. But now, inhabitants of the night do have regular prey," the girl licked her lips in a display of her predatory nature, as if to say she was personally eating the careless unfortunates.

Though, perhaps she really was. Who could say what kind of character she played? Clearly having noticed a change in my behavior, she said:

"Your eyes just grew wide in horror as if you'd seen a monster. I assure you, there's no reason to fear me at all." The woman looked at the stuck bag of gum drops and extended me a whole armful of cosmetics. "Here, hold this!"

Without a remark, I took the mountain of

bottles and tubes, while the woman walked over to the vending machine and extended a hand. The machine went into action. On the upper level, a spiral began spinning, moving forward the chocolate bar the beautiful redhead had chosen. Would you look at that! She had an implanted identification chip instead of any kind of document or bank card! I had heard of such technology, but this was the first time I had actually seen it.

The bar fell top-down on the trapped gum-drop bag and plunked down together with it into the slot.

"So, you see, I don't bite," she smiled, her curly bunches of fine wet hair bobbing as she stood up. "And don't worry about being too formal with me. I'm not much older than you are. By the way, my name is Kira."

"Timothy," I introduced myself and handed the cosmetics back.

She took the products in her arms and stopped to say something, but then... the woman's towel fell to the floor. An awkward situation. Her arms were full, so she couldn't pick up the fallen towel, or even cover her body.

"Kira, let me. I'll help!" With these words, I picked up the towel and wrapped the young woman in it.

Touching her skin, tender and hot after the shower, was insanely pleasant, but I didn't take too long. Even when she kissed me on the cheek in gratitude, I didn't hesitate. This was no place for impossible dreams. Kira and I were too different and had met for too short a time.

"Thank you, Timothy. Maybe we'll see each other around. You can have the chocolate bar. I don't eat chocolate, anyway."

Kira went back to her cabin to get dressed. I spent some time standing and watching her walk away. Before my eyes, I could still see the picture of her seductive curves frozen in time. Well then, now I knew where and when Kira worked, and arranging another meeting with her wouldn't be too much work.

An hour later, I was already jangling my key ring against the door of my rented apartment. I didn't ring the bell as not to wake up Val, but my sister wasn't sleeping at all and rolled out to meet me in her chair.

"Do you mind explaining what the hell that was? You blasted me off my feet and tore into the building as if there was a whole horde of demons after you!"

I saw no reason to hide the truth from my sister, so I told her the details of my character's dark side. Valeria's reaction was unexpected:

"Why were you being so stupid then, bro? You should have killed me with a bite right there at the respawn point, then used Veil to change my logs so no trace remained! At these low levels, a small experience loss for me would be absolutely nothing, but where are you gonna find another wood nymph for your Taste Tester achievement?"

I told her there was no way I would kill her. After hearing out my answer, though, Val shook her head in reproach.

"You know best. Alright, Timothy, go eat breakfast. Everything's warm. And, as this is how it is now, go get some sleep before another night shift. For now, I'll read up on vampires in *Boundless Realm* and think of how your character should progress."

Gray Pack

MY SISTER woke me up.

"Time to get up, Tim! How long can you possibly sleep, lazy-bones?!"

I pried open my eyelids and looked at the time. It was four thirty P.M.

"Why get up so early? In *Boundless Realm*, it only gets dark at nine, and it takes me just one hour to get to work. You should have woken me up closer to eight," I replied. In fact, I was already practically totally rested, and was moaning only to get a rise out of her, which my sister understood perfectly.

I lowered my feet onto the floor and started looking around for my perpetually lost socks. Valeria wheeled up closer to me and opened a dresser drawer.

"I threw your socks into the laundry. Take a new pair. By the way, the landlady came by today. She was quite insistent in reminding me of our three-months of overdue rent. Also, I sold all our characters from *Kingdoms of Sword and Magic* today for five hundred eighty credits. Technically, we could pay a month and a half of back rent with that."

"Let's just give her one month for now. We still need to live on something, after all. I'll send it to her today so she'll hold off a little bit. You're a smart cookie, Val. Did you find anything out about vampires in *Boundless Realm*?"

My sister acquired a look of despondency, rolled up to the computer desk and took out a sheet of paper covered in proper handwriting.

"This is all I found. At one point, there were a lot of vampires in *Boundless Realm*. NPC's and living players as well. In the very first months of the game, 'resettlement mode' was very popular. People would travel by boat to uncharted lands, build fortresses there, then hold the area down with their teeth, fighting back the constant attacks of legions of the unclean and undead. The *Boundless Realm* marketing team then made a successful ploy on human pride and attracted millions of gamers in a short time. I remember the ads from three years ago saying things like: 'Humanity is on the brink of extinction. Your blade could save mankind.'"

"Yes, I remember. As a matter of fact, when I tried to play *Boundless Realm*, it was just such an advertisement that drew me in," I agreed.

"Hm, alright. Well, at that time, vampires were one of the main threats to humanity, and there were many quests to destroy them. For example, human paladins of many schools were obliged to kill at least one vampire to pass an initiation quest. But what the developers back then didn't foresee was that there were suddenly too many people, and not enough vampires to go around. Vampire players were tracked down and simply not allowed to play, constantly getting killed before they could leave the respawn point. Whole hordes of hundreds and even thousands of players would gather to wait for the respawn of a known vampire, all of them hoping to be the one to kill it. There were many complaints, so the developers removed the ability to play as a vampire, and gave the ability to those that already existed to change race. I found a year-old interview with one of the directors of the *Boundless Realm* corporation. In it, he officially stated that there were just fourteen vampire players remaining, and they were all carefully hiding their true nature, as they understood perfectly what could happen if they were uncovered."

"And NPC vampires?" I clarified, putting on my clothes.

~ Video Game Plotline Tester ~

"They were left in, but made very rare and sneaky. They are very hard to uncover. That was why vampire missions haven't disappeared entirely. They were made unnecessary, though, and the reward was made very generous. As for NPC's, it's hard to say how many exist. According to the game mechanics, a dead NPC is dead forever, so discovering and killing an NPC vampire would be a one-time event."

Everything became clear to me. I wasn't wrong when I figured that I should be hiding the fact of my dark nature. But I had seriously underestimated the scale of the problem.

* * *

It might seem strange, but in our gaming partnership, my younger sister was always the brains of the operation. For me, games were just a fun way to pass the time and earn beer money. My sister, though, lived her whole life in virtual worlds. Reading through manuals, and figuring out magic and crafting systems brought her nothing but glee. She also enjoyed solving the puzzles we came across in games, so she usually did it for the both of us. She really liked coming up with the best possible path for our characters' progression, and working out the best way for them to behave. At this point, she probably thought of real life as some kind of virtual reality with good graphics but a horribly dreary plot.

Once upon a time, I had encouraged her interest in video games as an alternative to sinking into hopeless oblivion. I would back down in arguments and allow her to make all the important decisions. My trust in her made her happy, so she solved all our issues with great zeal, proudly presenting me with readymade solutions. Sometimes, her methods seemed questionable, but Valeria always proved to be right in the end. And now as ever, on my way up the granite steps into the *Boundless Realm* skyscraper, something my sister told me was turning over and over in my mind: "You can already level up agility and perception well with your skills. Strength, intelligence and constitution are important, but are still secondary to your character so, ignore them, no matter how scary that may sound. All your new stat points should go straight into charisma."

I walked up the stairs, went through the revolving door into the massive hall and stopped before a turnstile. I placed the magnetic card I was assigned yesterday to the reader, but it lit up red and a horrible buzzing sound rang out. Denied?! I tried it again, but the result was the same. I wasn't being let in to work? But why?! I walked up to the security window and told them my pass wasn't working. The dour muscular security guard took the plastic card from me and entered its number into his computer terminal.

"Your keycard has been blocked. Access to your virtual reality capsule as well. Your character has been banned. Mr. Lavrius ordered you brought directly to his office as soon as you showed up."

My heart simply stopped. It can't have been that I didn't pass the trial period, right? I had so many plans for *Boundless Realm*, and I had been fired on the first damn day! With my soul in a very gloomy place, I went up to the forty-fourth floor, where the special projects division was located. Alexandro Lavrius's office stood out from far away. There were several people milling about near his door. Among them were some of the testers I had been filling out surveys with yesterday.

The director's office doors opened, and the very same middle-aged accountant lady, who hadn't wanted to be a dryad ran out into the corridor with tears in her eyes. She led her troubled gaze over those gathered, then commented:

"I already knew this job wasn't for me yesterday. Today I made sure of that. It's good that I didn't waste too much time here."

The door of the director's office opened, and a fat young man in glasses came out. If I remembered correctly, it was he that had been offering a troll astrologer to exchange with any takers.

"Could anyone figure out how to take the chain off? I couldn't find any way! I spent all day suffering with those shackles on my arms before they stopped me and told me to climb out of the capsule."

"But you're a troll. Your Regeneration is the best of all races. You could have just gnawed your own hand off, and an hour later, left with a new one," I suggested to him, to which the fat man grew irritated, and answered:

"How was I supposed to know that trolls have Regeneration?"

I didn't explain to him that any player should have known that, even total beginners. I mean, how was he planning to play as a troll if he hadn't even taken the pains to read up on the special features of his race?! It seemed clear that the corporation was now sifting out the obvious losers like him. But then, why was I here? Over the director's door, a sign reading "Open" lit up, but no one from the crowd in the corridor had the balls to go in. So I, not giving a damn about whose turn it was, went inside and closed the door behind myself.

Alexandro Lavrius was sitting at a massive, old-fashioned desk. His huge picture window had an incredible view of the dark city from above.

"You wanted to see me, Mr. Director?" I asked, trying to conceal all traces of timidity in my voice.

The man turned around on his spinning chair, stared at me for a long time with a careful, studious gaze, then glanced up inquisitively at his assistant. To hurry him along, she handed her boss a folder and whispered barely audibly: "This is the vampire we were talking about." Comprehension came onto the director's face. He pointed me to a chair, then opened the folder with my dossier:

"So then, Timothy. In your interview, you told us a boldfaced lie. You said had never played *Boundless Realm* before..."

The conversation was going in the worst possible direction, so I took a risk and interrupted my boss. I had nothing to lose at this point anyway.

"That's not true, Mr. Director. I wasn't lying. At the time of the interview, I actually had no memory of the fact that I had played it. The raw, unfinished abomination I started up for a few minutes three and a half years ago was in such an early stage of development, I didn't even process the fact that it was the same game as today's *Boundless Realm*. The product has come so far in the meantime, that it totally slipped my mind. Actually, I already wrote this exact thing on social media, and the video hosting channel I made today as a way of promoting the goblin race."

"Wait. Is that true?" Alexandro Lavrius

turned on his computer screen and started searching. "Yep, that's right. There it is, a brand-new channel. No subscribers, and just one five-minute-long clip. Not much."

"All I've done for now is tell my future subscribers that I just left *KSM* after six years of playing and found myself a new, more entertaining game world. I described my first, unsuccessful attempt to play in great detail. I had to have some explanation for my one-word character name, after all. I thought it could be a good thing, actually. It will make my future viewers less likely to suspect that I work for the company..."

"Well that was a very good decision, Timothy," the director interrupted me. "There are hundreds of millions of normal players, and they don't always have a positive opinion of corporate players. Some see their ability to withdraw game money into the real world and try to bribe them or buy them out. Others complain that our employees level up too fast and suspect that they are using unfair methods, like unique quests unavailable to normal people or hidden treasure troves. Some even believe they can simply change their numbers around at will. That is all nonsense, obviously. But all the same, it is for the best to hide your affiliation with the corporation."

The director went silent and stared at me. I took advantage of the pause and continued my story:

"So, due to the specifics of the vampire race, I won't always be able to be in the game during the day. But, I figured I could spin that to my advantage and use those days to make interesting video clips for my channel. I've only spent one day or, to be more precise, night in-game. Even still, more than enough material has piled up: my unusual method of getting out of the chain, getting up on the galley deck and lowering the boat, killing the conman Trong Diver, my dangerous journey through the forest at night, the friendly wolf pack, making my own weapons suited to my race, and hunting a poison-spitting duck. If I edit it and add an appropriate soundtrack, it should be very interesting to potential viewers."

Alexandro Lavrius thoughtfully turned my dossier over in his hands and set it aside, but not on the pile of other papers. My heart was relieved. It seemed that my firing had been set aside for now.

"Alright, Timothy, your explanations have left me totally satisfied. I'll order the block removed from your character and your pass restored. I expect quality material from you on the goblin race by tomorrow. But keep two important things in mind. First, the viewers won't be interested in only night-time plots. Also, people may start to suspect you if you're only active at night. If you want to avoid revealing your secret, your character must be active during the daytime as well."

"But how, if the sun will turn me to ash in an instant?"

"Daytime doesn't have to mean sun. In our game, there are cloudy, foggy, and rainy days as well. Use them to the best of your ability. The second thing you should keep in mind is that, in comparison to normal players, it will take you a significant amount more time to level. Players who choose traditional, well studied paths, usually reach level eleven by the end of the first day and, by the end of the second, they're already sixteen. So, no matter how interesting your advertising of this alternate path may be, newbies will be forced to consider, above all else, the growth speed of the character. People tend to want everything right away, after all. I hope you have already thought through how your herbalist will gain experience, given that you won't be able to collect plants on sunny days like a normal person."

I nodded curtly, not planning to describe all the details of my leveling plan to my boss.

"Then that's great. By the way, I forgot to say right away that our corporation typically pays small prizes out to people who find new things in the game or discover bugs that we didn't know about before. You have already earned two such prizes: one for your unusual method of escaping the hand cuffs, and another for the class-change error. You get two hundred credits in total. We could give it to you via bank card, or as two thousand coins in the game."

"Bank card would be fine," I answered, my voice even crackling in anticipation. I had to repeat myself.

What perfect timing! I needed a deposit into my account so the bank wouldn't block my card. This was simply miraculous!

"Alright, you can expect the money by the end of the day. Have you got any questions about work?"

"Yes, Mr. Director. I wasn't able to find an answer to the following question in the forums: if a player kills me just because they dislike goblins or some other reason not related to vampires, but they have a quest to kill a vampire somewhere in their backlog, would the quest be completed?"

"Huh..." the director replied, thinking it over. "It would seem utterly illogical if the secret of vampirism could be uncovered so easily. As far as I see it, to finish a vampire-killing quest, you should have to fulfill some preliminary condition to make sure you actually uncovered said vampire first. Otherwise, quests to find undead in a certain village could be completed by just killing all residents wholesale. Alright, get back to work. My assistant will ask our programmers for the answer to that question."

* * *

I only finished editing the video around eight at night. Yes, it was quite the slog, but I can say without excessive modesty that it turned out quite well. In the fifteen-minute clip, I managed to convey the atmosphere of doom and gloom on the orcish galley, the raging sea, and the fervor of the battle with the naiad, as well as the spookiness of the forest at night. It was all overdubbed with ironic commentary by me. I pointed out all my errors and missed chances with no obfuscation whatsoever. For example, I directly said that "my big-eared freak is tongue-tied and pretty dumb." After posting the video, I was finally ready to continue the game.

I took a look at my character's stat sheet before starting my second day:

~ Video Game Plotline Tester ~

Name	Amra
Race	Goblin Vampire
Class	Herbalist
Experience	1280 of 1800
Character level	6
Hit points	57/57
Endurance points	45/45
Statistics	
Strength (S)	7 (7)
Agility (A)	8 (17.1)
Intelligence (I)	5 (5.8)
Constitution (C)	9 (9)
Perception (P)	3 (10.2)
Charisma (Ch)	8 (9)
Unused points	**2**
Primary skills (4 of 4 chosen)	
Herbalism (P A)	3
Trading (Ch I)	1
Alchemy (I A)	1
Dodge (A P)	5
Secondary skills (4 of 4 chosen)	
Stealth	6
Veil	2
Acrobatics	2
Exotic Weapons	2

No matter what the director said about my slow progress, I was proud of my big-eared Amra! I also liked his appearance. My sister had taken a shot at it during the day, and the result was a sweet little smile-inducing green goblin face, that no player would associate with vampires or danger. I had already loaded it into the game and confirmed that I wanted to change the appearance of my character. As my sister had recommended, I put my two free stat points into charisma.

And then, my second night in the game began. Well, actually, night had yet to fall. Just after the virtual reality capsule closed, I found myself curled up on the bed inside the blockhouse under a layer of heavy, stinking pelts. I carefully poked my head out and took a look around. The sun was already below the horizon. Through the arrowslit, I could only see clouds lit up slightly pink. Alright then, the burning sun was no longer a threat to me. I could start playing. Where to begin?

The first thing I noticed was that the dark bloody spot in the center of the room was gone, and the floor now harbored traces of mopping. I couldn't believe my sister sometimes. After that, I noticed that my goblin was hungry and, what was more, wanted to drink blood. I opened my inventory and fed my big-eared troglodyte the duck meat, sating my hunger. Now was time to drink the blood I had saved from the night before, and I could get on with my business. What the? I stared in incomprehension at the vial of duck blood. The liquid in it had coagulated and turned dark brown.

Spoiled blood (waste)

Come on! I looked in fear at the Quenching the Thirst bar. It was blinking an ominous shade of red at 1/20! I had less than an hour to drink some blood, otherwise I'd lose control! Time to get hunting before it was too late!

On the map, not too far from my building I saw Valerianna Quickfoot's marker. There were several red dots spinning loops around the wood nymph. Was my sister in combat? I had to help her! But the group of dots continued moving measuredly with her toward the building and was now near the stockade fence. I looked out the window. Next to my sister, there were three huge brown toads hopping along.

Level-7 Warty Toad

It didn't appear that the nymph was afraid of the beasts, so they must have been the beast master's new pets. I walked out onto the veranda. The toads froze abruptly and, after a command from Valerianna I couldn't make out, their markers on the map changed from red to green. It all made sense. My sister was telling them I was a friend.

"Greetings, big-ears. Oh, I see you drew yourself a new face. Was that so monsters wouldn't get so scared of you? I'm joking. Your new friendly countenance suits you. Why didn't you come around during the day? I've grown exhausted from boredom already. I've been all around the area. Are you ready to get going?"

My sister, it should be said, was playing a part we had agreed on earlier. The plan was to flip a coin to decide whether we would stay in the shelter for a few more days or not. But I didn't have time for that right now! I needed to find a victim and suck their blood right away! I tried to suppress my need to hurry, though, and replied according to our plan.

"Where we going?" I asked, faking incomprehension. "House be. Safe. Me want here, for see game."

Technically, my undergrown intelligence was now high enough that I didn't have to speak in this distorted way, but my sister and I had decided that this manner of speech gave Amra a certain uniqueness and even charm. And beyond that, it would give strangers the illusion that I was a totally moronic primordial creature. Sometimes, it's useful to seem dumber than you really are. It makes enemies underestimate you.

"But what is there to do around here? We're

in the middle of nowhere. It's just forest and swamp for kilometers. I mean, sure, there are two villages not far from here. One is human, seven kilometers from here. It's called Stonetown. I was there today. They greeted me cautiously, but let me through the gate. There didn't seem to be much to do there. There were only twenty buildings. They didn't even have their own blacksmith. Though they do have a healer, who buys herbs. Maybe you'd be interested in that. And there's also a goblin village to the southeast, but I didn't go there. I got attacked by the aggressive guards, who were level sixty or so and quickly died."

> ***Mission received: Socialization 1/3***
> ***Make contact with the inhabitants of the Human village***
> ***Make contact with the inhabitants of the Goblin village***
> ***Mission class: Chain, group***
> ***Reward: 800 Exp.***

"Hey!" My sister went silent, either from the new quest, or because she had just seen a large dark gray wolf at the dilapidated gates of our stockade. "Him again! That wolf has been a royal pain in the neck all day for me! This morning, he ate all my pets. Then, during the day, he did it again. But there's nothing for me to do. He's much higher level than me, and he travels with three other strays just like him. It's incredibly hard to level up beast master with monsters like this everywhere! Every time a pet dies, I lose two skill levels!"

Though my sister had managed to hit level nine today, she had no chance of taking down a level-twenty-seven seasoned forest wolf. It was all leading to the gray-furred predator treating himself to Valerianna's entranced creatures yet again. And it should be said that the wolf was green on the map for me, meaning it was friendly. Ugh, here goes nothing! I walked out to meet the predator, who was still sitting at the gate, not having made up his mind to enter our enclosure.

"Hunger? You for meat eating!" I threw the last piece of duck meat to the forest creature.

But the wolf gave a grudging shake of its tail to the meat, didn't touch it and walked away. Then, the female level-22 seasoned forest wolf trotted over in my direction. I immediately noticed her bulging belly and swollen teats. By all appearances, the wolf was in the very last stage of pregnancy and was getting ready to be a mother very soon. After quickly swallowing the piece of meat on the ground, she stared at me expectantly. The other two level-27 seasoned forest wolves strutted out of the forest behind her, and I now had four beasts staring me down with hungry eyes.

~ Video Game Plotline Tester ~

Mission received: Feed the Pack
Mission class: Rare, individual
Reward: Variable

Would you look at that! A rare quest with a variable reward based on how I completed the mission. Very intriguing. So then, the mission was to feed four hungry mouths.

"Nymph, where you be finding toad?" I asked Valerianna, who was standing on the deck ready to duck inside the building at a moment's notice.

"Not far away. I'll mark it for you on the map now. Go get 'em! But just so you know, toads scare easily. They dive into the water almost right away."

The player Valerianna Quickfoot would like to sell you: Local map
Price: free

Naturally, I agreed and opened my updated map. That's what I'm talking about! My sister had been very busy today: everything within a kilometer of the blockhouse had already been studied in detail, as well as roads in both directions as well. The human village of Stonetown, located seven kilometers from my current location, was also revealed, but the nymph had not gone further down the road than that. In the other direction, the discovered area along the road cut off sharply four kilometers from us.

There, she had placed a note: "Danger!!!" My interest was also drawn by the other notes my sister had placed on the map: "Cave, still haven't gone in," "Flower field," "Something's lair, horrible stench," "Copper vein in rock," and finally "Swamp with level-7-12 toads."

After placing a marker over the swamp, a direction arrow showed up with a distance number under it: eight hundred thirty meters. Approaching the wolf, whose opinion of me had increased to friendship, I looked him right in the eyes and said aloud:

"This toad, no bite. Other place, many-many same. I show and bring wolfies. You can eating all. We to road."

The wolf looked at me understandingly and lied down on the ground. I got up on the back of the forest predator and pointed the way with my finger, then fervently shouted out:

"We forward! Pack hunting!"

All four of the wolves tore off from their place and rushed off where I was pointing. I was slightly worried for the extra encumbered she-wolf, but she was also confidently keeping pace. A private message came in from my sister:

"Hey, how'd you do that?"

I didn't answer, as I didn't really know myself how I had been able to communicate with wolves. Just a minute later, the pack had reached the edge of the huge swamp and I ordered them to stop. I jumped down from the wolf and shouted to the predators, trying to make my voice louder than the deafening croaking coming from the swamp:

"Wolfies stay by pebbles. I shooting, lure to me. Lead here toad. Together, you biting."

As silent gray shadows, all four of the beasts split up in different directions and hid in the nearest bushes. I then went carefully forward, loading ammunition into my weapon. I didn't have to go far before seeing my first victim behind a set of nearby bushes:

Level 9 Warty Toad

The huge toad was the size of a fully-grown Doberman. It was croaking away with abandon, blowing bubbles out both sides of its cheeks. It didn't notice me until I shot:

Damage dealt: 53 (59 missile damage - 6 armor)

Just one shot had taken a whole third of the overgrown amphibian's life bar away. If the toad were a bit smarter, it would have realized that it shouldn't get into it with me, despite its level advantage. But in the game, just like in real life, amphibians didn't possess very impressive brainpower. I rolled to the side. When the toad had finished its jump, it landed with a huge squelching sound where I'd just been standing. Its long, sticky tongue shot out, but I saw it coming and easily turned away and ran a few steps back from the enemy. Another jump followed to the place I had just left, and its sticky tongue shot out another time into thin air. In theory, I could have dealt with such an immobile and predictable enemy myself, but I decided it would be a waste of time:

"Sic! Catching, bite!"

The predators appeared form all sides instantly and tore their prey to shreds.

Experience received: 58 Exp.

It was very little experience in total, given that it was split between five. But that was not the point. I was more concerned with its loot. Without paying attention to the terrible groaning and bared teeth of the greedily meat-devouring she-wolf, I walked up to the trophy with my vial at the ready, and filled it with blood before the wolves were finished gulping down their prey:

Toad Blood (alchemy ingredient)
Achievement unlocked: Taste Tester (4/1000)

I immediately drank the blood I'd collected, noting that the Quenching the Thirst bar went up by just three to 4/20. Not much. Either I was supposed to drink the blood straight from my victim, or the toad wasn't a great donor candidate for me. After noticing that my wolf partners hadn't left even a bite of their prey, I walked out to find another toad.

By experimentation, I figured out that toads lower than level-nine would dive fearfully into the water if hit, taking my ammo with them in their bodies, so I concentrated on the very largest individuals.

Level-12 Warty Toad

I didn't lure the beast to the wolves. I was just feeling too greedy to share experience with the wolves this time. Fortunately, the elevated level of my enemy had very little effect on its intellectual capabilities. This toad behaved just as predictably as the lesser specimens had. Beyond that, I discovered that the toad would quickly lose sight of me if I stood motionless. It was, as they say, my lucky day. It was no problem for me to shoot the toad from afar with my darts then kill it with a Vampire Bite.

Experience received: 640 Exp.

Objects received: Toad meat * 5 (food), Toad hide, Hand-made blowgun ammunition * 9

Level seven!

Racial ability improved: Taste for Blood (Gives +1% to all damage dealt for each unique creature killed with Vampire Bite. Current bonus: 4%)

Racial ability unlocked: 10% Resistance to Poison

Cool! And if you consider that I completely sated my Thirst for Blood to 20/20, and improved my Exotic Weapons skill to level three in the process, I couldn't have been happier! After calling over my furry helpers, I showed them to the toad's corpse. Two seconds later, there was nothing left. The she-wolf retched from overeating and walked up closer, licking my cheek good-heartedly with her bloody tongue.

Mission completed: Feed the Pack

Now, all four wolves on the map were shown as green markers. I waited for a few more "little bonuses" for completing the rare quest, but nothing further happened. Except perhaps the fact that one of the wolves laid down on the earth again, offering me a ride. The hunt can't seriously have been over already, right?! It would be too bad if that was true. I just got the taste for it. But with every second of delay, the wolves grew more and more nervous, and their anxiety transferred over to me. I had barely crawled up on the back of the gray-furred predator before it shot off like an arrow, its ears pressed to its head in panicky fear at something I couldn't comprehend. The other wolves were close on its heels.

"Amra, don't forget that night is about to fall."

Just as my sister's message came in, I heard a fell sound from the swamp behind me, somewhat like a laugh or croak. I turned around in fear. In the same small glade where the wolves had recently torn the first frog to shreds, there was a majestic creature:

Level-42 Fetid Bullfrog Patriarch

The reason for my canine friends' worry immediately grew clear. Now, I was in complete agreement with them, and couldn't get away from the swamp fast enough. The last thing I wanted was to die. A minute later, the wolves let me off near the broken gates of my barricade. I jumped down onto the earth and chummily clapped the back of my weary, panting mount. And it should be said that it was hard to not confuse him with his brethren. Before, I had differentiated this wolf by the color of its marker on the map, but now, the markers for all the forest predators were an identical green. I tried to make my own note under the wolf's name on the map. It turned out quite easy. The name I chose came up over his head almost instantly: "Akella."

"Give names to the others, too!" suggested the nymph, who was keeping her distance, and I followed her advice.

Next to Akella, appeared White Fang and Lobo, while the nameless female became Blanca. It was surprising, but the wolves clearly sensed the name change in some way, as they started exchanging surprised looks.

"Dumbo, the wolves are yellow to me now. They're no longer aggressive!" the wood nymph called out in surprise. "And they're all such pretty wolves, as if they were handpicked. Perhaps, when I get to be higher level than them, I'll take them as pets."

As if in reply to those words, from the depths of the forest there came a vile, bone-chilling howl, followed by a concert of yipping. The wolves all perked up their ears in unison and, staring into the darkness, bristled their fur and bared their teeth.

> *Mission received: Protect the Pack*
> *Mission class: Rare, group*
> *Required condition: Blanca must survive the night*
> *Reward: 800 Exp.*
> *Optional condition: All pack members must survive*
> *Reward: Variable*

A shudder ran over me. No matter who or what was approaching from the darkness, the wolves were panicking in fear of it. And their fear transferred to me. I looked at the fallen gate door. Well, I could pick it up and put it back on the hinges...

Your character doesn't have enough Strength to complete this action
Necessary minimum Strength of 200 to lift this gate door

.

Your character doesn't have enough Agility to complete this action
Necessary minimum Agility of 200 to put the door on the hinges

Alright then, I wouldn't be able to fix the gate and protect myself from the nocturnal beasts, after all. But if the outer ring of defensive structures couldn't save me, perhaps it would be worth trying to convince the wolves to hide in the building?

"Akella, go in home. Take friends. Door is locking in."

I didn't have to try very hard to convince the forest predators. One after the other, the wolves headed up toward the porch and began scratching at the step. My sister ducked into the house, then I let the wolves in, and quickly followed after them, locking the sturdy door behind myself with the heavy log. Valerianna Quickfoot made a comment, standing at the very top step and looking at the gray beasts quivering in fear:

"They should stay on the first floor. During the day, I got some water in a birch-bark bucket. It's down there. They can drink if they want. But don't let them upstairs..."

The end of the nymph's sentence was drowned out in a ghastly roar that rang out from the yard. The seasoned wolves, whimpering in fear like little puppies, rushed away from the entrance door and huddled in a corner of the kitchen. I glanced cautiously out the arrowslit. Inside the fence, there were a few tall hunch-backed creatures milling about on four long lanky legs. The creatures' eyes shone out in the darkness in a bright ruby-red.

Level-54 Warg

The sounds they had made earlier had made me somewhat cautious, sure, but now I couldn't even imagine leaving the building tonight. I was immediately reminded that my inventory still contained a huge number of various herbs with as-of-yet unknown properties. Also, it felt like time to start leveling my Alchemy skill. It had gone neglected long enough. So, in the end, being trapped in here wasn't such a loss.

"Amra, it's time for me to leave the game." By all appearances, my sister had just caught a glimpse of the monsters in the yard as well and had little desire to get any closer to them herself. "How about, tomorrow morning, we go to the goblin village? They won't shoot you on sight, after all, and you can tell them I'm, like, with you. We need to complete the Socialization quest, after all."

Tomorrow morning? My sister hadn't seriously forgotten, right? How could I go anywhere, if I could be killed by just one little beam of sunlight? As if answering my unasked question, Valerianna added:

"The wind will drive dense clouds over here. The whole sky will be fuzzy like a cat's tail. Tomorrow, it will be overcast and rainy all day."

So, that's what she was thinking! The inclement weather really had fully changed the situation! That was just awesome! I needed to take advantage of any opportunity to be active during the day, so no one would suspect that my goblin was a vampire, and a rainy day was an excellent opportunity for just such an outing!

"Alright. Amra there, be protecting nymph. I to see tomorrow. To go for village of my kind."

Socialization

THE NYMPH, her legs crossed, took a seat on the floor and froze — my sister had left the game. Thirty seconds later, Valerianna's body began to dissipate and, a few moments after that, was totally gone. Her three pet frogs disappeared along with her. Alright, so that's what it looks like from someone else's perspective! If a character didn't have any aggression penalties and wasn't a criminal, they would just disappear without a trace, becoming invisible to all other inhabitants of *Boundless Realm*. The hint I called up told me that aggression against an NPC would increase the time it took for a character to disappear to ten minutes, aggression against a living player that didn't lead to a character becoming a criminal (for example, a legally permitted duel or a fistfight in a tavern) would bring the delay up to thirty minutes, robbing others brought it up to two hours, and killing a player made it eight.

What? It was useful information for the future. We goblins were a weak and cowardly folk. A timely log-off could perhaps be the best way to escape certain situations. What did I care if PvP-focused players shrieked in indignation and told me off for using "unfair methods?" As if a fight between a high-level warrior and a noncombat character, doomed from the outset, had any fairness in it to begin with...

Before leaving the game, my sister had spoken of approaching clouds. Now, I could already see lightning all over the horizon and hear blasts of thunder. But here, over my shelter, the sky was still clear. The light of the moon was more than enough to avoid bumping into walls in the semi-dark room, but to do more delicate work, I needed to light candles or lamps. In that I didn't have either of those things, I tried something else: I activated night vision and got to work. I placed my empty vials on the table in the room upstairs, got clean water in a little baked-clay saucer I found in the kitchen and spread out a rag I had found among the bed pelts. Then, I hung bundles of herbs to dry around the room, as well as wreathes of flowers, rings of mushrooms and bunches of berries. It smelled nice in the room now, like forest flowers, and for some reason, honey. The room started looking like an alchemy laboratory or a healer's dwelling.

So, let's get started! I already knew that eating one bunch of swamp currant would restore one hit point. The juice I pressed from these berries had the same property. It took three bunches of berries to fill one vial.

Experience received: 4 Exp.
You have created a Minor Elixir of Healing (restores +3 HP)
New recipe added to Journal

I was able to determine the properties of the simplest alchemical potions despite my fairly weak intelligence, which made the work easier. The potions that restored just three hit points were total crap, but I was still proud of myself, because it was the first elixir I had made all on my own. After swamp currant, I tried preparing a potion made of swamp horsetail.

Experience received: 4 Exp.
You have created a Weak Botanical Poison (removes 3 HP)
New recipe added to Journal

Experimenting in that way, I quickly filled

all the vials I had. The time had come to try some more complicated recipes by mixing the elixirs together. I drank one of the useless mixtures down to free up a vessel and mixed the weak botanical poison and the weak elixir of confusion, which I had just made from slimy brown mushrooms.

Experience received: 8 Exp.
You have created an unknown beverage (potion)

Insufficient Intelligence to identify object

Alchemy skill increased to level 2!

Taking the vial in my hands, I looked at the cloudy white substance. I knew that, in the past, it was common practice to describe the taste of a new substance, not only for the alchemists of the far-off middle-ages, but also for well-educated chemists all the way up to the middle of the nineteenth century, who noted it in their lab journals alongside other physically observable properties. That rule had cost the inventor of Hydrogen cyanide, Wilhelm Scheele, his life as well as many other scientists. But unlike them, for me, death wasn't that big of a deal. And I also had a certain Resistance to Poisons. Welp, here goes! I drained the vial in one gulp, after which I stumbled and almost fell over.

Damage taken: 5 (poison)
Your character is paralyzed for 0.5 seconds

By all appearances, I had created a weak poison that caused temporary paralysis. Not bad, not bad at all. Then the light in the room went noticeably dim for some reason. I turned toward the window and jumped up in surprise. Looking in at me through the arrowslit, there was a huge yellow eye!

Level-48 Cyclops

How tall must this monster have been? It was staring at me through a second story window! I grabbed for my weapon and, alternating a few printable words with an abundance of curses, I promised the monster I would do to it exactly what Odysseus had done and create a new species of eye-less giants, if it didn't stop staring at me. The cyclops sighed in pity and walked away from the window. Based on the map, there were eight various kinds of beast wandering around outside my shelter. What could they want here?! Was it caked in honey?!

I threw off the unwelcome thoughts and returned to my experiments. My Alchemy skill leveled up. Now was the very time to check whether the level of this skill would allow me to make stronger potions. I set about pressing swamp currant berries into a vial again and looked at the result:

Minor Elixir of Healing (restores +4 HP)

Bingo! I shouted in joy. Sure, the effectiveness of the potion had grown by just one HP, but that was just the beginning! I needed to look toward the future: as my Alchemy skill grew, the potions I created would become stronger and stronger. They would be better at healing, restoring endurance and, the weak poisons I made now that caused half a second of paralysis... I started grinning from ear to ear. Because... what exactly did it say in the properties of Vampire Bite?

When attacking sleeping, unconscious, or paralyzed targets, chance of success is 100%, and attacker may choose an effect: (Instant death/6-hour deep sleep/Infect with Vampirism)

What an "imba" that would be in the future! After all, I just needed a few seconds of paralysis to get up to a victim and bite. And soon, I would be able to make potions that did just that. Beware, NPC monsters! This weak little goblin just discovered a path that, with time, would allow him to become a threat to the whole of *Boundless Realm*!

Some strange sounds coming from below distracted me from continuing my alchemy. The wolves were growling menacingly, trying to drive off an enemy I couldn't see. I heard gnashing and cracking. I picked up my blowgun and hurried downstairs. Akella, Lobo and White Fang were standing before the barred door, their fur bristling, and were baring their frightening teeth. Lobo was scratching up the floor and door from inside with his claws. What was going on? Did they want to get out and fight with someone? And though, based on the map, there were no less than ten enemies nearby, there were none shown right out the door.

Just then, my attention was drawn by incomprehensible slurping sounds from the kitchen and the sharp smell of blood mixed something else I couldn't recognize. I took a cautious look in that direction. Blanca was slurping down a flexible red tube with a dismayed grumbling. After swallowing it, the she-wolf lowered her snout and began licking a tiny blind puppy clean. I made a step forward to take a closer look at the newborn wolf pup, but Blanca bared her teeth and her marker color changed from green to yellow on the map. I then stepped back:

"Amra to understand. Not get in way."

I went up the stairs to the second floor and chose the menu option "Exit Game." After opening the top of the virtual reality capsule, I didn't even get out. I just extended my hand, took my cellphone from the table and called my sister.

"I know you're asleep. But Blanca is giving birth. She might need some help."

"Have you lost your mind, Tim? She's a wolf. She doesn't need any midwifery. She'll manage on her own. Although... I'll just log in quick anyway. I've never seen an NPC animal give birth before."

It was just after three in the morning. I wanted horribly to eat something. That's not to say that my big-eared Amra's food bar was getting low. I wanted to eat for real. I crawled out of the virtual reality capsule and took off the sensor net that sent electronic impulses to my body. I got out the bag of sandwiches and a bottle of mineral water my sister had put together. My hunger sated, I took a look down the row of cabins. Just like yesterday, there were two red lights on, and many green ones. Just Kira and I were still here. Right after I'd arrived this evening, after the conversation with the director, the situation was very contrasting. All the cabin doors were lit up red. Almost no free ones were to be found then.

* * *

When I got back to the game, my sister was already sitting next to the she-wolf and, for some reason,

Blanca wasn't trying to chase her away. After turning to me, Valerianna Quickfoot made a dismayed comment:

"Blanca is afraid of you, so you should go upstairs and stay out of this. Also, we were preparing to go meet up with your countrymen this morning. Do you really want to go practically naked in nothing but a loincloth? The other goblins will make fun of you! At least take a pelt from the cot and sew yourself a fur vest and some kind of pants."

I nodded and ran upstairs. While I was standing and looking pensively at the old stinking pelts on the bed, my sister appeared and took a pair of the widest pelts to the kitchen for herself. I had to make do with what remained. It wasn't at all hard to make a fur vest for my goblin. I simply cut a rectangular piece from the pelt and made armholes in it.

But the trousers took a bit more work. At first, I tried for a long time to scratch a pattern into the back side of the pelt. After that, lacking adequate needles and thread, I had to make little holes with a knife and manually attach the edges with rotting, constantly ripping thread. When I finally finished the difficult task, it had grown light outside. The morning was rainy and overcast, but that didn't stop the quest from finishing.

Mission completed: Protect the Pack

Reward: 800 Exp.
Optional condition fulfilled: Go to Blanca for reward

Level eight!
Racial ability improved: 15% Resistance to Poison

When I got downstairs, the wolves were half-asleep and looking calm. When they saw me, they jumped up abruptly, sniffing noisily, and stared me down with their eyes wide open in surprise. After that, White Fang got down on his back and began rolling around the floor. The behavior must have meant something along the lines of "LMAO."

"Amra, you may be a decent herbalist but, to be perfectly frank, making clothes is not your thing," my sister commented on my appearance, barely able to hold back her laughter.

With a shame-filled wave of my hand, I walked over to Blanca. The she-wolf was still laying in the corner of the kitchen. Next to her soft fur, there were four tiny wolf pups lying fast asleep.

"Blanca already gave me the black one second from the right. You can pick one of the others!" Valerianna Quickfoot warned me.

But I hesitated, not in any rush to make my choice. First, what did I need a wolf pup for? The baby forest wolf would clearly be advantageous to the nymph. She was a beast master after all, and she needed a pet to level up. But then, what did I need it for? Second, I had a feeling in my bones that Blanca was in no mood to give a wolf pup to me. I mean, if I demanded the reward for protecting the pack, Blanca would give me one of her pups without complaint, but the she-wolf was adamantly opposed on the inside. Third, how else could I understand the quest reward "variable?" They could have just written directly: "Reward: One wolf pup."

"Amra not taking child from mother. Blanca keeping wolflings."

CRITICAL ERROR!
The Boundless Realm *game client will* now *be restarted*
We apologize for the possible inconvenience

The world began to fade. Some technical code lines ran before my eyes. Twenty seconds passed and the picture grew clear once again. So, what happened? I was standing next to Blanca. The quest was already finished. No experience had been added, but the markers for all the wolves on the map had changed from green to blue. The popup hint told me that this color meant allies or fellow clan members.

Also, the fork and spoon crossed over a plate

image appeared. My big-eared troglodyte had grown hungry again. It was time to go back on the hunt. Morning had come, so the most dangerous enemies were gone now. I opened the entrance door and walked outside. The door and wall around it bore traces of fresh scratches on the outside. Last night's uninvited guests must have tried to break in. Some claw marks were very high up, and I got scared even imagining what kind of monsters might have left them. But the door held out, and that was what mattered.

"Pack, hunt toad!" I shouted fervently, and the wolves hurried to the exit. Just Blanca remained inside with her pups.

Taking my usual seat on Akella's back, I was already preparing to give the command to move out.

"Amra, do you think I could come with you?" The nymph asked timidly, and I gave my permission.

Lobo went down on his belly and the wood nymph scrambled up on top of him. I gave a rakish whistle and the pack tore off from their places. A minute later, we were back at our old hunting ground. Rain was falling. Visibility had fallen appreciably, and the croaking amphibians were many times greater in number than they had been the night before. After ordering the wolves to hide, I went to find a victim.

It soon became clear that only toads of level

eleven or twelve could be provoked into attacking simply by attacking them. All the others, including the large level-ten frogs simply fled to safety. Bad, very bad even. It meant that soon, as my character grew in level, the swamp would become a worse and worse hunting spot for me. Nevertheless, I quickly ate my fill and even sated my Thirst for Blood. But the wolves, being level twenty-seven, were still not full.

In our search for large toads, we went a bit further than before. And here, my sister pointed with her hand at some far off elevated area, barely visible through the sheet of rain. I couldn't figure out what it was, but it seemed to me that something over there was moving.

"Big-ears, it's shown on the map as a question mark. That means it's an unknown location. Must be interesting. We should go take a closer look..."

Mission received: Curiosity and the Cat
Mission class: unique, group, time-limited
Description. Investigate the mysterious island in the swamp within 2 days, 23 hours, and 59 minutes
Reward: 8000 Exp.

Eight thousand exp!!! My character had just 2976 experience points in total and just for completing this one quest, I was being offered this very generous reward! I would hit level thirteen just from that! The nymph was in just such a state of joyful elation:

"Ten thousand experience!!! That's what I'm talking about! That would put me up to level fourteen! But something about the name of the mission is worrying me. After all, we all know where curiosity gets the cat in the saying!"

We walked along the swamp shore to check for another way to access the island. Neither the nymph nor I could easily get through it on our own. Also, even though I couldn't get information on them from this far, seeing the monsters over there did nothing to increase my confidence. They looked like many-armed snakes or hydras of some kind.

"Alright, dumbo. Let's not waste time. Let's get out of this muck and go to the goblin village."

The predators took us back to the shelter, and Valerianna Quickfoot fed the hungry Blanca some toad meat. After that, I suggested that we ride the wolves there, but my sister cut me off sharply:

"If we do that, we'll lose the wolves. They'll be shot through by goblin bowmen. We'd better go on foot to make sure your countrymen see you and recognize you as one of their own. It isn't so far from here. We'll be there in an hour or so. And you can collect useful plants on the way. There's a crazy amount of flowers by the road."

* * *

The nymph yawned as she walked. My little sister had clearly not slept enough last night and was fighting back her weariness. Her three toads were obediently hopping behind her, waiting patiently as I stopped and ripped out forest or field flowers. We really did come across a great number of plants, and I easily raised my Herbalism skill to level four. We still hadn't even yet reached the place where goblin archers had shot the nymph from the bushes the day before when a harsh voice shouted out to me:

"Halt! Not a step further!"

I stopped obediently and made a hand motion to my sister so she would also freeze. From behind the trunk of a mighty giant tree, there came a large goblin with yellow-brown skin coloration and a full quiver of long darts on his back.

Level-48 Goblin Dart-Thrower

Lord what an ugly face! He had a huge uneven face full of small sharp teeth, wrinkly skin, and two huge yellow eyes. His right eye was torn as if by biting and his left ear was hanging broken. His nose was covered in scars. He reminded me of a fight-loving stray dog with scarred up snout attesting to all of his victories and defeats. But the ugly goblin wasn't looking at me at all.

"A mavka! Not another one! Just yesterday we killed one, and now we've got another."

Based on how the severe-looking goblin reached for a dart, the nymph could expect another death and respawn. I rushed to intervene:

"Stop! She is no enemy to goblins! The nymph is with me!"

Successful check for Goblin Dart-Thrower reaction
Experience received: 40 Exp.

"Mavkas are dangerous. They wait until the time is right and lure honest goblins deep into the forest, then attack and eat them," the scarred-up veteran mumbled, but still lowered his weapon.

I took advantage of the moment to introduce myself and my companion, after which I said that we were searching for a goblin village, and our purposes were strictly peaceful. The guard stroked his nose in contemplation and pointed his hand at something in the distance:

"Ah, well then you've arrived. Our village is right over there. Just past the bend in the road, you'll find Tysh. When you get there, make sure you introduce yourself to our leader Ugruem first. He must be shown the proper level of respect, or you'll upset him. And you must go to Kaiak right after that. He's the one who gives out jobs in the village. And don't let the mavka out of your sight. It'd be a pity for there to be any unfortunate misunderstandings!"

When we'd put a bit of distance between us and the dart-thrower, the nymph asked me what he and I were talking about. I even stopped in surprise.

"But nymph was hearing! You standing close!"

"Sure, I heard that you were talking, but I don't speak goblin!"

So then! That was it! Amra wasn't tongue-tied at all when speaking his native language. I explained the essence of the conversation to my sister in brief and, at the same time, asked why they had been calling her a "mavka."

"Well you see, to them, I am a 'mavka.' A 'rusalka' of the forest. It's all from Eastern European folklore. A mavka is a forest spirit that leads travelers from their path and brings them to the middle of nowhere, where they disappear forever. The devs must have given these goblins Slavic mythology."

I asked the wood nymph if there was a grain of truth in the scary campfire stories, or if they were all made up from beginning to end. My Amra barely got that complicated sentence out in his faltering language. The nymph laughed mysteriously.

"You may not have noticed, but I am carnivorous and eat raw meat. It could very well be that some other mavkas really do use magic to attract lone travelers into the depths of the forest. But nymphs don't have fangs or claws to deal with their prey. Whether mavkas kill their victims from afar with magic, sic forest predators on them or lead them out to more dangerous relatives, kikimoras and leshies, is of little importance. But then, there is another well-known folk tale, a purely invented one, that a captured forest rusalka can grant three wishes. That has absolutely no hint of truth to it."

We went silent, not finishing our conversation, because we had finally reached the first line of fortifications: rows of stakes driven into the earth at an angle. Some of them were still adorned with the hanging bodies of half-decomposed monsters. Behind this first line of defense, there was a wide dug-out ditch filled with stagnant water. The smell of decomposition from that ditch was so pungent that I had to hold my sensitive nose. The nymph also squeezed her nose with her hand and commented on all the fortifications:

"It would seem various beasts regularly attempt to break into the village. But few get up to the wall, and those who do are cleaned up by arrows from those two towers there."

And in fact, the village of Tysh was very hard to break into. There was a steep hill, then a line of stakes, a ditch full of water, and a wide ravine leaving the enemy just one way in: straight down the road past the defensive towers, each of which could hold a dozen archers. And just now, we were walking right between those towers. My sister pointed me to a set of huge metal spikes sticking a meter out of the gate doors.

Right next to the village entrance itself, there were ten huge goblins butchering the body of a huge creature for meat. I noticed a great many arrows and darts sticking out of the beast's hide. I overheard a bit of their conversation and figured out that this beast had been trying to bash down the gates, but was stopped by the village defenders. My appearance didn't arouse especial concern among the residents but the wood nymph, on the other hand, was met with shocked gawking. Still, though, no one tried to stop her.

"I need to find Ugruem," I said to one of the goblin butchers.

Successful check for Goblin Patriarch reaction
Experience received: 80 Exp.

"Consider him found, boy. What do you need?" the fat goblin butcher asked, turning to me. He was wearing a leather apron, carrying a cleaver in his hand, and was covered head-to-toe in blood.

I would swear on anything that, a second earlier, I had seen a black skull over his head, meaning he was over fifty levels higher than me. Just then, his name appeared as well:

Ugruem Butcher
Level-87 Goblin Patriarch

Level eighty-seven! I tried not to look too surprised and told him about my fleeing the slave-traders' galley and the two nights I'd spent in an old building. For some reason, near the end of my story, the faces of all the goblins listening looked clearly upset and even somehow afraid.

"So, that means you and the mavka hid in the house of the dead?" Ugruem asked and clarified that he was talking about a wooden blockhouse inside a stockade with the gates torn off their hinges.

I confirmed, not understanding what was so strange about it. The crowd of goblins began gasping in fear and chattering excitedly. Ugruem called them all to silence and said:

"Boy, that place is bad, cursed. That there house was built by ogres eight years ago. They also put up the stockade, and dug a well and cold storage for keeping meat. They were hunters. Five or six of the giants. And though they looked fierce, they lived peacefully with their neighbors. They traded with us and humans too. But then, one day, they up and disappeared. And their whole yard was just caked in blood. Since then, the same has happened to anyone who tried to live in their former hunting cabin. First was my father Uguzh. After he fought with his brothers, he decided to move into that house. He held out longer than anyone else: a whole eleven days. But on the twelfth morning, the only thing they found of him were bloody spots on the porch. And since then, both humans and goblins and all other kinds have happened upon that cursed house. But all of them died a terrible death within a few days. Our shaman Kaiak says that there is some kind of ancient curse there directed at the original ogres."

Mission received: Cursed Old House
Description: Find the reason for the many strange deaths
Mission class: Reputation
Reward: improved relationship with the village of Tysh

"Did that fatty just give you a quest?" My sister inquired, giving a chilly cringe, and then asked me to say a word for her, as the goblins in the village were still hostile to her.

More and more new goblins walked up to our little group. A large crowd started gathering. Then Ugruem wiped his bloodied palms on his dirty leather apron, after which he called over a fat, almost spherical green-skinned goblin woman with muscular arms and powerful column-legs. After pointing his fat finger at me, the local leader declared to the woman unequivocally:

"Let them live with you, Tamina. He's all weak and small. He won't take up much space."

Failed check for Tamina Fierce's reaction

The woman, her strong arms held to the side, disputed Ugruem's decision, speaking up in a shrill unpleasant tone:

"Ugruem, have you been eating too many mushrooms again? Where do you think he would sleep?! I have eleven children. There's not enough space to walk in my house as it is! Where could I put another new arrival?"

She dared argue with the local leader? I read the feisty heifer's information, and my eyes crawled up into my forehead:

Tamina Fierce
Level-78 Goblin Warrior

For me, she was marked with a black skull. It would have been a death sentence for me if she decided to be hostile. And though Ugruem surpassed this woman in level, he didn't want any conflict either and canceled his order.

"Alright then, Amra. Walk around the village and ask the locals if anyone can give you shelter. But as for your companion, there's no room for a mavka in the village of Tysh. They are crafty and dangerous beasts. I'd never even let one near me. Just yesterday, a mavka almost stole up to our very walls. The archers shot her up good."

I realized he was speaking about my sister, who had been killed yesterday from the bushes.

"Ugruem, this is the very same mavka as yesterday. She wasn't planning anything evil. She was just finding new locations for the both of us. And actually, it's useless to kill Valerianna Quickfoot. She's one of the undying. So, fighting with her is a very bad idea. Now she's small, just level-ten, but literally yesterday she was level-one. In about a week's time, this mavka will become stronger than most of the residents of Tysh, and a few months from now, will surpass everyone here, including you. So then, tell me, wise Ugruem: does it seem reasonable to fight with an undying mavka? She'll just respawn anyway. Do you want her to get angry in response and start to look on the residents of Tysh as food? Is it not better to make friends with this undying mavka and have her as a defender of Tysh to help the goblins who live here? Valerianna Quickfoot only asks the right to visit Tysh in peace, speak with goblins and buy the things she needs."

Trading skill increased to level 2!

Trading? I couldn't tell how that skill had anything to do with the negotiation I was holding with Ugruem but, according to the game algorithms, the chieftain and I were in fact engaged in Trading. I checked the information on my character. That was right! As I leveled up the Trading skill, my charisma had also grown by one, which was very useful in this situation.

Ugruem was sitting in contemplative silence as before, rolling his bloodied apron nervously with his strong hands as he did so. For some reason, I didn't doubt that the goblin was thinking up ways of breaking the dangerous mavka's neck. But my assertion that the wood nymph was invincible ended up working on Ugruem. He considered it seriously. He must not have been used to working with his brain. It looked like it even hurt him, as the patriarch's countenance was scrunched up in agitation.

While the chieftain thought intensively, having pushed those gathered out of the way, out came an old goblin with a curved staff in his hands wearing a cape adorned with the skulls of small vermin and necklaces of dried mushrooms. The old man walked in a funny-looking half-jumping gait. Also, his face was nothing but wrinkles, but the other goblins bowed their heads in respect when they saw him. Before he even started speaking, I guessed that I was looking at the local shaman:

Kaiak Badgerleg
Level-56 Goblin Shaman

Successful check for Goblin Shaman reaction
Experience received: 50 Exp.

The shaman was behaving in an unexpected manner: he bowed low, almost to the ground, first to the wood nymph, then to me. After that, he said with clear respect in his voice:

"It is with great honor that we accept two of the undying to the village of Tysh. The wood mavka shall receive the right of passage, speech and trade. In return, we expect from her a promise not to consume goblin flesh. You then, green brother, may also settle here in Tysh."

Mission completed: Socialization 1/3
Reward: 800 Exp.

Level nine!
Racial ability improved: 15% Resistance to Cold

What? How could the first mission of the chain have been completed? I still hadn't been to the human village of Stonetown!? Although... it was a group mission, and Valerianna had run up there yesterday without me. Clearly, that had been plenty. I bowed low to the shaman and answered that I was grateful for the honor he was showing us. After that, I assured him that Valerianna Quickfoot did not eat goblins, so the residents of Tysh had nothing to worry about. Just then, a private message came in from Valerianna Quickfoot:

"Dumbo, you convinced them alright! All the goblins on the map are yellow for me now. The hostility is gone."

And with that, the goblins gathered began to gradually get back to their own business. No one was paying particular attention to the "mavka" anymore. The shaman adjusted his cloak, threw a hood over his bald head and was clearly preparing to go away from us. What should my sister and I do now? Just hang around here by the gates of Tysh? As if answering my unasked question, Kaiak Badgerleg said:

"Speak with the residents. I'm sure they won't refuse a goblin a place for the night. And maybe someone will even agree to shelter the mavka. After that, both of you drop by my hut. I have something to offer you. Many missions have piled up that only an undying can handle!"

Mission received: Arrange a Place to Sleep in the Village of Tysh

Mission class: *Normal*
Reward: *160 Exp.*

The nymph and I were left to our own devices, and the goblins went on their separate ways. Everything was basically going the way it should in any game. We introduced ourselves to the locals, got acquainted and got a new quest... But the sensation that something was amiss just wouldn't leave me. After all, if you thought about it, what need did I have for a horrid cot in a house already overflowing with goblins? I already had a spacious blockhouse of my own, after all. And though some force came active there periodically and killed NPC's, my sister and I were living players, and our deaths wouldn't be final. In fact, if we were to see that strange something, we would complete the Cursed House mission, which would even be good.

I started getting the impression that we must have been going about our time in *Boundless Realm* all wrong from the very beginning. We were supposed to get on the road, and wander down it to one of the villages. In that case, all these quests to meet locals and find a place to stay made total sense. The abandoned blockhouse, was supposed to remain a location hidden in the woods, and the Cursed House quest was supposed to be for later. But due to my randomly meeting the wolves, I discovered the abandoned blockhouse before the normal villages, and even ended up moving into that very cursed house.

What was more, the situation suited me just fine. I had my very own Alchemy laboratory, where no one would get in the way of my experiments, and I had a pack of forest wolves as guards. Sure, I still needed to spruce the place up a bit and take certain safety precautions. At first, at least get the gates up to keep out uninvited guests. But there, I was master of my own domain, and could do whatever I wanted whenever I wanted. Here in Tysh, I had no idea at all what I could do at night with hundreds of watching eyes all around.

"Well then, big-ears, shall we go our separate ways or look for goblins in the village that would agree to give us shelter?" Valerianna hurried me along, not happy with my hesitation.

"Amra no wanting Tysh. Is home where Blanca. Amra walking shaman and to say 'no stay.'"

The nymph went silent for a long time, then agreed with my choice:

"I also don't like the idea of living here in the goblin village. Everyone I come across sees me first and foremost as a dangerous beast. Dumbo, we've got our own home, and we must start improving it, not looking for something else. I'll take engineer as a primary skill and come up with some defensive structures for our shelter. You should start training our wolves. They must get up at least to level forty. Then, they won't have to piss in fear every time they see night creatures! I have to wash the floor again after last night..."

Night of Miracles

THE CONVERSATION was going in a circle. The shaman Kaiak Badgerleg was worried by our refusal to settle in Tysh and was trying to figure out why we didn't want to help the residents of the village. My sister and I answered that we did want to help the goblins of the village with all our hearts and asked them to give us a mission. The shaman grew truly joyful at our preparedness to work and told us to go find somewhere to stay in the village. Then we were back to the beginning of the circle...

But my sister and I continued the seemingly useless conversation with the NPC, because we had both noticed independently that our relationship with the shaman was gradually rising. When we refused to settle in the village, his opinion of us fell by 10%. But, when we said we were ready to help, it grew by 15%. In parallel with the shaman's personal opinion of us increasing, the opinion of the whole village was going up as well. When the shaman had become blue for me on the map at a total of +80, a new message came in:

Mission received: Socialization 2/3
Reach a state of friendship (average opinion of 50+) with the village of Tysh
Reach a state of friendship (average opinion of 50+) with the village of Stonetown
Mission class: Chain, group
Reward: 3200 Exp.

The nymph and I exchanged glances, and Valerianna Quickfoot shook her head:

"Not now. I got a scarily low amount of sleep last night because of Blanca giving birth, and I'm still dozing off as we speak. Do this quest on your own, big-ears. You have an initial racial bonus of +20 to goblin opinion anyway. You'll have a much easier time raising their opinion to that level. I already looked around the map. There were just six key NPC's for the whole village: Chieftain Ugruem the two guards marked with black skulls at the gates, the badger-legged shaman, the feisty lady and another goblin at the other end of the village. You won't even have to pay the others any mind. Alright then, I'm gonna sign off. As soon as I'm rested, I'll be on my way to Stonetown. I'll try to get a mission to improve my standing there."

The nymph took a seat on the floor right next to the elderly goblin shaman and soon melted away. A few minutes after that, there came a private message:

"I almost forgot. I saw that you started your channel on that video site. I'll send you the video of the NPC wolf giving birth. Give it some production and upload it. They're rare scenes. The viewers will be sure to like it."

To be honest, my own eyes were already getting heavy, and I was also getting ready to take a break. So, I spoke with Kaiak Badgerleg, completing our cyclical conversation another four times and, on the fifth, got an error message:

SYSTEM ERROR!
Opinion variable of NPC-character $FF0076-AF5780 has surpassed allowable value
Error code #LOC/ER-002056
This message has been sent to Boundless Realm tech support.
We apologize for the possible inconvenience.

What was it that Alexandro Lavrius said

about incentives for every bug found? In an excellent mood, I followed my sister's example and also exited the game. After that, I spent another hour of time stitching together video and recording narration. All the interesting moments of my second game session added up to a total of fifteen minutes. After that, I left the building. And I was already in the hall by the revolving doors, preparing to exit when a call came into my phone from an unknown number.

"Good morning, Timothy! This is Jane, assistant to Alexandro Lavrius. Before you leave the building, Mr. Lavrius requests that you come to his office on the forty-fourth floor."

What did the Director need from me this time? I went up in the elevator, busting my brains over the question and coming up with the most improbable suppositions. But the reality was even more bizarre. When I went into the office, my boss was watching a video of Blanca giving birth on his monitor.

"Hey, read this and sign it," he said, not feeling the need to greet me and extending me a several-page-long printout. He pointed me to the guest chair by the wall and continued carefully studying the video I'd uploaded.

The document he passed me was headed: "Changelog for *Boundless Realm* patch 15.48." Getting lost in guesses as to why I'd been handed these papers, I nevertheless took a seat in the chair and began carefully studying the document.

"...Casting time for the spell Ice Sphere increased to 12.7 seconds... Average hardness of mithril chests increased by 70%... Maximum communication distance for using in-game messages increased to 10 kilometers... When a Chameleon player is gradually disappearing, it is no longer allowed to choose the last part to disappear as 'genitalia...' Damage done by all kinds of fans reduced by 20%..."

Why did I need all this information? I looked at the list of future changes to the game until one struck me like a lightning bolt:

"The special attack Vampire Bite no longer works on paralyzed or unconscious targets."

How could that be? I had so many plans for using this ability! After noticing by my reaction that I had found the point that concerned me directly, the Director of Special Projects made a comment:

"The other viewers of your video were not able to understand it, as they didn't have all the information, but I made the obvious connection. You could use Herbalism and Alchemy to make paralysis poisons, then your Vampire Bite would allow you to kill nearly any enemy. As such, I insisted these corrections be made to the game mechanics, and corporate management agreed with me. We could never leave such an unbalanced tool in the game to allow vampires to instantly kill any creature with no level limit. Sign at the end of the document that you have been informed of the upcoming changes and hold no grievances against the *Boundless Realm* corporation."

I absolutely loathed doing it, but I still took the gilded pen from the Director's table and signed at the end of the printout, as I understood perfectly well that, if I refused, I would be fired immediately. Jane, who walked up at that very moment, pointed to a blank space at the end of the page, and asked me to sign and date it, after which she took the papers.

"We need this for the legal department," the girl explained. "There have been precedents when normal players have taken the *Boundless Realm* corporation to court because they thought changes in the game mechanisms damaged their interests or virtual property they obtained for real money. But you, Timothy, are an employee, even if you are still in your trial period, so those compensation rules do not apply to you."

"Come now, Jane. No need to scare the man," Alexandro Lavrius cut into the conversation. "Timothy is still doing quite well in his job as a tester, and good work must be rewarded. We decided to let you and the nymph keep the high opinion of the NPC shaman, for example, despite the fact that you were obviously abusing a loophole in the game algorithm to get it.

And yes, Jane figured out the answer to your question from the programmers. If your goblin is randomly killed, none of the many existing quests to kill a vampire would be considered complete, and the secret of your vampirism would not be revealed. But you should at least try to be a bit more cautious about advertising your second nature."

"What do you mean 'advertising?'" I asked, not knowing what he was referring to.

The director pointed to the screen, showing a still from my video.

"Think up a more or less believable explanation for your viewers on where your goblin got Night Vision."

I froze for a few seconds in fear with my mouth open, then said with a satisfied grin:

"Lily-of-the-valley! It's berries, when consumed, give a short-term version of that same effect!"

"Excellent choice!" Alexandro Lavrius nodded in approval. "I would have suggested a different one, though: when generating a character, it is possible to choose a subrace. There are six options. Night goblins have night vision. But I like your choice better, as it explains why your Amra can see normally during the day. Make sure to write about using the lily berries in the comments to your video then, before the players start asking unpleasant questions."

The director entered some kind of service command, and the detailed statistics of my Amra came up on the monitor, including a list of objects in my inventory and current quests. My eyes climbed up onto my forehead in surprise. I had no idea that he could see such detail about my character so easily. On the other hand, though, how could I be surprised? The developers had to have some way of controlling things. Alexandro Lavrius tore himself from the screen and turned to me:

"Collect a bit more lily. Then, as if it's nothing, show how much you have in your inventory and comment on it in that your modern mocking style. But, all in all, great job. Your imagination will be sure to keep coming in handy for you. Your inventive solutions to problems show great promise. Also, you've gotten pretty lucky, Timothy, which is of considerable importance in your profession. Getting a unique quest at the very beginning of the game is a great stroke of fortune. What's more, the corporation wasn't involved one bit. Your character discovered the very rare random location all on his own. But there is one hitch: to fight your way through the Curiosity and the Cat mission, you'd need a well-equipped character of a much higher level than your herbalist. Literally one hour ago, I was arguing with some of our specialists on this very topic. Some of them think you will be able to complete the mission as is, though it will be difficult. If you are able to finish the mission, you can consider yourself to have passed the trial period. And just to up the ante a bit, the programmers set the reward to this quest as something truly amazing and I am very interested to see if you can take full advantage of it."

* * *

"Get up, Tim! Time for work!" Valeria was in an excellent mood and clearly had spent a large amount of time primping before a mirror.

I smiled at my sister, trying not to reveal the fact that my heart was filled with regret. Valeria was looking excellent at her fourteen years. She had wavy chestnut hair in little ringlets down to her waist, proper facial features, huge joyful brown eyes, a flawless smile and two rows of ideal, snow-white teeth. If her life had come together differently, boys would be swarming her. If it hadn't been for that horrible accident...

"You look wonderful," I admitted.

"I just got enough sleep, and found the time to comb my hair and put on makeup," Val laughed heartily. "I also haven't gone into the game yet today. I wanted to talk about our plans first."

"Did you find something interesting?" I inquired, and my sister nodded with a satisfied look.

As I was standing before the mirror shaving, Valeria told me what she'd found. It seemed that, over the last day, she had gotten six private messages at once from *Boundless Realm* players. The letters were all different, but they were saying nearly the same thing. For various reasons, they were all asking my sister to sell them her map. Some promised to help her complete missions, others offered speedy leveling on local monsters, and a third wanted to see Blanca and the wolf pups with their own eyes. Some players were simply offering money for the map. It should be said that it was utterly insignificant amounts: from thirty to one hundred coins.

"Naturally, my interest was piqued by my sudden, strange popularity and especially at the fact that everyone needed my map. I was on guard, so I started scouring the game forums and, look what I found," my sister invited me to the monitor.

They were old messages from the classifieds section of the *Boundless Realm* game forum:

"Offering five thousand coins for an invitation into a group engaged in the Curiosity and the Cat mission."

"Six-thousand-coin advance for a group to take on Curiosity and the Cat. No matter the loot, you can keep the money."

"Five thousand for the coordinates of the location from Curiosity and the Cat. You'll get

another thirty thousand if the loot is what it should be. No scam, everything above board."

My eyes shot up into my forehead. Thirty thousand game coins was three thousand credits in real life. That was the price of a mid-range electric car, or a year of rent for the kind of room my sister and I were now living in. I typed "Curiosity and the Cat reward" into a search engine, but couldn't find the answer.

"It's no use, bro. I already ran through all kinds of different queries on this quest, but I didn't find anything worthwhile. That said, some players must know something interesting about this mission, because they're offering a huge amount of money just for the ability to participate. And look at the characters I got these messages from: level-one-hundred-fifty, one hundred thirty, even one hundred eight! You must be able to find an item that would be useful, even to a very high-level character. So then, my advice to you is not to give your coordinates to anyone, and not to sell the map of locations you've discovered. If there truly is something valuable there, the high-level players will simply take the reward from us by force. Perhaps we can later ask some cool players to join us on the Curiosity and the Cat quest, but first we have to figure out the true value of the reward, then try selling tickets. It might be better to keep such a valuable object for ourselves."

I started thinking hard, then looked at the

view number from the video file I'd uploaded earlier today. Over three thousand views in just one day! Not bad! This was the exact video I had received Curiosity and the Cat in, and all these viewers now knew about it. What exactly had the director meant when he said "something truly amazing" would be the reward for this quest?

"Alright, Val. I'm heading for work. When I get there, I'll call and ask you about the weather. You blow through Stonetown and finish the second part of the Socialization chain. Meanwhile, I'll do the same in the goblin village."

Valeria nodded, rolled her chair over to the computer desk and picked up her virtual reality helmet. I walked up to my sister and ran my hand through her thick hair.

"Val, when we get some more money, I promise I'll buy you a real virtual reality capsule just like they have in the *Boundless Realm* corporation building. Then it's really full immersion!"

My sister gave me a good-natured punch to the shoulder in response:

"You're an incurable romantic, Tim! The cheapest capsules out there cost six thousand credits, and the best models are at least fifty thousand. Just worry about paying off our debts first."

"And I will! This morning I got my first four hundred credits for my work in exposing bugs in the game. I already got a call from the bank and they said that my loan was extended by a year. And as for the virtual reality capsule, I wasn't joking one bit. Val, I absolutely will buy you the very best one out there one day, so you can really feel what it's like to be fully in a virtual world!"

* * *

"It's overcast, but the sun is peeking through the clouds in places. You could play, but be careful."

I thanked my sister and started getting undressed before my third game session. The top of the virtual reality capsule had barely come down when, before my eyes on the dark background, there came a text on the new game update, after there came a long list of changes. I skimmed it and confirmed that I was familiar with the rule changes. After that, I opened my eyes and found myself back in the home of the old goblin shaman. Kaiak Badgerleg was right there in the room crafting something of feathers, resin and thin twigs.

"Good evening, wise shaman!" I said. I didn't think I'd spoken in a particularly disarming way, but the old goblin still shuddered in fear and dropped his craft to the floor.

"Ah, it's you, Amra! Don't scare me like that!" The goblin bowed and, with an upset look, glanced at the strange broken object, then started looking toward the door, which was still closed from the inside. After that, he stood up straight with a groan. "I have heard that the undying reappear in the same place they disappeared, but this is the first time I've ever seen it. Have you already spoken with the residents of the village and found shelter for the night?"

That same old shtick?! I had been hoping that the programmers had fixed that bug. The decision came to me suddenly:

"That's what I'm here to talk to you about, wise shaman. You have a spacious home which could easily accommodate another bed. I will only need to stay here on very rare occasions. Usually, I plan on living in another house. I won't make a racket, and I don't plan on eating you out of house and home. Will you let me spend the night here, Kaiak Badgerleg?"

Successful check for Goblin Shaman reaction
Experience received: 50 Exp.

"How could I say no to such a debonair young goblin? You can stay with me as long as you want!"

Mission completed: Arrange a Place to Sleep in the Village of Tysh
Reward: 160 Exp.

In the end, finishing the quest couldn't have been easier. Evidence of Kaiak Badgerleg's +100 opinion of me, obviously. I thanked the shaman for agreeing to provide me shelter and went outside. Night hadn't come yet, and the residents of the village hadn't yet gone back to their own homes. Now was the best possible time to get to Socialization.

I remembered what my sister had said, that just six key NPC's defined the village's average opinion. They were the only residents of Tysh that it was really important to talk to. Now, I had a relationship of +100 with the shaman Kaiak Badgerleg, +25 with Chieftain Ugruem, +20 with the huge Tamina Fierce, and +20 with the other three key goblins of the village. The arithmetic mean now was +34, which was my exact standing figure in the village of Tysh.

Based on the map, one of these highly-placed goblins was just around the corner. I could tell by his black skull marker. What could I say? He was perfectly good enough for me to continue with the Socialization quest.

Tarek Bigfoot
Level-77 Goblin Warrior

The goblin was sitting on a bench next to a small fire stirring the contents of a pot with a stick.

In the pot, there was something thick and black boiling and bubbling. Tarek's feet really were disproportionally huge like two tree trunks. I was immediately visited by the thought that the huge boots stored in the chest of the cursed house could have been made specially for Tarek's bare feet. I stopped two steps from the key NPC and tried to figure out what he was doing. It didn't look like he was cooking food. The smell coming from the pot was pungent and unappetizing.

Then, on the very same street, there appeared a green-skinned girl, and I realized for the first time that goblins can be pretty. She had a good figure and was wearing a modest blue apron. She had a magnificent copper-red hairdo with ears that poked out into a refined point. Yesterday, my sister had admitted that she had spent forty minutes creating my ugly mug. I suspect that the programmers and designers who created this kind of beauty had spent no less time. There was just no way she could have been a randomly generated NPC. She just stood out too strikingly from the other cringe-worthy faces of Tysh's residents. Nevertheless, the information on the girl was utterly typical and was in no way different from the dozens of others I'd seen:

Level-22 Goblin Villager

"Did you bring the resin?" Tarek Bigfoot

asked the villager as she approached.

"Father, I found just one piece, next to the road. And I didn't go deep into the forest, as you didn't give permission."

The girl handed her father a golden lump of tree sap, and the big-footed goblin threw it right into the pot.

"It's not enough. I won't be able to seal all the cracks in the boat with just this," Tarek grumbled in dismay.

If this wasn't beginning of a mission, I'd never played a computer game before in my life! After taking a few steps toward the fire, I stated:

"You must be such a proud father! Your daughter is simply a treasure of the whole goblin race! Tarek Bigfoot, would you please tell me the name of this charming creature?"

The wizened goblin just opened his mouth in surprise and froze like that. His daughter answered for him:

"It's nice to hear such kind words, Amra. My name is Taisha, but my friends call me Spark."

"Does your nickname come from your excellent hair?" I posited and the girl confirmed my theory with a nod. "Spark, I couldn't help but overhear your conversation with your father. I was just preparing to head for the nearby forest, so I thought could help you gather resin. How much do you need?"

"Five times as much as Taisha just brought,"

Tarek Bigfoot finally joined the conversation.

> **Mission received: Collect tree resin for Tarek Bigfoot**
> **Mission class: Normal**
> **Reward: 80 Exp.**

The mission was clearly made for characters of the very lowest levels. I just needed five minutes to gather the necessary amount of resin from the trunks and return. But Taisha had already managed to go somewhere else, so the rest of the conversation was just with her father. After passing the resin quest, I took a seat near the fire and watched the viscous mixture bubbling in the pot.

After that, the goblin brought a small flat-bottomed boat in from the back yard and Tarek and I sealed it. It was another small quest to raise his opinion of me. With satisfaction, I noted my relationship with Taisha's father growing gradually. When I was over 60, Tarek Bigfoot suddenly declared:

"Amra, you're a good guy, but I have to advise you against trying to win my daughter's heart!" he barked out in a threatening tone, not at all in line with his previous manner of speaking. But I didn't let that throw me one bit:

"Why not, Tarek? Your daughter is gorgeous. I've never seen such a beautiful goblin in my entire life."

Taisha's father furrowed his brow in dismay:

"Look at yourself, Amra. You're weak. There are small children in Tysh stronger than you. What's more, you're poor and barely clothed. You are not capable of protecting my daughter, much less providing for her future! The best suitors of the whole village are all after my daughter. Boys even come here from the neighboring village of Tyrym just to catch a glimpse of her rare beauty, so a ragamuffin like you has no place here!"

Mission received: Earn the Respect of Tarek Bigfoot

Mission class: Personal, reputation

Required conditions: Tarek Bigfoot must have a +100 opinion of you

Give Tarek Bigfoot a trophy from a creature level-50 or higher

Pay Tarek Bigfoot three hundred coins

All equipment slots must be filled with articles of clothing

Reward: 4000 Exp., permanent improvement of Taisha's opinion of you by +50

I was reading into the conditions of the unusual mission when a message came in from my sister:

"I just met Trong Diver not far from Stonetown. He's hit level ten and is now trying to

hunt us down. His intentions are not good. After seeing me, he started saying nasty things and immediately drew his weapon. With the help of White Fang, I sent him to respawn."

I grew alarmed and began thinking. For thousands of kilometers all around me, there was nothing but little-known lands. How had the naiad managed to find us? We had already gone quite far from the shore, after all. It couldn't be... I clicked on "Exit Game" and called my sister.

"Val, we totally forgot about another risk: in our videos, I mentioned the names of the villages Tysh and Stonetown! There must be some way of finding a certain place by the name. Or at least figuring out the continent and province!"

"Hold on, brother. I'll check now."

But I had already found a way myself. I typed "Stonetown Tysh" into a search engine and checked the first link that came up:

"Stonetown. A small human village in the Lars province, Southern Continent. Three hundred seventy kilometers to the northeast of the nearest city, Weiden. Approximately one hundred residents from levels 40-70. They give a few standard quests for increasing standing in the village."

The information on Stonetown in the *Boundless Realm* player-made database had been added a year ago by a half-elf ranger named Garret BeerLover, who was now level-two-hundred-twenty. As for Tysh, I found nothing in the database, but that already made no difference. It was enough that the players knew the location of Stonetown.

I checked the search engine statistics. Yesterday, neither Stonetown nor Tysh had been of any interest. But today, that combination of words had been searched for by one hundred seventeen people. Probably, some of these players, using city portals and teleportation scrolls were already going full steam ahead toward the Lars province and the city of Weiden and would be going due northeast from there. If my sister and I didn't hurry, these high-level players would find the secret location with the unique mission and take the still-unknown reward from the Curiosity and the Cat quest.

When my sister called again, already having found the information on Stonetown, I said decisively:

"Drop everything and run to the blockhouse. I'll be there soon, as well. Together we can go to the swamp and think up how to be first to finish the quest."

* * *

"Where are you off to, tiny?" asked the owner of the boat, quite thrown off. "We still need to make sure the boat won't leak. There's a stream right nearby.

We can test it there."

It looked like the next quest for further increasing my relationship with Taisha's father was being given, but it was just such bad timing! There was less than an hour to sunset, and trying to find a way through the swamp in the dark would be far too dangerous. Although... if I had a boat, it would be a great way to get around on the water. I just had to convince Tarek to drag the boat there, as I personally wouldn't have enough strength.

"Tarek, you can't seriously be telling me that you want to test your boat in that stinking ditch, right? Your neighbors will laugh at you. Why not just put it in that puddle in the middle of the village? To really put it to the test, you need a big body of water. One with waves, where we can also test the oars."

The goblin stroked his bald head with his fingers, trying to think up an appropriate location not far from the village of Tysh.

"We could test it in the swampy lake near the Cursed House. That's right! Alright, let's do the test right there!" I suggested.

"What do you mean lake? That's nothing but a dirty swamp. Also, it's pretty far, and it's already getting dark out."

"What's that I hear?" I grew artificially surprised, egging the goblin on. "Are you afraid of the dark, Tarek? You could kill the toads there with one left jab!"

"I'm not worried about the toads. They're the least of my concern," the wizened goblin said thoughtfully. "It's thick muck over there and so full of squirming leeches you can barely see the bottom. It's just horrible to walk there with bare feet. Also, if you get a bit farther from the shore, the creatures start getting scarier than mere frogs..."

But I had gotten the idea, and couldn't be stopped:

"I have a pair of huge leather boots. Exactly the right size for your big stompers. I'll give them to you, if you drag the boat to that lake and scare away the biggest toads so they won't trip me up. And as for the predators in the depths, don't worry. I'll row the boat on my own and tell you whether it's good or not. They won't be able to kill me, as I'm undying. And if anything happens to the flat-bottomed boat, I'll pay you ten coins' compensation, and you get to keep the boots no matter what."

Trading skill increased to level 3!

Mission received: Test Tarek Bigfoot's Boat
Mission class: Normal
Reward: 160 Exp., +15 to Tarek Bigfoot's opinion of you

"If you sink my boat, you owe me fifteen coins," the goblin moaned in dismay. He then hoisted the flat-bottomed boat onto his shoulders as if it was light as a feather and started walking. "Amra, go fetch the oars and my club. And don't delay!"

Tarek went directly to the cursed house, cutting off a big bend in the road. I was barely keeping up with the goblin, in fact. We walked up a steep slope and through a big patch of viscous swampy earth, but he just kept his pace as if on flat asphalt. A half hour later, we were already next to the blockhouse, and I ran in to get the boots. I couldn't see the Gray Pack anywhere, just Blanca feeding her pups in the kitchen, and the nymph Valerianna crafting candles from wax and wound thread.

"Goblin drag boat. Nymph helping me for go through night swamp."

My sister understood without any questions and jumped up, getting ready. In the yard, there was a surprise waiting for us. Tarek Bigfoot had set the boat aside and, holding the heavy gate door in his hands, was trying to hang it on the hinges. I ran over to help, and Valerianna came after me. Unfortunately, it was in vain — Tarek had easily enough strength to lift the gate door, but even the three of us taken together didn't have the agility to put it on the hinges. Taisha's father swore and set the gate back on the earth. But when he saw the boots, he started smiling in joy and even bowed to me.

"Great shoes! I've never had the like! I simply cannot wait to show my neighbors!"

A few minutes later, we were already at the swamp shore. Night had come, and creatures were crawling out, all marked with red skulls on my map. In the distance, I saw the monster that had scared the Gray Pack half to death yesterday:

Level-42 Fetid Bullfrog Patriarch

"That green bighead is in our way. I'll chase him off," Taisha's father decisively took his spiky club in his hand, but I stopped him.

It would have been stupid to lose out on the free experience from the level-40+ monsters he would kill, and I didn't want to waste the chance. I laid out a hunting plan for the wizened goblin and he didn't object to my taking the frog meat as a trophy. The nymph and the goblin warrior hid in the bushes and I grabbed my blowgun and went off to lure the fetid bullfrog patriarch away from the swamp.

Damage dealt: 3 (Missile damage 58 - 55 armor)

Holy crap! This creature had uncommonly thick skin, which swallowed up almost all the damage I did to it! The huge green patriarch turned toward me in disbelief.

Damage dealt: 0 (Missile damage 34 - 55 armor)

Dodge skill increased to level 6!

My big-eared Amra, who looked like a midget in comparison with this enemy, barely managed to react when a wad of acidic spit hummed past me. A dark cloud popped up where it landed, probably poisonous. Right after that, the bullfrog jumped forward. I even felt the earth shake when its big body flopped down right where I had been standing a second earlier.

An icy arrow flew into the snout of the huge frog. That was my sister joining the fight. I guess Water Magic was not the best choice against an amphibian. The bullfrog's life bar didn't even appear to go down. Then, a second later, Tarek Bigfoot ran in and, with a swing of his spiked club, took away two thirds of the bullfrog's health points in one blow. Then, with his next strike, he debrained the monster.

Experience received: 15520 Exp.

Level ten!

~ Video Game Plotline Tester ~

Level eleven!

Level twelve!

Level thirteen!

Level fourteen!

Level fifteen!
Racial ability improved: 30% Resistance to Poison
Racial ability improved: 30% Resistance to Cold

Oh, gods! I fell to the earth, not feeling strong enough to stay standing. An intense quivering overtook me. Six levels in one go! Thirty stat points for my character! This feeling was better than sex!

* * *

"If you hadn't rolled in mud, like a seizure victim, you could have also lured in the other bullfrog," my sister chewed me out for my lack of restraint and she was totally right to do so.

The burst of energy was very unexpected and abrupt. For some time, I truly lost control of my character. Tarek Bigfoot looked at my squirming and, spitting in shame, quickly gathered everything of value from the body in a business-like manner and started off back to the village of Tysh. And though there were more toad-like monsters not far away, the nymph and I were in no condition to fight them without the wizened goblin.

And so, the boat now in the shallow water, I took a seat in it, wrapped myself up in the frog's skin and tried not to move. Valerianna Quickfoot, meanwhile, was kneeling in the cold muck gathering the wet branches and bunches of cane that were all around, building a huge blind to hide the boat and oars from unwanted observers.

In that I was unable to help my sister with the camouflage, I set about assigning my stat points. Strength and constitution had grown by six points by default, but as for the remaining eighteen free points, I had to think. On the one hand, a targeted increase in charisma would bring certain fruits, helping me to speak and revealing unusual plot lines for my big-eared Amra. That was very important, in that only truly unique and unusual stories would attract viewers and the interest of my employer.

On the other hand, I was strongly upset and on guard about the fact that my character was incapable of wounding more serious enemies. The damage done was so pitiful that it was totally absorbed by the armor. To fix the situation, I needed a serious boost to agility. After carefully weighing all the factors, I put eleven free points into charisma and seven into agility.

Beyond that, when I reached level ten, my goblin got the ability to take another primary and secondary skill. I immediately moved Stealth (A C) from secondary to primary skills. The viewers of my channel already knew that Amra often had to move in the dark, and I had told them that I had this skill in my secondaries.

You have taken Stealth as a primary skill
Skill level: 6
Primary skills taken: 5 of 5

My agility grew immediately by almost eight points. The eighteen extra hitpoints it gave me would also be quite welcome. But then, with the two secondary skills I could now choose, I paused to think. Shamanism, Lock-Picking, Diplomacy, Leadership, Silent Step, Fishing, Leatherworking, Farming, Light Armor, Animal Empathy, and hundreds of other skills existed in the game... My eyes were spinning from the abundance of options, and I chose to just wait a bit with this choice.

"I took Illusion Magic for myself," my sisters voice came in, drowned out by the branches. "I'll make myself look like a toad now, and I'll cast an illusion around your blind so it looks like a small hill. It'll make ideal camouflage. I should have done this at the beginning... Woah! Big mistake! The huge toads sense the use of magic! Amra, run! Make sure to finish the mission to compensate me for the loss of experience!!!"

I felt my boat get shoved forward, and overheard a distant fast squelching. After that, my little boat rocked on the waves. A frightened squeak carried to me from the nymph and, next to the green dot on the map, there came a red skull. It was all over in an instant. The sign next to the name Valerianna Quickfoot, that showed her online changed to a gray circle. The player was dead...

It was eleven thirty at night. Due to the heaped-up weight of the wet branches, my flat-bottomed boat was seriously low in the water. The black liquid was almost coming overboard. Very carefully, making sure the oars wouldn't creak or squelch, and so the swamp water wouldn't come over the sides, I turned my overloaded boat around. After that, I very slowly began moving toward the far-off marker on the map showing the unique mission location.

Moving through the swamp teeming with horrible freaks didn't scare me one bit. But it did take a long time and was hard to enjoy. I was navigating the red skulls on the map and trying to avoid the large clusters of monsters. I had to go as unhurriedly and carefully as possible so the inhabitants of the swamp wouldn't perceive the bunch of branches boating through the swamp as anything but a natural hill.

Stealth skill increased to level 7!

My boat had now entered the visual radius of a whole group of red markers. My Stealth bar, even after reaching level seven, continued to quickly fill and, a few minutes later, I was nearing level eight. What kind of creatures were lurking here in the expanses of this swamp-side lake? I wanted horribly to move the branches blocking my view just a little bit and look, but the name of the quest gave me pause, so I didn't. I went unhurriedly onward, just one or two paddles per minute. Yes, it was slow going, but none of the local monsters noticed my camouflaged boat.

Stealth skill increased to level 8!

In front of me on the map, I could see a small island, thickly sewn with red and black skulls. But I wasn't interested in them at all. In the very middle of the concentration of beasts, there was a golden triangle! That must have been the target of my adventure! I called up a hint and read the description.

A golden triangle marker signifies a unique

creature in Boundless Realm. *As a rule, these creatures are intelligent, and a great many rare missions with very unusual rewards can come from finding and working with them.*

As the map showed, the direct path to the island was blocked by a thin shoal and a few hillocks. On the island, there were many dangerous beasts as well. I had to take a slow wide arc boating around the obstacle. When my overloaded flat-bottomed boat had already managed to get near the island, it was five in the morning. I already realized long ago that my boating venture would be a one-way trip, as there was no way I could manage to return to my shelter before the sun came up. And morning, no matter how unfortunate, was expected to be sunny. Even through the twigs I could see the sky steadily growing pink in the east.

Very slowly, I neared the shore, teeming with red markers of deadly dangerous monstrosities. I wonder what distance is needed to complete the unique quest? A thud rang out. My little vessel had hit on the bottom and stopped. There was just seven meters between me and the nearest monster. But the mission still wasn't completed.

Stealth skill increased to level 9!

What did I have to do to get the reward? I probably had to at least see the unique creature and recognize it, I guessed. I began cautiously moving the branches aside, widening a viewing window. First, I saw the monster nearest me and looked at it in detail from close up:

Level-51 Swamp Wyvern

It was a three-meter-tall toothy black lizard wound into a ball with wings furled up on its back. And only later, having raised my eyes, did I see HER: a huge winged snaked of a malachite-green color:

Kayervina, the Mother of Flying Snakes (unique creature)

The snake mother was incredible. Her flexible thirty-meter long body covered in scales that was constantly in motion, sometimes winding itself into a tangle, other times falling into rings as if carrying out an endless dance. The snake's pointy head had two whitish unblinking eyes with vertical black slits for pupils. Its two pairs of clawed feet looked like those of a lizard. And on her back, there was a pair of huge wings with bright red skin membranes! I took a few screenshots to remember the deadly dangerous beauty by.

But the mission still wasn't finished. Why?

I wrote out a private message to Valerianna Quickfoot. The nymph was already supposed to have respawned long ago and, based on the green marker next to her name, was playing. But I didn't wait long enough for her to answer. Most likely, my sister was already sleeping in bed, simply having left the game running. I had to think on my own.

So then, I had reached the prophesied island. I could see on it a plethora of wyverns of levels forty to seventy and one giant winged snake by the name of Kayervina. My mission was to finish the unique quest and get the reward. Time limit: forty minutes. After that, the sun would come up and my goblin vampire would inevitably die as the burning rays of the sun penetrated the piled-up branches over me.

"Sorry, I was sleeping. I found information on other similar missions. The unique creature has to see you. Even if it attacks and kills you, the mission will still be considered finished."

Woah! That meant it would be enough for me to attract the attention of Kayervina in any way possible. I now had a clear idea of what I had to do. I had to make sure the other wyverns didn't kill me before the snake mother noticed me!

I looked at the wyvern nearest me. It was sleeping, wrapped in a ball on a grass-covered hill. I realized I really did have a very effective method of attracting the attention of all the island's inhabitants. There was just seven meters between the neck of the flying snake and myself. By the way, my potential victim was level-fifty-one, so I had to be sure to take some kind of trophy from it for Tarek Bigfoot's mission.

After first opening my inventory and moving the window to the side so it wouldn't block my vision, I set about removing branches and clearing myself a path. I took a heavy sigh, preparing my body for activity. Now! With all my might, I tore off toward the sleeping wyvern and took a drink with my fangs from the snake's throat.

Experience received: 4080 Exp.

Racial ability improved: Taste for Blood (Gives +1% to all damage dealt for each unique creature killed with Vampire Bite. Current bonus: 5%)

Achievement unlocked: Taste Tester (5/1000)

Level sixteen!
Racial ability improved: Resistance to Poison +35%

Like a flock of startled crows, the winged snakes all rocketed upward at once, flapping their wings with a deafening roar. That was all. I had been noticed. My goblin had just a few seconds left to live. But why had it given so little experience?! The amount of experience I'd gotten from killing the level-42 bullfrog with a group leveled me up six times, so for solo killing a level-51 wyvern, I was expecting to get at least ten more...

Mission completed: Curiosity and the Cat
Reward: 8000 Exp.

Level seventeen!

Fame increased
Present value: 1

Racial ability improved: Resistance to Cold +
35%

So, that was it?! I got just one level for the unique quest, and no loot whatsoever? Hurriedly, not even looking, I popped the trophies I'd gotten from the wyvern into my bag, when I suddenly saw IT. In the place where the huge snake mother had just been sitting, there was a strange glowing yellow object:

Wyvern Egg (unique object)

My legs were thrown forward to the loot before my mind recognized what I had seen. So, that was the amazing reward! I dodged abruptly, letting the wyvern diving at me hit the bare ground. Then, I rolled forward as not to fall beneath the stream of sizzling poison from the other enraged snakes.

Dodge skill increased to level 7!

Acrobatics skill increased to level 5!

I jumped forward, slipping on the damp clay soil and letting one of their scaly bodies fall over me. After that, I jumped over a long tail sweeping under my feet. I turned away from a set of jaws snapping right in front of my nose, jumped and let a wing strike pass over my head. I tripped over something moving and leapt, extending my arms forward. I made it! Not losing even a single second, I stuck the invaluable trophy into my inventory and raised my head just as the snake mother breathed a stream of poison directly at my face.

You have died
3015 Exp. lost
You will respawn in 59 minutes, 58 seconds at the last respawn point you set

A Big Fuss Over an Egg

WHEN I CLIMBED OUT of the virtual reality capsule, I was feeling groggy, tired, and barely able to stand. My arms and legs were shaking, and my shoulders hurt like hell. I had just spent the last six hours rowing an overloaded, sagging boat with a pair of very unwieldy oars. This must have been how the slaves on an ancient Greek trireme felt after a long day's work. When I turned back to the virtual reality capsule I had just left, I discovered that the interior was all wet from sweat. Fortunately, in modern game capsule models, there was a self-cleaning function, so I started it up. My own body was shimmering with sweat as well, even the hair on my head was completely soaked. I threw a towel

I'd brought from home over my shoulders and hurried into the shower. Morning had yet to come in *Boundless Realm*, and I wanted to wash up before Kira, who usually finished playing just after dawn.

"Good morning, Timothy!" The sonorous woman's voice rang out from behind my back as soon as I'd left my cabin.

Based on the bath robe, towel and whole armful of cosmetics she was holding, she was also headed for the shower. I greeted her politely and froze, letting her go first. But Kira stopped next to me and said with a wily smirk:

"Did I scare you that bad the day before yesterday, Timothy? I feel like you're avoiding me. To be honest, after our first encounter, I was expecting you to look desperately for a reason to see me again. I was even a bit worried about it and had a bunch of sharp words ready to brush off the brazen dandy I took you for. But yesterday, you didn't leave your cabin all morning, and today you hurried to finish playing early as not to cross paths with me. To be honest, as a woman, I was actually somewhat offended to be so totally ignored like that."

I didn't even know what to say to Kira now. Should I have told her she was wrong and I wasn't avoiding her at all? That would be a lie though. Today, I had actually left a bit early for that very reason. Kira cracked up laughing:

"Timothy, you're so funny when you get embarrassed! I mean, look at you. You're blushing. But you've got nothing to be embarrassed about. You have a handsome, muscular body. Do you work out?"

"I used to do artistic gymnastics. I even competed in a few tournaments back when I was still in shape," I admitted honestly.

I had dropped the athletic club when Val and I moved to the outskirts of the megalopolis. I no longer had the money or time to keep it up. Recently, I had found it harder and harder to make it out to the stadium, but my body still had yet to lose its shape and really drown in flab. The girl came closer, outstretched her hand and slowly led it across my shoulder. Then she looked at her sweat-dampened fingers.

"I adore the sight of an overworked young man's body!" Kira cracked up laughing again, watching my reaction, then suddenly grew serious and changed the topic. "You look like a stallion fresh from the races. Your body isn't supposed to react that way to things happening in the game. Timothy, is your virtual reality capsule set up wrong? Or do you have health problems? In any case, they shouldn't have let you play like this!"

Afraid of being fired, I hurried to dash Kira's doubts and answered as honestly as I could:

"I'm doing just fine. I was just rushing to finish a quest before someone else did. I had to row a boat for a few hours. That's why I got so sweaty..."

Kira looked at me in disbelief, then said thoughtfully:

"I must say, you've got me intrigued. A quest available to a day-three player that must be completed at night and also involves rowing... To be honest, I thought I knew all the game missions for new players. But for some reason, nothing fitting that description is coming to mind."

"It was a unique quest, called Curiosity and the Cat," I told her, and her eyes shot up in surprise. "I finished the mission just three minutes ago. But right after that, a huge flying snake named Kayervina killed me."

Kira suddenly became unusually serious and frowned.

"That is all very, very strange. Let's say you're not lying. Then what are you doing wasting time here with me, dummy?! If you've got a unique quest, you should be making money on it! Timothy, do you have any idea how many players there are in *Boundless Realm*, who would sell their own mother just to find a unique creature and raise their fame?! And also, the loot there would have to be interesting, given the unique mission. If you can't handle the rare monster or get the valuable treasure, at least try to sell your map of the location. That's what I always do. I assure you, Timothy, if you advertise it well on the forum, your character could be swimming in coins by this evening!"

It now seemed that bathing would have to take the back seat. I thanked the experienced player for the valuable advice and hurried back to my gaming cubicle. I had high-quality screenshots of a most rare thirty-meter flying snake and a video of myself completing the unique mission Curiosity and the Cat. I also had pictures taken at a long distance of wyvern egg. If I edited the video well, took out my attack on the sleeping wyvern and the part where I picked up the unique egg, then gave it the right voiceover, it could really blow up!

I spent half an hour making a condensed video overview of my third work session. A video of the goblin village of Tysh, the beautiful Taisha and her severe father, my six-fold level up when hunting the bullfrog and, after that, a detailed section on my night-boating adventure, the flying snake Kayervina and my "unsuccessful" attempt to acquire the unique egg. The video ended with a striking scene of the snake mother attacking me followed by my death. At the end of the video, with pity in my voice, I said: "This quest was too hard for a beginner: my character would never have been able to handle Kayervina. But, if an experienced player wants to try to take on this thirty-meter-long snake, they could download my local map with a marker showing the place Kayervina lived and where her egg was for just one hundred coins."

I chose my words very carefully to make sure no buyers could accuse me of lying. That's right, I sold a map with a marker showing where the wyvern's egg *was*. I could hardly be blamed, if it weren't there anymore, right?

* * *

A call came into my cell phone, jerking me from a hectic dream where I was escaping from a swarm of snakes. With massive effort, I peeled my eyelids back and glanced at the clock. It was nine thirty in the morning. And that was at the fact that, after my night shift, I had gone to bed only at eight. It was Jane.

"Good morning, Timothy," she said. Despite her polite words, Jane's voice didn't contain even a drop of kindness. It sounded more like badly hidden annoyance. "Mr. Lavrius would like to see you in his office at once. How soon can you get here?"

"The commute takes me about an hour. But, what's the rush?"

"I do not know the reason, Timothy. But our boss has been in a very bad mood since he got here this morning. He just left to go to a meeting, but before that, he was gnashing his teeth in anger. And I heard him mention your name a few times, often in combination with curse words. I haven't seen him this mad for some time. If I were in your place, Timothy, I wouldn't want to make him wait."

Jane hung up, leaving me in a state of deep confusion. Why did the director want to talk to me, and also, why so quickly? What had I done wrong? I yawned, driving off my weariness and took a look around. My younger sister was sitting with her virtual reality helmet on before an inactive monitor and, based on the movement of her hands in the sensor gloves, was either climbing something, or crawling through thick vegetation. I touched Valeria's shoulder, and my sister shuddered then took off the helmet.

"Val, for some reason I've gotten an urgent call into the office. I just wanted to tell you, so you wouldn't worry where I went."

"It must have to do with the turmoil now being stirred up at the wyvern island," the girl supposed. I perked up my ears and asked her to tell me about it.

While I was getting dressed and making myself some strong coffee, my sister turned her chair toward me and started turgidly explaining the events now underway in the game. She had noticed an unusual activity in our normally quiet, unpopulated part of the world at around eight this morning. The local chat suddenly lit up with players talking and trying to gather a group together for an assault on the wyvern island in the swamp. In that very chat, I read that a certain player had enchanted a bunch of portal scrolls in Stonetown and was selling them in the nearby city of Weiden for one thousand coins each. The gamers were incensed at the outrageously inflated prices, but still, most of them had made use of those very scrolls to get a leg up on their many competitors who were lagging behind on foot or riding various mounts.

By eight thirty, a group of thirty of the most impatient players was first to reach the island in the swamp, but they all got killed, having underestimated the strength of the mother of flying snakes. The level of the unique snake, based on her level-forty-seventy minions, was judged to be around one hundred, so they came up with a combat strategy based on that. All the same, Kayervina easily wiped the whole group of "tanks" out in one breath, then took down their ranged support a few seconds later. The chat filled up with acrid comments: the dead warriors respawn points were, in the best case, in the city of Weiden, and some were much farther away.

After the first group's bad luck, a second group started forming, but it had problems of a totally different type. In Stonetown, a huge group of PK-ers, specialized in murdering other players started showing up, having bought the portal scrolls themselves. The village of Stonetown was suddenly inundated with Stealth-mode ninjas, thieves, and assassins, who instantly killed lone players or any player who even blinked. Some even saw members of the *Goons* and *Scum* clans, hated by the other players for their pathological tendency for senseless murder simply for murder's sake.

Now, most of them were hiding in the homes of NPC residents making further plans. The rumor was that the stone-faced level two-hundred-fifty dwarf Headshots_For_All was seen in Weiden. He was one of the main tanks from the *Keepers* clan, which was in the top ten strongest clans on the Southern Continent. Such famous warriors didn't even take a piss without dozens of support players following them, so it was expected that a huge assault force of high-level *Keepers* would soon arrive in Stonetown.

"I sent the Gray Pack away so our wolves wouldn't accidentally become the victims of someone's hot temper. I'm next to the swamp now. I can see some flashes on the island of wyverns. There's a serious battle there with lots of magic being used, but I cannot tell who is taking more hits. I'm pretty far away"

"Gotcha, Val. That's all. I've got to run to work now."

* * *

I'd been sitting on a little bench in the hall for two hours already, enjoying the view of the metropolis from way up on the forty-fourth floor. From up here, the city looked like a benchmark of cleanliness and order. It had emerald-green squares, a blue lake with dozens of pleasure boats, and ideally even highways with endless lines of electric cars rushing to and fro. Among the green and roads there rose up the faceted crystals of skyscrapers housing the largest corporations on the planet. Between those tall buildings, civilian flying cars and quadrocopters darted about like so many buzzing flies. Hovering at regular intervals, there were police drones maintaining public order. Everything here in the downtown of the megalopolis spoke to the presence of lots of money and confidence in the future.

I took a heavy sigh and, for the umpteenth time, glanced at the director of special projects' office door. Alexandro Lavrius still hadn't returned from his meeting, and his assistant Jane couldn't say when her boss would be back. With every passing minute, I grew more and more worried. Something extraordinary must have happened, given that it required an emergency meeting with the senior executives. I was feeling dead tired. There was really nothing I could do to stop myself from yawning anymore. Finally, I ran out of patience. I stood up and walked over toward the director's door.

"Jane, I'm going to go get to work. When the director comes, call me. I'll come straight up on the elevator."

The director's assistant gave a very slight nod. She was busy painting her long, well-kept nails. It seemed that evenly applied polish was a much higher priority for her than the personal problems of a corporate drone like me.

I took the elevator down to the basement and headed for my cabin. But I barely managed to take out my electronic keys before I heard several people call my name. I stopped and recognized some of them — they had been in the room where I'd filled out the work questionnaires. There were about a dozen men and women standing in the break area at the end of the walkway. The testers must have been taking a lunch break.

"So, there's the mysterious 'number sixteen!' It's our third day here, but this is the first time I've seen you at work," joked a young woman, motioning for me to join them. She was the one who had traded for a dryad dancer.

I walked up and greeted my colleagues. It turned out that we were the only ones left from our initial group of forty testers. The rest had already been fired by Alexandro Lavrius. I had to answer their tough questions about my character and where I'd been for the last three days.

"Level-seventeen goblin herbalist," I introduced myself. At these words, my colleagues nodded in respect.

"Cool! The only one doing better than you is

Veronica. She's already level twenty-five," said a redheaded mustached man of forty years, pointing at the dryad girl.

She laughed happily and said, without a drop of shame:

"My character's profession has limited applications, so it was obvious what I should do from day one. I purposely provoke passers-by with my sexual appearance and behavior. Any issues with NPC's can be solved either immediately on account of their highly positive reaction, or in bed. I passed all three steps of the Socialization quest on the very first day. To be honest, my dryad has been sexually assaulted a few times, but I guess that comes with the territory. It's just in a video game, after all, so it doesn't really get to me. On the first day, I put my video channel in the category 'strictly 18+' and, since that time, I've been doing live streams. I've already gotten eight thousand paid subscribers. On top of that, many viewers have sent me considerable sums of money and want to meet me in real life. Mr. Lavrius told me yesterday that I had already passed the trial period and hired me on as a permanent employee, so I now have the ability to turn game money into cash. Yesterday, with the money I've earned, I bought myself a penthouse with a pool on the roof of a skyscraper. This evening, after I buy myself a flying car, I'll never have to use the elevator or come down to earth again..."

Veronica, who was playing the dryad, cracked up into careless laughter. The redheaded man standing next to her looked quite dejected:

"I'm glad it all turned out so well for you. But I'm still just level eight, and that's in the middle of my third day! Mr. Lavrius is very unhappy with me. He said I might get fired, if I don't get to level twenty by the end of the week. Where can I get experience, though? No one will let my ogre fortifier within a kilometer of their village! I've already tried going to a human village and an arachnid one! They both killed me on sight! There's no one else near my spawn point, either. All around me is nothing but dangerous forest full of level-twenty monsters. They kill me at least three times a day, so I just keep losing experience! I'm not a hunter or a fisherman. My slow-moving giant can't even catch prey in the forest, nor hide or flee from danger. I need a normal job. Digging, building, cutting stakes, things like that..."

Something in the words of my despairing coworker caught my attention. An idea took root in me and immediately bore fruit. If I were in a cartoon, there would have been a light bulb popping up over my head. I spoke in an intentionally boring, ambivalent voice:

"You've got it easy: you're strong. You just need to find an adequate employer. I, though, have the opposite problem: I'm in desperate need of a fortifier to make better defenses around a house I found in the forest. There's spooky monsters all around. They come right up, scratch at the door and peer in the windows. I need to renovate it. And there's a lot of work: fixing the stockade, digging out trap pits, building a watchtower, getting the outer gate back on its hinges... Suffice it to say, there's plenty to do. My character is a goblin, so I have a penalty to leveling strength, and it would take me centuries to even dig out a suitable pit..."

The balding redheaded man stood predictably to his feet like a hunting dog that just caught the scent of a pheasant:

"Hey, what are the coordinates of your house? If it's not too far, I'll come to your place and set you up exactly what you need. You provide the tools and the grub, and I'll give you my honest work! I need that job so bad!!! Toss the coordinates of your forest house to a character named Shrekson Bastard."

I went into my cabin and sent the message. I noticed right away that eighty-four players had already taken advantage of my offer and bought the map showing where the wyvern island was for one hundred coins. It wasn't too many, to be honest. I was expecting at least a couple hundred buyers. But, eight thousand in-game coins wasn't bad at all. Although... I hadn't really thought this through. I hadn't received the money directly in coins. For now, it was just in the form of promissory notes from two different banks: "The

Subterranean Bank of Thorin the Ninth" and "The Most Reliable Bank of Gremlins." I would have to find branches of these banks, if I wanted to actually turn these papers into usable money.

I went back onto the elevated walkway and said that everything was ready. Shrekson ran to see, and a minute later came a joyful voice:

"That's right near me! Just forty-seven kilometers away! Alright, guys, I'm off to play! Hopefully, I'll be there by evening!"

The door of his cabin closed. The little red light bulb above it lit up over it.

"I really hope Leon can pass the trial period," said a freckled young lad with an earring in one ear. "I've only been working with him for three days, but I feel like I've known him my whole life. It's a rare thing to meet such an honest and open person. He worked his whole life as a construction worker and, a month ago, they had an accident. Someone didn't buckle their safety harness and fell to their death. After that, the construction company fired the whole brigade. Must have figured one bad apple spoils the bunch. Leon actually worked a totally different shift and had nothing to do with what happened, but he was fired too. He didn't even get severance pay. Anyone else in his place might get angry or drink, but not him. Picture this: this morning, Leon found a gold woman's ring with a huge ruby in the shower room. He showed it to me. It must be worth at least sixty thousand credits. Trust me, I know this stuff. He could have just quietly hidden it and lived out the rest of his days in comfort, but Leon went and brought the ring to the security guards at the building entrance so they could find out whose it was."

"Kira must have dropped it," I slid into the conversation. "She's a young woman who works the night shift in cabin twenty. She has fancy rings on all her fingers, actually."

"That sounds right," Veronica supported me. "I've seen that woman here a few times. Just one of her hats is worth as much as my new apartment. I have no idea what character she plays, but all my achievements are simply worthless in comparison with what that hussy earns!"

By the end of the sentence, Veronica had clearly been overtaken by a fit of anger, no longer holding back her extreme envy. To be honest, it shook me. I made an excuse about having to work and locked myself in my cabin. Without closing the lid of my virtual reality capsule, I set my telephone on the table and simply lay down to sleep.

❋ ❋ ❋

In a stroke of deja vu, I was again awoken by the sound of my phone. And again, it was Jane. But this time, it was already five thirty PM, and I was actually feeling quite well rested. Had the directors' meeting really lasted this long?!

"Timothy, the Director is expecting you in his office on floor forty-four."

"I'm already on my way," I blurted out. I quickly threw my shirt on, buttoned it up and rushed to the elevator.

Three minutes later, I was walking into the office of the director of special projects for the *Boundless Realm* corporation. When I got there, though, Alexandro Lavrius was not in the room. Sitting in the director's chair was a man I didn't know. He was quite corpulent and wearing an expensive suit. There was another stranger in the room as well. He had blond hair and was well-groomed like a soldier, clearly having done a fairly long stint in the army. He perched himself on the edge of the director's desk, even though there were two perfectly good armchairs next to him. Searching for an explanation on what was happening, I turned to Jane.

"This is Mark Tobius, the new Director of Special Projects for the *Boundless Realm* corporation. Just today, he was appointed by the board of directors to replace Alexandro Lavrius, who's been fired," the girl introduced me to the portly man. "Next to him is Andrei Soloviev, head of in-game security for the corporation."

"I see you are surprised, Timothy," my new

boss was studying me shamelessly, simply drilling into me with his gaze. "Yes, there has been a bit of reshuffling in our leadership today. You see, early this morning, one of our experienced testers came to the virtual security department with some evidence. They asked us to take control of a developing situation with the rare quest Curiosity and the Cat, as they suspected the potential for large-scale fraud. The in-game security service was quite alarmed by this, and looked into it closely. After a good deal of investigation, we were forced to admit that the aforementioned tester's instincts were well founded. There was, in fact, a large-scale attempt at stealing virtual property from the corporation involving an organized group of highly-placed employees."

"The wyvern egg?" I supposed, and both of the men nodded in unison.

The head of the virtual security service took a piece of paper from the table. On it, there was a screenshot printout: my goblin, arms outstretched, lying spread-eagle in the nest of the queen of flying snakes. Also, next to that, there was an open inventory window showing one slot occupied by a golden egg. In the corner of that printout, you could see the time in-game: 05:44:37.148.

"Timothy, with your desperate lunge for the egg, you upset the fraudsters' plans. No less than four minutes later, that very same location was visited by another employee of our company: a high-level illusionist, who wanted to take the reward. When he got there, though, the wyvern nest was empty. We traced a phone call from the second underground floor of the building to Alexandro Lavrius and, soon after that, a call came to the director from one of our highly-placed programmers. We then detected an attempt to duplicate the egg. But it is a unique object, so there can only be one copy in the game at a time. Alexandro Lavrius quickly discovered where the original was. That was followed by a number of attempts to hack into your inventory and remove the egg. Unfortunately for them, any attempt to meddle with the inventory of a dead player is automatically blocked. Naturally, by that time, we already knew everything except the name of the end customer. Now we know that as well. It was a very respected player, the leader of one of the top clans of the Western Continent. This person has invested quite a good sum of real money into the game, and doesn't seem to have done anything wrong."

"Yes, I personally spoke with them and explained the situation," the heavyset man stated, trying to get comfortable in his predecessor's chair, which was clearly not wide enough for him. "I was able to stay in his good graces, and the high-value player will continue putting money into *Boundless Realm*."

~ Video Game Plotline Tester ~

The head of the in-game security department cringed:

"By all appearances, this was far from the first instance of these crooks withdrawing money from the game in such a fashion. But, all the same, the board of directors decided to let the players keep the rare objects they'd already bought. Their fraudulent scheme was finely tuned and simple: when an inexperienced player happened to get a rare quest with a potentially very valuable trophy, Alexandro Lavrius would find out and tell his inside man, a programmer. He then would change the quest settings. You see, normally, quests have completely random rewards. After his meddling, though, the most valuable possible prize would be dropped automatically. The new player would then be given a chance or two to try to cut their teeth on, and the valuable prize would be taken by a different corporate employee. After that, there followed a private or even public sale. The valuable object would end up going to one of our many rich players, the employee would withdraw the game money as real money and the take would be split between all participants in the scam."

Both of the men went silent, so I piped up and asked:

"Could you tell me, does the board of directors' decision to let players keep rare objects apply to my case? After all, I got the egg fair and square. I even died getting it."

My new boss, having again begun to drill into me with harsh tenacious eyes, answered:

"Timothy, the chance of that egg appearing on generation of the Curiosity and the Cat quest, is just three percent, so we can't exactly say you came by it honestly. The surrounding events played into your hands quite nicely, but it wasn't really your fault. So, it was decided that you could keep the egg and, given the massive game event now underway near the wyvern island, you will also be given thirty minutes of protection on the artifact, but you cannot trade or sell it under any circumstances. The same limit shall apply to your sister as well."

I froze in fear, and Andrei Soloviev looked at me and laughed good-heartedly:

"Timothy, it was naive on your part to hope that the corporation wouldn't check all our coworkers' calls and contacts, both in-game and out-of-game. The security forces found out the identity of Valerianna Quickfoot on your first day. Your sister used service commands to start the game in a specific location with a specific person. She also circumvented the standard age-check procedure. Instead of providing an identity card, she used her disability card to register her character, and it doesn't show age. And it should be said that this error has already been corrected."

"But, for my disabled sister, virtual worlds are the only way of forgetting about her bleak existence! She feels like they allow her to live a full life, traveling around and talking to different people! And, without my sister, *Boundless Realm* would lose all meaning for me!" I grew very afraid that Valeria would be forbidden from playing.

"We have no problem with your sister playing," my new boss reassured me. "Today, I even suggested hiring her officially as a tester with some kind of fixed salary, as she's playing quite a rare race anyway, and quite skillfully at that. But, the higher-ups decided against it. Your sister is underage, and *Boundless Realm* is rated 18+. It's one thing to 'not notice' her real age, but another thing entirely to officially hire a child to test adult content. Then, it starts to smell criminal. So, you can keep playing together. Our corporation has no issue with your partnership."

I exhaled a bit freer, but then Mark Tobius dropped a turd in the punchbowl:

"All the same, I must warn you that you and your sister should be careful not to share in-game property. Coins especially. If your goblin is detected in possession of your sister's in-game money, it would be a criminal offense, and you could expect a lifetime ban on your characters and a very real trip to court. I trust you understand that?"

I confirmed that, before starting my job as a tester, I had signed a warning to that effect. My new boss nodded in satisfaction.

"That is excellent, Timothy. Because for some reason, many look on work in the *Boundless Realm* corporation as nothing more than a way of helping players withdraw virtual capital, naturally, for a certain cut. Even in the group that was hired just three days ago, half have been terminated for getting involved with criminals specialized in the withdrawal of game currency. And it is very good that you honestly disclosed your past sin. These connections were checked carefully and found to be no obstacle to your work."

The large man, in the end, admitted the impossibility of his sitting normally in the armchair, stood up wearily and went over to his new assistant.

"What's your name...? Jane, order me a normal chair for tomorrow. I have no need for this abomination. And put on a strong pot of coffee. The work day is almost over, and I just can't get my head straight."

"And bring me some coffee as well, would you?" asked the head of security and the girl went to prepare some.

Supposing that the conversation was over, I also stood, but my boss stopped me.

"Wait, Timothy. There are a few other organizational issues. I've already been informed that you were promised successful completion of the trial period, if you finished the mission

Curiosity and the Cat. Unfortunately, I cannot uphold my forbearer's promise in that regard. I first need to get my bearings here and get to know my coworkers. Whether you stay or go now will depend in large part on what you do with that valuable egg. Do with it what you will, but you must never sell it!"

"I'll do something with the egg no one is expecting. What if I just ate it?!" I chuckled.

Mark Tobius gagged on his coffee. Jane, with a composed look, got a napkin, wiped off the coffee sputter and said that she would be going now to make another cup. Just then, Andrei Soloviev clarified with slight lack of confidence:

"Timothy, I suspect you were joking but, all the same, I do not think you would actually be able to feed your character one million credits."

I tried very hard to not reveal my shock.

"To be honest, I didn't think the wyvern egg was worth that much."

The head of in-game security finished his coffee unhurriedly and looked at an abstract picture on the director's wall, then said thoughtfully:

"It's always hard to assess the value of a truly unique item. For example, this picture. I saw reports that Alexandro Lavrius bought it for one hundred thirty thousand credits. But, if you think about it, how does this paint smear differ from the hundreds of others sold for nothing in underground passageways? Only in that it found a buyer prepared to invest one hundred thirty thousand in it. When talking about a set of bytes in a computer game, the situation is the same. The value is determined only by the presence of demand. There was a buyer prepared to pay that exact amount for the wyvern egg: ten million game coins. A similar item, a griffin egg, which also was given to a player who completed the Curiosity and the Cat quest half a year ago, was sold at auction for six million seven hundred thousand game coins. Beyond that, the appearance of the very first flying mount, the giant silver dragonfly, led to serious criminal investigations in the real world and cost three people their lives."

The security officer went silent, but his thought was immediately picked up by my new boss:

"At present, there are just seventeen flying mounts in all of *Boundless Realm*. What's more, on the Southern Continent, where gamers in our time zone live, the only flying mounts are five snow-white pegasuses. The *Steel Legion* received command of them last year for victory in a PvP clan tournament. Your wyvern could have been the sixth on the continent and the eighteenth in the whole world. And I said 'could have' not at all because I truly believe you might eat the egg. The doubt in that sentence was caused by the combination of words 'your wyvern.' I'll put it directly: the chances of your weak goblin retaining possession of such a valuable object are very low. Many, many people will want to steal the egg. If they find you, they will kill your character again and again, until the valuable loot finally drops. Also, it creates the possibility you could be doxed, opening the door to real-world harassment, which you surely wouldn't want."

I stayed silent a bit, then asked how players could find out I had the egg, if I didn't advertise the fact in the video. Andrei Soloviev answered my question:

"Only a few of our employees know who truly owns the egg, but they all signed a nondisclosure agreement. No other players could possibly be sure of this. But top clans are interested in gaining the wyvern mount and, in the next few days, will be working out lists of all the players who took part in the event, as well as those who were near the wyvern island. The battle ended two hours ago in Kayervina's death. It was the fourth attempt, but the egg was nowhere to be found. Right now, *Boundless Realm* tech support is answering thousands of requests with identical responses:

'The event took place in full accordance with game mechanics. The Wyvern egg will remain in the game, and is now in possession of a most crafty player, whose name we cannot disclose for obvious reasons.'"

My boss's tablet, lying on the table, gave a

beep. The fat man picked it up, quickly scrolled past a few screens and melted into a smile:

"An evaluation of the events from the point of view of *Boundless Realm* upper management has come in. Despite the spontaneity, the mass event turned out quite well. Nine and a half thousand players were present, and just one hundred seventy didn't die once. Add to that the fact that three of the top one hundred players were killed today, losing lots of experience in the process. Such occurrences are quite rare and encourage competition. Thousands of items and pieces of equipment changed hands, including many rare and two legendary ones. There was also a direct conflict between the *Keepers* and the *Lords of Chaos*, the second and third strongest clans on the Southern Continent respectively, in a swamp teeming with underwater beasts. That was just the cherry on top. Recordings of the battle are now being shown on many news channels. Viewer interest is colossal. The *Lords of Chaos* won the battle, and they were then able to take down the snake mother, at the same time sharply increasing the authority of their clan, which will have serious political consequences in the future."

Mark Tobius set the tablet aside and turned toward me.

"All in all, the senior executives are quite satisfied. Given that, as the organizer of all this activity, you have earned some kind of bonus from the company. Jane will figure out an appropriate payout. You can expect the money by tomorrow morning. I then will close my eyes to your use of an NPC village guard for an illegal frog hunt. Split experience for killing aggressive beasts is calculated by a different formula for key village defenders. The reward is increased for the whole group to make sure recently spawned NPC's get to a high enough level in good time. Using these kinds of 'steam trains' for farming is flagrant cheating and, if you use this exploit again, there will be very serious consequences..."

The director went silent, as a short telephone trill rang out in my pocket. It was a message from my sister:

"Trong Diver is back. He's up to level eight. I took care of him. Will you be coming back soon?"

"My sister is worried. She's asking when I'll be back," I told him, apologizing for the interruption.

"Answer her that it will be very soon indeed," my boss chuckled back. "This meeting is over, Timothy. You can get back to work. And I remind you that you have just one half hour in which the artifact will be protected."

Finding Myself

"*I SEE NOTHING bad in the fact that the administrators know of our relationship. We still shouldn't advertise it to players, though. Let them keep thinking we're independent. Log on. The weather right now is great for you. Cloudy skies! There will be a thunderstorm tonight! I have very important guests near the blockhouse. We can talk about it later.*"

After thanking my sister for the weather information, and without asking about unexpected guests, I laid down in the virtual reality capsule. And so began my fourth game session. Before I started playing, I looked at my character's information:

~ Video Game Plotline Tester ~

Name	Amra
Race	Goblin Vampire
Class	Herbalist
Experience	27450 of 31000
Character level	17
Hit points	150/150
Endurance points	122/122
Statistics	
Strength (S)	18 (18)
Agility (A)	15 (39.7)
Intelligence (I)	5 (6.7)
Constitution (C)	20 (24.5)
Perception (P)	3 (12.75)
Charisma (Ch)	30 (33)
Unused points	**6**
Primary skills (5 of 5 chosen)	
Herbalism (P A)	4
Trading (Ch I)	3
Alchemy (I A)	2
Dodge (A P)	7
Stealth (A C)	9
Secondary skills (3 of 5 chosen)	
Veil	2
Acrobatics	5
Exotic Weapons	3

I was slightly embarrassed that the skill I had been assigned, Herbalism, was far behind Stealth and Dodge, which spoiled the legend of my being nothing but a peaceful plant gatherer. But it was nothing. One or two fruitful nights or cloudy days spent practicing Herbalism, and the imbalance would be corrected.

With the six stat points I had sitting around... I decided not to reinvent the wheel. I continued the development path I had been on by putting four points into charisma and two into agility. As for the two unused secondary skill slots, I hesitated for a few minutes, but still didn't make any choice. I could make up my mind on this as the game progressed. So then, loading... Before the world loaded, a message popped up on the dark background detailing last night's death. A link at the bottom allowed me to familiarize myself in more detail with the reasons for the fatal outcome. I clicked on the link and saw the following logs before my eyes:

Damage taken: 107888 points (165981 poison damage from Kayervina, 35% Resistance to Poison)

Damage taken: 230891 points (230891 acid damage from Kayervina)

Damage taken: 123893 points (123893 fire

damage from Kayervina)

You died at 05:44:37.889
3015 Exp. lost

You may now respawn

The mother of flying snakes gave me a good little whipping! To be more accurate, she'd given me an acid burn. I mentally corrected myself, as the acid damage Kayervina had done had the greatest effect. As far as I knew, that damage type had a very nasty side effect. It could ruin and even totally destroy your equipment. I could only imagine the storm of curse-words coming from the other players who got hit with Kayervina's breath!

After closing the information window, I chose the menu point "Continue Game." The screen lit up and I found myself sitting on a slightly buzzing rune-covered stone. I didn't have time to look around before I overheard a surprising and comical voice right next to me:

"What kind of green abomination do we have here?"

Literally a couple of meters from me, leaning on a long, carved staff, there stood a man in a dark blue wizard's robe imprinted with silver runes. His face was half hidden by a hood. I saw only his angular chin, grown over with a dark stubble.

~ Dark herbalist Book One ~

Klaus Flawless [GOONS]
Human
Level-55 Elemental Mage

I tried to maintain my sangfroid, even when I saw a bright red criminal marker over the wizard's head and the *Goons* clan name.

"Hey Klaus, isn't this that goblin what sold you the map?" I turned toward the voice of the second player and saw a boy sitting not far away on a wooden block in dark leather clothes. He had two long, hooked blades on his back, and his face was obscured by a mask with eye holes, telling me that I was seeing an assassin even before I read into the character's information:

Perros Ruthless [GOONS]
Human
Level-44 Assassin

The very same criminal marker was hanging over his head and the very same *Goons* clan tag. These were some bad dudes. Relentless PK-ers, who killed just for fun. Now I'd really put my foot in it... There was absolutely no point running, even less fighting. I tried to play the part of the naive fool, with no idea what was going on.

"Humans! You is maybe two only player I meeting for alls game! When first I start, there two with Amra: naiad and nymph. But I running away and, after, where they? I alone boring, to play with robots. You no understand how happy is to find more real living."

"Yep. That's the one alright. He makes those videos with the dope commentary!" said the assassin, growing happy at recognizing me. "He shook a hundred coins from every player for the map. Probably got rich on that..."

I was a bit shocked. I was just meeting my first fan and he was a criminal assassin.

"No, he's really poor. Just eleven coins. I could hardly bring myself to take it." A third person appeared from invisibility behind me. It was a short Asian-looking human in a black cloth robe and dark skin-tight clothes.

Lee Fast_Fingers [GOONS]
Human
Leve- 50 Thief

"You didn't happen to see a wyvern egg lying around his inventory, did you?" the mage asked in a joking tone, though I noticed distinct anxiety on his face as he waited for the answer.

I froze in horror. This was it. Now, the contents of my bags would shake out, and the valuable egg would be discovered and taken. And the worst thing was that there was nothing at all I could do. We were just too unevenly matched.

"There's no egg. I looked right away. A lot of

different kinds of herbs, berries and flowers, though. Basically, he's a botanist. The most valuable thing he's got are three pieces of wyvern hide, material for a leatherworker."

I could see the golden egg in my own inventory, though. In its properties, there was also a countdown timer showing twenty-eight minutes. That must have been exactly how the artifact protection was working. Other players couldn't even tell it was there. Slightly coming to, I commented on the thief's statement:

"Is snake skin for mission. I be in wyvern island walking before. Flying snake destroy fur jacket and shorts. Now I will for making new clothes."

At these words, all three robbers and murderers took another look at me. I really was standing before them in nothing but a loincloth. The developers of *Boundless Realm* had made the last article of clothing absolutely indestructible. Nothing could damage its fabric, not the strongest acid, nor the fire of volcanoes, nor even the sharpest of blades.

"I'm not trying to get my hands dirty on this little goblin. How long until your marker goes away?" Klaus the mage asked the assassin.

"One hour seventeen minutes," Perros answered after a second of pause and cringed in dismay. "I'm not feeling it. Taking a four-hour penalty 'just because?' We won't get any experience or loot from big-ears, here. I pass."

The thief agreed with his henchmen and turned to me: "It's your lucky day, big-ears! We won't touch you. Go on your way."

I didn't tempt fate and hurried away from the dangerous trio. But I didn't even make it forty steps before a spark of light lit up behind me and I hurriedly turned around. On the buzzing rock, there appeared an armor-clad swordsman, clearly having just respawned. I didn't even look at his name, concentrating only on his level. Fifty-nine. Too low to stand up to the three killers. That's what you call bad luck! Instantly figuring out what was happening, I started running for my life.

As I had predicted, the recently returned cuirassier was powerless against the three *Goons* and, ten seconds later, was on his way to another respawn. The trio of PK-ers, their criminal timers reset, now had nothing stopping them back from killing me.

"Hey, greenie, come back over here. I've got something to tell you!" The mage's shout reached me.

Ha! Dream on! By that time, I had already come down from the hill and was booking it through the tall grass into the safety of the forest. Another thirty meters and I'd be out of reach. As if reading my thoughts, the assassin launched something at me. At first, I noticed the danger on the mini-map. It looked like a bright fast dot.

Quickly turning my head as I ran, I saw a magical blue grenade flying at me from the hill. I rushed to change my trajectory to get out of its possible strike zone. A dull plunk came from behind me and a bright spark lit up the evening forest.

Successful Agility check
Experience received: 8 Exp.

Successful Agility check
Experience received: 8 Exp.

Successful Agility check
Experience received: 8 Exp.

I dodged the dark blue shards, but a pressure wave from their explosion knocked me off my feet. I fell to the ground and rolled in the grass.

Damage taken: 134 (203 cold damage from Level-20 Ice Sphere, 35% Resistance to Cold)
3 second freeze effect

Successful Constitution check
Experience received: 16 Exp.

Health level: 16/150

I was lying on the frozen-solid dense blue grass inside a large circle mowed down by the fifteen-meter-diameter explosion. But worst of all was the fact that, just one outstretched arm from me, there was fresh, fragrant, juicy green grass just waving in the breeze. Just a few steps further and I would have been safe!

Three, two, one... The freeze timer had barely passed when I abruptly jumped up and, crunching the crispy breaking grass underfoot, slunk into the forest. I even overheard surprised shouts from the bandits behind me, who clearly weren't expecting how agile I turned out to be. That was it. There was dense vegetation separating me from my enemies now. Also, which was fairly important, I had a racial ability that kicked in just then:

+30% bonus to movement speed in forest and swamp tiles

I started dashing faster and faster, noting with worry that one of them had disappeared from the mini-map. Either the thief or the assassin had gone invisible. I wonder if he was following me, or just sitting on the hill? How could I possibly find out?

"Amra, a level eight ogre came to our blockhouse. He says you hired him to fix the fence. Should I kill him or is he telling the truth?"

I was caught off guard by the private message from my sister and, crucially, it was at a very bad time. I almost ran head-first into the trunk of an ancient tree, not having noticed the obstacle due to the pop-up window. I had to optimize the frame position while running and answer her.

"Good. Feed him, then. He's very hungry, so let him work. As a matter of fact, I have a bunch of ideas for him. He can help us defend the house from nocturnal monsters."

Thankfully, Shrekson had managed to reach my house. I hoped my sister would find him suitable. I really wanted him to make it to level twenty by the end of the work week. By the way, what an interesting partnership they would make: the engineer could draw up the buildings and defenses, and the fortifier would bring them to life. As a result, both of them would level their skills, gain experience, and everyone would be satisfied. Hey! Immersed in thought, only at the very last moment did I jump away from a creature lying in the bushes.

Successful check for Seasoned Tusker reaction
Experience received: 20 Exp.

The toothy little level-23 boar was following my crazed goblin with a surprised gaze as I went through the woods over hill and dale. Hey, sorry, didn't mean to scare you. I was looking at the mini-map, so I saw what followed in detail. A few seconds later, next to the yellow marker of the forest creature, there appeared a red triangle. A second later, and the seasoned tusker was no more. After quickly scooping up the loot, the criminal-marked player went invisible again. The question of whether I was being followed was settled, then. There was a *Goon* after me for sure.

The shameful thought to stop and allow him to kill me, keeping the artifact at the cost of my life, I dismissed out of hand. It wasn't in my habit to just throw up my hands. Also, respawning would only mean I would meet the same PK-ers an hour later. So, I would have to run, run, and run, trying not to leave the forest and lose my speed bonus.

Where could I run to? Obviously not to the blockhouse. Even a forest creature knew not to lead a predator to its lair. That would lead the ruthless PK-er to my sister and the newly arrived builder, which I couldn't allow under any circumstances. I opened the map wider and added the desired endpoint for the route: the village of Tysh, where there were more than enough high-level goblin NPC's capable of stopping my pursuer in his tracks. After correcting the set route to make sure it went through the forest and swamp at all times, I closed the map and concentrated on running.

"You'll never get away from me, goblin. I see

you on the map, so running is useless."

The private message was from the player Perros Ruthless. That meant it was the assassin after me. I didn't answer him, observing my gradually draining endurance points bar. The sprint was sapping my strength. Obviously, my pursuer noticed that as well:

"It's stupid to run. Sooner or later, you'll run out of endurance and you'll have to stop."

Every minute of running took away five endurance points. Now, I had 92 EP of my total of 122, giving me enough time to run for eighteen minutes. I opened the map again and tried to calculate how long it would take me to get to Tysh. I came up with twenty-three minutes. Not good! If I were to do nothing, I would run out of endurance before reaching safety.

First and foremost, I would have to finish drinking all the elixir of endurance I'd crafted. +4 EP was thin gruel, but it was still helpful. Beyond that, I had blackberries in my inventory, each of which could restore one point of endurance. Together with the berries, I popped down one of the four pieces of wyvern meat I was still holding onto. The meat didn't give me any endurance, but it sated my hunger and restored fifteen hitpoints.

Would you like to take Runner (C S) as a secondary skill?

It had been some time since the system had offered me a new skill. What did "Runner" do? I read the description. It increased running speed by 1% for every level gained. If the assassin and I had been running a marathon, perhaps I'd have taken it. But in this situation, a few extra meters of running wouldn't save me. Though there was something to the idea... I was reminded of a skill offered to me in the middle of yesterday's several-hour rowing session. What was it called? Athletics? That was right, Athletics! It increased the number of endurance points by one for every skill level.

You have taken Athletics as a secondary skill
Skill level: 1
Secondary skills taken: 4 of 5

And almost right away, before it had even been five seconds, my investment paid off:

Athletics skill increased to level 2!

Great! On the way to Tysh, I would manage to level this skill up two or three more times. I did the calculations again and melted into an ear-to-ear smile. I now had more than enough endurance to make it.

"Amra, do you have any strength left? Stop

and I'll let you die easy."

"Suck on my little green pee-pee!" I actually said something altogether different, close in meaning, but appropriate for polite society. All the same, the automatic goblin language translator had chosen these very words.

Perros made no secret of the fact that he didn't like my answer. The assassin let forth an uncensored invective, recalling all his past intimate relations with members of the goblin race at the speed of a printer. I just laughed. If the enemy was so easily upset, he clearly didn't see the situation very clearly, and so was capable of making errors and doing obviously stupid things.

"Attention! There are two PK-ers next to the respawn point southeast of the wyvern Island. A mage and a thief. Levels 55 and 51," wrote a level-62 elven bowwoman in local chat.

The chat instantly came to life and was splattered with offers to help the elven lady kill the PK-ers.

"Perros, leave that little goblin alone and get back here at once. Without you, we didn't have enough damage to kill the bowwoman. Now, she's gathering others to stop us. We need to get back to the castle."

"Klaus, you idiot, you wrote that in the public chat! Both of you get out of there. I have a scroll with a portal to the city," said a message from the assassin, who was still hot on my trail.

I suppose that was an error on his part. I abruptly rethought taking shelter in the village. Now, I wanted nothing more than to kill my arrogant pursuer.

* * *

Athletics skill increased to level 5!

The chase was coming to an end one way or another. I had just enough endurance for another few minutes of running, but the road leading to Tysh was already showing on the map. I led my hunter to the far watchtower, where the goblins surveyed the road heading to their village, and where I had first met a member of my own race. I just hoped someone was there…

Bingo! On the map, I saw three NPC's, and all three of them were marked with black skulls. I was saved!

The trio of goblins were zealously digging a pit for a roadside boundary pillar, loosening the dry soil with sharpened stakes, then scooping out the earth with their wide hands. The pillar itself was lying right by the roadside, adorned with frightening faces carved into its light wood. Chieftain Ugruem was sitting wearily on a log, holding the soil-covered, wind-bleached skull of a horned animal. When I appeared, the goblins got on guard. The excavators climbed out of the pit. Among the workers installing the pillar, I saw a level-47 goblin dart-thrower and Tarek Bigfoot. Next I saw a worker, a tall slender goblin in a leather vest, who I was meeting for the first time:

Shikir
Level-69 Goblin Berserker

All four of the goblins were watching my approach carefully. They knew perfectly well that one of their countrymen wouldn't just be running wounded down the road for no reason.

"There's a goblin-killer on my trail!" I yelled out to them from afar. "He's following me, but he's invisible. He's a hundred steps back. Tarek, this is the bastard that broke your beloved boat! Chieftain Ugruem, he called you an earthworm! He also promised to make a doormat out of Shikir's hide to wipe his dirty feet on!"

It worked! The goblins bared their teeth, grabbed for their weapons, but then looked at the empty road behind me in incomprehension. The most quick-witted of the bunch, much to my surprise, was the berserker. With his wide palms, he scooped up a handful of fine roadside dirt and threw it high in the air. The wind obediently carried the wisp of dust down the road and we all saw the outline of a moving figure. One hundred steps?! By the end of the chase, there was just twenty meters between me and my pursuer. On the flat road, the assassin had managed to seriously close the gap. I grabbed for my blowgun and, after putting some distance between us, took a shot, making sure to consider the assassin's movement speed. I hit him!

Damage dealt: 31 (108 missile damage - 77 armor)

The dart-thrower hit our target at the same time. A nearly meter-long sharpened missile pierced the assassin's knee, causing the man to stumble and fall to the ground.

"Don't let him get away!" I howled out, reloading, but my compatriots already understood perfectly that we couldn't allow the enemy to get to his feet and run away in invisibility.

The berserker, and just a second later the chieftain as well, demonstrated their ability to leap forward long distances, bringing them in direct contact with the prostrated killer. Perros Ruthless finally became visible. His life bar was hovering in the red zone after the simultaneous hit from two high-level goblins. Tarek Bigfoot, who ran up a second later, split the assassin's head wide open with his spiked club.

Exotic Weapons skill increased to level 4!

Experience received: 13440 Exp.

Achievement unlocked: Player killer (2)

Level eighteen!

Level nineteen!
Racial ability improved: 40% Resistance to Poison
Racial ability improved: 40% Resistance to Cold

This time, I managed to stay on my feet, though my knees were still shaking from the energy burst. Tarek Bigfoot looked carefully at me, and his green face suddenly melted into a satisfied craggy smile (Taisha's father was missing a lower left fang).

"Wow, Amra, you're growing so fast! I feel like I've grown stronger as well!"

And in fact, the goblin warrior had reached level 78, which his information bore witness to. The dart thrower also leveled up and was nearly jumping for joy. But Chieftain Ugruem was less elated:

"He was undying. He will soon be reborn. And he'll be back with a vengeance..."

"That's it Amra. It's curtains for you! I won't rest until I've killed you ten times! I'm also gonna

dox you, find you in real life, and break your arms and legs!!!" Perros, no longer in the game, wrote me in a private message.

"He won't be getting revenge on you," I reassured the chieftain. "He's really only mad at me. Even though Tarek Bigfoot made the last strike, the assassin thinks I killed him, because I'm also undying. Such are the laws of the undying: all our squabbles stay between us. We don't get mad at others. But seriously, thank you guys! You saved me!"

The goblins started smiling in satisfaction at my words of gratitude. Their opinion of me had clearly improved.

Mission completed: Socialization 2/3
Experience received: 3200 Exp.

That fast?! I checked the information, somewhat skeptical. It was exactly right! The average opinion of my big-eared Amra in the village of Tysh was now 51.6! My character had just 785 experience points left to reach level twenty. And that was precious little. I just had to finish a few simple missions and I'd hit it!

Before taking care of other business, I put Perros Ruthless in my observation list so I would always know if my enemy was online, and also to mark him on the map by default. By the way, the information on his character showed that, with the loss of experience after dying, the assassin had fallen to level 43. And that was just the beginning. I called up the public chat window and wrote:

"*Small weak Amra was can killing strong assassin (here I included a link to Perros Ruthless). Any who hate* Goon *come at time 20:19 to reborning point south from island wyvern. You can killing Perros again. And next hour also killing Perros. Four times you can killing him. You all teach lesson for assassin. Him brains get smartened up.*"

The local chat exploded with elated commentary. Players were quickly lining up to take out the PK-er, as there were many with a taste for *Goons*. And that even included some who had suffered at my enemy's hands today. What could I say? If the assassin was really so reckless that he had chosen the closest respawn point, this would be a lesson he'd never forget.

While I sat smiling dumbly at my thoughts, Ugruem bowed over the body of Perros Ruthless and took a gold ring from his hand with a large shining blue stone. The chieftain measured the ring on his sausage fingers, but it wouldn't even fit on his pinky.

"I'll give it to my wife. She loves this kind of crap," the hardened goblin stuck the trophy in his pocket with determination.

Here I froze! He might have had some very valuable loot! I walked over to the corpse, but Tarek Bigfoot was blocking my way:

"Back off. We take loot in order of seniority around here!"

I didn't dispute him and took a step back. Of all the dead assassin's things, though, the only one that remained for me was some kind of magic scroll, which I couldn't even read about:

Insufficient Intelligence to identify object

That said, I did manage to collect two vials of human blood and, to the surprised stares of the goblins, stuffed them in my bag, explaining that I needed the blood for alchemy. That technically could have been true, but I was actually alarmed at how low my Thirst for Blood bar was (7/20). I couldn't bear this night without blood, and hunting for forest creatures to feed on, given the fact that the forest was teeming with players, was a very risky proposition.

"Alright, let's get back to work. We need to mark the border of our holding to stop other marauders from crawling in!" Chieftain Ugruem Butcher headed decisively back to hole in the ground.

The berserker Shikir looked skeptically over the dulled wooden stakes they'd been using to break up the dry earth.

"Ugruem, you could just ask Nyle for a normal shovel, then we wouldn't have to stay out here until nightfall!"

"Yeah, I already asked!" The chieftain snapped. "Nyle told me to get out of there. Three years have gone by, and that old miser still remembers the time we broke his good saw trying to get that knight out of his plate armor. He won't give me anything now, and I'm not gonna stoop to bartering!"

If that wasn't a new quest, my big-eared Amra was Pope of Rome! I offered my services to help them acquire tools. Shikir and Ugruem exchanged glances and nodded.

Mission received: Get a Shovel for the Diggers
Mission class: Normal
Reward: 80 Exp.

Despite the paucity of the expected reward, I didn't get upset. I had been meaning to speak with the local trader for some time, and here I had found a reason to do just that. After walking a short distance from the four goblins, I drank down one of the vials of blood, slightly sating my Thirst.

Achievement unlocked: Taste Tester (6/1000)

The merchant's house was in no way different from any of the others in the goblin village. It was a small squat construction dug into the earth. Its walls were made of lashed poles, interwoven with time-darkened boards. My attention was drawn by a colony of death caps growing from its lopsided hay- and fur-covered roof. There was no sign outside advertising the commercial nature of the structure, nor product displays, nor even a door on the entrance. Just a hole in the wall that would let in anyone who wanted! If it weren't for the mission target marker, stubbornly pointing me inside the hut, I would have walked right by.

"I won't give up the shovel!" barked the wrinkled old goblin, clad in a ragged soiled robe, just after I crossed the threshold of his residence.

Nyle Miser
Level-59 Goblin Trader

Paying the cold reception no mind, I politely greeted him and introduced myself, at the same time noting the disarray of the local trader's home. It was more of a warehouse than a residence. Half of the room was packed full of bags containing either peat or lignite. The remaining half was taken up by crudely heaped boxes, leaving just a narrow passage to the bed on which Nyle Miser was now sitting. At that, above this corridor, there was a wooden boat hanging upside-down over the boxes, careening dangerously and threatening to collapse on the head of a passer-by like the Sword of

Damocles. My goblin, already nowhere near the tallest of his race, would have found it quite impossible to sit down in here, or even stand up straight for that matter.

"The travelling merchant will come soon. I'll be able to unload some of my wares and that should bring down the clutter," Nyle began justifying himself, seeing my bewilderment. "What'd you want then?"

"I thought I'd try to sell these two pieces of blue wyvern hide, and buy some things for myself, if I took a shine to them." I took the items from my inventory and showed them to the trader.

Nyle Miser's eyes lit up on seeing the trophies from the wyvern island, so I immediately realized that the item had caught the trader's attention. But the old goblin demonstrated nothing but utter indifference in his words:

"What am I supposed to do with raw, unworked pelts? They'll go bad in a day. It's such a bad purchase I'd be throwing my money to the wind. I'd have to look for a leatherworker, and gods know where I'd do that. Though... I could take the lot for six coins. Maybe I'll be able to find them a good home..."

It wasn't even funny. I hadn't come across such an obvious scam in a long time.

"Nyle, I watched Chieftain Ugruem Butcher breaking down an animal and tanning its hide with my own eyes. So, I know Tysh has a leatherworker. I guess I'll have to go to him..."

Trading skill increased to level 4!

"Alright, you tricky youngster. If that's how it is, I'll take your wares for thirty coins," the goblin smiled, standing from his bed with a groan.

I shook my head reproachfully:

"Shame on you, Nyle! I'm a trader too, you know. I may not be the most experienced, but I have a good enough understanding of what my goods are worth. Let's drop the jokes and talk seriously!"

"Well Amra, to be perfectly honest, I could buy one piece of wyvern pelt for two hundred coins, or both for three hundred. And there's no reason for you to keep bargaining here — that's all the money I have. In fact, there are only three hundred coins in circulation in this village, and they're all in my hands at the moment."

"Three hundred coins and that boat," I pointed to the lopsided watercraft, which was threatening to become an instrument of death.

Trading skill increased to level 5!

"Take it. I've been wanting to get rid of that rubbish for ages. But you'll have to take it down and bring it outside yourself. Or even better, call the children of Tamina Fierce. Her little madcaps are always hungry, and milling about nearby. They'd agree to any work. For a silver coin, they'll not only take your boat down, they'll run around the village a thousand times holding it over their heads singing and dancing."

The old trader took me outside and looked around. And in fact, a crowd of green-skinned kiddos were on the neighboring street. The group of goblin boys and girls was dressed in reeking rags. Meanwhile, the babies with them were totally naked. The bunch was chasing a level-three rat down the street with screams and shrieks. Our appearance stopped the panic-stricken vermin's torture from turning deadly, as it managed to scurry under a wood pile while we had them distracted. I was thrown off by the kids' high level. Even the smallest, bare-bottomed little tykes were level-twelve minimum. The teenagers were all no less than twenty-two. I called the oldest of them over — a thin young boy by the name of Irek.

"I've got a job for you: get the boat down from the rafters of Nyle's shop and take it to Tarek Bigfoot, who is now pounding in a pillar on the road to Stonetown," I said, tossing him a silver coin that disappeared imperceptibly from thin air with a deft snap of his small hand.

"Hosh, Tsak and Shim, come with me," Irek called the next three biggest boys after him. "Yunna stays here to watch. She's oldest."

While the children were hauling the boat

under the watchful gaze of the miserly trader, I looked over his goods. First and foremost, I was interested in clothing. It was improper for a nearly level-twenty character to trounce around in nothing but a diaper. A simple vest, a straw hat, old fingerless leather gloves... I chose the cheapest things I could find while Nyle Miser was still blabbering on endlessly about how he did business even with human merchants from Weiden.

"Wait up. Are you telling me they come all the way to this village?" I grew interested. "Are you seriously telling me this little bush village is worth them slogging five days down a washed-out road?"

"It's true, the city-folk don't come through these parts often," Nyle corrected himself. "But middlemen do. They come around quite often. In the city, you can sell any goods for more: fish, mushrooms, pelts, dried meat. But Weiden is far away. There's a whole chain of intermediaries, who take goods from village to village, and they all crank up the price a bit. Ugh... those skinflints have been stiffing me on copper ore for the last two years! They don't even pay me a quarter of what it's worth anymore," the old goblin pointed at a pile of dirty bags, "but you'd get a good price for it in the city."

"Nyle, you seem to know a lot about commerce and merchants. Tell me, are there gremlin and dwarf banks in Weiden?" I asked, barely able to hold back my excitement.

"Of course. In every large city, there's a branch of the Subterranean Bank of Thorin the Ninth and a Most Reliable Bank of Gremlins. Sometimes, we even get their promissory notes out here. Out-of-town merchants often use them. They're afraid to carry large sums of coins down the road. But, if you're hoping to pay in notes instead of silver, know that I only accept them for half their value. It's too hard to turn those pieces of paper into coins."

"I've got an even better offer!" I replied, pulling out the scroll that had dropped from the recently dead assassin. "I've got a feeling that this is a magic portal to the city of Weiden. Check it. You can see the properties of objects, right?"

"Checking the properties of objects costs fifty coins!" the cheap goblin declared. But I just waved it off:

"You'll be charging that to yourself, then. I was planning to give this scroll to you. If it really is a portal, you can go to the city and take as many things with you as you can carry or fit on a cart. Bypassing all the middle men, you could sell your goods at their true value!"

The old goblin stroked the bridge of his nose in contemplation, lifted an old-fashioned monocle to his eye and stared at the scroll for some time. Then he confirmed that I was not wrong and this really was a single-use magic portal to the city of

Weiden.

"What do you want for it?" asked the old goblin, his voice trembling anxiously.

"I'd like to be able to buy not just pitiful old garments, shaking over every coin, but nice expensive clothes, paying in bank notes. You'll be able to exchange them at full value in the city, so it's no difference to you. Then, I'll be able to get more goods from you. No matter how you spin it, you're doing quite well."

Trading skill increased to level 6!

"Do you have a lot of these notes, then? I mean, why bother?"

I looked over my sales reports. My map of the wyvern island had been purchased by a total of one hundred fourteen people. Multiply that by one hundred, subtract the *Boundless Realm* admins' take, a one-percent fee, and... I used the built-in calculator.

"I've got notes worth eleven thousand two hundred eighty-six coins."

The miserly trader could barely stay on his feet. His opinion of me instantly increased. Despite my unpresentable appearance, Nyle finally started looking on me as a rich buyer.

"Alright, Amra, deal! You can pick whatever you like. Just ask, and I'll open any of these boxes."

"Wait, last question. What's the story with the shovel? I mean, the first words you said to me were: 'I won't give up the shovel!'"

"Oh, nothing. An old story," said the old goblin, growing obviously embarrassed. "Ugruem came around to borrow my handsaw, and to be honest, I was reluctant to give him a good metal one. It was new, without even a single scratch on the blade. So, I gave him an old bone one, which my great grandfather used to use. It wasn't very good, so it broke. Its serrations had lost their edge with time. It was just sitting around the pantry. I didn't wanna throw it out, either, though. But, in order to stop my neighbors from trying to borrow tools from me for free, I started claiming that the bone handsaw was of immense value, and that its breaking needed to be compensated. Ugruem didn't want to pay for it, though, so now, I don't give any of my things to him or any of my other neighbors. But, if you want to buy the shovel or any other tools, I'd be nothing but glad!"

* * *

I left the trader's house in a suit of brand new clothing. I had a black metal helmet giving a +2 bonus to perception, a thick vest and light chainmail shirt. On top of that, I was wearing a dark brown cloak giving +1 to Stealth. I had two copper rings, one giving +2 agility and the other +2 intelligence. Around my neck, I was wearing a bronze medallion that increased my visual radius by 15%. My wrists were adorned with a pair of bronze bracelets, each giving +1 to Alchemy. On my legs, I had thick leather pants, held up by a belt with a sheath for a metal knife. My new soft boots gave a 4% bonus to movement speed, and my medium bag had 30 inventory slots. As for weaponry, I'd acquired a new blowgun made of ebony giving 2% critical hit bonus. I'm not sure how, but the big shovel also fit in my inventory along with the other tools I acquired, including fifty empty vials for my alchemical needs.

All my purchases totaled to nine hundred seventy coins, and I had to negotiate until I was hoarse over every single one. I even raised my Trading skill to level eight. I also wanted to buy some equipment for my sister, but the wood nymph wouldn't accept. She said I'd never known how to pick out pretty clothing for her, and that she had already dealt with her own outfit.

In my absence, the diggers had done basically nothing. The depth of the pit hadn't changed a bit. I handed the tool to Shikir, and the chieftain sitting nearby on the overturned boat, jumped up and rubbed his hands together in satisfaction:

"Finally! These loafers are getting lazy as hell. They say they're tired. They can't even dig one damn pit in a day!"

Mission completed: Get a Shovel for the Diggers
Reward received: 80 Exp.

After pointing Taisha's father to the new boat, I stated:

"I promised you fifteen coins if anything happened to your old flat-bottom. I am accustomed to keeping my word and am prepared to return the money right now. But I decided that a new boat would make better compensation. Which do you prefer?"

Mission completed: Test Tarek Bigfoot's Boat
Reward received: 160 Exp., +15 to Tarek Bigfoot's opinion of you

The big-footed goblin raised the boat, looked it over carefully from all sides then started tearing up in joy. I checked the conditions for the mission on raising Taisha's father's opinion of me:

Tarek Bigfoot must have a +100 opinion of you: complete!

Give Tarek Bigfoot a trophy from a creature level-50 or higher: trophy in inventory.

Pay Tarek Bigfoot three hundred coins:

sufficient coins in inventory.

All equipment slots must be filled with articles of clothing: complete!

I extended the last piece of wyvern hide in my pack to Tarek, along with three hundred coins. The wizened goblin froze for a few seconds then, slipped the money in his coin-purse, and stuck the hide in his bag.

"I'll make sure to tell Taisha about you today. My pretty daughter will be glad to see another worthy goblin suitor. If you want to, feel free to come by my house today. We're having a celebratory dinner. We're letting it all hang out!" Tarek clapped his hands on his coin-packed purse, which gave a dull jingle.

"I'll be there with bells on!" I promised and smiled. "But just make sure you get that post in. It's getting closer and closer to sunset and dinner hasn't even been made."

Tarek spit in his hand, grabbed the shovel and jumped into the pit. Clumps of dirt started flying all around.

Mission completed: Earn the Respect of Tarek Bigfoot
Reward received: 4000 Exp., permanent improvement of Taisha's opinion of you by +50

Level twenty!

Attention! You have reached level 20. From here on, every ten levels, you can improve your character's survival ability by choosing one of the following modifications:

- ***Increase health (+1%, +2%, +3% etc.)***
- ***Increase endurance (+1%, +2%, 3% etc.)***
- ***Resistance to one type of damage 10% (9%, 8%, 7% etc. per type)***
- ***Increase movement speed (+1%, +2%, 3% etc.)***
- ***Health regeneration (+1, +2, +3 etc. Hitpoints per minute)***
- ***Strength regeneration (+1, +2, +3 etc. Endurance Points per minute)***
- ***Mana refill (inactive for your character)***
- ***Keen sight (+1%, +2%, 3% etc. to vision radius)***
- ***Invisibility (-1%, -2%, -3% etc. to detection radius)***

I was finally level twenty, having met the requirement before my week was up. Technically, for our group, the third day hadn't even ended yet, and I had already reached the target. Sure, I'd gotten off to a bit of a head start, but who was stopping them from doing the same thing?

I didn't have to think long over the choice offered by the system. Trying to guess the type of damage I would most often be killed by wasn't exactly sensible. Theoretically, physical damage should be met more often, but I'd already been spit at with acid, poison, cold and boiling water. My character was not made for an honest exchange of blows, and all the enemies around were high-level. It was best to simply avoid battle. That was why I chose Invisibility.

Green Bride

WE WERE ALREADY back in Tysh when a popup warning flashed up saying that Perros Ruthless was back in the game. And literally three seconds later, a new message came in that he had been killed. The local chat began filling with enthusiastic lines and acrid comments. Perros had dropped a pair of leather pants and a solid chunk of coins this time around. The reborn PK-er from the hated *Goons* clan had been anticipated at the respawn point by many determined players, so the assassin was instantly sent out of the game again.

My interest piqued, I opened the information on Perros Ruthless. My enemy had lost two levels that time, and was now just level-forty-one. If my calculations were correct, Perros could expect to die another three times tonight. That would be a serious loss of experience so he'd go down another few levels. A good lesson for the assassin. He'd think twice before getting into it with a little goblin next time!

"Amra, I'm gonna go buy some good meat and wine for dinner," Tarek Bigfoot said just after we'd passed the village gates. "If you want, you can wait for me here. Or, go to Taisha and bring the boat with you. You know where my house is. It's right next to the place where we sealed the flat-bottom."

I estimated the weight of the boat and was forced to refuse. To this level-78 strength-focused warrior, it must have seemed easy to carry, but I could barely lift the thing. In order not to spoil the wizened goblin's opinion of me, though, I thought up a good excuse:

"Tarek, I would be remiss to show myself to the beautiful Taisha without a gift. While you're out buying groceries, I'd better quick run to the trader and buy something worthy of your daughter."

Tarek snorted in approval, tossed the boat toward the gates and went up the narrow, dirty alley. He was barely out of view when Tamina Fierce's familiar children surrounded me:

"Uncle Amra, we could carry the boat up for you. It wouldn't even be hard! We could help you keep the Cursed House clean as well, but only when it's light out. Our mom won't let us go at night."

Would you like to take Foreman (Ch P) as a secondary skill?

What did "Foreman" do? I read the skill description. It gave me the ability to hire friendly NPC's for various tasks. Unlike Slave-Owner (the ability to control slaves with fear and terror), hired workers had to be paid, either in money or some other reward, and the size of the payout depended on the difficulty of the work and opinion of the employer. The skill level governed the maximum number of workers you could have at once. Alright then, why not? I've always got something to do, but never enough time to do it. I could use some little helpers.

You have taken Foreman as a secondary skill
Skill level: 1
Secondary skills taken: 5 of 5
Your character may take one more primary and secondary skill at level 25

"Good. Take the boat to the house of Tarek Bigfoot," I said, extending a coin to Irek, the oldest kid in this gang. "And tomorrow morning, if your mom'll let you go, I'll be waiting for you at the Cursed House. Perhaps I'll even find work for a few of you."

Foreman skill increased to level 2!

I chuckled in satisfaction and walked toward the trader's place to buy a gift for Taisha. I found Nyle Miser next to his house. He was loading heavy bags into a big cart. With surprise, and even doubt, I looked at the whole mountain of bales, boxes and rolls that the cheapskate goblin had gathered to bring to the city all at once. And I even expressed my confidence that the merchant wouldn't make it very far without four of the strongest mules.

"It's nothing. The neighbors here will push the cart into the portal, and I'll be in Weiden just like that! Once there, I'll sell all my goods along with the cart, then I'll get on my way back home. The return journey is quite long, so I won't be back in Tysh for five days, maybe even seven."

"A little advice for you, Nyle: You've probably heard how many undying came to Stonetown today to kill the huge flying snake. That was all because mages made up a bunch of portal scrolls from Weiden to Stonetown and sold them today to the undying for a thousand coins each. But that activity is over now, and no one needs portal scrolls taking them to some useless village anymore. I suspect that their price will soon fall sharply. You should be able to pick up one of the leftovers for practically nothing. You could buy yourself a scroll and be back to Stonetown in an instant. It only takes two hours on foot to get from there to Tysh."

Trading skill increased to level 9!

The miserly trader began smiling and his opinion of me grew to +80. Finally, Nyle Miser inquired why I'd come to his hut. I had barely managed to mention the name of Tarek Bigfoot's daughter before the old goblin cut me off and assured me:

"Forget about jewelry and pretty outfits. In Taisha's case, they won't help. I have just the thing for her! I bought it with her in mind some time ago."

The old, wrinkled goblin opened one of the boxes and laid some dark soiled rags right on the hay-covered floor. There were form-fitting pants, a jacket with a hood, a short black robe, and a pair of soft boots. I looked at the clothes in confusion. I couldn't believe these things would really be to the village girl's taste. I noticed a ring of lock picks and a thief's mask with eye slits lying among the clothing.

"What is that?!"

The goblin could only chuckle craftily and

offer me the thief's set for "just a mere thousand coins." The offer was so out of place that I was taken aback. A thousand *Boundless Realm* coins was equivalent to a hundred credits in real life, the price of an average sized refrigerator or an intelligent robot maid. Was I really going to spend that kind of dosh on virtual rags from an NPC I barely knew?! But I still didn't refuse right away, asking the merchant to explain the meaning of the gift and, at the same time, give a basis for its high value. Nyle Miser just laughed:

"Yeesh, you're a crafty one! That information will cost a lot. Judge for yourself: Taisha is gorgeous, a true gem of the goblin race. She will soon choose herself a groom from among a great many admirers. There are many candidates, so her father Tarek Bigfoot is preparing to set up many difficult tests to weed out weaklings and losers. He will choose the strongest, most agile and capable of the bunch. No offense, Amra, but you won't be able to win. You're too weak and have too little experience in comparison with Taisha's other suitors."

"But I *am* undying and progress very fast!" I disagreed. "A few days or weeks from now, I won't have to fear any competitors. I'll just outgrow them all."

"That may be so, Amra. But what will you do if Tarek Bigfoot decides to hold the tests two days from now at the big midsummer festival? Or even tomorrow? Such a notion could easily come into his head. And now, any of the contestants would be able to beat you to a pulp! But if you listen to me, even if you don't win the competition, the right gift could help you win the girl's sympathy. And in the end, after all the quests are over, Tarek's daughter just might choose you. If you don't make too much of a fool of yourself in the competition, that is."

The hard-nosed huckster spoke very convincingly. Perhaps these rags and lock picks really would come in handy with Taisha. As a bride, the NPC was of very dubious value to me, but having a fun pretty companion would give the viewers something to tune in for and would have a very positive effect on my work. But also, my inner cheapskate was screaming out that I shouldn't hand him another thousand silver in bank notes... I tried to negotiate, but Nyle Miser stayed firm in his offer, not lowering the price by even one coin. There must have been a programmed-in limit to stop a player from buying the valuable items for less than the advertised price.

Alright, sorry Val. We'll have to get along without a robot maid for now. And forgive me also for the fact that I bought a pair of golden sapphire earrings with the thief's outfit. After all, there was no guarantee the trader's tip was actually good.

* * *

They were expecting me when I arrived. Tarek Bigfoot had long since returned to his small hut and given the groceries he'd brought to his daughters. They were now hard at work preparing the celebratory meal. It was a surprise to me, but Taisha also had two older sisters. One look at them, and I perfectly understood what made the youngest so unique. My opinion was particularly spoiled when one of the older daughters, whose fat frame had been crammed into tight clothing with significant effort, placed a dish next to me with stewed vegetables and smiled at me happily, revealing a set of yellow fangs and giving off particularly bad breath from a mouth that hadn't been cleaned for some time.

Level-33 Goblin Villager

When the goblin was back behind the screen separating the "kitchen" from the "main room" in Tarek Bigfoot's small hut, the house's owner, who'd already managed to guzzle down a fair amount of wine admitted something:

"Taisha is a constant headache for me. Why couldn't she just have been born like all the other girls?! After all, you know the traditions of goblin families: the youngest daughters are supposed to wait patiently for their older sisters to get married. But all the suitors who've come change their plans when they see Taisha and opt to wait in line for her instead. How am I supposed to get rid of the older ones?!"

The older daughter appeared again, carrying a dish with delicious smelling roast meat on it. In fact, it smelled so delicious that the goblin pulled a few pieces from the plate as she walked and, not really hiding it, popped them straight into her mouth. She could have kept standing there next to our table swallowing the food she'd brought, but her father gave her a firm slap below the belt to show her back to the kitchen, telling her not to stick her nose into our serious conversation.

"Here's what I think," Tarek Bigfoot said, not stopping chewing. "Taisha has many suitors, but my two other daughters have few. To be more accurate, they have none. So, here's what I decided: I'll give away all three of my daughters together! I'll put on a suitor competition in a few days, and the winner will get the right to choose any of the three girls. The second will get his choice of the remaining two, and the third will get whoever's left. And then, if one of the suitors doesn't suit the girl he goes with, she can refuse, but the suitor himself cannot. What do you think, Amra?"

Mission offered: Suitors' Games
Mission class: Rare, racial
Description: Take part in three tests set

forth by Tarek Bigfoot

Stage one: Strength Test

First place: 3 points, second place: 2 points, third place: 1 point

Reward for participating: 1600 Exp., +10 to Taisha's opinion of you, +10 to Tarek Bigfoot's opinion of you

Stage two: Agility Test

First place: 3 points, second place: 2 points, third place: 1 point

Reward for participating: 1600 Exp., +10 to Taisha's opinion of you, +10 to Tarek Bigfoot's opinion of you

Stage three: Luck Test

First place: 3 points, second place: 2 points, third place: 1 point

Reward for participating: 1600 Exp., +10 to Taisha's opinion of you, +10 to Tarek Bigfoot's opinion of you

Required condition: The three participants with the most points may choose a companion in the order of the number of points they have.

Reward for winning after three tests: 8000 Exp.

Extra condition:

If mission refused: -50 to the opinion of all Goblins in the village of Tysh

If mission accepted: +800 Exp., +10 to Taisha's opinion of you, +10 Tarek Bigfoot's

**opinion of you, +10 Ugruem Butcher's opinion
of you**
Accept mission (Yes/No)?

I cursed ornately to myself. It's all been a
setup! After all, I'd already figured out that NPC
beauties like Taisha didn't come around by
chance. They were clearly created by programmers
from the *Boundless Realm* corporation as decoys
to get players to spend their money on expensive
gifts and put them in awkward situations like this
one. I was sure the other playable races had
similar invented beauties (or handsome men) to
draw players' attention and force them to complete
these quest chains leading to "Suitors' Games."

What should I do then? Refusing would lead
to a serious penalty to my big-eared Amra's
standing in the village. Taking part in the games,
though, against high-level NPC rivals would be a
very big challenge, and could lead to my receiving
one of the two green crocodiles as a constant
companion or even bride. Although... if the
situation came together unfavorably, there would
always be the option of throwing it so I wouldn't
come in the top three. Sure, I wouldn't get Taisha
in that case, but I would also avoid her two ugly
sisters. The reward of a few thousand experience
points just for participating would just be the icing
on the cake!

"Tarek Bigfoot, it is with great joy that I

agree to take part in the games! I am confident I will be able to prove my prowess and abilities to the whole village!"

Experience received: 800 Exp.

+10 to Taisha's opinion of you, +10 Tarek Bigfoot's opinion of you, +10 Ugruem Butcher's opinion of you

In the kitchen, I heard a joyful shriek from the girls. All three sisters approved of my choice.

"That's what I like to hear! We need to drink to that!" the wizened goblin exclaimed, inspired. "Taisha, bring some more wine!"

Finally, for the first time all evening, it wasn't one of the older sisters coming from behind the screen, but the youngest, Taisha. Her dress and apron may not have been new, but at least they were clean. I immediately noticed that there was something wrong with the girl. She was making completely sure to turn her face away from me. Only when Taisha had set the bottle and two bowls on the table was I able to notice that the goblin girl's left eye would barely open, and was surrounded by a huge, bright purple bruise. After noticing my interest in his daughter's black eye, Taisha's father commented with a laugh:

"The older girls gave her a bit of a whooping, sure. They're angry that she takes all the good suitors away from them. They damaged the goods slightly, but I already voiced my fatherly disapproval. It's nothing, really. In two days, all this fuss over my three daughters will be over, and I'll be able to breathe freely once again!"

Taisha, clearly embarrassed at her appearance, handed me a fired-clay bowl already full of wine. But I didn't manage to take the cup before Tarek extended his huge hand and took my wine:

"Hey! That's my cup! Daughter, fill another for our guest."

It seemed to me that the black-eyed beauty grew slightly afraid, but filled me another, absolutely identical bowl of wine from the vine-enmeshed bottle without hesitation. Tarek Bigfoot, without any kind of toast, silently threw the whole container of wine into his gaping maw and hiccupped loudly. His eyes quickly began drooping. I also took a sip of the ruby-red drink.

Successful check for Poison Resistance.
Experience received: 80 Exp.
Successful identification. Weak Potion of Sleeping (effect of level-11 Sleep spell)

Alchemy skill increased to level 3

I froze in fear. They were trying to put me to sleep! They wanted to rob their carefree guest blind! A worrying thought came instantly to mind that my artifact was no longer under protection, and I could now easily be made to part with the valuable wyvern egg. The strange cup-trading maneuver was probably all part of it! I raised my eyes and met the gaze of Taisha, who was clearly watching my reaction in fear. The green-skinned beauty clearly knew what it was in my cup. But then, her father was either an excellent actor, or was totally unaware of the poisoning attempt, so naturally was playing the part of a drunk.

But what if this was Taisha's secret plan, and the sleeping potion cup was intended for her father? But why would the youngest daughter have wanted that? Still not understanding what was going on, I decided to play along.

"Tarek, what are we doing sitting here alone? Why don't you invite your daughters to join us? After all, they probably want to celebrate the upcoming end of their maidenhood. Taisha, fill two bowls for your sisters and pour some for your father. Can you not see that the master of the house's cup is empty?!"

The green-skinned beauty looked apprehensively at her father, but Tarek Bigfoot confirmed my words, shouting at his daughter:

"Did you not hear our guest? Do it at once! I have to teach you everything... But you, Amra, are a great guy! The shaman is also an admirer. I'm sure you'll quickly find a place in our village."

Mission received: Socialization 3/3
Reach a state of respect (average opinion of 75+) with the village of Tysh
Reach a state of respect (average opinion of 75+) with the village of Stonetown
Mission class: Chain, group
Reward: 8000 Exp.

A minute later, the whole family was at the table, their glasses filled from the vine-wrapped dark bottle of wine. I wanted to say something appropriate to the celebratory circumstances, but Tarek and the two older daughters had already drunk their cups down. Sensing Taisha's attentive gaze on me, I poured my wine out under the table into a pile of food scraps. A second later, the green-skinned beauty was doing the same.

* * *

"So, what made you do that?" I asked Taisha a few minutes later, when all her relatives were snoring on the floor.

The girl was pacing around the hut by this time, hurriedly filling a canvas bag over her shoulder with food, extra clothing, a ball of twine, a kitchen knife, a flint and other objects, clearly preparing to leave.

~ Video Game Plotline Tester ~

Successful check for Taisha's reaction
Experience received: 40 Exp.

"Honestly?" The girl stopped in the middle of the room and stared at me. "I wanted to put my father to sleep so he wouldn't make any more promises about me, and couldn't stop me from leaving home. Did Tarek even ask me if I wanted to be the top prize in that idiotic suitor contest? My sisters, then, are dumb as rocks. I was planning on filling their heads with silly talk about how we were just going on a walk by the village. Once past the gates, I was gonna bonk you with something heavy and run from my abhorrent fate. With your interference, though, you helped me neutralize my sisters along with my father. Now, there's nothing stopping me from running away. My relatives are all asleep and you're too weak to stop me!"

"I wasn't thinking of stopping you," I chuckled. "But are you sure you'll get far? Night will be here any minute and the monsters will come out to hunt. You will be visible for a thousand steps in your white dress like a flame in the night. Your backup outfit is also white and won't help you hide from the predators, either."

Taisha froze for a second, then grumbled back in dismay:

"It's none of your business! I'll get undressed and cover myself in dark mud, if that's what it takes to walk unnoticed through the forest."

"I've got a better idea," I said, taking the set of thief's clothing and lock picks from my inventory and setting them on the table before her. "Take it. It's a gift from me."

Tarek Bigfoot's youngest daughter tried to put on a show of how little she cared for the gift, but the girl's burning eyes and voice wavering in anxiety gave her away very easily.

+10 to Taisha's opinion of you
Experience received: 200 Exp.

Successful check for Taisha's reaction
Experience received: 40 Exp.

"How'd you know this might be of use to me?! And especially I mean the lock picks! After all, I've never shown anyone my lock-picking skill! Answer me, Amra! It's important for me to know!"

Ugh, here goes nothing! The fact Taisha had a +100 opinion of me gave me a good chance of getting her agreement to most sensible propositions. Why not try to make friends with Taisha and get her on my side?

"Well, you see... Just don't get mad before I finish talking. All your father's talk about games is complete bullshit! First, your opinion of me won't get any better, even if I can win all three of the tests. Second, I'm not interested in you as a bride at all..."

"What?!" Despite my warning, the girl's hair still stood on end like an enraged kitten. "Am I not good enough for you, Amra?"

-10 to Taisha's opinion of you

"That's not the problem. In my opinion, you cannot force someone to act against their will in matters of the heart. Taisha, I met you yesterday. We don't know each other very well. How can we even start to talk about feelings? Sure, you're a rare beauty. That's obvious. Capricious, adventuresome and impulsive. I've figured all that out. But that's all I know about you for now and it's not enough for me to look on you as a potential mate. That said, I realized at first glance that you weren't cut out for the role of a villager suffering daily beatings from her husband. You're too good for that and too smart. Your flexibility, light touch and graceful movements told me that you are much more suited to the role of dancer, assassin or thief. I've been thinking over the issue all day. You haven't left my mind and, in the end, I decided to take a chance that you'd wanna be a thief. I was looking for someone with such abilities anyway, so I went and bought this outfit from Nyle Miser. I wasn't at all sure of how you'd react to the strange gift."

+10 to Taisha's opinion of you.

The black-eyed beauty grew embarrassed and even began blushing slightly, which looked very strange on her green skin.

"You know how to give a compliment, little goblin. I noticed that right when we met. But tell me, why were you looking for a thief?"

Yikes! The hardest part of the conversation was over. I had her interest, and now I just had to build on that.

"Well you see, I am undying, so nothing scares me. I am constantly searching for interesting adventures. But dangerous trap-filled crypts with chests full of valuables, stash houses, locked doors leading to treasure chambers — none of that is worth a damn, if my team doesn't have a skilled thief in it. I mean, I'm just an herbalist and my companion is a beast master. We've also got an orc fortifier with us, but none of us can open locks, so I was looking for a good thief to join the party. But only a truly good and capable thief. One we can count on."

Trading skill increased to level 10!

"Well, gosh. I'm not that good of a thief," Taisha lowered her eyes. "Also, I do not have the qualities of the undying. But I would very much like to join you, if you'd take me."

"Your share of the loot and experience, a life of adventure and no more tiresome suitors. That's what I can offer you, Taisha. You can live with us in the Cursed House as an equal, manage your own affairs, clean up, work honestly and defend the house in the case of an attack."

"In any case, it's more interesting than cooking, cleaning and doing laundry for my family day after day, all the time hearing cursing and mockery from my older sisters."

"If you agree, we can go right now. Once beyond the gates of the village of Tysh, change into your new clothes." I stood from the bench, preparing to leave.

Taisha looked at me and inquired with distinct surprise in her voice:

"What, Amra, you're not even going to ask for an oath that I will obey you, follow the rules you set and not steal from your companions? What if I suddenly run off with all your money and trophies?"

Oops... What? Was that really possible? I looked at her and noticed a wily glimmer in her eyes. It looked like she was testing me, trying to see if I would limit her in any way.

"Stealing from companions is not accepted practice, even among thieves, but I'm not preparing to pile any limits on you. I need a free companion who can make her own decisions, and not some mere obedient slave. How about you think up a set of rules for yourself, then you can strictly follow them."

Taisha suddenly froze in the middle of the room, her eyes glazed over.

LOGIC ERROR!
Infinite recursion
NPC $FF0076-BB0733 is waiting for external commands originating from its own logic
Error code #LOC/ER-009955
This message has been sent to Boundless Realm *tech support*
We apologize for the possible inconvenience

SYSTEM ERROR!
Opinion variable of NPC $FF0076-BB0733 has surpassed allowable value
Error code #LOC/ER-002056
This message has been sent to Boundless Realm *tech support*
We apologize for the possible inconvenience

Mission received: Taisha's loyalty
Reward: #ERROR! Variable not defined

Mission completed: Taisha's loyalty
Reward received: #ERROR! Variable not defined

For crying out loud! So, this is what I got for

trying to run off. As a tester, I was very glad at finding errors, but they'd happened at such a bad time! I hoped Taisha's opinion variable shot upward, not down, otherwise I'd have a surprise waiting for me when the girl stopped lagging. What could I do? Just then, Taisha's father started twitching in his sleep, which made me give a scared shudder. Had he drunk enough of the weakly soporific wine? He was a very high-level character, after all. Tarek Bigfoot was waking up more and more with every passing minute, and it was very difficult to guess his reaction to seeing his younger daughter standing stiff but ready for a long journey and his two older daughters just lying on the floor. I had to make a radical move. I gave him a Vampire Bite, but not to kill him, just to put him to sleep!

Achievement unlocked: Taste Tester (7/1000)

So, now I had a certain amount of time to think through what to do next. Above all else, I had to get Taisha out of Tysh somehow before the village gates were closed for the night. Could I drag her out in my arms? I tried to lift the goblin girl. Failure! I had barely enough strength to get the girl up off the floor. I suppose the most my weak Amra would achieve was to drag the "frozen" beauty to the door of the hut and place her outside the threshold. But what could I do from there?

I got an idea! I had a whole gang of kids at my beck and call, and they would be willing to drag the motionless Taisha as far as I needed, though perhaps not very far beyond the gates, as night would soon be falling, but still she would be outside the bounds of the village. And there, I'd have to look for another strong hauler. And, as a matter of fact, I knew just such a titan.

I sent my sister a private message asking if Shrekson was still there.

"Yes, the ogre is here. He's been working tirelessly. He's replaced the fallen stockade beams, dug out three trap pits near the gates and now he's whittling stakes to place at the bottom of them. By the way, twenty minutes ago, the Gray Pack returned. They're starving. They haven't eaten a thing all day. I showed our wolves the traps. They seem to have understood."

"Val, I need Shrekson near Tysh. I need him to pick up some valuable cargo and bring it to our house before nightfall."

"I can send the ogre to you, but the Tysh guards don't know him and will probably just kill him. Also, Shrekson walks fairly slowly. He won't be able to drag his ass all the way there and back before dark. He has no Stealth, either. At night, the predators will find him from afar and devour him. The ogre is just level eleven now. He can't deal with any of the local monsters."

So, the ogre option had fallen through, but a different idea came to mind.

"I'll need you, then, Val. Ride Akella and bring the Gray Pack to the village of Tysh. I'll meet you on the road. I've got something for the wolves to eat."

* * *

There was a little hitch with bringing the body out of Tysh. No, Tamina Fierce's children didn't refuse to help me, nor did they ask unnecessary questions. But Irek noted reasonably that the guards at the village gate wouldn't let us leave with the girl's body as it smacked distinctly of kidnapping.

"We need some kind of mat, bag or old rug to wrap Taisha in," suggested Yunna, the youngest of Tamina's girls.

"Shaman Kaiak Badgerleg has an old ragged doormat!" Irek remembered. "How about I run over to him and offer my help to beat the dust out of the doormat. I bet Kaiak will agree."

The shaman really was glad at the unexpected help and, a few minutes later, the kids and I were already on our way to "beat the bedbugs and dust out of the rug." For two pieces of silver, the goblin children helped me drag the heavy roll to the freshly planted border marker, and most of the children hurried back to Tysh. Just Irek, Shim and Yunna stayed with me. They weren't so much there to beat the doormat as they were burning with curiosity and waiting to see what would happen next.

"Hey, wolves!" Yunna was first to notice the Gray Pack and nimbly climbed up onto the carved post. Her brothers followed after her a second later.

The wolves stopped next to me. Akella sniffed me and gave his tail a few timid dog-like wags.

"I see that you've upgraded your outfit, big-ears!" The wood nymph, also in new equipment, jumped off Blanca and looked around.

The bunch of children hanging off the top of the post were of little interest to her, unlike the senseless Taisha lying on the road. Her body had already caused an unhealthy interest in the wolves as well, who were now sniffing around it. Valerianna chased off the overly curious White Fang and Lobo, then asked me:

"Who's the doll? D'you rob a goblin sex shop?"

"This is cargo I saying. She my girly, be frozen. Bring in we house before dark-time. Nymph helping load up to wolfie back."

"If this is 'your girly,' how could I not bring her?" my sister cracked up.

And while we were talking, Akella

impudently stuck his shaggy snout into my bag. That's where I'd put most of the meat left over from dinner. After remembering that the wolves hadn't eaten all day and were frighteningly hungry, I began doling out chunks of meat. Most of them went to Blanca who, as a nursing mother, needed more food. But the meat ran out quickly, and the wolves clearly hadn't eaten their fill.

"Today night is of hunt! Time to grab big piece of loot. Our wolfies to growing," I declared to the wood nymph, and she agreed with me.

"I've been telling you for a while, big-ears, to try and level up our wolves so they could be truly effective security and wouldn't be afraid of night monsters. By the way, when a pet or mount reaches levels twenty and fifty, their master can choose a specialization for them, which creates very interesting possibilities. These wolves aren't considered mine, so that function is not available to me. But if you could rename them, then it should be somewhere in your stats menu."

I looked at Akella and called up detailed information on him. That's what my sister was talking about. The beast had a specialization called "Silent Step." It made sense now that he had managed to sneak up on me that one time! I took a quick look around at the other predators and figured out that it was already too late to choose a specialization for the wolves. They'd already all taken one at level twenty.

And at that, the automatic system's choice was typical and even boring like "Increased Health," "Tear Damage," and "Thick Hide," even though there were other options that had a lot more potential and were quite unusual. For example, "Chameleon," which allowed an animal to blend in with its environment. Or "Bloodthirsty," which made wounds heal as the wolf bit. You could even make a wolf into a very unusual type of mutant with the specializations "Poisonous Bite," or "Deafening Roar." I was also interested in the "Pack Hunter" specialization, which improved all combat stats of the individual for every ally in the pack with the same specialization. If I gave all of Blanca's pups that specialization, with time, they'd become a very fearsome force indeed.

"Amra, what is it? Are you frozen too?" Valerianna Quickfoot's unhappy voice distracted me from looking through all the leveling options for the wolves. "Clearly it's contagious, and you've been infected by 'your girly.' Night will fall in ten minutes. It's time to get going!"

I apologized and went to lift the motionless goblin girl. My sister helped me set the petrified Taisha on Akella's back. I sat behind her, keeping the paralyzed girl from falling with one hand. My sister jumped up on Blanca, looked over at me and frowned in dismay:

"Hold on to the wolf, dummy, not her tits. Akella has convenient hand-holds as well!"

"Uncle Amra, do you think I could come with you?" asked an inquiring girl's voice, sounding out from somewhere high up. I'd almost totally forgotten about the children sitting on the post. "I could help you with all kinds of housekeeping, washing up, cooking, cleaning, and tending the garden."

"Yunna, we're on our way to the Cursed House. And to make matters worse, it's night time. Even if the ghastly monsters don't eat you on the way, your mom will give me a walloping in the morning!" I thought that just one mention of Tamina Fierce would be enough to get the girl to rethink her plan.

But I was wrong. The chubby goblin girl skillfully jumped down and walked fearlessly up to Lobo, who even grew confused and staggered back from the impudent girl. I hurriedly marked Yunna as a "friend" to the Gray Pack to avoid any tragic incidents. And after that, Irek followed his sister down.

"Uncle Amra, take me too!" The green-skinned lad begged. "I'd be so jealous and mad, if my sister got to ride a wolf and I didn't! I swear I'd die! My brother, Shim can bring the doormat back to the village and tell mom and Tarek Bigfoot that we're just fine. But if you don't take us, my sister and I will get angry and tell everyone you kidnapped Taisha!"

"What's the hold up? What are these kids

babbling on about?" Valerianna Quickfoot asked, not understanding a single word of their goblin speech.

Not wanting to give such a long explanation in my broken language, I wrote a private message to my sister:

"These little blackmailers are asking me to take them with to the Cursed House. They promise they'll work honestly doing chores for us. But if we refuse, they threaten to bring us a visit from the enraged Tarek Bigfoot with his spiked club. He's the father of the frozen girl."

"But the kids say they won't accuse us of kidnapping, if we agree to take them with us? The little scoundrels! If we do that, not only will Tarek Bigfoot be running after us, but the whole village of Tysh, and they'll bring torches and pitchforks."

"Well, we'll see in the morning. They probably won't, though. I mean, technically, these kids work for me. I'll feed them and even pay them a bit."

"It's up to you, brother. You made your bed when you kidnapped 'your girly.' Now you've got to lie in it."

I looked at the children, who were patiently awaiting my decision, and waved my hand:

"Alright, you urchins. I'll find you work, but only if you behave yourselves in the Cursed House and don't make the wolves mad. Otherwise, I'll send you all back on foot this very night."

~ Video Game Plotline Tester ~

Foreman skill increased to level 3!

Irek and Yunna couldn't wait a second longer and, with joyful shrieks, got up on the forest predators' backs. As they did so, their classes both changed from villager to wolf rider.

"We going home!" I shouted fervently, and the Gray Pack tore off at full speed to the Cursed House.

Big Plans

"WE'RE NOT GONNA make it. We have to pick up the pace!" Valerianna Quickfoot called out with obvious anxiety in her voice.

I was also glancing constantly at the clock. Night would fall in a few minutes, yet we weren't even half way to our shelter. Our wolves also understood the danger of night falling and were rushing down the forest road to the Cursed House with their ears pressed down on their heads in fear.

It was time! The electronic digital clock face in the lower right corner of the screen had barely hit 9:00 when I saw a constellation of red markers in front of us on the mini-map. A second later, my sensitive ears were cut through with a fell barking and yapping sound given off by the many beasts. After making a mental note to myself that, in *Boundless Realm*, sound traveled at approximately the same speed as in the real world, I sharply pulled Akella to the right, taking him off the road.

"All following Amra!" I called after the others and led the wolves around the dangerous obstacles, making a big detour through the swampy forest.

Unfortunately, we didn't make it out unnoticed. The array of red dots on the map tore off toward us at full speed. Our wolves, who seemed to have been running as fast as they could already, noticeably picked up the pace. Akella started periodically whimpering in terror below me.

"Where am I?" Taisha twitched fearfully in my embrace and tried to wriggle free. In surprise, I nearly dropped the awoken girl.

"Sit calmly! Otherwise, you'll fall off and get eaten by night creatures!" I had to raise my voice and shout at Taisha. Only after that did she turn, recognize me and stop trying to wriggle free.

With anxiety, I looked at the mini-map. The distance between us and the monsters on our trail was quickly closing. Taisha, looking closely at something behind me, quickly widened her eyes in horror. I turned sharply. Now, even without the map, I could tell what the far-off dark shadows were. There were red skull markers hanging over them, too. Though the difference in level may have been less than fifty, there was no way we'd be able to manage all of them.

"There's a bog near the road there. I marked it for myself on the map a few days ago. Now, our pursuers are flying straight toward it. I hope they drown..." said Valerianna Quickfoot, but I didn't sense much faith in such an outcome from her tone.

The eleven red markers really did slow down, though. After that, they stopped entirely, but a few moments later, they continued after us, having gone around the dangerous area. Well, alright. That gave us a few extra seconds of safety at least.

"Ahh! Why didn't I stay home?! I don't wanna die!" Irek, riding next to me was shedding floods of tears, and wiping them away on the sleeves of his dirty shirt.

His sister Yunna was behaving much calmer. She was just periodically looking around and quietly whispering something, either praying to the goblin gods, or trying to do magic. Taisha, though, was just pressing herself to me in silence, but I could hear her little heart pounding in fear.

Athletics skill increased to level 6!

Would you look at that! Riding atop a wolf, it seemed, also raised my Athletics skill. A pleasant surprise. But my attention wasn't drawn to that for long, as I quickly got distracted by the frenzied ride through the forest. The red dots on the map went around the marshy area and were again approaching us, with every second noticeably closing the gap.

"No afraid. We making it. Real, real very close!" I assured the others.

"We won't make it, Tim. You can see it yourself. But I wrote Shrekson, and he confirmed that he was ready to close the gates as soon as the Gray Pack was inside. I'll jump off Blanca now to distract them. That'll give the rest of you time to get away."

"Nymph, don't dare! We making it! Where's you pet frog?"

"My toads all died just before I got to you on wolfback in Tysh. Basically, just like always. Amphibians make bad pets. They're slow and dumb. They are afraid of the wolves and die as soon as you take your eye off them. Every time they die, that's two levels lost, which is very hard to restore afterward. But you're right, Amra. Now is the exact right time to call my toads to feed our pursuers."

Next to the wolf pack, there appeared three huge brown toads. I was barely able to read the information on one of them before they were left in our dust:

Level 7 Warty Toad

The beings chasing after us, and I could already clearly make out their long-legged sinewy bodies, really did get distracted by the released pets. Just one second more and the overgrown toads were no more. The monsters stopped and set about tearing the flesh of the three toads to pieces, greedily swallowing the bloodied hunks of meat.

"That meat won't stop them for long. Those are level-54 wargs. The very same ones that were chasing our wolves before and made them so panicked," my sister told me. Her Cartography skill allowed her to identify markers on the mini-map at a much greater distance than I could.

Mission received: Horror of the Gray Pack
Mission class: Rare, Group
Description. Find the lair of the Wargs and exterminate all of them
Reward: 8000 Exp, +1 to maximum Gray Pack member limit (up to six)

Why up to six? Akella, Lobo, White Fang, Blanca and the four wolf pups already added up to eight! What I wanted to do was object out loud, but my sister cut me off. There was unhidden elation in her voice:

"My wolf pup can be an extra fourth pet to

the three I already have. Cool! I've been wanting that so bad! Amra, we have to complete this mission, no matter what!"

Did that mean my sister was getting offered a totally different reward for completing the quest? That was completely possible, but the circumstances didn't allow me to find out. The wargs following us quickly reduced the distance. There was now no more than one hundred meters between us. I turned around and could see their four long-legged bodies distinctly, their toothy maws and burning red eyes glistening in the darkness.

"Heads up, big-ears! We've almost reached the Cursed House. Follow me carefully, so we don't fall into the traps dug out by the ogre! Anything but that! Woah, naiad at the gates!"

I looked forward and noticed that there were two players standing near the far-off stockade holding the heavy gates, preparing to close them. Gates?! But how?! Who had hung the gates and when? They'd been on the ground last I'd seen them! After deciding to find an answer to the question later, I looked at the players' standing there. And though the level-eleven ogre, all caked in mud, was the first of his kind I'd seen, I had already met a naiad before. For a moment, Trong Diver came to mind. We clearly didn't have a very smooth relationship from our first day in the game. If this was Trong thinking of revenge, this was the best chance he'd get. He could just slam the gate shut right in our faces and let the wargs eat us up. I grabbed for my blowgun, though I understood perfectly that there was nothing I could do to stop them from slamming the gates now. But... it was a different player altogether! Also, based on the name, it was a Frenchman:

Max Sochnier
Naiad
Level-10 Trader

The fish-man waited patiently for all the wolves of the Gray Pack, together with their riders, to get inside the enclosure. Only after that, did he and the giant close the heavy gate and lock it with the strong beam, shutting it tight. It was very unexpected help. I even grew confused, not knowing how to treat the newcomer. I suppose that, above all else, I should have a talk with him and get acquainted. But before that, I had to take this naiad from the Gray Pack's KOS list (kill on sight), so he didn't die from a misunderstanding.

I still hadn't totally figured out the fairly difficult control system for their protecting my place of residence. It had many different access levels, so I'd just ignored it, because I hadn't been expecting to see a crowd of players and NPC's here. That was why I had simply set the Gray Pack to consider any stranger near the house an enemy.

Now, I needed badly to correct those settings, as the wolves were already snarling and approaching the fish-man with unambiguously aggressive intentions.

Yikes! Just in the nick of time! Right after I did it, the wolves stopped baring their teeth and started just observing the naiad attentively. I didn't manage to get away from the gates before a bunch of identical messages jumped in:

Experience received: 880 Exp.
Experience received: 880 Exp.

Akella next to me lit up in colorful flames, signaling that the wolf had reached level 28. Based on the other light shows I saw, Blanca, Yunna and Shrekson had also leveled up.

"You made it, friends!" exclaimed the ogre fortifier, rubbing his huge hands together in joy. "Two of them even fell right into a trap!"

For some reason, it wasn't much experience for a level-54 warg. Although... given we were sharing the experience with the ogre, who'd dug the pits and the whole group I'd rounded up, including the four wolves who led the nocturnal monsters into the traps, it seemed reasonable. I recounted the participants and whistled. I now had between nine and eleven people and animals sharing every reward. From behind the wall, a heart-rending cry rang out, which gradually gave way to a fading gurgling groan.

Experience received: 880 Exp.

"Another one!" the ogre laughed. "A bit more of that and I'll hit level thirteen! Almost five levels for less than three hours' work! At this pace, I'll be sure to hit level twenty by the end of the week!"

Hearing the enraged snarling and twitchy yapping on the other side of the barrier just five steps from us, I looked doubtfully at the three-meter-high stockade and asked the construction worker:

"Beasties no can jump fence over this side? Warg having longinging leg. They run, run jumping..."

The ogre hurried to reassure me:

"Out there, almost the whole perimeter of the stockade is thick with thorny ivy. You can't touch it, or get up the speed to jump over it for that matter. And, in the places without ivy, I dug out pits with sharp stakes at the bottom. So, that means these long-legged hyenas have no chance whatsoever. Let them go mad with impotent rage and try to burst in. We'll just get more experience and trophies. But, there are other nocturnal beasts, who could easily get over the barricade. I've seen some with legs as long as a giraffe's, for example. Also, predatory birds and anything else with wings could just fly over."

The wargs grew suspiciously quiet. Either they'd thought up some kind of trick, or they'd just walked away from the dangerous area. Maybe, something even more ghastly than them had spooked them off. On my mini-map, it looked like the eight red spots had just torn off sharply from their places and were now hurrying to run away.

"Can we see to behind fence? What doing big-bads?" I asked the fortifier. He just made a helpless gesture, looking guilty:

"For now, we cannot, boss. Even though you could maybe see something through the stakes, or build a quick ladder out of poles. But, we've got plans to build a watchtower next to the gates in the next few days. It's just a few hours' work, given the right tools."

I opened the trading menu and placed all the tools I'd bought from Nyle Miser into it: a handsaw, a big ax, a chisel, a sledgehammer, an adze for stripping beams, a shovel, a pick, and a whole package of big wrought-iron flat-head screws. I set the desired price to zero coins and offered a trade to Shrekson. The ogre accepted the offer and blossomed into a satisfied ear-to-ear smile:

"Now, I'll be able to build everything in a few days, boss! I'll make a barn in the fenced-in area for storing grain and other food, then I'll make a doghouse for the wolves to sleep in if the weather gets bad. After that, I'll make a workshop and a sawmill for making beams, a shed for storing stuff, then I need to dig a well..."

"Stop, stop!" I remembered the words of Ugruem Butcher. "Well is we having. Big basement with ice for meat storing also be once-a-time. Trusty goblin telling me this."

The wood nymph, who had walked away to let Blanca into the house to feed her pups, had already returned and discovered the ogre and I talking. Valerianna Quickfoot exchanged glances with Shrekson, and the titan just shrugged his shoulders in surprise. My sister commented on the builder's incomprehension:

"You're just confused, big-ears. Our fenced-in area isn't very big. And though it is overgrown with tall grass, we've cleared it all in the last few days, so we definitely would have noticed a well or a way down into a basement."

Mission renewed: Old Cursed House
Description: Find the entrance to the Ogre Hunters' underground construction to discover what's behind the many strange deaths
Mission class: Reputation
Reward: Improved relationship with the village of Tysh
ATTENTION: Recommended character level for mission: +50

In that the other players had obviously not

received that message, I took screenshots of the quest description and sent it in private messages to Valerianna Quickfoot and Shrekson Bastard. The huge ogre froze for a few seconds, then thoughtfully stroked his bald spot and looked around.

"Alright then. Looks like we'll have to dig this all up again."

"Not yet!" my sister intervened, also already familiar with the details of my quest. "In the description, it's pretty clearly stated that this quest shouldn't be done by characters of lower level than fifty. That means there must be something dangerous down there."

"But that must be for people who want to do it alone, and look how many of us there are!" the ogre gasped, pointing to all the people and NPC's around. "I bet even just the four wolves could handle one level-fifty monster."

I hurried to add:

"In goblin legend, they say all resident of this house dying in night. A few days living here, then bam, died. Live here longest is Uguzh, goblin warrior. Eleven days he living here, but then also bam, died. Friendses, Amra no wanting force you in doing mission. But, if riddle of haunted house no is solve, then wolfie pack die, three goblin die too. Is big pity."

"Yes, we'll help, of course," the wood nymph supported me. "I mean, we have to protect the wolves no matter the cost. They're a very valuable resource. Also, 'your girly' is worth something. And you brought those kids, so they're your responsibility. You'd be answering for their heads before all the goblins of Tysh."

After hearing themselves mentioned, Yunna and Irek walked up to me.

"Uncle Amra, we're ready to start working. But it would be nice to have a bite to eat first. My tummy is grumbling."

I translated the goblin speech for the others and asked my sister if she had any food in her inventory.

"I fed it all to the ogre. He was hungry," my sister sighed helplessly. "But we could get the stuff that fell into the trap pits and split it up!"

It would have been a good idea, if it weren't for the fact that, based on the mini-map, eight of the wargs had survived and were still circling around not too far from our house. What was more, there looked to be other dangerous creatures very close by as well. Too many to safely leave our shelter. Taisha threw up her hands guiltily. I was hoping she had something left in her pack. She was hungry, too. She hadn't actually managed to eat at her house and, while she was lying unconscious, the wolves had managed to treat themselves to the contents of her bag. Obviously, it hadn't been the petrified girl herself that caught the wolves' attention as much as her tasty smelling knapsack.

I then heard a coughing sound come from the naiad. It seemed he was trying to draw attention to himself.

"I've got fish in my inventory, both fresh and dried. Actually, that's one of the reasons I came here."

Max Sochnier took a few steps in my direction, but then a trio of wolves, who had been resting calmly until that point on the grass, all jumped up at once and blocked his path, baring their fangs and growling unambiguously. The naiad gave a short nervous giggle, throwing his trident to the side and showing his empty hands.

"Calm down. Let him pass!" I said, marking the fish-man as an ally for the Gray Pack. After that, the wolves instantly lost interest in him.

"There!" Max set about stacking fish on the grass. "I've got mackerel, rainbow trout, and flounder. I've got a lot of other stuff too. Next to the place where the broken Orcish Galley was, near the cliffs is the underwater city of Ookaa. All kinds of newts, merpeople, sirens, naiads, nereids and oceanids live there, but they're all NPC's. They catch fish and gather pearls. You can come by this kind of stuff very cheap there. And, not far from the rocky shore, there's a dock where, a trade frigate comes once a week and buys the goods from the undersea residents or trades them for various baubles, like fish hooks or harpoons made of forged metal. And it should be said that five high-level players live by that dock as well. All humans bitten by the fishing bug. I figured out they're a group of old men, who worked for many decades together on the same net-fishing boat in the Arctic and Atlantic Oceans. They're not interested in anything in *Boundless Realm* other than fishing. From morning to night, they sit on the cliffs and fish, betting on who'll catch the most. The loser treats the others to dinner in real life. I tried to compete with them, but it was no use. Their fishing skill is leveled up far beyond one hundred, and they've also taken all the supporting specializations and levelled them up as well."

The naiad finally finished placing the fish on the grass and offered some to the goblins to go and cook. Taisha decided she should be the one to take charge in the kitchen. Irek and Yunna helped her. Together, they gathered the catch and went into the house. I whistled to myself in surprise. Max had set over fifty fish down, and some of them were very large indeed. The value of his catch must have been quite high, and it was somehow uncomfortable to accept goods worth so much from a trader I barely knew. I voiced my concern.

"Come now, by Ookaa prices, this is all less than seven coins," the fish-man smiled with two rows of razor-sharp teeth. "It's just that, there isn't much to do there. You can only either catch fish, or gather mussels and oysters. Also, there's just one NPC trader you can sell your catch to, and his prices are miserable, as I already said. I asked around. The locals there are generally not against selling their catch to me for more, but where am I supposed to unload a whole shipment of fish?! I was getting ready to come up onto the dock, when a human frigate tied up on it. They practically took me captive again, but I was able to figure out that, up the nearest stream, there is a village called Stonetown and I headed there on the boat. I didn't even make it to Stonetown, though. I was shot full of arrows by some damn PK-ers and had to leave the boat with a large part of my wares and dive underwater. And after that..." the trader abruptly fell silent and looked at the ogre.

"Go ahead. You can say it. Amra already knows. The problem is that Max also works as a tester in the *Boundless Realm* corporation. Yesterday evening, we were both called into Alexandro Lavrius' office, and he gave us both a talking-to over the fact that we had no interesting material, and our characters didn't seem to be progressing. He set us both the condition that we had to hit level twenty within seven game days, or we'd be out on our asses looking for new employment."

"That's right. He worked us over good. I've never been chewed out like that in my life..." the naiad agreed, shivering nervously from the unpleasant memories. "I mean, it's just the third day of the ogre's trial period. For me, it's day five! I've just got two days left. 'No quality content,' they say. Where can a trader even find that, huh?! Around Ookaa there are just aquatic-race fishermen. Nothing but herring and pike interests them. The only living player I've seen down there came five days ago, and he turned out to be a complete moron. He was also a naiad, by the way. At first, it made me happy. I thought that we could make something happen together, but the first thing he did was kill me with a stab in the back and take my stuff. Then, he contrived a way to make the whole village mad at him and he fled Ookaa on day one."

My sister and I exchanged glances, and Valerianna Quickfoot guessed out loud that the "moron" he'd been referring to may have been named Trong Diver.

"You've met him too?" The fish-man chuckled unhappily. "Yes, the very same. You'd think he was a grown man, as he plays *Boundless Realm* but, based on his intellectual and psychological development, I'd be inclined to think he's still in elementary school. He decided to 'nab a bunch of experience all at once' by walling up an underwater newt cave. Unlike the other residents of Ookaa, newts have to swim up to the surface periodically and breathe real air, even though they can remain under the water for a long time and breathe with their skin. So, Trong Diver thought up a way to kill them all at once: he sealed up the entrance to their house, making it impossible for them to surface. He even tried to get me to join and help him with his flagrantly illegal activity. Actually, he killed me for refusing to help. What happened in the end with the newts, I do not know exactly. I was waiting to respawn at the time, but the aquatic court decided to feed Trong Diver to deep-ocean predators. And because he is undying, he was also forbidden from ever returning to Ookaa..."

"It seems to me you've gotten a bit off track, Max," the ogre fortifier interrupted the story. "Back to the story. We both left the director's office, and both of our arms were trembling so much that we couldn't even button our shirts. I mean, picture this: I haven't smoked for twenty years, but I was reaching for a cigarette. It's a good thing there's nowhere to buy cigs in the *Boundless Realm* building, or I definitely would have been running straight for it. Max and I just went to make ourselves some coffee. As we went, we got to know one another. And today, he unexpectedly sent me a private message in the game. Max was simply cursing at the fact that those ragamuffins had stolen his wares near Stonetown. I read in the rules that, in order to send such a message successfully, the sender has to be within ten kilometers. So, that meant Max must have been somewhere very near me! I opened my map, found that damn Stonetown on it and told the naiad how to get to me. Having a construction partner suited me just fine. After all, we've got big plans!"

"Using a professional player and trader as a simple laborer is basically like using a microscope to hammer in nails," Valerianna Quickfoot cringed in dismay. "And also, it's the most reliable way of failing the trial period, because a trader, unlike a fortifier, doesn't get experience just for digging and sawing."

I was in complete agreement with my sister in this matter. Along with that, such misuse of his character would hardly have been to the liking of the management.

"Today, they find Alexandro Lavrius was bad cheater. Him was fire, kick out on ass. I already seeing new fat boss, Mark Tobius. He say old arrangement no work and now he will look see who of testers be staying."

"Excellent news! Simply wonderful!" Both players lit up with joy, practically starting to dance.

But I rushed to reign in their glee by saying that the new director seemed even stricter than Alexandro Lavrius. So, we all had to try very hard to show our very best sides.

"Shrekson, I finding ogre other helpers. Maybe Irek, maybe other mob. But Max is no dig. He be sell-trader. Must inventing trade scheme for profit. Will to best for all. We go all in house and discuss shared game of four-player and many mob."

* * *

The smell of roast fish was clinging stubbornly to the inside of the blockhouse. Taisha and two of her other helpers had gotten to work in earnest, setting up a true assembly line. Yunna was cleaning and gutting the fish, Irek was threading them onto a rod and feeding wood into the fire, and Taisha was putting the fish over the fire, turning them when they'd picked up some color, and taking them off when they were finished. At the other end of the kitchen, a half-sleeping Blanca was thawing out in the warmth and feeding her four pups. To describe the scene in one word, it was idyllic.

The ogre reached for one of the finished skewers, but Taisha slapped his hand away:

"First wash your mitts! Also, wait for everyone to sit at the table!"

I thought the giant would get offended, but his reaction was unexpected. He opened his mouth in surprise and asked, not believing his ears:

"So, does this mean goblins can talk normally?"

"Some can. But they don't talk to everybody,

only to those they consider friends," Taisha said, also in human language. What was more, she spoke totally distinctly and without the slightest accent.

"It depends a lot on intelligence," I confirmed, also in normal language. "But distorting speech and talking with strangers in hard-to-understand 'goblin-esque' phrases is useful. It makes others consider you stupid and not take you seriously. Why don't we go up to the second floor? I'm drooling here from the delicious smells."

We went up the steep stairs. Due to the absence of adequate furniture, I laid out some pelts right on the floor and told everyone to take a seat. My sister lit the candles she'd made by hand, and it became surprisingly cozy.

"This place looks like a medieval laboratory," Max Sochnier chuckled, looking at the wreathes of drying plants and the alchemy table.

"Well you see, I'm an herbalist by trade," I answered with a smile and suggested we immediately begin a serious conversation. "Given we've got so many plotline testers together in one place, I'll be direct: in the days that remain, my sister and I will help you get to level twenty. But don't think of this as only a one-time thing. We're hoping for long-term collective gaming and mutually beneficial cooperation."

"Sister?" Max caught on my words.

"Yes, I see no reason to hide it. Valerianna Quickfoot is my sister Valeria. Though she's not an employee of the *Boundless Realm* corporation, she is completely aware of the trial period situation and has helped me in many ways. In particular, she's been very helpful in development issues for my character, and could help you as well. She's been specializing in this topic for years and can find something of value in even the bleakest situations."

My sister stood up, bowed to everyone and immediately asked for a word.

"I'll be as honest as possible; your characters leave you all little to celebrate. No herbalist, fortifier, or trader would ever be able to create especially interesting unique gameplay all on their own. This is serious money we're talking about here, and no viewers would be interested in watching a trader sit for days on end in a stall or an ogre who just digs holes. I don't know who would ever want to watch some goblin milling about gathering flowers, either."

"But what can I do? We were given these characters by the system!" the ogre objected.

My sister made a pause and smiled:

"We should use the characters we received to build something bigger! We need to think something up and name a goal that will take your viewers' breath away. For example, for a trader, create a monopoly delivering fish to the cities of the Southern Continent by squeezing out and destroying all the competition. Will it be hard? Very. Undoable? That very well could be. But it would certainly make for an interesting story!"

I cut into the conversation, apologizing for interrupting my sister:

"As a first step in our big strategy, we need to start delivering fish to all nearby villages and the large city of Weiden for trade. I'll need both of your discovered-territory maps..."

"Sorry, bro, but even that isn't actually the very first step. Initially, we'll have to deal with their skills and stats. Look at Max Sochnier's. It's just a muted horror!"

On my sister's advice, I looked at the trader's primary skills and stroked my head in thought. Alright then...

Trading (Ch I) level 4
Polearms (S A) level 2
Fishing (P A) level 3
Amphibious (C S) level 9
Thick Skin (C S) level 1

Where were the skills to improve charisma and intelligence, the two most important components of a trader's success?! Beyond, obviously, Trading itself, which was at level 4, there was nothing.

"Polearms and Trading I had no choice on!"

the fish-man began justifying himself.

"And those skills are fine," my sister, wise beyond her years, reassured Max. "It's hard to imagine a naiad with anything other than a trident. A two-handed hammer would look ridiculous. It'd be almost as hard as imagining a merchant who cannot negotiate. The Amphibious skill allows you to live outside the sea, and is used constantly, so I get that also, even though I may have put it in secondaries. But Fishing and Thick Skin!?"

"Well, in Ookaa, everyone's a fisherman! So, I chose that skill on the first day to fit in. I figured I could trade the fish I caught. And thick skin I took literally this morning in the boat on my way to Stonetown. The whole riverbed there was lined with flies the size of my fist. They each took like one or two hitpoints, but there were whole clouds of them. They were gonna bite me to death!"

The nymph shook her head in reproach and lowered her gaze to the floor, not having said a thing. But I understood perfectly and continued her thought:

"Max, all that happens if you die is that you lose a bit of experience. You could have made it up in a few hours. But I don't get why you'd take it as a primary skill and ruin your character's whole future. If it was so hard to bear the flies, you could have taken Thick Skin as a secondary!"

"Well my secondaries were already all filled

up. Light Armor, Diplomacy, Diver, Strong Back and..." here the naiad went silent for a second, clearly embarrassed, "Lothario."

"Lothario?" the ogre started whinnying so hard that he fell on his back and began rolling on the floor.

"Well sure, what's the big deal?" the trader objected. "I figured it wouldn't hurt my character to learn to talk to women better. Half of my customers are women, after all."

Valerianna Quickfoot took a heavy sigh and said with badly hidden fatigue and annoyance in her voice:

"Truth be told, I'd like to take a wooden rolling pin, or better yet a heavy shovel handle and really help you learn to communicate with the opposite sex, as well as thicken your skin up a bit."

Taisha saved Max Sochnier from having to further discuss his skills, as she appeared with a whole mountain of roast fish on a large wooden platter. The following few minutes, the only sounds were jaws munching away in unison. Finally, Taisha broke the silence:

"Irek and Yunna are finished and have already dozed off, tired after the endless, anxiety-inducing day. So, I set them up a bed in an empty room to the right of the stairs. The little kiddos fell asleep as soon as their heads hit the pillow."

"Thank you. So, why haven't you changed your clothes yet?" I wondered.

The goblin girl smiled an exhausted smile and shrugged her shoulders imprecisely. I still couldn't figure out what that body language was supposed to mean. Was Taisha embarrassed in front of the undying, or had she simply not had the time to equip the thief's outfit? Perhaps she was afraid she couldn't take it back. I mean, if I understood correctly, donning the outfit should have changed her class.

"Do you want Valerianna to help you change?" I suggested.

Successful check for Taisha's reaction
Experience received: 80 Exp.

"To be honest, I don't know the wood nymph at all, so that's why I'm embarrassed. I'd rather have you help me, Amra," the redheaded girl answered.

Is that so? I set an unfinished piece of fish aside, carefully wiped my hands on my pants and helped her up. We walked down to the first floor, and Taisha went into the kitchen... and sharply stopped, her face stretched out in fear. I looked behind her and also froze, not knowing what to do. Blanca was eating her puppies!!!

"Hey, wait up! Woah! Leave them alone!" I shouted. After the initial shock at what was happening, I threw myself at the puppies, but stumbled after meeting with the utterly mad eyes of the predator.

The seasoned she-wolf, her snout covered in blood, swallowed the piece in her jaws, slowly stood from her bed and came forward in a cowardly fashion. In any case, I took a step back, putting myself between her and the terrified Taisha. Blanca stopped before the entryway, staring inquiringly at me and starting to scratch at the door. I looked at the mini-map and the she-wolf's marker was blue for me on the map, meaning ally. And next to her, there was another blue marker... I turned to the little bed the female had just left.

Level-1 Wolf Pup

After letting the scary predator out and locking the door behind her, I wanted to walk up to the wolf pup, but Valeria Quickfoot got in my way. My sister simply knocked me off my path, ran up to the little animal and picked him up:

"That one's mine! Blanca promised him to me!"

Almost instantly, above the head of the sleepy pup, squinting from the firelight, there appeared the name her owner had given: "Pirate." Why my sister had wanted to give the pup that nickname precisely, I had no idea. But at that, after thinking over what had happened, I commented to everyone:

"That was all how it had to be, unfortunately. The Gray Pack now has five members. When the newborn wolf pups grew up a bit and became independent creatures at level one, a program script kicked in. The pack wasn't allowed to contain so many individuals, so she simply brought the number to within acceptable limits."

"I didn't get even half of what you just said, Amra," Taisha admitted.

But everyone else did. My sister even continued my thought:

"It's very sad for the pups, but this is how it had to be. After we find and destroy the lair of the wargs, Pirate will be a helper to Gray Pack, without taking a place in it. We'll be able to add another wolf to the pack!"

"Two wolves even," I corrected the nymph. "The reward for finishing the Horror of the Gray Pack quest is increasing the size of the Gray Pack to six."

"I still don't understand a thing! Can you not speak more simply?" the villager complained.

Valerianna Quickfoot looked thoughtfully at Taisha, then with pity at me, and went upstairs, calling on the naiad and ogre to continue their discussion of skills and development plans for their characters. Taisha and I were then left alone.

"She doesn't like me," the goblin girl whispered.

"Not at all, Taisha. The nymph is very smart and sees a high value in you. She's just a bit angry that you're getting involved in matters of the undying, even though you have no understanding of our lives. Don't worry, I'll tell you all about the undying when the nymph, ogre and naiad have all disappeared."

"Disappeared?" she asked, not understanding. "Did you mean to say 'fallen asleep?'"

"No, disappearing is exactly what they'll be doing. Taisha, one of the things that makes the undying different is that we are not always in the realm we call *Boundless*. Sometimes, we take our leave from it to sleep, rest or take care of other business. Also, the undying temporarily disappear from *Boundless Realm*, if we get killed. But we always come back."

"And will you also disappear, leaving me here all alone for the night?" Taisha asked, her voice trembling in fear. "Amra, I'm very scared to be here in the Cursed House alone! Don't go, please!"

Basically, I hadn't been planning on exiting *Boundless Realm* before morning, so I promised the girl as honestly as possible that I wouldn't leave her alone at night in this scary house. Taisha took a step closer and kissed my big-eared character right on the cheek, whispering:

"Yunna isn't asleep. She's watching. So, make sure to turn away when I get dressed."

I didn't argue and dutifully faced the other

direction. Behind my back, I heard a rustling, then the sound of her dress falling to her feet. Another minute of shuffling and Taisha told me I could turn back around. Wow!

Taisha Spark
Goblin
Level-23 Thief

Her lightweight dark clothes were so thin that I could make out all the lines and shapes of her young feminine body. It looked appealing and erotic. I suppose even a bit too erotic. Taisha's clothes weren't so much covering her feminine wiles as they were underlining them. Even her totally naked figure wouldn't have looked this sexual.

"Well? How do you like it? Why aren't you saying anything? Does it suit me?" the girl asked timidly.

"I'm overcome with the desire to paw at your body," I admitted.

Despite the rudeness and clumsiness of the compliment, Taisha still laughed happily:

"Perhaps I'll let you paw at me one day, if I find you worthy. But I absolutely refuse to take weak and awkward admirers seriously."

Mission received: Reach a Higher Level than Taisha

Mission class: Standing, Rare
Reward: 2400 Exp., +20 to any check of Taisha's opinion

Mission received: Reach a Higher Agility Level than Taisha
Mission class: Standing, Rare
Reward: 48000 Exp., +20 to any check of Taisha's opinion

While I was reading into the mission conditions, not believing my eyes, I checked the number of zeros in the quest reward several times. The newly-minted thief was pulling her white villager dress up from the floor and, a second later, bunched it up and threw it on the fire. It flared up bright, literally devouring the fabric fed to it in the span of two seconds.

"Alright. I've made my choice and will no longer return to the past. Let's get back to the others!"

On the second floor, the discussion of skills was over. We caught the very end of it. Valerianna Quickfoot was giving advice to the ogre on his future progress:

"Shrekson, with Trapping, you made a simply excellent choice. That was the exact skill you needed to get the rest of the way to level twenty. But don't rush picking a fifth main skill. Yes, I agree with you that Athletics would give you extra endurance and would be useful in your tiresome work. But still, don't rush it. Let me think it over until morning so I can take everything into account. Woah! Look at you! Amra, aren't you afraid that the men in our group won't be able to concentrate with Taisha around? All their blood is gonna flow out of their brains to a different part of the body!"

As you could easily guess, the last few bits of her speech were directed at Taisha. The beauty really did cause quite the sensation with her new look. Everyone in the room could now only discuss the thief's new appearance. A minute later, Valerianna Quickfoot whispered to me:

"I approve, big-ears. The viewers will be sure to like her as a companion. And the most interesting thing is, look at her skills. There's nothing out of place. You could learn a thing or two from Taisha, like how not to spread yourself too thin and concentrate on the most important factors!"

To my great shame, only after my sister's words did I look at the beautiful redhead's skill information. Before that, I was too distracted by her appearance. Obviously, Valerianna's words on my mental capacity falling in Taisha's presence were true.

Lock-Picking (A I) level 14
Trap Disarming (A I) level 6
Dagger (S A) level 8

Stealth (A C) level 15
Dodge (A P) level 21

That's what I'm talking about! Four primary skills with a priority in agility and another with agility as the secondary! Considering the goblin racial bonus of +30% to agility-growth speed, just from the skills Taisha already had... I called up the built-in calculator and made some calculations. They showed that the redheaded beauty's agility had to be at least 77 from her skills alone. She also would have gotten a significant amount of stat points in her level twenty-three levels, which were probably also placed directly in the statistic that made the most difference to a thief...

Off the top of my head, I made a very crude approximation and figured Taisha's agility must be around 120-130. I opened my stats and looked with pity at my own agility, which was just 45, even with all the bonuses I had. Hmm... I couldn't see an easy way of finishing the quest with Taisha at all. I mean, how could an herbalist possibly get more agility than a thief?!

When the oohs and aahs on the beautiful thief had gone quiet, the naiad told us that it was time for him to leave *Boundless Realm*, as it was already late, and his family was waiting for him at home. We all wished Max a good trip and my sister added:

"Don't forget what we agreed on. Right after

you get out of the capsule, write to *Boundless Realm* tech support. Tell them how little time you've been playing, and how little experience you have with games. Say you made a mistake when you chose the skills Thick Skin and Lothario. Blame it on the unfriendly interface and lack of warning that it would be irreversible. Be sure to tell them that it's been less than a day since you chose the skills. You haven't leveled them further and haven't gotten any benefit from using them. If they try to waffle out of it, send them the links to the precedents I sent you. I'm practically a hundred percent sure your request will be approved. That's all. Good luck!"

The ogre also bid us farewell, blaming it on the late hour. Both players took a seat on the floor and closed their eyes.

"Taisha, do you think I could ask you to heat up some fish? It isn't very tasty when it gets cold," the wood nymph asked, handing the redheaded beauty a platter of skewers.

The goblin girl didn't argue and headed down the stairs. She was barely out of the room when Valerianna pointed me to the two motionless figures:

"What are you waiting for? Bite the ogre now, before it disappears! When are you gonna get the chance to try ogre blood again!"

My sister was right! I turned on the half-forgotten, long-unused Veil skill and leaned over toward the sitting giant's neck, having chosen the option of a six-hour deep sleep.

Achievement unlocked: Taste Tester (8/1000)

While Veil was still active, I did the same with the naiad trader, but nothing happened. I quickly called up the game logs for editing and deleted the record of both bites.
Veil skill increased to level 3!

"I have to admit, that looks very gross from this perspective!" my sister commented with a look of disgust on her face. "And now, you're marked for me with a red criminal marker. But, I guess that's fine. As long as no one else saw it. But explain, why'd you bite the naiad as well? I mean, every one of your bites, even if not lethal takes a small number of hitpoints from the victim. The ogre is fine. He has regeneration and, by morning, he'll be good as new. But the naiad might notice!"

"I needed to sate my Thirst for Blood a bit more. Those weak bites give me very little blood. I need to drink my fill before morning, and every hour is important. You don't have to worry about him noticing, though. Max forgot one very important detail: he's a fish-man and shouldn't have left the game on dry land. Our acquaintance's Amphibious skill is still quite weak and tomorrow, when he logs into *Boundless Realm*, he won't be feeling too great. He'll be quite dried out. I'll prepare a couple health potions for him tonight, and get him a trough of clean water. That way, the naiad won't just straight-up die but, in the morning, he won't be able to notice a few hitpoints missing."

"Ok then. I approve. By the way, brother. At least show me your trophy from the wyvern island! There was just so much turmoil around it today! The local chat has been full of talk about it. A whole group of players from *Lords of Chaos* even came to our shelter this evening asking for you. They were all well over level-two-hundred. They searched the house, checking every nook and cranny. They even searched me. But, all in all, they behaved themselves, and were even polite. They took selfies with the feeding NPC she-wolf, fixed the gates and went on their way. What happened, Taisha?"

Just then, the goblin girl ran up the stairs with a look of horror.

"There... this room doesn't have any windows, so you can't see it but, from the kitchen, I saw a strong glow to the northwest."

"Maybe that's the night storm we were promised?" my sister supposed.

"What, do you think I haven't seen a storm before?" Taisha exclaimed, offended. "My home village is over there. Tysh is on fire!"

"She's right," I agreed, having noticed an intense flashing from the closed chat window. I opened it and read the messages. "Valerianna, look at the local chat. Some undying have found our goblin village and are now committing genocide there! They say they're cutting up anything alive!"

Little VIXEN

THE HARDEST PART was convincing Taisha not to do anything rash. The girl was chomping at the bit, wanting to run to Tysh as fast as possible to save it from the fire. She was especially worried for her father and two sisters, drunk on sleeping-potion wine and not able to sense the danger. All my admonitions that Taisha wouldn't be able to get to the village due to the dangerous night creatures were duly rebuked.

"I can get around unnoticed. I have good Stealth! And my dark clothes will help me stay invisible! I'll be able to run there!"

"Sure, alright. And what then? Based on the chat, there's practically twenty undying there!"

"I'll talk with them! Ask them to leave Tysh

alone. We goblins didn't do anything to them! We're a peaceful village. We aren't at war with anyone. We have good relations with our human neighbors. Their merchants even come to our village."

"They won't even listen to you. They'll just kill you on sight," I said, trying to talk the girl down from the deadly adventure once again.

"But why? I've never seen any of them before. I've never done anything bad to them. Why do they wish death on me?"

My sister looked on me with reproach and, straining to hide a yawn, said wearily:

"Taisha is asking questions that seem believable for a real person, but are totally unexpected and even inappropriate for an NPC. And I don't know how to explain the world of *Boundless Realm* to her in a way she'll understand. Amra, you dragged her here. It's up to you to explain this. I'm done. I'm off to bed. Tomorrow, starting in the early morning I've got to draw all the blueprints for the ogre and find new pets for myself..."

The wood nymph took a seat on the floor with a sleeping puppy in her hands, covered her eyes and, thirty seconds later, had disappeared together with the tiny wolf.

"She's so callous and heartless! The nymph couldn't care less that our countrymen are being slaughtered in Tysh right now! I mean, right?"

"You're wrong, Taisha. Valerianna is very kind, sensitive and thin-skinned. Once, she saw a baby bird that fell out of its nest and her mood was spoiled for days. If her favorite doll gets broken, that's cause for a day of tears."

I went silent, remembering unwillingly. I hadn't been exaggerating on the doll one bit. After her terrible accident, to celebrate her release from the hospital, I bought my sister a big robotic doll. She was very pretty and almost as tall as Valeria herself. The toy was self-teaching. It could sing, dance, find its way around the apartment, answer her owner's questions and keep up a conversation fairly well. My sister, not yet able to even get out of bed, was insanely happy to get such a gift. But all it took was me leaving her alone with it for one second and Valeria was reaching for the kitchen knife and lopping off both of her doll's legs above the knee. After that, she wailed all day without end. I even had to give her a sedative. After that, Valeria couldn't even look at the crippled doll without immediately falling into hysterics. She made me promise I'd never buy her more toys or pets.

"How do you know that much about the nymph?" asked the gorgeous NPC, distracting me from the sad memories.

"Valerianna Quickfoot is my little sister."

"How is that possible? You're a goblin and she's a nymph."

I took a heavy sigh. It was too hard to explain to this virtual character. How could she understand that the world around her wasn't real and was made just for entertainment? Would she ever truly be able to understand that the attack of the undying on Tysh was not part of some massive crime spree, but just a totally innocuous experience farm? Or the fact that the players didn't even think they were doing something bad when they killed her relatives?

"When the undying come into *Boundless Realm* they change appearance and look completely different from normal. That's how I became a goblin and my sister a wood nymph. But most of the undying look like humans. That's why they didn't touch the population of Stonetown, buy and sell goods there, and even help the residents with various quests. To them, goblins are completely foreign, and the undying do not think it shameful to kill them simply for loot or just fun. If you go to Tysh, they'll kill you too."

"And what if you went? Amra, you're also undying, after all! They'll listen to you and leave the goblin village in peace."

I shook my head doubtfully. I mean, sure. They'd listen. Then they'd make a "screw loose" gesture and beat me so I couldn't get away. They'd look on me as nothing but a moronic low-level player.

"And why did so many undying come to our

quiet gods-forsaken corner of the world? Until now, I hadn't met any my whole life. Then, yesterday, you and the nymph showed up, and a day later there was a whole invasion. Was it you that called them here?" Taisha asked with a certain apprehensive suspicion in her voice.

I had to answer her difficult question, trying to give the girl a neutral story in which my role in the sale of the map and calling thousands of players to the middle of nowhere wasn't mentioned.

"Do you remember yesterday when I was resining that boat with your father? Well, after that, I tested out the flat-bottom on the swampy lake, and got attacked and killed by a huge flying snake named Kayervina. She is a very rare creature in *Boundless Realm*, so every undying desires the honor of hunting her and taking the snake's treasure. Information on such a valuable monster being discovered spreads fast. When I was reborn, the area was already lousy with undying. In the end, they took Kayervina down, but they're still trying to find out who got the trophy."

"Amra, what's happening right now? Can you feel it? It's like the world is twitching. Your words come to me with a delay."

I also noticed that the game had started to lag quite badly. That was what happened when the efficiency of the game cluster processors was too low to process events. During mass-scale battles, for example. Clearly, there weren't enough computing resources dedicated to this backwoods location, as the attack of the players on Tysh had gobbled them all up. Calculating the flight path of missiles and damage radius of spells, constantly tracking which player sees which NPC, or hit, missed or dodged. Processing the graphics and all the effects from fire, smoke, houses being destroyed... That all required processor resources. Generally, if those resources ran out, the system could automatically devote some extra power to a region. And that was what happened this time. The lagging passed fairly quickly.

I didn't manage to give Taisha an explanation of what was going on that she could understand, because I was trying desperately to figure out how was she able to see the choppiness if she was actually part of this world? Players, sure. They were outside the game, and could see. But how would a piece of code, inseparable from *Boundless Realm* itself, understand that it was "lagging" together with the surrounding reality? Were there different independent processes responsible for the intelligence of an NPC and the rest of what was happening nearby? That must have been. Before I could think up a better explanation, my virtual friend asked me another question that shook me:

"Amra, could you show me the snake's

treasure?"

How did she know about that?! Fear probably was shown on my face, as Taisha cracked up laughing:

"Even if I wasn't sure from overhearing you, your facial expression would have given it all away. I'm not wrong. No, Amra. I wasn't rifling through your bags, and I cannot read thoughts. It's just that, when I was hurrying to tell you about the glow far away on the horizon, I heard some of your conversation with your sister. Valerianna asked you to show her the treasure from the wyvern island. At that time, I didn't understand what she was talking about, but after your story, I guessed."

Well then, that explained everything. I opened my inventory and set on the table before Taisha a huge, soccer-ball-sized golden egg. Its shell wasn't like that of a chicken egg, but more like rough skin. Now, with the egg lying on the table, I could see that it was pulsating slightly. The girl didn't even hide her disenchantment. She was clearly expecting to see something more unique and exquisite.

"So, this is the treasure?" Taisha asked, carefully taking the egg in her hands. "I wonder how valuable it is? If you offer it to the undying, would they leave the village of Tysh alone?"

Devil! That was the last thing I needed! She really was foolish enough to try! I didn't answer her provocative questions, instead calling up the

Gray Pack control window and removing Taisha from the friendly list. I couldn't allow the goblin girl to run off with my treasure.

"You don't have to answer, Amra. I know what you'll say. It's very, very valuable, as the undying spent all day today killing one another over it. If you show the egg to the undying near Tysh, they'll get distracted for some time from robbing the village and will start fighting amongst themselves. Maybe that could even save some goblin lives. But then, the undying would start to regularly visit Tysh and kill its residents, because they'd start to think they could find similarly valuable things in the area. Right?"

"Yep. Couldn't have put it better myself. You described it well. Both the value of the treasure and what would happen if you brought it to Tysh."

Successful check for Taisha's opinion.
Experience received: 80 Exp.

The girl turned the egg over in her hands thoughtfully, then returned it to me.

"Don't worry so much, Amra. Even if it was a thousand times more valuable, I still wouldn't take it from you. Thieves don't steal from their own. You told me that yourself. But, if I'm not mistaken, it isn't so much the egg itself they're after as what's inside. If you look, the little wyvern was just about to hatch, but now is gradually dying."

"Do you know how to help it?" I asked in alarm.

"Yes, I know. But as the treasure is so important to you, let's make a deal. I understand perfectly that there's nothing we can do for the goblins of Tysh now. First, we're far from the village and wouldn't get there in time. Second, we're weak. But I feel in my heart that a relative of mine died in that despicable attack. I will get revenge on the murderers! Even if it takes my whole life, I'll search all of *Boundless Realm* until I find them. So, that's my offer: I'll help your little wyvern hatch tonight, and you'll help me get my revenge. Agreed?"

"*Boundless Realm* is huge. It could take months and even years to find the killers!"

"Well, as far as I understand, revenge is a dish that is often served cold!" the redheaded thief declared to me harshly. "No matter how long the search takes, I won't stray from the path. And know, as long as you work toward that goal, I'll never leave your side. But hurry with your choice. The little wyvern in the egg is about to breathe its last. She needs help!"

"Good! I agree to your conditions!" I barely managed to say these words before lightning struck right next to the blockhouse followed by a deafening thunder blast.

"The gods of *Boundless Realm* must have

heard our oath," Taisha commented.

* * *

"Are you sure?" The idea to surround the egg with raw meat and wrap it in a pelt looked, to put it lightly, strange.

"The old shaman Kaiak Badgerleg once said that he caught a glimpse of the wyverns in the swamp hatching their eggs. The flying snakes hunt, bring their prey back to the island still alive, eviscerate their victim and stick the eggs in its corpse. Then something strange happens. The flesh disappears before your very eyes. All that remains is a skeleton with skin stretched out over it. After that, the wyverns go back on the hunt and put their eggs in another dead creature, and so on and so on until the tiny wyverns hatch out of the eggs. The shaman said that they have to consume life force to ripen."

It all seemed very doubtful, but I didn't know any other way to save the life of the wyvern in the egg. And the fact that the embryo was in danger was no longer in question. The pulsations were gradually becoming less frequent. It wouldn't be too hard to test Taisha's method, either. In the trap pits outside the barricade, there were the fresh corpses of three wargs and it hadn't even been two hours since they died.

After setting Taisha as "in-group" for the Gray Pack once again, the girl and I went out into the yard. The night was dark and gloomy. There were low-hanging black clouds crawling slowly overhead, completely obscuring the stars. Somewhere in the distance, I heard thunder. The horizon would occasionally light up with lightning flashes. But next to the Cursed House, it was already raining. The soil was getting washed out and squelching horribly under my feet. There was an advantage in the bad weather, though. The deadly predators of the night were now taking shelter from the rain. I couldn't see even a single red dot on the mini-map.

With Taisha's help, I removed the log that was keeping the door locked and we went out to take a look around. The nearest trap pit was literally five meters from the gate. I went toward it.

Successful Agility check
Experience received: 40 Exp.

An unprintable expression tore itself from my lips as I nearly fell down onto the sharp stakes, having slipped on the damp clay and straining to hold onto the edge.

"Don't come near, Taisha. It's very slippery here after the rain!" I admonished my companion, but she just snorted in a very arrogant manner, having ignored my warning, and walked up to the very edge.

It had been quite dumb on my part to point out the risk to her, actually. Her agility was easily high enough to stay on her feet on the slippery, inclined surface.

"I could jump down into the pit and string up the upper of the two dead wargs. After that, you lift me out and together we'll try to drag the monster's body out," Taisha suggested.

After remembering how hard it had been for my big-eared Amra to lift Taisha in the home of Tarek Bigfoot, I refused. I had a better idea. I remembered just in time that my Exotic Weapons ability gave me skill with more than just blowguns, but also throwing nets and lassos. I grabbed the rope, tied it into a slipknot, and threw it on my first try over the neck of the dead warg.

Exotic Weapons skill increased to level 5!

Hot diggedy! I first tried on my own, then with Taisha's help to drag the corpse of the warg from the pit. But we weren't strong enough. I had to call the Gray Pack for help. I made a few loops down the length of the rope and harnessed Akella, Blanca, Lobo and White Fang. Then, they all pulled! Got it! The first dead warg, caked in blood and mud, was pulled up to the very porch.

I took out my knife and was preparing to cut

the trophy's pelt off when I remembered the skills and stats needed to do it. After that, I clapped my palm on my forehead. In *Boundless Realm*, players didn't have to actually cut up the dead, bloodied bodies of the beasts they'd killed. I opened the loot window and removed the black warg pelt into my inventory, as well as five large pieces of raw meat and filled my alchemy vial with blood. It became hard to move. I was over-encumbered!

Doubling over from the heavy pack, I got up onto the porch step, went into the house and strained to climb up to the second floor, cursing at every high step along the way. When I was already in the second-story room and standing, trying to catch my breath, Taisha commented acridly on the pathological greed and stupidity that must have stopped me from giving some of my items to her.

"Alright, that's enough laughing at the less fortunate. Yes, I was definitely being dumb. But I still got the meat in, and that's what matters now. Let's try your method of growing a wyvern."

I spread out the glossy black fur on the floor right in the center of the room, set the egg on it and covered it in pieces of meat. At first, nothing happened, but then the leathery egg started pulsating noticeably faster and the meat around it started dissolving without a trace.

"It's working!" I was ready to jump for joy. "But the meat we have won't last for long. Let's bring the other two bodies in!"

We got the second warg from the pit, brought it in and butchered it in the same way. But complications arose with the third. Our wolves helped us get them but then, baring their teeth and growling, they sent me an unambiguous message that they thought the last of the three trophies their rightful share. I didn't disagree or ask for trouble with the four seasoned wolves, and the last body disappeared without a trace including the skin and bones, lost to the toothy maws of the Gray Pack.

"We should cover the pit traps with poles and branches again. Maybe we'll catch something interesting!" I suggested to Taisha, to which she agreed eagerly.

It wasn't the easiest work. While Taisha and I were covering the trap with poles and spreading torn-out grass on it, I received another two messages about successful agility checks and one failed check. But it was a blessing in disguise. It allowed me to level Acrobatics to six by jumping off the unstable ground as it shifted away underfoot. I had already placed a piece of bait in the middle of the trap, a pleasant-smelling roast fish, when I got another message:

Stealth skill increased to level 10!

I couldn't see any red dots nearby on the mini-map, but that was the scariest part. There was probably an invisible player walking around somewhere nearby, though it was also possible that it was a high-level Stealth predator. In any case, any desire that remained to stay outside the barricade quickly left me, and I ran to shelter. I locked the gates with the log, and immediately hurried into the blockhouse to check on how the golden egg was doing.

The wyvern egg was still pulsating and periodically giving sharp shivers. Its leather grew thin and soft. Inside it, I could sometimes make out a moving, dark body. The meat was gone, sublimated without a trace, so I packed some fresh pieces in.

"The baby snake will soon hatch," Taisha assured me, also watching the behavior of the wyvern embryo with curiosity.

Tarek Bigfoot's daughter was surprising me greatly with her calm. After getting very naturally worked up because her village was burning and wanting to run straight out and save the goblins in Tysh, flying in the face of all reason, the girl was now demonstrating a simply unbelievable restraint. I suggested that she go to sleep on the bed, and even laid out a luxurious black warg fur, but Taisha refused to rest, saying she was still too worked up about what was happening in Tysh.

"Amra, tell me about the undying," the thief asked, crouching on the floor next to the quivering egg.

And really, why shouldn't I? So, as I got to work at my alchemy table, trying all sorts of new elixir combination, I also told the NPC girl about the real world. I mean, I didn't actually tell Taisha anything to suggest *Boundless Realm* was less than real, I simply described the other reality. It had people in it who went to work every day in tall stone buildings and huge cities with giant steel wagons that flew through the sky. Taisha was entranced by my tales, not interrupting me once, even though I was in deep doubt that the girl understood even a fifth of what I said.

"Hey, look! The egg is cracking!" Taisha's voice distracted me from checking the effectiveness of the healing potion I made with my now level-nine Alchemy skill.

I set the vial of pinkish liquid aside and took a seat on the edge of the dark fur on the floor. She was right! The leather on the egg was now stretched to the limit, and a small crack had appeared, and was now gradually widening. Another minute passed and, through that little opening, a dark, tiny thin head poked out with microscopic black eyes. The head twitched back and forth and stuck another few centimeters out.

"She's so little!" Taisha whispered very quietly, but the tiny snake heard and began shivering in fear, trying to escape the prison still holding her body in.

"You're scaring her!" I snapped, extending

my hand to help the little snake by breaking the egg up.

Hey! That hurts! That jerk, not even yet fully hatched, bit my finger with its sharp little teeth.

Damage taken: 4 (Bite from Royal Wyvern)
Health level: 167/171

Successful check for Poison Resistance

So, you're already poisonous at birth? I carefully unlatched the wyvern's fragile jaws from my finger and, after tearing a bigger opening in the leathery eggshell, pulled out a half-meter-long snake. Neither its front or back legs could be seen yet, but there were two little protuberances on its back pointing to where the wings would be.

ATTENTION! Open creature settings menu to set mount statistics

I opened the window on the little snake trying ceaselessly to get out of my hands and found its settings.

Level-1 Royal Wyvern

Leave default Swamp Wyvern subrace (Yes/No)?

Would you look at that! Show me the whole list, please! I opened the list that came up and read the descriptions. As a matter of fact, there were just five options: swamp wyvern, mountain wyvern, forest wyvern, polar wyvern and twilight wyvern. The subraces differed in the type of damage they dealt, skin coloration and a few minor perks. And though the polar wyvern had full immunity to cold and breathtaking snow-white scales, and the twilight wyvern had the best name coupled with very worthwhile death magic, I ended up deciding on forest wyvern. It was a bit smaller and weaker than the others, but its emerald green scales suited my habitat, and I liked the fact that it did poison and acid damage. The most important thing, though, was this:

"Second fastest flying creature in Boundless Realm *after the legendary Phoenix."*

That was the factor that made the decision for me.

Would you like to change subrace to Forest Wyvern (Yes/No)?

Yes, please! I'd barely made my choice before the little snake in my hands changed color from copper brown to emerald green and immediately grew calmer. Without closing the settings menu, I made sure that my little snake was a female and chose a name for my little poisonous baby: "VIXEN."

VIXEN
Level-1 Royal Forest Wyvern

* * *

Near morning, Taisha fell asleep despite her earlier resistance. The lack of sleep and worry had really done a number on her. She was lying in the fetal position on the black fur on the floor. The girl had stubbornly ignored the bed, thinking it mine and clearly feeling embarrassed to sleep in a man's bed.

I then, leaving Taisha to sleep in peace, took VIXEN out into the yard. There was absolutely nothing to do in the building. I was out of herbs for Alchemy practice. The thunder had long passed and the air exuded freshness. The sky was clear and starry. And that was bad for me. The next day would probably be sunny.

The appearance of the tiny wyvern didn't draw the attention of the Gray Pack. Just Blanca came over and sniffed the new creature, giving a scant tail wag, and went back to sleep, stretched out near the porch. Obviously, the wolves simply took the little snake as a part of me. Once in fresh air, VIXEN first got confused and even made a threatening pose, either afraid of a little breeze that brushed past her, or a little level-2 moth that flew by. But after that, the wyvern grew more brave and dived into the tall weeds that grew abundantly in our yard. I wasn't at all worried for my little pet, as I'd already read that a mount cannot die permanently, and it dying would only be penalized with a five-percent experience loss. So, that meant if VIXEN came upon something predatory and dangerous in the grass, it would be nothing more than a life lesson.

Stealth skill increased to level 11!

My complacent mood instantly went up in smoke. As before, I couldn't see any enemy markers on the mini-map, but the game message meant that there was an enemy somewhere very close to my shelter. The Gray Pack also sensed the uninvited guest and the wolves awoke and, looking timidly at me, alternating between baring their teeth at someone unseen on the other side of the fence and looking at the door to safety in the blockhouse.

As before, I couldn't see any markers on the mini-map, but I could guess by the wolves' behavior where approximately the cloaked character was. He was walking unhurriedly along the outside of the stockade, periodically taking short breaks to test the wall for weak spots. One time, I even seemed to hear a curse word fly out in human language. I could easily understand why the stranger would do that. The earth there was unstable, and he was probably up to his knees in mud. Also, there were a few thick bushes of thorny ivy growing up around the edge of the stockade, so I hadn't even managed to walk all the way around it myself.

"Aaahhh! Mother... (what followed was unprintable)!" the exclamation rang out suddenly. I shuddered in surprise.

On the map where I'd marked the third pit trap, a player marker appeared. After hearing the shrieks of pain, the wolves immediately grew braver and came together into a sound that wasn't so much a bark as it was a yelping growl, jumping at the gates and demonstrating their preparedness to run outside and kill the unfortunate enemy. Over the fence, it became possible to see a black skull marker and a quickly dropping life bar. I read the player's information:

Valentin Wise_Wizard
Half-Elf
Level-96 Illusionist

Well, I'll be damned! Level ninety-six!!! It was the first time I'd ever encountered such a strong player. It appeared that the experienced mage was moving in Stealth but had fallen carelessly into the trap and landed on the sharpened stakes. The illusionist's health bar jumped up a few times, replacing the lost hitpoints, but quickly fell back down again. It seemed the mage must have had healing potions with him, but they only prolonged his suffering. He wasn't able to cast any spells that could really get him out of the tragic situation (for example Levitation or Teleportation) because he was constantly taking damage, breaking the cast.

I never would have managed to help the man, so I just observed his vain attempts to get free with measured curiosity. That's why I noticed when, next to the player's yellow triangle marker, there appeared a red dot denoting an NPC monster. A moment later, the high-level player was no more!

Experience received: 2304 Exp.

Level twenty-one!
Racial ability improved: 45% Resistance to Poison

A second later, the unknown monster also disappeared. The nocturnal predator hadn't died, though, unlike its victim. It had just gone invisible again and was now back on its savage hunt. While I was frozen, shocked at what I'd seen, a new system message came in:

Mission renewed: Old Cursed House
Description. Follow the night monster's path to the entrance of the Ogre Hunters' underground construction
Mission class: Reputation
Reward: Improved relationship with the village of Tysh
ATTENTION: Recommended character level for mission: +50

Stealth skill increased to level 12!

If it hadn't been for the last line, bearing witness to the fact that I was still in the sight radius of the ghastly being, I might have even risked going out and looking at the site of the tragedy. But now, there was too much riding on that horse. I mean, in case of my death, I would have lost just some of my experience, but if I opened the gates and, at the same time, let the monster get inside the shelter, everyone would die: Taisha, Irek and Yunna, the entire Gray Pack... I couldn't let that happen no matter what, so I decided against trying to track it down. The monster's ability to take down a nearly level-100 player so quickly inspired a certain respect. I wanted to find out some more about it first, if possible, so I wrote a private message to the player Valentin Wise_Wizard:

"I tried to come out and help you, but I didn't make it. Say, what kind of beast was it that attacked you? Toss me your game logs if it isn't too much to ask."

I wasn't at all sure that my message would reach him, or that he would answer. But, as they say, nothing ventured, nothing gained. After assigning my remaining stat points: two in charisma and one in agility, I went to search for VIXEN. My poisonous mount, just as I'd set, got ten percent of the experience I received as well as whatever it could get on its own. And VIXEN, already having reached level three, was now engaged in an unequal battle with a level-4 night hornet. I even had to intervene and cut off the hornet's stinger to assure my tiny wyvern's success in the badly progressing duel. Sure, it wasn't sporting, but I couldn't just sit idly by and watch. The huge black wasp was holding my wyvern at a distance with its jaws and stinging her over and over. She couldn't even fight back.

"Don't be afraid to call me or the Gray Pack in to help!" I strictly warned my green snakelet, which just then reached level four, fully restoring its lost health before it went off once again in search of adventure and tall grass.

* * *

Only near morning, with a few minutes left before sunrise, did I risk going outside. I had to struggle against the locking beam. I could barely get it up even a centimeter without Taisha's help. I suspect that, if my character's strength hadn't increased by one as it grew in level, my big-eared Amra wouldn't have even been of much help. In the trap pit where the careless illusionist had stumbled, I managed to collect a bit of half-elf blood in a vial. There was no other loot that dropped. Making use of the fact that no one could see me, I drank down the prepared vessels of blood from the warg and the half-elf.

Achievement unlocked: Taste Tester (9/1000)

Achievement unlocked: Taste Tester (10/1000)
Regeneration improved to 2 HP/Minute

Woah! Taste Tester, it seemed, wasn't just some mere virtual achievement with no practical application. It had a real benefit! Unfortunately, I hadn't found any additional information on Taste Tester in the in-game hints or the *Boundless Realm* forum. And it wasn't like I could just go around asking that question, for obvious reasons.

That meant, as the Taste Tester number grew from here, I would get more and more of these perks. I looked carnivorously at the nearest forest, which was full of bird, mammal and insect species I had yet to bite. Only the fact that morning would soon be here could save the animal world from total taste testing. I managed to get back into the blockhouse before the sun came up and, rattling Taisha awake and warning her of my exit from *Boundless Realm,* I took the sated level-5 VIXEN in my arms and chose "Exit Game" in the menu.

I opened the virtual reality capsule lid and sat up, turning the events of my last game session over in my mind. I'd managed to do so much in just one night! I escaped the PK-ers, took a beautiful girl from her home, participated in a frantic ride through the forest at night, and found new friends and helpers. But the main thing was that I'd gotten a unique creature as a pet, and there was no other like it in the whole of *Boundless Realm*! I thought everything over well and weighed the pluses and minuses, then decided not to tell my viewers about the existence of VIXEN yet. Let their passions calm a bit first after the mass event with Kayervina. Soon, the remaining players would leave the vicinity of Stonetown. I had plenty of interesting game moments already without the royal forest wyvern, and my viewers would be satisfied. Taisha alone would have been enough!

After editing the video clip, I went out into the hall and unexpectedly met with Kira, who was already totally dressed in an unbelievably chic outfit and hurrying to the elevator. I greeted the young beauty politely and she stopped next to me with a smile.

"Hey there, Timothy! You'll never believe it, but I managed to find you in *Boundless Realm*! A goblin herbalist with a very short name. Arbie! Antie? Anton? I can't remember right now, but I put you in my contacts..."

"Amra," I told her, and Kira grew obviously joyful.

"That's right, Amra! After our last conversation, I wanted to find information on the quest Curiosity and the Cat and I found some newbie selling a map of the wyvern island. I cross-referenced the time in-game and figured out it must have been you making use of my advice. I even bought your map, though I didn't rush to go there. It was just too far. More than seven thousand kilometers from my palace."

"I have to thank you, Kira. The new director of special projects, Mark Tobius, told me that you intervened on my behalf to stop the cheaters from getting my reward from the Curiosity and the Cat quest."

For some reason, Kira frowned. The smile instantly left her face and her gaze grew cold.

"Timothy, you must be confused. This is the first time I'm hearing about a 'Mark Tobius,' and I suspect that he also knows nothing about me. In the whole corporation, there are only a few employees aware of my work, and even fewer who know the whole story. My character in *Boundless Realm* is quite famous, but only my direct boss knows it's me who controls it. There's a lot of money involved here, so it's important that I maintain my anonymity. I even prefer not to go up to my office too often, which is why I work here. Otherwise, interested parties could calculate who my character is just by lining up when my character is active with the times I am at work. If the corporation allowed it, I'd work from home and never show my face to the parking-lot cameras again."

"I must have misspoken. The director didn't actually mention you by name. He only said that the in-game security service got a message from an experienced tester and employee who asked them to check on the situation with the Curiosity and the Cat mission. But you're the only person I told about the unique quest, so I guessed it was you."

The girl relaxed and even smiled at me:

"Yes, it was me who wrote to the in-game security service. Although, if the security guys worked the way they should, their alarm bells should have already been going off from a simple analysis of game logs. A newbie like you isn't supposed to get such complicated quests, after all."

The beautiful woman adjusted her bag on her shoulder and asked:

"Did you drive here, Timothy? Do you want a ride home?"

This was an excellent chance to get to know Kira a bit better! I could have told a little lie about my car and residential address, but I didn't. I just answered truthfully:

"I don't have a car yet. And I wouldn't refuse a ride, but I live in such a bad neighborhood that you'd refuse to bring me there."

I told her my address and the name of my neighborhood. Kira agreed instantly that it was better not to poke her nose around there in an expensive sports car, because the risk of simply losing it was too high. And I chuckled back:

"And knowing my neighborhood from experience, I'd say you could count yourself lucky, if the only thing you lost was your car. More likely, you'd also lose your jewelry, expensive clothes, and have your bank account drained. And by the way, speaking of jewelry... You didn't happen to lose a ring in the shower, did you?"

"You found my ruby ring?! I thought it must have fallen off in the garage. I dug through all the nooks and crannies there, and looked under the cars next to mine. Security even asked what I was doing. But that little bauble is valuable both intrinsically and because it was a gift from a close friend."

I told her that her ring had been found by a tester named Leon, and he had brought it to the security post at the main entrance of the corporation building.

"I don't know this Leon. So, I think I'll thank you for finding it," Kira quickly clicked on a tiny screen on her golden bracelet and my cell phone gave a beep, indicating a change in my bank account balance. "Timothy, this is to you from me personally. If you want, share it with this Leon. If you don't, feel free to keep it. It's up to you. I just ask that you go to the security post and pick up my ring. I'll call them right now and warn them you're coming. Then leave the building. I'll meet you at the main entrance. I won't be bringing you all the way home, but I can let you off at the highway exit."

The underground parking lot elevator beeped, announcing its arrival. Kira quickly gave me a smack on the cheek and hurried into the elevator. Only after the doors closed did I take out my phone and look at the message. She'd sent me six thousand credits! No, no, no. I couldn't accept that! It was too much for what I'd done. My elevator arrived and the whole way to the security post, I was mentally composing a speech for Kira on why I had to refuse her money. But at that, my hand just couldn't lift itself up to cancel the transaction and return the huge sum of money to its rightful owner. At the security post, they gave me the ring without questions and I hurried outside.

"Timothy, I'm here!" I saw a car parked next to the stairs. It looked futuristic and was flat and black with huge attachments that were either wings or a spoiler. Its tinted window went down and I saw Kira in the driver's seat.

The door on the passenger side opened automatically. I took a seat in the deep passenger's chair and immediately gave the ring to its owner.

"About your money for the ring..." I began timidly. In response, Kira put her finger decisively to my lips.

"Not a word about the money, agreed? Otherwise, you'll be going on foot. Sit down and buckle up."

I didn't manage to grab the seatbelt before the car started abruptly, pressing my back into the seat, and then... it took off into the morning sky almost vertically, like a firework! So, this is a flying car? But why is it so miniature, and why does it have wheels?

"This is a hybrid. It's a whole new concept," Kira stated, as if reading my thoughts. "It does four fifty on the road, and seven in the air. I saw it last month in a flying car dealership and couldn't resist. Its maximum altitude is, truthfully, just seven kilometers, but that isn't important."

Kira straightened out the car and I saw the height indicator on the dashboard showing 3100 meters and a flight speed indicator that was quickly going down. Two hundred ten kilometers per hour. One hundred thirty. Seventy. Forty. Zero. Kira pressed a key and the roof of the flying car slid noiselessly back, revealing the blue sky overhead. I had never really been afraid of heights, at least, not until today, but now I was frantically clenching the door handle.

"Look Timothy, it's so beautiful! The megalopolis is just now waking up. There aren't even any traffic jams on the highway yet. And if you look hard, way over there, through the smog, you can even see a bit of the sea."

Kira suddenly undid her seatbelt and stood all the way up, her arms stretching up to the heavens.

"Though I play *Boundless Realm* at night, I just love the morning and the sun!"

The girl looked at me and suddenly, after giving a happy smile, stepped over my legs and took a seat on my lap, facing me. Without any warning, Kira leaned forward and kissed me right on the lips.

"Why are you so tense, Timothy," the young beauty chuckled. "Don't you like flying cars?"

"No, I don't," I admitted honestly, trying not to think about my parents' death in the crash of just such a vehicle.

"Well alright, I'm sure you can bear it for a bit. We'll only be up here for a few minutes. They don't let you stay for long. Patrol drones will fly up soon and start writing out tickets one after the other for breaking the rules of air transportation. But my mood is great today and I wanted to have a little fun. Also, tomorrow is my birthday, and I wanted to invite you. Nothing official, don't worry. You can wear whatever clothes you want. The only people there will be my best girlfriends from college and their beaus. They don't know anything about my job. As far as they know, I own a small designer-clothing store. And I would like for them to stop asking me questions about my personal life, so I thought you could play my boyfriend for the night. Figure out the situation, spin them some yarn about yourself, basically just blend in. Can you handle that, Timothy?"

Alright then, why not? I agreed effortlessly. Kira kissed me once again and suddenly, looking somewhere far behind me, frowned:

"The patrol drones are already on their way. We'll have to drop down. We were having such a good talk!"

After turning around, I saw some quickly approaching dark spots in the distance with little blue sirens flashing on top of them. With clear satisfaction, Kira went back to her place in the driver's seat, put the roof back over the car and let it drop down. A few minutes later, the girl was letting me out at the exit from the high-speed highway a half-kilometer from my house.

"Don't forget, Timothy. You promised!" Kira said and, after sending me an air kiss for the road, raised the window on her door and abruptly took off into the morning sky.

A Step Forward

I WAS AWOKEN by the sound of my alarm clock. Three PM. Time to get up. I had slept well and felt amazing. In the other corner of the room, Valeria was talking to someone in *Boundless Realm*, her virtual reality helmet clipped on, and sensor gloves on her hands. My sister was laughing happily into the microphone and saying it was of no use to train the Lothario skill on her. Max Sochnier must have managed to convince technical support to change his primary and secondary skills around. I didn't distract my sister from her business, or even worse, listen to their conversation.

I washed up and ate my fill of microwave lunch, which had been prepared earlier by my sister, then got to business. First of all, I went out and paid up with the landlady for our room and even paid her two weeks in advance. Then, I went to the grocery store and bought some food for later. It wouldn't have been fair to make my sister do it. It's hard to carry around heavy bags in a wheelchair, after all.

"D'you get a job, Timothy?" the elderly clerk asked in surprise, being accustomed to me sweating over every penny.

"You could say that. I'm still in the trial period, but I got an advance," I answered him cheerfully and went outside with big bags in my hands.

God, damn it! This was the last thing I needed! Near the store, a windowless car stopped, painted all over with graffiti skulls and symbols of the local youth gang. I really didn't like the long, attentive gaze the two fully-tatted skinhead teenagers led over me. They were members of the gang that controlled this and the two neighboring blocks. They must have come to shake their "protection money" from the owner of the grocery store.

The young criminal groups usually didn't touch Valeria and I, as there wasn't anything to take from us. One time, right after we'd moved to the outskirts of the megalopolis, a group of bandits broke down our door at night. They had scared the crap out of my sister and I with their appearance, that was for sure, but the careful search of our room they carried out found that we didn't have any valuables or real money. They'd taken thirty credits, though, for wasting their time, and the racketeers even helped us put our door back on the hinges.

I brought the bags into our apartment and was finishing putting the groceries in the refrigerator when a call came in to my cellphone. Based on the number, it must have been Jane, my boss's assistant.

"Good afternoon, Timothy! Do you think you could come into work a bit early today? The director would like to see you," the girl lowered her voice to a whisper and continued. "Mark Tobius just asked HR to draw up a permanent work contract for you, so they want you to come in and sign it. But that's a secret for now. You don't officially know why I called. But all the same, congratulations, Timothy! Also, literally one minute ago, I sent a letter from the boss to the accounting office saying to send you a bonus for organizing the mass event on the wyvern island. It's all they've been able to talk about for the last two days on all the game channels. They're giving you five hundred credits!!!"

After thanking Jane for the good news, I said goodbye and began getting ready to go to work. I didn't want to force the director to wait for me, all the more so when the reason I was getting called was so pleasant! After leaving the room into the hall, I locked the door and hurried down the stairs.

"Hey, you. Stop! Come over here! We just wanna talk!" The same two gangsters I'd seen outside the store earlier were standing on the first-floor stairwell landing.

Well, shit... There was no point to run. They could easily find out from my neighbors where I lived, and just come after me later. I walked up to the tattooed, clean-shaven thugs.

"I heard you found work. Is that right? Does it pay well?" the shorter member of the pair asked. As he spoke, his strong, muscular partner of Middle-Eastern appearance was playing idly with a butterfly knife.

"I'm still just in the trial period. I was paid an advance just today. It was enough for groceries."

"Oh yeah? Because we heard that you paid off a few months of back rent in the last few days and even paid a bit into the future," the shorter one said while the knife-holder chuckled, showing me his scarce, rotten teeth. "And Cocker from the East crew said he saw you getting dropped off in a Black Crystal at seven this morning. He told me: 'A badass whip dropped down from the sky, and that guy came out of it, the one with a crippled sister who lives in entrance thirteen.'"

Here, for the first time, the other bandit started talking. He was a head taller than the first, but scrawny and clearly occupied a secondary role:

"Cocker is a huge bullshitter! If he wasn't sleeping this morning, that means he was high on angel dust. And you see all sorts of shit on that!"

"That's true. I took PCP a few days back and felt like I was swimming in the sea. It turned out I'd just pissed myself. So, what he said about seeing a Black Crystal by the highway exit is obvious crap. In the news, I heard they've only sold three of them so far. But this guy got some money. I can smell it on him."

And then, it just had to happen that at that very moment, my phone beeped to tell me the money had arrived! What bad luck! Both of the racketeers immediately lit up like hounds who'd just caught a fresh scent.

"I know that sound! Well then, let us see your cell phone!" the Arab said, waving his knife threateningly, and his partner also demonstrated his readiness to take my phone by force in case I resisted.

I had to give it to them, even though the incoming message text was still on the screen. The smaller one read it and shouted in surprise:

"Check this out! He just got five hundred credits! And in total... ho-lee shit! You've got six thousand five hundred credits, but you're playing poor! Man, this is a dangerous neighborhood. If you don't want bad things to happen, you've gotta pay for protection!"

I took a heavy sigh and said in a stubbornly confident voice:

"I'll talk about this in the evening. But not with you. I want someone higher up. I mean, this is serious money, and I need guarantees," I responded, extending my hand decisively for my phone.

The Arab gave my phone a couple of spins in his hand but, in the end, returned it. Walking outside, I headed in a hurried gait for the far-off bus stop, sensing the attentive gazes of the racketeers on my back. Once in the electro-bus, I called Valeria:

"Val, listen to me as close as you can. The local gang found out we've got money. I think our landlady ratted on us. They want to catch us by surprise tonight and demand we share it with them. But you know how racketeers are. You pay them once and they never stop coming. They just keep asking for more. Basically, we need to move out of the apartment ASAP. Bring the most valuable stuff you can carry and come out to the bus stop on your wheelchair. Also, try to look calm and natural, because there will be people following you. Take any route toward downtown and get out in two stops. I'll meet you there."

My sister is just such a great kid! She didn't get worked up, or make any badly timed inquiries. Twenty minutes later, Valeria was already rolling out of an electro-bus in her wheelchair. She had a small full backpack on her back with a colorful design. She also had a traveling bag behind her chair, which was pretty packed.

"I took the virtual helmet and gloves, your tablet and my comp. Of your clothes, I could only fit a jacket and one change of underwear. I set the alarm on the door, so if anyone tries to open it, a message will come to your phone. There were two gangsters watching the door, but they let me past."

"You're a smart cookie, Val! It's time to leave our slum life behind and move to a more respectable and peaceful neighborhood. While I was waiting for you, I looked through some ads. We could afford some rooms in private hotels or some rental apartments in commuter areas. The prices start at four hundred credits a month."

"Do we have that kind of money? Or are you hoping to get another loan from the bank?" my sister looked at me with doubt.

" I've got a little over six thousand in my account right now."

Valeria couldn't hold in her surprise and even started cursing. I always told my sister off for rude words, so I made sure to advise her against such language before continuing.

"There's money on the card. But the problem is that three thousand of it belongs to Leon. He plays the ogre fortifier in our camp. He doesn't know about it yet, and might never find out, but fair play, the money should go to him. And there's another thing. There's a girl. You don't know her. She invited me to her birthday party tomorrow. So, I need to buy some fancy duds. I can't go in this T-shirt and old jeans! And that's to say nothing of the gift I need to buy. I think around eight hundred credits will go towards that. What do you say?"

I went silent, waiting for my sister's reaction. Valeria shrugged her shoulders:

"What can I say? Other peoples' money won't make you happy. The faster you give it away, the better. And as for the girl, do you really think you have to play my nurse all the time? You need to get on with your own life. I understand perfectly how girls always blow you off because of your non-walking sister... The main thing is, just keep in touch with me when you're gone, alright?"

At the end of Val's sentence, her voice was quivering. Tears welled up in her eyes. I crouched down next to my sister and said reassuringly:

"You're not understanding me right, Val. Not even the most gorgeous woman in the world could get me to leave you alone in this world. I'll only be gone one night, and I'll be back right after. I promise. Don't cry, dummy! Everything's fine!"

Valeria dried her tears with her sleeve and nodded in silence. She then embraced me tightly in her arms, squeezing and not letting me go for a long time. Only a minute later, clearly embarrassed at the emotional display, did my sister back away, saying in a deliberately spirited voice:

"Tim, what are we wasting time here for?! Let's go look at our new place!"

* * *

Jane met me in the hallway outside the director's office with a look of extreme disapproval on her face:

"Timothy, what took you so long?! We were expecting you at four, and it's already six fifty! Mr. Tobius already called his wife and promised he'd be leaving work in a few minutes. And he won't wait. He's got a family outing planned today to the robot drama theater to celebrate his promotion."

"I know, Jane. Thanks. I just had to move to a new apartment today, and for some reason, it took an indecent amount of time. You see one thing online, but when you get there, it turns out they've only got more expensive options left."

"So, how'd it go? Did you find one?" Jane grew surprisingly interested. "I mean, I was looking last month for a place downtown near work, but I couldn't find anything for less than seven hundred credits a month for a tiny little box. I've already paid for that little room upfront for the next couple of months but I'm still looking for something a bit better. Alexandro Lavrius promised me a few times in private conversation that he would send my issue to the accounting department and the *Boundless Realm* corporation would start paying for my place as a valuable employee. He even said that, if the financiers refused, he'd pay for my room out of his own pocket. But now, I've got a new boss, and it's not a good time to raise that issue yet. I need to let Mark get settled first..."

Jane's rent was seven hundred credits a month?! Apparently, directors' secretaries could live pretty well! I tried not to show my surprise. I also didn't ask the girl what service she provided to prompt the director to promise to pay for her apartment out of pocket. Instead, I told her about my recent tribulations:

"I wasn't looking the very center of the metropolis, just in residential areas. I went around to three places before finding a more-or-less ok one. It is a two-bedroom furnished apartment on the one hundred seventy-fourth floor. They reamed me for it, too. I'm paying four hundred thirty credits a month, there's no kitchen and the view is horrible. It looks out right onto the mirrored wall of a neighboring skyscraper. But at that, it's just half an hour from work, and there's cheap places to eat in the building as well as a bunch of shops. Rent also includes security and housekeeping."

The director's assistant started thinking

about something else, then smiled at me and promised:

"Alright, I'll try to talk to Mr. Tobius and convince him to hold on for another few minutes. He's talking with another employee right now, but I'll say you've been waiting for a long time, and that you had a good reason to be late."

"I owe you a chocolate," I promised, but Jane furrowed her brow in dismay and showed with all her proud appearance that she was above such trifles.

All the same, as she was disappearing into the office, the girl turned to me and added:

"My favorite is milk chocolate with hazelnuts."

Jane didn't close the office door tight, so I involuntarily overheard a snippet of the director's ornery bass. Mark Tobius was telling someone off in a raised voice and, I very quickly realized who.

"...and after all that, you ask support to help you get free?! Veronica, don't you think that's an illustration of the abject failure of your gameplay style!? You signed an affidavit acknowledging the fact that you are now incapable of escaping captivity. But the only reason you're in such an extreme situation in the first place is your actions!"

"I don't think this was really my fault. My audience isn't going to question it. It's not like I'm asking for something outrageous. All I need is a little interference in the game world, like a pirate siege, an invasion of warring tribes, or a wild animal attack. It doesn't really matter what. Just enough to distract the local NPC's for a few hours so I can get out. My viewers are bored stiff! I've been in the same area for four days! But if I could just get to a new location, interest in my character's story would start growing again."

"No, Veronica, I'm still not convinced. The problem isn't our world; it's the shortcomings of your methods. Sure, in the first two days, we saw explosive interest in your explicit clips. But at that, your dryad was cracking quests like nuts, quickly gaining experience and showing that you were on a viable path. Getting your character to level twenty-three in two days was very impressive, and I understand perfectly why my predecessor considered you to have passed the trial period. But after that, your scheme broke down, and you didn't even notice! On the third day, you only leveled up three more times, then that maniac killed you and your character started regressing. And today's been a complete dead-end! Your once frivolous and happy dryad dancer is now nothing more than a sad-eyed sex slave for teenage NPC's. The net result of today: zero experience, zero profit, and all your property was stolen. Then, after your attempt to flee, you were physically restrained. Tomorrow, you'll get more of the same. It will never end. What's more, if you do get free, you'll just attract more perverted sickos as the rumors spread. And you're trying to tell me everything's fine?!"

"I didn't say that," Veronica objected timidly. "I just asked you for the chance to run from the NPC village and start the game in a different place with a clean slate. Audience interest in my videos has gone down, sure, but it's still high. I could easily find a way out of this situation. And, after that, I'll just be an unarmed dryad trying to survive alone in the wilderness. Doesn't that sound like an interesting story?"

A long pause followed. Based on what I heard, Jane took advantage of it and told the director about me.

"Oh yeah? Good. Invite Timothy into my office in a minute. Just warn him that I have to leave very soon."

In order not to be caught listening in, I walked a bit farther from the door and took a seat on a couch in the hallway, so I didn't hear how the director and Veronica's conversation ended. A minute later, the young lady in the horrible situation left the office and, after giving me a scant nod, walked toward the elevator. I was then invited in.

"Take a seat, read and sign," Mark Tobius said, immediately extending me a permanent employment contract. "Congratulations, Timothy! Excellent work."

I quickly signed both copies of the contract

and set them back down on the director's table. On doing that, my gaze fell on a similar document that had yet to be signed, and I caught a glimpse of the name "Leon" and the words "Ogre" and "Fortifier." My attention didn't go unnoticed by the director:

"Yes, you can congratulate your friend. Tell him to come here tomorrow morning to sign. Who could have thought that an ogre fortifier would be so interesting, multifaceted and, most importantly, in demand in *Boundless Realm*?! Leon got off to a pretty hard start. It took him a long time to find a gameplay style. But every day, it started looking more and more positive. Then, when he chose Military Machinery as a fifth primary skill, it was just a stroke of genius! Now he's just got all these possibilities opening up before him. I mean, we'll practically have to nerf his combination of race and professions, or even make it against the rules. As it is, it's very imbalanced."

My phone beeped. I apologized and reached to turn it off, but looked at the screen before doing so. It was a message that my home alarm had been set off. Someone just broke down the door of my old apartment. I guess my sister and I left at just the right time!

"Now, let's have a very quick chat about your goblin herbalist," the director said as he was already getting moving, starting to change his clothes before leaving work. "Personally, I've got three questions and one request for you. First question: why a forest wyvern? Rock is stronger and has more health, so it's a better fit for fighting NPC's or players both solo and in a group. And the swamp wyvern is perfectly suited for the kind of places your character will live. And that's to say nothing of the polar wyvern. It's the best possible companion for a vampire! It could breathe frost on a group of enemies and you would just go and bite the ones you want, leveling up your vampire stuff. Twilight wyvern is the stealthiest and, with time, would get the ability to be invisible while flying. For a player such as yourself, who doesn't want to advertise his coming and going, you could hardly dream up a better mount. But for some reason, you took forest wyvern. You must have had something in mind when you chose it!"

My boss just stared at me, waiting for an answer. It seemed that my choice of forest wyvern had disappointed the director. Mark Tobius himself clearly would have gone with a different option. I had to explain, describing the advantages of my little VIXEN:

"Forest wyvern was the best choice, if you ignore immediate gains, and focus on long-term perspective. Flying mounts are extremely rare, but they do exist. And with time, there will be more of them. A forest wyvern is a guarantee that I can catch any player or, if need be, run away from any unwanted encounter. It is a way to evade pursuit and keep valuable and even unique items in my possession. It gives me the ability to flee from an attack by any winged NPC, whether it be a griffin, a harpy or even a dragon. And also, it's just a way to cut down on flying time. *Boundless Realm* is huge and, over long distances, the speed of a creature is its main advantage."

The fat man cracked up in satisfaction:

"Timothy, you should work in the marketing department! In just a couple sentences, you managed to convince me that all the other options are total garbage, and players should only ever want the forest wyvern! Alright, I agree with your choice. Second question: tell me about your further plans now that you've passed the trial period and you no longer need to rush or bust your butt?"

"I definitely don't plan to sit in the same place and grow blackberries and cranberries in the swamp. The viewers want to see interesting gameplay, but for now, all my serious plans are still held up by a simple lack of money. So, my very nearest plans are to arrange the delivery of ocean fish from the underwater city of Ookaa to the nearest seaside villages and the city of Weiden with the naiad trader Max Sochnier."

"Max Sochnier?" The director asked thoughtfully. "I feel like I've seen that name before. Is he a tester from a different group? I'll have to take a closer look at him tomorrow."

"Yes, he works in a different group, but he found me in *Boundless Realm* and suggested we play together. He had an idea for an ambitious project to establish trade routes between the underwater and terrestrial cities of the Southern Continent. It seemed interesting and large-scale to me, and also necessary to provide a decent cashflow in the desolate country my big-eared goblin ended up in."

"What can I say then? The viewers are sure to love it. What's more, there's very little material on underwater races or settlements so, in any case, the story will arouse interest. And now for the last question. Timothy, tell me about Taisha. Why did you and Alexandro Lavrius add her to the game? What was the purpose?"

I stayed silent, batting my eyelids in surprise and not hiding my confusion. Taisha was created by Alexandro Lavrius?!

"To be honest, I thought Taisha and other clearly custom-made beautiful NPC's were a way of getting players to part with their money. I met other goblin girls, and they looked so dramatically different from Taisha that, she stood out to me, like it or not, and I wanted to have her as a companion. I've spent one thousand five hundred coins in the last two days just on gifts for that cute little redhead. And if you suppose that there are hundreds of thousands of such characters, and even millions, specially rendered for players of every race in existence, that would mean a multi-billion-credit cash flow for the *Boundless Realm* corporation."

Mark considered it briefly and shook his head:

"It's too much work for too little payoff. There are much easier ways for our corporation to provide itself with a stable income from our hundreds of millions of players. For example, the tax on trade operations. You don't need to put any work into creating anything, and yet you are always provided with a stable, passive income. Beyond that, registering the rights to virtual property, renting houses in cities, fees for creating player clans, maintaining castles, checking for emblem uniqueness... There are hundreds of ways for us to make money! There is no reason whatsoever to create sexy NPC's with the goal of pulling another hundred coins from players. No, this is something else..."

Mark already had his raincoat on, so I decided the conversation was over. But the director, turning around before the mirror, looked back to me and continued:

"This morning, we got a complaint from the DPC (data processing center). Yesterday evening, there were two abnormal computing power draws in the Lars cluster, and they had to devote some extra resources. The programmers told me that the reason for both surges were awkward logic algorithms and memory leaks from one and the same NPC, known to you as Taisha. At its peak, the goblin girl's simulation program alone was using more resources than the whole rest of the game cluster. Unfortunately, Taisha's programming code is encrypted, so the programmers weren't able to figure out the reason for the error. But based on the number of libraries and modules supporting her, she has much more complex algorithms and goals than would be required of a simple beggar. I tried to make sense of the story, but it all came back to the fact that the technical specifications had been written by Alexandro Lavrius, who was fired together with the programmers who handled the project. No documentation was retained, either. By the way, Timothy, I almost forgot. You completed some quest with that Taisha, but you didn't get the reward. The thing the programmers wanted to write in as a reward, they didn't actually manage to put into the game, and clearly will not be able to now. We don't like leaving players with no reward after they complete a mission. Do you have any wishes on that?"

I didn't even have to think for a second before I gave my answer:

"Other than Taisha, I have a pack of forest wolves, which also behaves unconventionally. I think they are the unharmed companions of some dead player or the remnants of a failed quest, as they're obviously not from the surrounding forest, and the local monsters are quite driven in their attempts to destroy them. I need total control over the Gray Pack in order to be able to correct errors in their behavior."

"I'm well aware of the Gray Pack. They were part of a game event six months ago. As a matter of fact, it was developed by the same team that later created Taisha. At one time, the Gray Pack contained hundreds of wolves and wargs under the control of the giant wolf Fenrir. The members of the Pack were famed for their clever intellectual behavior algorithms, joint collective play and ability to soberly assess their forces, avoiding battle when necessary. The Gray Pack was a real pest for the Urtez and Lars regions. It quickly replaced any losses, easily evaded pursuit and, time and time again, put players in bad situations, if they were accustomed to seeing NPC monsters as nothing more than dumb nonresponsive sources of experience and trophies. At the end of the day, the players had to join together and resist the threat as one, attracting the best strategists and soldiers from the top clans to solve the problem. A little while later, Fenrir was killed, and the *Boundless Realm* board of directors considered the Gray Pack mission over and disbanded it, while all the employees who participated in creating it received gratitude and very generous bonuses. I also got my share, even though I only joined the project at the very end. What can I say? I agree to give you control over the wolves living near your shelter. Janey, write the programmers. Tell them to give Amra control over the Gray Pack. Not administrator privileges, just the ability to correct skills and behavior. That's all, I've gotta run. I'm running very late as it is!"

I left the office together with Mark Tobius and, already on the way to the elevator, asked him a belated question about what request he had in mind when he said he had three questions and one request. The fat man smiled good-heartedly:

"My request? Collect more herbs and flowers. It's starting to look weird seeing a goblin herbalist with Herbalism as the least leveled skill."

* * *

"Tim, as unfortunate as it may be, it's sunny out. The sun is already starting to set, but there aren't any clouds in the sky, so for the next half hour, there's no reason for you to log in."

"The ogre fortifier wouldn't happen to be near you, would he? Maybe ask him to leave Boundless Realm *for a few minutes. I could give him the money."*

"The ogre's here. Hard at work as always. He's built so much in the last day that you won't even recognize our old Cursed House. But actually,

there are a lot of people waiting for you here. And, if Leon finds out you're near your cubicle, how would you explain why you aren't logging in? I'll send him to you when the sun goes down."

I thanked my sister for the advice and said goodbye. What could I get up to while my character, who would die from a single beam of direct sunlight, couldn't log into *Boundless Realm*? I scoured the game forums for information on vampires and the Taste Tester achievement, but didn't find anything I didn't already know. Just then, I was reminded that Kira had told me she had bought my map of the wyvern island. I opened the list of buyers. Just one hundred thirty people had bought my map of the snake treasure island, and I saw them all by name. That meant I could perhaps figure out who Kira's character was from among them.

I filtered out all male buyers as, in *Boundless Realm*, your character had to correspond to your legal gender. There were just forty-three women. Not so many, if you thought about it. All the same, twenty minutes of close reading didn't get me any closer to solving the riddle of Kira's in-game identity. Humans, light elves, one half-elf. There were some high-level ones among them, but I still felt that they weren't her. Kira wasn't there. What was I doing wrong?

It occurred to me that Kira was a very careful and guarded individual. She kept the secret of her character very fastidiously. She could hardly be so careless as to buy a treasure map from me directly, then tell me about it. But she also had no reason to openly lie either. Maybe she bought the map through some inconspicuous middle-man? Sensing that I was on the right track, I removed the gender filter and again looked at the map buyers. This time, I was looking for noncombat characters who would never manage to handle the wyverns or Kayervina, but who had bought my map all the same. There were six such characters. But one of them caught my attention above the others:

Larsen Lucky
Human
Level-221 Trader

In this player's profile, among many achievements, it was said that he had been granted a royal favor for his services to the Land of Gloom that allowed him to trade there, even though it was off limits to all other humans. I opened the additional information on the Land of Gloom and figured out that it was the name for an expansive region surrounded by a ring of high, impassable mountains called the Boundary Ring. There weren't any roads into the Land of Gloom in the traditional sense, though there were some underground tunnels dug out by dwarves connecting the area inside with the world beyond. The population of the Land of Gloom was all nonhuman: minotaurs, mountain titans, trolls, harpies and even dragons. The ruler, then, of the isolated country was Kirra'ellita, Huntress of the Night, the wise elder harpy. I called up a portrait of the ruler and gasped. There could be no doubt about what was looking down at me. It was a half-woman-half-bird with huge eagle wings, terrifying claws, powerful talons and... Kira's face!

So then, that's who she was! But I didn't think you could play flying races?! How did this make sense? It was against the rules! But an even bigger surprise awaited me when I opened the guide on Kirra'ellita, Huntress of the Night. She was a unique creature in *Boundless Realm*, the Ruler of all Harpies, Dragon Whisperer, Keeper of the Boundary Ring... She had many epithets, but her level wasn't shown, and also, the information made her look more like an NPC than a player. But could you play an NPC?

I was distracted from further investigation by a knock on the door of my cubicle. I turned the screen so my visitor wouldn't see that I was investigating the ruler of harpies and unlocked the door. Leon was standing in the doorway wearing a tracksuit, all red and damp with sweat.

"Hello, Timothy! Your sister told me you were at work and wanted to see me for some reason."

"Greetings! Yes, I did. I've got two pieces of news for you, and they're both good. First, here you go!" I chose the option "send funds" on my phone and, finding the only person nearby and making sure it was Leon precisely, transferred him three thousand credits.

The former construction worker, still overheated and not yet having caught his breath, felt in his pockets, took out his phone and read the message. He then stared at me in surprise, waiting for an explanation.

"I know what you're thinking, but it's no accident, Leon. It's just that the person who works in game cabin twenty asked me to send you her gratitude for finding the ring. But that's not all. I just saw a contract on our boss's table to hire you on as a permanent employee of the *Boundless Realm* corporation. The new director said he was very satisfied with your playing and wanted to see you tomorrow morning in his office."

Leon froze for a few seconds, but then his face stretched out into an ear-to-ear smile.

"I just can't believe it! This is the greatest day of my life! Although... I still haven't hit level twenty. I'm just eighteen."

"Clearly, the director thought you'd have no problem hitting twenty in the next three days, so there was no reason to draw it out," I supposed.

He agreed, but somehow not very cheerfully:
"It's not about level twenty. I could even hit

thirty in three days if I was really trying. I was in Tysh today..." the smile finally crawled off Leon's face. "They're rebuilding at a frantic pace after the fire. There's just a whole heap of work to be done. Two or three of the village houses burned to the ground. It's just ghastly how many died. Everywhere, no matter where you look, there are burnt bodies. And they don't disappear with time. That smell of burnt flesh... I mean, what's the damn point of having such detailed reality in a game?! I don't understand goblin speech, but there was so much crying and wailing that my heart was just aching. I couldn't stay there. Communication was a challenge, but I talked with the new chieftain and offered my help in fixing the village as soon as the goblins finish their mourning activities. And right after that, I ran back to your forest house where I spent all day hard at work trying to forget the horror. And Taisha also ran back to the Cursed House an hour later. She couldn't stand being in Tysh. She's been pale all day and just bawling. If I understood correctly, your green girlfriend had two sisters die in the fire, and her dad was badly burned."

The melody of my cellphone ringer cut off Leon's speech. It was my sister calling.

"Tim, I need you here now. A disgruntled goblin woman just came to our house. I only understand a third of what she's saying, but it looks a lot like she's trying to claim the Cursed

House as her property."

"Tell her to get bent! Tell her that the owner of the blockhouse will soon return and give her a kick in the ass."

"I would say that, but she's level-eighty. She's got a black skull for me. She brought another four smaller goblins with her, and they're between eighteen to twenty. Beyond that, Irek and Yunna have joined her side. If it comes to blows, they'll take us down in a matter of seconds."

I considered it. It must have been that Tamina Fierce had come to stake her claim on the Cursed house with her children. It wasn't clear what she was doing so far from Tysh, but there was no way we could count on ending the conflict by force.

"Gotcha, Val. Hold on. I'll be there in a few minutes."

After turning off my phone, I met eyes with the construction worker who was listening in apprehensively on our conversation.

"Leon, we both need to get back in the game right now! It seems like someone's trying to kick us out of the Cursed House. Every defender counts now!"

Night of Blood

I DIDN'T HAVE to repeat myself. My friend hurried back to his cabin. As soon as the door closed behind Leon, I donned my sensor suit and climbed into the virtual reality capsule. Before the game loaded, I discovered two unread messages. The first was from the illusionist who'd died in our trap last night, Valentin Wise_Wizard, who had lost a level after dying in the pit trap. Based on the time of the answer, this morning, the high-level mage was still roaming around the area near Tysh and Stonetown, within ten-kilometers of my shelter.

"Amra, did you want to help me?! You must be kidding! The difference in levels between us is too great. But as you wrote me so politely, very well,

I'll reply. I won't give you my game logs, sorry, that's too personal. I don't reveal my armor and or damage-type resistances to other players. But the beast that attacked me was called a midnight wraith. I didn't notice it's level. It attacked me from behind. I can only say that it looks like a ghost and uses long-range death-magic spells. I hope this information will help you somehow."

The second message came from a character I didn't know and contained an emblem in the header that looked like gold coins. That must have meant the sender had sprung for paid postage. I heard that there were various ways of sending messages long distance in the game, even for a thousand kilometers, but the price of the service, as a rule, was prohibitive to a normal player. All the same, this player could afford the indulgence:

Mariam Standing_Right_Behind_You [GOONS]
Moon Elf
Level-197 Assassin

Even before I'd opened the letter itself, I could already tell by the clan name that something unpleasant was awaiting me. And I wasn't wrong:

"Little goblin, you killed one of my Goons. *To make matters worse, you made a laughing stock of my clan by throwing my player to that cohort of cowards, who only managed to take down my PK-ers as a group. Such offenses cannot be forgiven.*

Perros Ruthless has been kicked out of the Goons, because he brought shame on the clan. There are always plenty of players waiting to join us, though, so the vacant place will soon be taken. I have placed a bounty on your head of five thousand coins. The player that manages to get the prize is guaranteed a spot in the Goons' ranks. And it should be said that I promised to seriously consider all those who kill you after that, even though they will not receive the bounty. That will be valid for the next two weeks.

I wish you the best of luck, goblin! Your next fourteen days will be unforgettable!
Mariam Standing_Right_Behind_You, Leader of the clan [GOONS]"

What a witch! She paid for my murder, and also declared that taking my life would serve as a kind of entrance exam for all kinds of mindless killers, as savage as her. I read in the *Boundless Realm* forums that there was very severe competition between players for the right to join the top clans. And the *Goons*, with all their nasty reputation, were in the one hundred strongest clans of the Southern Continent...

What could I say? I had to spend the next two weeks constantly thinking up ways to make the lives of the murderers coming after me as hard as possible. I'd have to travel a lot, not stay too long in one place, avoid meeting players, only come into the game at night... Basically, I could no longer leave work due to the constant attention of PK-ers!

Alright, unwelcome thoughts aside, I needed to get down to business. For some reason, Tamina Fierce limped up to the Cursed House and was claiming it as her own. Where did I stand at the beginning of my fifth game session?

Name	Amra
Race	Goblin Vampire
Class	Herbalist
Experience	54535 of 64000
Character level	21
Hit points	183/183
Endurance points	156/156
Statistics	
Strength (S)	22 (22)
Agility (A)	21 (55.4)
Intelligence (I)	5 (13)
Constitution (C)	24 (30)
Perception (P)	3 (12.7)
Charisma (Ch)	42 (52)
Unused points	0
Primary skills (5 of 5 chosen)	
Herbalism (P A)	4
Trading (Ch I)	10
Alchemy (I A)	11
Dodge (A P)	7
Stealth (A C)	12
Secondary skills (5 of 5 chosen)	
Veil	3
Acrobatics	6
Exotic Weapons	5
Athletics	6
Foreman	3

Yes, the director was absolutely right: my Herbalism skill was in an embryonic state and looked abominable in comparison with my Stealth. I would have to correct the imbalance and pull that skill up, as it was considered a priority for my herbalist. So then, the world around me lit up and I found myself on the second floor of the Cursed House. Even from here, I could hear the shouts and swearing in the yard. My immediate intervention was clearly needed. But, before going down the stairs, I drank some elixir of beauty I'd prepared just in case. I discovered the recipe last night. It was a three-ingredient potion and was fairly hard to prepare. It raised my character's charisma by a whole nine points for a few minutes, which, along with persuasiveness, was key for the conversation I was about to have.

The sun had already dipped below the horizon, so I walked out fearlessly onto the porch. In the yard, Tamina Fierce was standing and shouting hysterically with her hands on her hips. Around her were her children, who had determined looks on their faces.

"Here's the owner of the house!" shouted the wood nymph, blocking the way onto the porch, her green hair bristling threateningly. She stepped aside with clear relief. A little level-9 wolf pup hurried off after its master, along with a whole swarm of tiny multicolored wasps that flitted before my eyes. They must have been my sister's new pets.

I got down from the porch and looked at the high-level goblin. First of all, I noticed that Tamina Fierce's hand was badly burned and wrapped in rags, and her dress and leather apron were gaping with a lot of burn holes. The goblin woman was also wearing a black mourning scarf on her head. How many children did she have? Eleven, I seemed to remember. Now I saw only six, though, including Irek and Yunna, who were also standing next to their mother.

Taking my silence as a signal to spring into action, the big fat level-eighty goblin warrior took a decisive step toward the door, starting to howl as she moved:

"What is the meaning of this? I'm a widow with many children and I don't even have a roof over my head. These undying, meanwhile, built themselves a real mansion! Huh? You better find you tongue now, tiny, before I get really mad and wreck everyone here!"

The woman made a resolute charge forward like a tank, but I didn't let her pass by. Tamina stopped literally a step from me, towering over my short character by a whole head. I didn't see any weapons on the goblin lady, but a warrior of that level could kill my big-eared Amra even with a simple punch. Sensing the danger, VIXEN hissed and came down from my arm to the ground, striking a threatening pose. Also, White Fang was standing at my legs, baring his teeth at the uninvited guest.

"Tamina, you have lost five children and your house in last night's deplorable attack on Tysh. But what do I have to do with this? I was always good to your children. I gave them work and paid them fairly for their labor. The fact that Irek and Yunna are alive and well right now is down to me and me alone. I gave them a roof over their heads, food, safety and well-paid work. And after that kindness to your children, you still dare come to me with grievances?!"

Successful check for Yunna and Irek's opinion
Experience received: 80 Exp.

.

Successful Charisma check
Experience received: 80 Exp.

Foreman skill increased to level 4!

VIXEN, at my feet, lit up in colorful sparkles, having reached level six and growing immediately by ten centimeters in length. Through the skin on the sides of the small wyvern, two pairs of rudimentary protuberances started sticking out — the first signs of her future feet. While Tamina was looking at my evolved mount, Taisha stood up decisively behind me, and Akella and Blanca also came closer, no longer preparing to sit this out. Not losing any time, I tried to build on my success:

"Tamina, this forest blockhouse is mine! Only I have the right to decide who may settle here. And only I know the horror that inhabits the Cursed House and has been killing its inhabitants. If I leave, the Cursed House will very quickly become a tomb for you and your children. Think about that before you try to kick me out."

Successful check for Tamina Fierce's opinion.
Experience received: 400 Exp.

My argument clearly hit its mark. Irek even joined my side outright, leaving his mother and coming to stand next to me. The older son's opinion of what was happening had a strong influence on Tamina. She unclenched her fists and slumped right over, now looking somehow about half as big as before.

"But what else can I do?" The spite and rage had left the woman's voice, now bearing only immeasurable weariness and desolation. "Last night, I lost everything. I have nowhere to go..."

Tamina Fierce was only a computer program, just like her children. Nothing but a soulless array of zeros and ones. You might think, "hey, what do any of their made-up problems have to do with me?" But all the same, I couldn't just turn away and leave the NPC woman in a difficult situation. I had to help her. But, considering Tamina's high level, I had to make sure her position in my group was clear from the outset, so the strong warrior wouldn't try to make a claim for more later.

"Listen carefully, Tamina. I will only help you under these terms. There won't be any negotiation, and I will not repeat myself. You and your children may stay on the first floor of the Cursed House for precisely three days, and not one minute longer. And at that, you and your children are categorically forbidden from entering the second floor. Up there is my personal bedroom, along with other things you have no business going into. That includes my alchemy laboratory, which has many dangerous and deadly ingredients, so one false move could end in your death or the complete destruction of the whole building."

Trading skill increased to level 11!

That message came in at an odd time, confirming that I was on the right track. So, I continued my speech:

"Over the next three days, this ogre fortifier," here I pointed to Shrekson, "will build a spacious house for you and your children in the village of Tysh. He, of course, won't be able to do it alone, so you and your oldest children will help the ogre.

This is in your own best interest. It would be even better if your goblin neighbors helped as well."

Tamina Fierce began thinking and answered me with sadness in her voice:

"Sounds good, but I have no way of repaying the ogre for his work..."

Yunna tugged on her mother's sleeve and whispered something into her ear. Tamina asked her something and Yunna nodded in response.

"The only thing I can offer, Amra, is to leave Yunna here as a maid for as long as it takes to pay you back."

I didn't manage to answer, as my attention was caught by the strange behavior of the Gray Pack. The wolves next to me turned their heads in unison, as if tracking something moving in Stealth mode. Remembering what had happened yesterday with the high-level illusionist, who had somehow found his way to my shelter, I put up my guard and tried to put the wolves between myself and the potential invisible player. And it was just in the nick of time!

Successful Agility check!
Experience received: 80 Exp.

Dodge skill increased to level 8!

Perros Ruthless fell out of Stealth mode, having tried and failed to stab me in the back with a dagger. Literally one moment later, VIXEN stuck her teeth into the assassin, not letting the enemy run away. A second later, the unfortunate assassin took a powerful punch to the ear from Tamina Fierce and flew toward the blockhouse wall, falling to the ground like a broken doll. He was immediately swarmed by the wolves of the Gray Pack, and ripped to shreds.

Experience received: 15300 Exp.

Level twenty-two!
Racial ability improved: 45% Resistance to Cold

Achievement unlocked: Player killer (3)

The others gathered were obviously confused and only now, when it was all over, did they begin squawking animatedly. I though, was slightly losing my mind from the abundance of experience that fell into my lap. As far as I knew, this was a repeat of the situation where I'd gotten extra experience for killing a player together with an NPC village guard. But this time, instead of it being the goblin warrior Tarek Bigfoot, it was Tamina Fierce, a different goblin warrior. I was reminded of the fact that the director promised me lots of trouble if I purposefully took a key NPC guard out of a village to farm experience. But how was I at fault for the fact that Tamina and her children had wandered over to the Cursed House on her own initiative?!

"What a strange snake..." the naiad even got down on his haunches, looking at VIXEN, who was curled up in a ball at my feet. "She's... unique! That's actually no snake at all!" In the voice of the fish-man there was a mixture of delight and surprise.

And then, I was visited by a thought that almost made me shout out loud: my enemy had also seen the wyvern! And, even if he'd been rushing to kill me and hadn't looked particularly hard at the surrounding NPC creatures, he would soon see in the logs that he'd been bitten by a royal forest wyvern, and he'd know everything! I needed to edit his logs right away!!! I selected the Veil icon and barely managed to correct the logs in time. Now, it no longer said "VIXEN. Royal Forest Wyvern," but "Venomous Whipsnake."

Veil skill increased to level 4!

I wasn't totally sure I'd managed in time, though. Perhaps the secret of my flying mount was revealed, but I was still breathing a bit easier. And by the way, how had we allowed a murderer to attack me in our defended enclosure? I frowned and asked harshly, turning to everyone at once, and no one in particular:

"Why gates is like unbutton pants?! That Perros is clown. Dumb like oak. Want killing me yesterday, idiot. Have taste for me. But other undying walking here-by, too. And close is living midnight wraith. For he, eat flesh of us in Cursed House is big tasty treat. Order for all! Door is locked all of time. When gate need opening, call wolves Gray Pack. They smell hidden one!"

The ogre and the naiad ran to close the gates. Tamina's children also dashed off to help. When I had calmed down a bit, I looked at the time, noting when my enemy would be respawning. It was important. Having attacked me, he gave himself the "Criminal" marker, depriving himself of the ability to leave *Boundless Realm* until it was removed.

Yesterday, I'd been hoping that a few deaths in a row would be a good lesson for Perros Ruthless not to mess with my little bat-eared goblin. But the incident today showed that I was seriously mistaken, and the assassin was still trying to get his revenge. Even if the motive for the attack was not personal revenge, but a desire to earn forgiveness and rejoin the *Goons*, it didn't change a thing. This mental midget apparently hadn't figured it out the first time, and that was all the worse for him. It wasn't that I was feeling vindictive, but for my own mental state, I needed to teach my enemy another lesson. I decided I would meet him at the respawn point and punish him a few times, reducing his experience and levels. And, if this was how it was... could I by chance invite Tamina to help us, and make it even more worth our while?

"Tamina, thank you! Your timely interference helped me dispatch the killer. With your help, you fully paid for the building of the house. And, if your children manage to gather the forest plants I told them to, I'll make you a healing balm for your burns."

The austere woman smiled. Her opinion of me had clearly improved.

Mission completed: Socialization 3/3
Reward: 8000 Exp.

Level twenty-three!
Racial ability improved: 50% Resistance to Poison

Wow, a real red-letter day!!! VIXEN, at my feet, wound herself into a Christmas wreath, having reached levels seven, eight and nine in the last few minutes. The wyvern's front legs were now fully formed and good enough to walk on. And also, the little beads on her back had grown larger. Through the thin, almost transparent skin, I could see the contours of her future wings.

In that neither Tamina nor the others were approaching the corpse of Perros Ruthless, I was first to take a look at the trophies dropped by the assassin. Other than seventy coins and a vial of human blood, I discovered an object, the contours of which were outlined with a green halo:

Elegant Dagger of Blood-Spilling (object from the Shadow Killer set)
Damage: 2-5*Agility, +3% chance of critical hit, 16% chance of causing 5 seconds of bleeding damage

It took me some time to realize what I was seeing. A hand-held weapon that had agility instead of strength governing the damage it dealt! What a rarity! In that my Trading skill allowed me to have a good idea of prices, I saw that the value of the dagger should have been no less than one thousand coins, and more likely was near two thousand. But for me, without the Dagger skill, it wasn't very useful. And also, the chance of losing such a valuable object was too high, given that I would be killed repeatedly for the next two weeks on orders from the *Goons'* clan leader.

So, I called Taisha and handed the dagger to her. The beautiful redhead looked at me incredulously, then quickly hid the weapon and took a decisive step forward, giving my big-eared Amra a kiss to the hooting and hollering of Tamina Fierce's children. And then, after taking a step back, the girl suddenly burst into tears:

"Amra, I'm a blithering idiot! Today, I was in Tysh and saw the remnants of the burnt houses and all the corpses first-hand. I helped my father bury my older sisters. And then, in shock from what I'd seen, I was powerless to refuse Tarek Bigfoot. I promised that I would go to a suitor competition tomorrow and agreed to marry the winner. Amra, I made the promise, and now I cannot break it!"

God, damn it! All my joy from leveling up twice flew away in an instant. Taisha was too valuable a companion to let her go to some coarse NPC goblin, who surpassed my character in nothing but strength and agility. I got an idea...

"But Taisha, what about your other promise? To stay with me as long as I kept working to find the people who murdered your sisters? I will not drag your husband along on our journeys!"

The girl took a heavy sigh and started thinking. And together with her, the whole world around also "started thinking." The image started looking like a slide show made of individual slides.

"I'm lagging really bad over here!" said the wood nymph, confirming my feeling. "Should I log out and start the game up again?"

"That won't be necessary. It will pass soon. The same thing happened yesterday. The programmers said that it's some fault in Taisha's logic, making her use a huge amount of system resources." I said in normal language, as I wasn't sure my friends would understand such a complex idea if I were intentionally warping my words.

"Amra, admit it, what did you say to her to make 'your girly' freeze up instead of answer?" my sister laughed, mocking me for my sharp tongue.

"Would you look at that! She really did freeze up!" Max waved his hands a few times before the eyes of the redhead and, before Taisha reacted at all, brazenly pawed at the paralyzed girl's breasts, the shapes of which were perfectly visible through the thin, form-fitting fabric.

And he got a smack from me for his wandering hand.

"What was that for, Amra?!" objected the naiad with blind sincerity. "That wasn't just for fun. It was to check something! My Lothario skill is frozen and I can't train it on anyone!"

"Well, you didn't have to train it like that..." what I wanted to do was point to Tamina Fierce, but I met with an aggressive look from the high-level goblin and didn't finish my sentence. For obvious reasons, I was not going to suggest Yunna or her very small sister whose name I'd forgotten, so I just squashed the topic.

Instead, I walked over to the frozen Taisha and, after a heavy sigh, suggested the ogre carry her inside the house. A slightly mean-spirited thought flickered through my mind. It occurred to me that it would be better if the girl didn't reactivate until tomorrow's suitor contest, and I even thought I should perhaps give her a couple of Vampire Bites to make her sleep through the objectionable event. But still, I refused such an inelegant approach. Sure, my character didn't have much strength or agility, but I did have something that separated all living players from NPC's: human cleverness.

*   *   *

The order of the day for the players on the second floor of the Cursed House were four basic questions. First: how to help the naiad trader get the last four levels he needed before the end of the last day of his trial period. Second: what should we all do given that there was a bounty on my head and, in the near future, we could expect attacks from all kinds of off-kilter murderers. Third: the quest with the suitor contest had gone from a mere formality to being quite important, and my Amra had to take part in it and win in order not to lose the unique NPC companion, Taisha. And fourth: night would fall in one hour, and I suggested we deal with the wargs once and for all today so they wouldn't terrorize our Gray Pack even one more night.

I was primarily the one who spoke, and the other players listened carefully. Above all else, I told my friends the story of my getting VIXEN, then told them about my plans for the near future:

"This will be quite a night of blood, but the experience we all get from it should be considerable. To start, in a half hour, we should meet Perros Ruthless when he respawns and send that goon back for another hour of inactivity. The assassin is missing one of his daggers, but still presents a serious threat. The problem is that we won't be able to bring any NPC helpers with us. They have a programmed-in rule saying that they can't come near the respawn stone. So, we'll have to handle the high-level player with our own strength, then repeat the trick another three times before daybreak. With every death, the enemy will lose levels, and become a worse experience farm, but still, Max Sochnier has to use this source fully if he wants to pass the trial period."

Everyone went silent. No objections or commentary followed. My voice lowered to a whisper, as if someone might actually have overheard us. Then, I continued:

"There's one other important aspect that I discovered by chance. If Tarek Bigfoot or Tamina Fierce, key NPC guards of the village of Tysh, do fight on our side, the experience will be calculated by a different formula, and we would get several times more. I'm planning to bring Tamina into the scrap with the wargs at least. But why shouldn't we play around with the rules a bit? Tamina could stand as far away from the respawn point as the laws of *Boundless Realm* allow, then when Perros Ruthless appears, she could simply hit him with a rock from a slingshot. That would mean the NPC guard was technically participating in the battle. What do you say, Max? The experience is more important to you than the others, so I'd like to hear your opinion."

The fish-man spent a long time wriggling his fleshy lips in a funny manner, thinking over the situation and making calculations in his head, so he answered nowhere near immediately.

"I need twenty-three thousand experience points to hit level twenty. On the one hand, that is a great amount, almost as much as I've gotten in the last six days put together. But I've got a few interesting quests in the old war chest, and I'm counting on them all coming through. First of all, I've got a mission from a Stonetown elder to dive in the swamp at the location of the battle of the two clans and search for treasure there. I plan on doing that tomorrow morning. Another quest I got from the village of Tysh. I have until tomorrow evening to take the place of their dead merchant, some old miser or something."

"Nyle Miser died?!" I shouted in horror. "How can that be? I mean, he had a portal to the city of Weiden. He could have fled at any moment!"

"What I was able to find out was that, during the attack on the village, the old goblin trader threw everything he was preparing to sell off his cart, loaded it up with wounded goblin women and children and sent the whole mess through the portal to safety. He himself stayed to defend Tysh and died alongside the chieftain in the defense of the main gates. His trading house, as strange as it may seem, was undamaged and not even too badly looted by the undying. The trader was survived by a nephew who is already aware of the death of his uncle and should soon take his place. I was given the mission of temporarily overseeing the goods and helping his takeover of the business. The quest was quite rare, and coincidentally went with my profession. It gives four thousand experience points, but much more importantly to my future, it gives me the reputation of an honest trader with good bonuses in negotiations. And the second stage of the Socialization quest is also connected with completing both quests, as it will give enough increased opinion to finish it as well. So, in one day, I will be able to get twelve thousand experience, which is half of the total I need. If my calculations are correct, for killing the assassin and the pack of level-fifty wargs, I'll get another fifteen thousand minimum. That's more than enough to pass the trial period, and I see no reason to fudge the rules and ask for trouble. We could all get fired for cheating, after all. Basically, I'm in favor of playing honestly!"

"Then we should hurry!" The ogre fortifier stood up from the floor with determination.

"There's just a half hour left before the assassin comes back, and we still need to get to the respawn point. Don't forget, friends, I have to go on foot. The wolves won't be able to carry me."

* * *

"Oof, we barely made it! Let me get some rest now!" gasped Shrekson, flopping back onto the humming stone, his arms thrown to the sides and his heavy hammer on the ground.

Despite his significant reserve of endurance points, our ogre was completely worn out from the run. For such a massive creature, moving quickly was highly unnatural and wasted a great deal of strength. Not good! Not good at all! With alarm, I looked at the timer. There was just two minutes before my enemy would respawn, and our biggest soldier, who I was planning to use as a tank to absorb damage from the dangerous high-level enemy, was completely burned out and couldn't stand.

Max Sochnier, our other close-combat fighter, felt alright and was showing optimism and readiness for battle, stretching out his muscles, trident in hand. But I wasn't especially counting on the naiad. I actually should have been protecting him. He couldn't afford to die. He just needed one or two stabs from his long weapon to be considered a participant, nothing more. As for me and the wood nymph, though, we were supposed to attack long-range in the upcoming battle, me with my blowgun and my sister with her combat magic. We were supposed to deal most of the damage to Perros Ruthless while the close-combat fighters handled the assassin up close.

The Gray Pack wouldn't be taking part in the battle and was lying on the grass a bit down the hill. For the umpteenth time this game session, I opened the wolf-control interface. In comparison with the previous day, nothing had changed. No additional functions or privileges had been added. Where were the changes the director had promised?! Were the programmers sleeping or something?

I walked up to the middle of the humming stone and looked around. It was quickly growing dark. After the battle, we would have just twenty minutes to get back to the shelter before night fell. Hopefully, the ogre would have enough endurance to reach the Cursed House in time. So, there was just one minute left...

"One minute," my sister confirmed, flexing her fingers to prepare to cast a spell.

And then... From the corner of my eye, I caught some movement flying past from the right and instantly turned toward it, but didn't see anything there. Was I just imagining things? Or... Without thinking it through, I jumped forward, my arms splayed to the sides.

Successful Agility check.
Experience received: 40 Exp.

Acrobatics skill increased to level 7!

My fingers caught on something mobile, and I managed to grab onto it. Perros Ruthless appeared literally right in front of my face and, I grabbed him tighter and I rolled over the rune-engraved stone. Ow! That hurt! The assassin worked his dagger into my flesh below the ribs up to the very handle.

Damage taken: 178 (204 Dagger strike from player Perros Ruthless - 26 armor)
Health level: 17/195

If it hadn't been for the leather vest Amra was wearing and the chain mail under it, one blow would have been more than enough to send my big-eared goblin to respawn. But now, the situation was critical. My character had no chance of surviving another dagger strike and, after that, the assassin would go invisible again, then mow down my companions one after the other. With both hands, I latched into Perros Ruthless's wrist, not letting the assassin remove the dagger protruding from my body.

~ Video Game Plotline Tester ~

Successful Strength check.
Experience received: 40 Exp.

Damage taken: 6 (32 Dagger strike from player Perros Ruthless - 26 armor)
Health level: 11/195

Ha! My enemy's strength wasn't so impressive, after all! The killer was not able to free his hand, and the punches Perros Ruthless threw after that, which depended on raw strength, were not at all crushing blows. Clearly, the assassin's statistics were skewed severely to agility, which explained the daggers with their unusual damage stat.

+2 HP from Regeneration

Just in time! And just then, VIXEN came to my rescue, sinking her toxic teeth into my enemy's leg. It wasn't coming together so terribly. I was still alive and my friends would probably be coming to my aid at any second. Despite the shooting pain in my side, I smiled at my enemy. Perros, his face distorted in rage, tried to pull his dagger out again, and again it was of no use, but then... he tried to bite me! I barely managed to jerk my nose out of his way before the man's teeth clapped into thin air. A foolish thought crossed my mind that I should show my opponent how to really give a proper bite, but I threw it out on the spot. Even death wouldn't be as terrifying to me as revealing the secret of my vampirism. For some reason, he didn't try to land another punch. Instead, the assassin stretched his left hand around my back.

I didn't understand what Perros was thinking, and that scared me more than anything. But where were my allies? They should have come to help me long ago and attacked my enemy while he was still visible and I was holding him! My head turned, I saw the naiad ten meters from me gripping his trident confused and frozen, and the ogre just barely getting to his feet. Not good! They were both too far away to help me. All my hope rested only in the wood nymph. But, instead of casting something deadly and destructive, Val just sent her bees in our direction. In the second that followed, I saw Perros's hand flying at my chest with another dagger, clearly taken from his inventory. There was nothing I could do to stop my death now. The world went dark.

You have died.
8064 Exp. lost
One level lost!
Current character level: twenty-two
Resistance to Poison decreased to 45%
You will respawn in 59 minutes, 58 seconds at the respawn point you set

I threw back the top of my virtual reality capsule and crawled out, banging my fist on the wall of my cabin in vexation. Devil! It was four against one, but we did a bad job staying coordinated, so we failed the simplest task! Now, all that remained was to wait until the invisible Perros killed all my allies. Then, if he wanted to, he could just wait for us to respawn and go back into the game and kill us another time.

I mean, where had we learned to bungle a battle so epically?! The naiad and the ogre, sure. They had no PvP experience at all. But Val and I knew computer games inside-out, having gone through thousands of battles and should have been able to act more reasonably. I didn't even get a single strike on my opponent. I had only taken damage. Meanwhile, Valerianna could have at least sent one icy arrow or tried to freeze him. I mean, she could have gotten at least some use out of her magic. Ugh...

I noticed the flashing of an opened chat window on the screen. Someone wanted to start a conversation with me. The player's name was something strange — support_092, just one word instead of two, and the class wasn't shown. It took me only a few seconds to figure out that it was no player at all.

"Hello! I made a way for you to control the wolves of the Gray Pack. Take a look. Is it what you

wanted, or not? It was just that the technical specifications from your division weren't very clear. In the game algorithms, there's no 'not totally admin privileges' option available."

Ugh. Where was he before?! I'd been checking regularly all evening to see if the Gray Pack control functions had appeared, but now... How could I look? I was dead, and I had a black screen instead of *Boundless Realm*! Nevertheless, I didn't voice my concerns to the corporate employee, instead writing politely that I wasn't able to answer his question for the next hour or so, as I was dead and waiting to respawn. His reply came back almost instantly:

"Well, I've gotta run. My official work day ended a while ago. So, I'll explain to you in words what I did and you tell me if that's good enough or not, and whether I can mark the request as complete. In old versions of the game, there was a Fenrir profile. I took that as a basis and made it possible for you to change the wolves' perks once a day and give them orders at a distance of up to ten kilometers. It doesn't give admin privileges, or increase the Gray Pack's limit or level, but it basically does solve all the issues from the technical request. In order to attach these abilities in some sort of tangible form, I added the indestructible Ring of Fenrir to your inventory, which gives these powers. It's unique, so no one else can take control of the Gray Pack. Sound

good?"

I could barely hold back the cry of glee that was tearing itself from me. It was even more than I'd asked for! I could now control the Gray Pack at a distance, and change their abilities once per day to suit whatever task I was working on. But I didn't agree right away, instead telling him my wish:

"I've got a serious conflict with PK-ers here. I'm being hunted and I'm on the run. So, there's a risk the Ring of Fenrir will drop if I get killed again. Is there any way you could protect the artifact?"

"I can't protect it all the way. That would be against the rules. As it's an object with active properties, I cannot hide it fully, either. Other players from Boundless Realm *will at least visually be able to see your ring. As a compromise solution, I could give the ring the attribute 'Cursed Unremovable.' That way no one could take it without your permission. But it would also be quite torturous to you if you ever wanted to take it off. Getting rid of cursed objects is very, very difficult. Even if you chopped off your own hand, the ring would remain with you."*

I thought it over and agreed to that option. The man stayed silent for a few minutes, then wrote:

"Alright, that will be all. As soon as you put the ring on, its properties will be activated. And, it should be said that another complaint has come in from the Data Processing Center. It seems that your

NPC companion is constantly freezing up? I've reset her. But perhaps, if she keeps freezing, could I just delete her?"

"No, no. Not on your life!" I grew afraid for Taisha's fate. "I provoked the last lag on purpose. We were looking for an error in the logic of the advanced NPC and we made a situation where two mutually exclusive actions came into conflict. Thank you for resetting her. And, by the way, the next predictable character freeze-up could be avoided. To do that, you should make sure it's cloudy tomorrow from six in the morning until sunset in the area around the NPC village of Tysh in the Lars province. Otherwise, there will be two mutually exclusive quests, and another logic error."

"Thanks for the warning. That's easy. The weather is simple to adjust. Would you like rain or not? What radius from the village?"

"Rain won't be necessary. It would actually be better without. The most important thing is to make thick clouds in a radius of twenty kilometers from Tysh so the sun won't peek out for even a second!"

He promised to arrange for the weather I needed and signed off. Great! Simply wonderful! I had managed to make sure tomorrow would be a cloudy day for the suitor competition. I wasn't worried about negative consequences, as I easily could prove to the director that it had been a necessary measure. If my Amra wasn't at the competition, Taisha would freeze up again because she wouldn't be able to keep a promise she made before the gods themselves. My cell phone rang abruptly, tearing me from my contemplation. It was my sister. I tensed up inside, expecting to hear that my team had been completely defeated, so Valeria's first words forced me to shout in glee:

"All in all, we managed, though we did lose you and Shrekson. You did an awesome job holding the assassin at the very beginning, keeping him visible. After that, I sicced my hornets on him, to keep him visible. Then, the naiad made a successful strike with his trident, holding him in place, and the ogre held the assassin in his big mitts while I cast spell after spell. Shrekson, unfortunately, didn't make it. We just needed a few more seconds. But the drop from Perros Ruthless was rich: a rare belt improving agility and almost fifteen hundred coins. Your chainmail dropped from you. I grabbed it. I'll set it on the stone before you reappear. We didn't go back to the Cursed House. We'll wait for you to come back for the next battle with Perros."

* * *

There was a large amount of time remaining until I would respawn, so I got dressed and left my work cabin. First of all, I noticed that the red light above the door of box number twenty was lit — Kira was already at work. After that, I noticed Leon standing near the coffee machine rifling through his pockets in search of a coin. I walked over to my friend and placed my card against the machine, paying for his purchase. Leon thanked me, then suddenly got embarrassed and lowered his eyes.

"Timothy, I shouldn't have died. It's just that Perros got a crit, and I only had a few hitpoints left, then a second later, I had none..."

The former construction worker waved his hand in vexation, having totally forgotten that he was holding a cup of coffee in it. Leon went silent, looked at the spilled drink and grew even more embarrassed. I ordered another and gave it to him.

"We all made a couple dumb mistakes. The fight went by so fast. At least our deaths weren't in vain. The enemy didn't escape. The naiad and the nymph managed to take him down. Our friends didn't go back to the Cursed House, so there will be another round of battle with the assassin and we need to make sure we're better prepared next time. Above all else, we need to figure out how to hold that tricky bastard in place and keep him visible. Otherwise, he'll just camouflage himself immediately."

"Hmm... Maybe we could get him trapped in a net?" Leon suggested, not at all confident.

I raised my eyes to him, my interest piqued,

as I waited for him to finish, but the burly construction worker totally lost his nerve:

"Well... you see... I made a new warg trap today... From the tower near the wall, if you shoot a net from the ballista, you can cover a big area in front of the gates. I have one net left. I folded it near the wolf house..."

A throwing net? That could be quite the interesting prospect. It could be used with the Exotic Weapons skill, which I just so happened to have! There was no more need to get near the dangerous enemy and expose myself to his strikes. With every passing second, Leon's plan seemed more and more appealing. I took out my phone and called my sister.

"Val, Leon thought up a great idea! Before night falls, ride Blanca as fast as you can to the Cursed House. There, next to the wolf house, Leon set a throwing net. You should bring it to the respawn point and set it on the stone so I can pick it up. We've got a plan to kill Perros Ruthless without any losses this time."

For the umpteenth time, I found myself in admiration of my sister. Valeria didn't even ask any questions, just added that she'd make sure the net was properly folded when she placed it so I could use it right away. When I'd already put my phone back in my pocket, I was suddenly visited by a belated thought: why should the former builder have been looking for coins when I'd just sent him three thousand credits?

I asked Leon that question. He grew all the more embarrassed and sputtered out something indistinct about already having lent the money to a good friend of his. Just then, Veronica walked out of the seventh cabin and immediately locked the door behind her with a magnetic card. She gave a friendly nod to the husky Leon and noticed me only after, then stopped abruptly.

"Timothy, I really want to talk to you. Could you please walk me to the elevator?"

Though I was surprised, I followed after the beautiful woman. Veronica got a small mirror out of her purse, fixed her fashionable chestnut hair, and handed me her surprisingly heavy bag. As soon as we'd turned a corner and were out of earshot of Leon, the girl stopped abruptly and blocked my path with her arm.

"There's a big mirrored cabinet next to our boss's office door, and you can see a bit of the hallway in it. Timothy, I saw you there when the director was blowing up at me."

The girl went silent, expecting me to react to her words in some way. But I stayed silent, not confirming Veronica's words, but also not denying them.

"I don't know what you managed to hear, but I want to let you know: everything is fine with me. I'm still the most successful tester of our group and the only one who has reached level twenty-five. The new director appreciates me. But in large part, I don't need to work here anymore anyway. I've got enough money to live the rest of my life on already. I've got almost eight thousand subscribers, who pay around ten credits per day for the privilege of watching my streams. I could just start playing *Boundless Realm* as a normal player and provide them more of the same content they've come to expect. But I would prefer to stay with the corporation for now. So, I ask you, Timothy, don't let any of our coworkers know about my temporary hardships. Yes, today my character was in a difficult spot, but the dryad has already gotten out of it. And she did it on her own, without any help from tech support. Got it? It's important to me. If need be, I could pay you off to stay quiet."

Who did she take me for? A no-good blackmailer? I hurried to dispel my coworker's fears.

"Veronica, I did in fact overhear a small fragment of your conversation with the director. Something about pirates and a wild animal incursion. It is not in my habit to talk about someone behind their back, though. And I'm even less prone to spreading gossip, so you don't have to worry about me. Play however you like. I'm not planning to interfere with your gameplay in any way. But if you're looking for my advice, if I've understood your situation correctly, you could ask tech support for much less than a pirate attack. A new loincloth or a chastity belt should do the trick... or what do dryads have by default there? Tech support would surely agree to that."

I was basically saying rational things, but Veronica just laughed a happy sonorous laugh in response:

"What made you think I lost my loincloth? I've got the situation under control. My clothing is in my inventory, and could be put on at any time. It's just that I don't want my viewers to know that."

The elevator arrived. The girl took her bag back from me, sending me a kiss in the air to remember her by, then disappeared behind the closing doors. I returned to the break zone just then and found Leon sitting in deep thought with an empty glass of coffee in his hands.

"I'm trying not to fall asleep," he commented. "All day, I've been digging, sawing and building... And there's also the burned village of Tysh. There are still ruined homes and burned corpses everywhere. I've never been this tired before in my life. I'm yawning. I just have no strength left. But it's nothing. We'll deal with Perros and the wargs, then I'll sleep right here in the virtual reality capsule until morning. I can help you with the suitor competition tomorrow, but then I'm taking a whole day off to get some proper sleep."

"Leon, you still need to build a house for Tamina Fierce," I reminded the construction worker, and he nodded wearily.

"I'd totally forgotten. Alright, I'll help with that house. You are counting on me, after all. But after that, I'm taking a few days off. I want to bring my kids to the sea. That should be right after I get the loan back, too."

I thanked my friend for the help, then asked him a question that was on the tip of my tongue:

"That 'good friend' you loaned three thousand to wouldn't happen to be Veronica, would it?"

The weary giant nodded in silence, not beating around the bush or denying it. I started thinking seriously. For some reason, I didn't like that whole story with Veronica. If the girl earned eighty thousand credits per day with her subscribers, why did she take a three-thousand-credit loan?!

Level Twenty-Five

I GOT A MESSAGE that made me cringe before I even opened it. Perros Ruthless had gone so far as to write me. It was the very same assassin who'd just sent my big-eared character to the grave.

"Venomous Whipsnake? That was a good one. I don't know how you hid your wyvern from my logs, but it doesn't matter now. You need to give me a thousand coins today, and another hundred for every day you want me to keep silent. If I don't get the money even once, all of Boundless Realm *will find out about your flying mount. And then, you won't be able to play at all anymore. It will just be an endless cue of constant deaths and respawns. If I see any of your group at the respawn point when*

I come back, you'll get the same. And I expect my dagger back from the set. Set it on the stone. I'll get a reward of five thousand for your head and the word of Mariam Standing_Right_Behind_You [GOONS] herself, promising me a place in the clan as your killer. That will bring me glory and compensation for all the losses. And I will soon get my lost levels back. The Goons clan helps its members grow quickly. You lost, Amra. I won."

My initial instinct was to simply ignore the message from the extortionist, but I decided to answer nevertheless. I just had too much pent-up bile.

"You still aren't getting it, Perros, so I'll explain the situation the way all other players see it. Before you met me, you were a successful assassin at level forty-four. But now, you've fallen to thirty-six, and that's not even the end. We'll bring you down in experience another three times in the next few hours and, after all these encounters, you'll hit level thirty-two, or maybe even thirty-one. You'll have lost thirteen levels in one day. You're an obvious candidate for 'Boundless Realm's most infamous loser.'

Now, as for the money. If you didn't know about the wyvern, that's just evidence of your doltish ignorance. All players interested in the matter already know about my mount and, today, in my next video clip, I'm gonna tell everyone all about my pretty little girl. So here it is again, 'suck on my little green pee-pee.' You don't deserve the money. What's more, five thousand coins is technically what you'll be getting, but your total will be much less. You've already lost more than fifteen hundred coins to us, and in the next three deaths, you'll lose the rest. Beyond the dagger, you've also dropped a belt from the Shadow Killer set, and I'm sure you'll lose a good deal more valuable items before this is all over.

And as for Mariam Standing_Right_Behind_You [GOONS], I'll write to her. I'm not sure the leader of such a famous clan will want to take you back after all the shame you've already brought on her clan. Now that you let yourself get killed by a low-level noncombat character again, all the more so. And yes, just for the record, if you try to attack me or any of my friends after three deaths, we would be more than happy to make sure you fall all the way down to level twenty-five.

I wish you the best of luck, assassin! Your next three hours will be unforgettable!

Amra"

I wrote the letter in an intentionally mocking style, trying to tease my opponent and get a rise out of him. After sending the message, I went and got a can of energy drink in order to chase off my sleepiness, after which I crawled back into my virtual reality capsule. The ogre and I were not criminals, so we could have avoided the risky encounter with the assassin just by waiting to start playing again. But I was fed up with Perros Ruthless and, in that such individuals understood only the language of force, the time had come to prove my threats in practice.

Time! I appeared on the huge, palpably vibrating stone. Over my head, the night sky stretched out, illuminating the earth below with millions of bright stars. I didn't even have to activate night vision, because there was more than enough light already. Near my legs lie my chain mail and the throwing net wrapped into a tight bundle.

"Grab the net and get ready!" I heard my sister cry.

In the real world, taking off my leather vest, putting on the chainmail under it, and putting the vest back on would have taken way too much time. But in *Boundless Realm*, it was all much simpler. I opened my equipment window and placed the chainmail into my empty armor slot, then put my blowgun into my backpack and picked up the throwing net. A few seconds later, I was ready for battle! Max Sochnier was standing next to me with his trident at the ready.

"First, Shrekson will appear, then a few seconds later, our enemy," the naiad warned me.

"Amra, don't you dare go dying again!" Taisha cried, standing at the foot of the hill.

I didn't get distracted from my preparation or ask my sister and the fish-man how the NPC thief had gotten here. Though I restrained myself with much effort, harsh words were ready to rip themselves from my lips. After all, unlike the rest of us, Taisha wouldn't just lose experience, if something went wrong again, but her only life, once and for all. Perros Ruthless would be very out of sorts after reading my message and wouldn't give quarter to any of my companions, if he got the chance.

A few meters from me, Shrekson respawned, turning his head blindly and growing accustomed to the darkness. I then began unraveling my weapon, looking around with my eyes peeled wide. There he was! The assassin appeared for just one second, but that was plenty for me. The throwing net landed neatly on its target, spreading out as it flew.

Exotic Weapons skill increased to level 6!

Trapped in the net, Perros stumbled and rolled on the stone right under Shrekson's legs. With a bang, the ogre fortifier's heavy hammer smashed the assassin's head like a ripe watermelon. To be honest, it almost made me nauseous to watch.

Experience received: 1296 Exp.

My small wyvern began scintillating with colorful little flames, indicating that she had reached level ten. My mount's back legs were now fully formed, and VIXEN now looked like a meter-long emerald green lizard with a hump on her back.

"Hey! You were supposed to be helping me level,'" Max Sochnier said indignantly. "I didn't get a grain of experience!"

"That was too fast. I didn't even manage to get a spell off!" Valerianna Quickfoot walked up to the corpse wrapped in the net and cringed as she saw the pool of blood forming under its mangled skull.

"What can I say? I happened to get a crit. It was my first one..." the huge ogre said, nudging the lifeless body squeamishly with his foot. "How horrid! I barely even want to take trophies from him. I got myself back to level eighteen, and that's good though. Amra, if you want to dig around in those brains and scraps, be my guest."

"So, this stiff is what had you all so scared?" Taisha asked, walking up totally unencumbered to the dead assassin and stopping a meter from his corpse. "Would anyone mind if I took his boots? They look like they were made specially for me!"

I strained to push my fallen jaw back in place. The NPC had walked into a zone that was supposed to be totally off-limits to any computer-controlled creatures or characters! Based on the widened eyes and outstretched faces of the other players, all my companions had also noticed the fact that this should have been impossible.

"Is something the matter?" the attractive goblin asked in surprise, having noticed the reigning silence.

"No, no. Everything's fine," I assured Taisha. "Except for the fact that only the undying are supposed to be able to get near the vibrating stone. Take the boots, just let me look at them first."

Taisha shrugged her shoulders and handed me the pair of soft leather knee-high boots. The trophy footwear was enchanted and gave a bonus to agility, but it wasn't actually from the Shadow Killer set, or even rare. Pshh, the peasant! I was expecting more from Perros Ruthless. Twelve hundred coins, two vials of human blood and a flask of brains (alchemy ingredient) rounded out the take from the assassin. Having decided there were no strangers nearby, I explained in normal, undistorted language:

"Friends, we have a whole hour until our enemy comes back. Feel free to rest for now. I'm going to collect night plants under the protection of the Gray Pack. I need to bring my Herbalism up, and collect ingredients for the burn cream I promised Tamina Fierce. Taisha, I have a big favor to ask you: could you wait for me here on the vibrating rock? You're not ready for night walks through the forest yet."

~ Video Game Plotline Tester ~

I was expecting incensed replies from Taisha, but the beautiful redhead was surprisingly accommodating today and didn't argue.

* * *

After getting away from my companions, I drank down both containers of blood. Half measures, of course. I had long needed to bite someone to death to really sate my Thirst for Blood, but this procedure did give me a few more hours of calm.

After that, I put the Ring of Fenrir on my pointer finger and tested the wolf-control functions. I could give commands from a distance both to the whole pack and to every wolf individually. I could edit the external appearance of each one individually, and change the selected perks. Cool! I didn't change anything yet, just gave the Gray Pack a command to hunt nearby and guard me and VIXEN, who had fled off somewhere in search of adventure.

I had barely begun gathering night plants when I heard an incoming call. A tech support worker called support_211 wanted to have a talk with me.

"Amra, we got a complaint about your in-game behavior. It says here you were engaged in intentional harassment and intimidation, accompanied by multiple murders."

"Well, I guess I'm quite popular with tech support today... Yet I'm not sure I remember pestering or threatening any players, who didn't deserve it."

"His name is Perros Ruthless. According to game logs, he has been killed eight times in the last twenty-six hours and, what's more, four of those deaths involved your character directly. So, the player is fully within his legal rights to complain of harassment and murder."

"So, this cute and fuzzy homicidal maniac is complaining that he's been offended by a low-level non-combat herbalist? Obviously, I've been forcing him to follow me around for two days in a row now. I thought it was allowed to kill players with active criminal status, anyway!"

"Mhm. Of course, it sounds crazy," the employee agreed with me. *"But he did write to support, and he has been killed many times, so we have to show some kind of reaction. Perros Ruthless spends real money to buy game objects, so for the* Boundless Realm *corporation, this client has value and we cannot simply poo-poo his problems. The player is asking us to change his respawn point to another place. Do you agree with this solution to the conflict?"*

"No, I do not. The player you mentioned has caused me five thousand coins in financial damages, which were supposed to be for my head, and for which I had other plans. As an employee of the *Boundless Realm* corporation, I easily could have exchanged this money for real cash, so it's actually real material damage. Beyond that, because of that assassin, I lost eight thousand experience points, of which I have only restored a bit over a thousand. Third, my companions, a naiad and an ogre, also employees of the *Boundless Realm* corporation are counting on getting compensation from the assassin. He wasted our time, and for testers, time is a very valuable resource. Fourth, I am interested in his unique dagger, paired with one already in possession of my companion Taisha, whose growth is one of my priority missions. This has been agreed on with the director of special projects. Only after these demands are met can the player Perros Ruthless change his respawn point."

"I guess that's what this killer gets for messing with corporate testers... Alright, I'll try talking with him. As for the dagger, I'm not sure. That demand seems too extreme to me, but I'll tell him your terms in any case."

For ten minutes, nothing happened. I went back to gathering plants and even raised my Herbalism to level five. Finally, the support employee came back online.

"Amra, I read your correspondence with Perros Ruthless and that explained a lot. So then, your opponent agreed to give up all the money he has left, two thousand three hundred coins, and

agreed to leave the left-handed dagger from the Shadow Killer set. In addition, he agreed to accept a programmed-in restriction that prevented him from visiting the Lars province again for the next six months.. Every member of your group will be compensated with one thousand experience points, as well. You wouldn't have gotten any more than that from the assassin anyway. Perros Ruthless' respawn point, was changed to his previous one, in the castle of the Goons clan on his request. One last question: is the illusionist Valentin Wise_Wizard, who is also present near the respawn stone, in your group? Shall I send him experience as well?"

"Yes, him as well," I wrote, not revealing the fact that his presence was news to me.

"Good. I put almost five thousand kilometers between you and Perros, and you should not be meeting one another for the next six months. I consider this matter settled."

He hung up. I didn't even manage to tell him that Perros had chosen a fairly risky respawn point this time as well. Mariam Standing_Right_Behind_You [GOONS] hadn't yet accepted him back into the clan, and she wouldn't be likely to do so before morning. Almost all clan castles had some kind of security systems in them to kill outsiders, too. So, one more death, and maybe two were practically guaranteed.

Experience received: 1000 Exp.

~ Video Game Plotline Tester ~

2300 coins received

Object received: Luxurious Dagger of the Poisoner (object from the Shadow Killer set)
Damage: 2-5*Agility, +2% chance of critical hit, 10% chance of causing 5 seconds of poison damage

So, my opponent had fulfilled his end of the deal. It felt almost unfair now not to tell the support employee my fears on the assassin's poor choice of new respawn point. So, I called him back.

"I know he made a bad choice. But Perros Ruthless insisted on that exact respawn point. I don't like blackmailers, so I didn't try to talk him out of it. Best of luck to you, colleague!"

I probably should have gone straight back to my friends to tell them we didn't need to stay watching the respawn point any longer. But I held off for a bit. I called up the Gray Pack control window and called the wolves over. At the same time, simply as an experiment, I changed all their coloration to hot pink. The forest predators looked so stupid that I couldn't even look without laughing. That mistake reversed, I tried one of the camouflage options for the Gray Pack suggested in the preset options, made of spots of black, gray and green.

+5% to camouflage in the forest during the day

+7% to camouflage in the forest at night

That's the ticket! I also changed the predators' eye color to bright red, making them a true terror of the forest! I saddled Akella and whistled for VIXEN. The royal forest wyvern came down from the canopy and landed at the trunk of a tree in front of me. In her absence, my emerald green baby had managed to reach level eleven. I commended my excellent pet for her quick development and hurried back to my other friends.

"Amra, for some reason we all just got a thousand experience," Val said when I got there, looking at the camouflaged wolves with some trepidation.

"Yes, this is Amra knowing. Assassin much fearing us. Him praying for gods to help, and now is respawn in other place. Them giving us all thousand experiences. They no want us mad. And Valentin Wise_Wizard mage invisible getting too. Hey, Valentin. Where being?"

On the side of the hill, the level-95 illusionist appeared fifteen steps from me wearing a glistening silver robe with a hood and carrying a carved staff in his hands.

"Oh well. I was just enjoying the fact that I could level my Stealth and Illusion Magic at the same time..." mumbled the half-elf, upset. He then wondered how I'd learned of his presence.

"Man so much powerful like demigod name of 'support.' He tell weak goblin about you. He say he following you close. Too much strong is wizard. Strange for this country."

Of course, I was embellishing the tech-support worker's words, but I really was bothered by the question of what such a strong illusionist was doing in our region, where the monsters were so weak compared to him. He could hardly be here farming experience.

"Dammit. They're watching me... Well sure, I guess I understand. You don't have to worry about me. It wouldn't be worth it for me to hurt any of you. I just came here two days ago on a mission from Alexandro Lavrius. You must know him..."

My big-eared character nodded distinctly. I hadn't forgotten that the head of in-game security had told me a high-level illusionist was supposed to take my wyvern egg on an order from our previous boss.

"Personally, I did not manage to take the snake's treasure from the island and, in that I wasn't involved in the other machinations, when it came time to assign blame, I was just let go quietly. The character was not blocked. They left me with him as a reward for my past service. And I wanted to take the flying mount just for myself, as it would be a free pass into any clan, even the most prestigious. But I saw that you had the green wyvern and I realized I was again too late. I could have just left the region, but now there's something else holding me back. The monster that killed me. Did you find information about it in the bestiary?"

I shook my head, as I hadn't managed to give that much thought yet. But he didn't understand my body language.

"Not surprising that you didn't find it. I've been pouring over all the sections of the *Boundless Realm* bestiary for the last few days, looking at all kinds of ghosts and wraiths. But there was nothing of the sort. Do you follow? It's a totally new beast, and whoever can add information about it will gain fame! I've been trying to track it all day. I even found its lair. But it was empty. It must be a strictly nocturnal creature, which simply doesn't exist during the day. So, I waited for the sun to set, walked around the edge of your forest home and... almost right after nightfall, got killed by that creature once again. It sneaked up on me, attacked me from behind and killed me in just a few seconds, just like the first time. When I respawned, I first thought you were a group of PK-ers hanging around the respawn point, and I wanted to punish you as an example. But there was no criminal marker on any of you, so I just stood and waited."

A private message from my sister distracted

my attention from the high-level illusionist.

"Tim, it would also be great for you to add information on the undiscovered creature into the bestiary. That would raise the fame of your big-eared character and your value to the company. But, it occurs to me that our new acquaintance might be playing a game with us. An unknown beast that lives in a location for new players and can take down a nearly level-one-hundred player in a matter of seconds is something much bigger than just another undiscovered phantom. From what I've read in the game forums, this looks like the beginning of a global quest chain, which should soon sweep over the whole continent. That would be quite the tasty morsel. The tastiest you can find in Boundless Realm, *as a matter of fact. So, let's figure out a way to do this without Valentin Wise_Wizard."*

✽ ✽ ✽

We parted ways with the illusionist uneventfully and peacefully. The high-level wizard was going back to the place where he'd last died to collect some valuable items that had fallen from his inventory. In that it was not far from the Cursed House, Valentin Wise_Wizard agreed to escort our ogre fortifier back to the forest blockhouse at the same time. The wizard refused to show us where the midnight wraith's lair was on the map, and we didn't especially insist.

Shrekson's mission was to prepare his traps for the packs of wargs and crack open the gates for us. Beyond that, the ogre had spent the whole day assembling a huge ballista and he wanted to drag it up into the watchtower by the gates. He didn't have enough strength to carry out his plan alone, but together with Tamina Fierce and her children, Shrekson was able to raise the weapon and attach it to the tower.

The rest of the group was to play the role of "live bait," just like the day before, and lure the wargs to the Cursed House. Considering that we had only survived yesterday's chase by a miracle, the plan looked very dangerous. For that very reason, I wanted to send Taisha back with the ogre. But the thief refused to leave my side, and the extreme danger involved did nothing to convince her. Gifts could sway her, though, and I finally managed to get her to go back safely by giving her the other dagger from the Shadow Killer set and a soft wide belt my sister had picked up, which was from the same set.

"When yes all can ready, ogre write in chat to me," I instructed Shrekson. "After ready your message, we looking wargs. Then we running and lead beasties to blockhouse."

The ogre fortifier and Taisha wished us luck and went with the illusionist to the Cursed House.

We then went to the nearest small river, no more than a humble stream. Max asked us to make this small detour so he could bathe and wet his gills before he dried out. While the naiad was splashing around in the freezing water, I walked along the bank collecting clay, lily pads and other river plants *until* my Herbalism skill reached level six. The experience that gave me brought my character back to level twenty-three. The stat points from that were assigned automatically, just as I had them before. My Resistance to Poison also returned to 50%.

"We are here. Everything is ready. Shrekson Bastard."

The local chat message distracted me from chasing a level-9 river newt. Despite its frightening size, the meter-long black and orange amphibian didn't even think of trying to fight back, it just immediately ran away down a branch of the small stream. I could have killed the newt with one shot from my blowgun, but I wanted to catch up to it, so I could kill it with a bite. I had to level my Taste Tester achievement and refill my Thirst for Blood bar. My prey almost buzzed away from me, but then VIXEN appeared from out of nowhere and intercepted it, clamping down on the newt's back ridge to hold it in place.

Damage dealt: 114 (Vampire Bite)

Experience received: 180 Exp.
Object received: Newt meat (food)

Achievement unlocked: Taste Tester (11/1000)

Racial ability improved: Taste for Blood (Gives +1% to all damage dealt for each unique creature killed with Vampire Bite. Current bonus: 6%)

I was concerned that VIXEN might react negatively to such a clear demonstration of my vampirical nature, but my mount didn't seem to mind my untoward gastronomic urges. She had her own shocking tendencies where food was concerned. And just then, VIXEN, looking very snake-like, unhinged her lower jaw and pulled herself over the newt like a glove.

"What a smart cookie!" I said, praising my emerald wyvern. "You let me sate my Thirst for Blood, and waited your turn to eat. But now, take a seat on my shoulder. We have to ride quickly on wolfback. Woah. Look how heavy you've gotten! It looks like you'll be eating me next. Tomorrow, I won't even be able to carry you anymore."

And so, our small band set out to seek the deadly wargs. Valerianna Quickfoot suggested we begin our search along the road to Tysh where we'd first met the predators. Trying to bring down the danger level somewhat from yesterday, I assigned all members of the Gray Pack the perk Fast Run (+20% to speed). Even though the wolves would still be slower than the long-legged wargs, this would be a great leg-up.

"This is where we encountered them yesterday," said the wood nymph, jumping deftly off Blanca's back and looking down the road. "There are a lot of clawed footprints here. I wish we could figure out who left them and when, or where they lead... Ugh, I wish one of us had the Pathfinder skill or high-level perception. Then, we could make some sense of all these confusing tracks."

At those words, my sister looked at me hopefully, clearly having remembered the goblin racial bonus to perception growth, but I had to disappoint her.

"My effective perception is just sixteen. It's not enough." She herself had told me to put stat points primarily into charisma.

"Amra, stat points have nothing to do with this. If your herbalist did more of what he was made to do, collecting berries and flowers and leveling Herbalism, your perception would be very high, and we wouldn't be in such a difficult situation now."

My sister was right as always. My big-eared green goblin had left Herbalism by the wayside. Even the Director of Special Projects had noticed.

I jumped off the wolf and walked over to the intersecting trails. No, it was useless. I didn't have the requisite stat points to figure out anything. Although... perhaps our companions could help us!

"Akella, I need to figure out where the wargs went. We want to follow them."

The camouflaged wolf looked at me incredulously with his fire-red eyes, as if doubting my order. But all the same, he walked up and started sniffing the grass. Turning around and around near the road, he headed further into the forest with confidence. I caught up to the seasoned wolf and climbed up on his back. Akella spent twenty minutes sniffing and weaving through the forest, gradually getting farther from the road before suddenly we were stopped by the voice of Valerianna Quickfoot:

"You shouldn't go any further. I can see them on the map, three hundred meters to the northwest. Eight red dots in a very tight bunch. It looks like they're feeding. I'll lure them over here, and point them toward the Cursed House!"

My sister waved her arms, and the hornets swarming around her flew in the direction she pointed. I turned Akella toward our house in advance and started waiting for my sister's word that her tactic had worked. Max Sochnier, riding White Fang, was also ready to take off at any second. Finally, Valerianna dug her heels into

Blanca, ordering the she-wolf to move.

"Alright, let's get out of here! The wargs are running in this direction! They see us! They'll be here in ten seconds!"

As the nymph spoke, we heard many creatures howling in unison. Our trio of wolves abruptly burst from their places and carried us at full speed toward the Cursed House. I didn't see our pursuers for quite some time, I only heard their yapping and howling. But a few minutes later, their red markers appeared on the map. The wargs were gradually closing the distance between us. And that was at the fact that our wolves were "modded" for speed. Yesterday's chase through the forest started looking even more senseless and deadly.

Valerianna Quickfoot, racing beside me, tried to talk in short, clipped sentences:

"I can see the Cursed House in front of us. Amra, we're going too fast. We need them to be closer. To get them in the trap! Otherwise, we won't catch the whole pack. We'll have to go on another hunt tomorrow!"

Athletics skill increased to level 7!

My useful increase in strength reserves noted, I answered my sister:

"Good. Amra is agree luring enemy. I say Akella go slower, so they almost-almost is catching we. You just be sure gate get closed behind, so predator pack is not get inside."

My wolf took my idea with extreme disapproval. He was very much opposed to letting the wargs catch up to us in any measure. I suspected that, if it weren't for the Ring of Fenrir on my finger, Akella wouldn't have obeyed. But with it, after a few barks either at me or simply to release his anger, the camouflaged wolf gave a fairly authentic limp with his front left paw and immediately started lagging behind his packmates. From behind me, I heard a triumphant howl. The wargs on our trail, nearing the end of their chase, were really stepping on it.

I steered Akella between the two rows of tall stakes that the ogre fortifier had dug in just today. The narrow corridor was fifteen meters long and ended at the gates themselves.

"Move it, Amra. You're not gonna make it!" Shrekson yelled down from the watchtower. He was manning the ballista and doing his best to hurry me along.

But I didn't push Akella any harder, as I could see the mini map. The first of the wargs had pulled ahead of the pack and was quickly bearing down on me. The remaining seven predators were somewhat behind. It was better to allow one enemy to get dangerously close than to reveal the trap prematurely and let the other seven go. Unfortunately, though, not all of my companions thought the same.

Tamina Fierce, on seeing the warg racing toward her, started closing the gate. Taisha tried to stop her and shouted that I needed to get through first. A commotion arose, preventing the goblin ladies from closing the gates, and the deadly warg burst inside the enclosed area.

Tamina's children, in the yard, scattered with a shriek. I stopped my mount and took the throwing net in my hands but, just then, the warg reached us. Its steel jaws gnashed at my right leg. Akella squealed in pain and fell on his side, rolling over onto his back.

Successful Agility check.
Experience received: 80 Exp.

Dodge skill increased to level 9!

Acrobatics skill increased to level 8!

I jumped off the wolf just in time, rolled over on the grass and jumped to my feet, ready to fight or flee depending on the circumstances. I threw the unfurled net, which I thought would stop the razor-toothed beast. But it was no longer necessary. The black warg was pinned to the ground with a massive arrow like a bug under a thumb tack. The ghastly monster gave a few twitches, and its eyes closed.

Experience received: 2640 Exp.

"Thank you, Shrekson. Perfect timing! That monster could have really made a mess here," Valerianna Quickfoot shouted, jumping down from Blanca's back.

The ogre fortifier gave us a salute from the tower, himself not fully believing he had managed to hit the level-55 warg from the ballista on his first try. I then walked up to Akella, who was still lying on the earth. The wolf was severely wounded. On his back-right leg, a nasty tear wound was pumping blood. The predator's life bar was down in the orange and slowly falling.

The bleeding was an ugly sight, but it wouldn't be deadly. It could be stopped with a bandage, and the wolf's health could be fixed with food. In fact, Tamina Fierce's oldest daughter Yunna had already begun bandaging the wounded beast. What was worse was that Akella had taken a two-day debuff:

Back right leg crippled
For the next two days, this animal will not be able to climb cliffs, perform jumps or be ridden
Movement speed reduced by 50%

I would have to find myself a new mount for the next two days or just go on foot. All the other wolves of the Gray Pack already had other riders, while my VIXEN was still too small to be a suitable mount. I gave Akella a grateful slap on the shoulder and assured the wolf that he could eat his assailant.

"Amra, come on over here! There's an interesting scene that would be good for your video clips!" Shrekson shouted, calling for my attention. I climbed up the ladder to the watchtower.

First, my attention was caught by the ballista. Unfortunately, I wasn't able to control the weapon by myself, as my character did not have the Military Machinery skill, or enough strength. Earlier, I had seen this ballista disassembled on the ground, but now I was looking on the heavy weapon in all its glory. The arc of the gigantic bow was four meters long, and it was attached to a massive sanded-down wooden beam with a special cocking lever attached. The ballista was installed on a rotating mount and used two-meter-long stakes with four-sided wrought-nail tips as ammunition. On the arrow shafts, the ogre had made spikes to cause bloody tear wounds. Assembled, the whole construction weighed probably half a ton, and I looked with respect at Shrekson and Tamina, who had somehow contrived a way to lift the ballista onto the watchtower. From up here, an excellent view of our enclosure revealed itself. Outside our completely walled-off yard, there were seven enraged wargs trying to find a way in.

"As soon as they came after you into the stake corridor, I raised the far wall and locked them in tight. The wargs cannot escape now. The fence is too high, and they don't have enough distance to get up the speed for a jump. They might be able to bite through the thick poles, but that would take a very long time. The easiest way to kill them is with this ballista. The damage from one average shot is about fifteen hundred HP, which is plenty to kill a level-fifty-five monster in one shot, as you've already seen."

I took another look at the ferocious wargs below. They made quite the ghastly spectacle. Despite the ogre's assurances, I had no doubt that the predators wouldn't be held in the enclosure for long. They all needed to be killed before we missed the chance.

"Before animals killing all, we must for be sure that experience is go to those who need," I said and Shrekson nodded in agreement:

"I'll get experience no matter what, because I built the trap. If I understand the *Boundless Realm* algorithms correctly, all the people who were in the chase will also get a share. I suggest we take one shot and check to see if everyone who needs it really will get the experience."

Getting two thousand and some experience seven times was great, but I still wanted to try bringing Tamina Fierce into the action to increase the reward even further. The goblin woman agreed to climb up on the tower with us after a brief talk, though she moaned and groaned as she did so.

"The ogre fortifier thinks you should try the ballista. If it is convenient and effective, you can also install one in Tysh to deflect the attacks of nocturnal monsters or even the undying."

On hearing the word "undying," Tamina clenched her fists and her eyes narrowed in hate. The ogre loaded the ballista and showed the goblin lady how to aim it, after which the woman took a shot at the nearest warg.

Experience received: 14291 Exp.

Level twenty-four!
Racial ability improved: 50% Resistance to Cold

Mission completed: Reach a higher level than Taisha
Reward: 2400 Exp., +20 to any check of Taisha's opinion

Would you look at that! It worked exactly as I predicted! And we had another six wargs to repeat the trick on! That meant... I almost felt unclean imagining the aftermath. I would reach level thirty in just a few minutes! My boss would surely notice my character growing that fast. And that realization sobered me up abruptly.

"Thank you, Tamina. We'll take it from here."

When the goblin woman was back on the ground, Shrekson admitted to me:

"It was good that you sent her back down. I leveled up twice just from that! I hit twenty! It was so sweet! I understand perfectly that you cannot play using cheats, but it's very hard to say 'no,' once you know they're there. I personally don't know if I'd have had the spirit to do what you just did. Thank you!"

The ogre fortifier reloaded the ballista with determination and set about aiming at the rest of the wargs in the trap one after another.

Experience received: 2640 Exp.

Experience received: 2640 Exp.

Experience received: 2640 Exp.

Level twenty-five!
Racial ability improved: 55% Resistance to Poison

Experience received: 2640 Exp.

Experience received: 2640 Exp.

~ Video Game Plotline Tester ~

Experience received: 2640 Exp.

"That's all. We can go down and gather trophies now!" the level-twenty-two ogre fortifier, his endurance sapped, slouched down onto the base of the rotating ballista mount.

"Thank you, friends!!!" Max Sochnier shouted, having hit level twenty-one before his deadline. He extended his bright red back fins and simply lit up with joy, prancing about the yard like a young goat.

I got down from the tower and sat on the porch to assign my new stat points. There was something to think about here, too. Beyond distributing six stat points, on reaching level twenty-five, my big-eared goblin had gotten another slot for primary and secondary skills. In that I wouldn't get another such addition until level fifty, which was not coming any time soon, I needed to think very seriously about what my Amra needed for the game now. First and foremost, I needed high agility. As I grew in level, all my enemies were going to start having better armor and higher resistances, so I had to level up the damage I could do with my weapon as well. Also, I needed high agility so I could eventually catch up to Taisha in that and finish the opinion-improvement quest.

After giving the matter considerable thought, I moved Exotic Weapons (A P) from secondary skills to primary. My agility jumped up to seventy-four, and my perception to twenty. Now, I had to decide what to fill my two free secondary-skill slots with. The first of them wasn't especially troubling: I was constantly riding wolves, and soon would also be flying around on VIXEN, so it would have been stupid not to choose the Riding skill, which would be automatically leveled in my journeys.

Would you like to take Riding (A C) as a secondary skill?

Would I!? But how should I fill the last free slot? There were lots of options, but I couldn't make up my mind. The level-26 wood nymph sat down next to me and whispered quietly so no others would hear:

"Tim, have you thought about Taisha? Almost everyone around, even the wolves of the Gray Pack got experience from the wargs and leveled up. But 'your girly' was totally left out... She was obviously hurt by that. She feels cheated, and I noticed. Taisha's just too proud to show it."

"Are you saying I should speak with her?" I inquired, as my sister clearly had a better understanding of women's psyche than I did.

"That is one thing you should do, yes. But more than that, you should take Taisha with you for some serious business so she'll feel useful. We killed all the wargs, but the Horror of the Gray Pack quest isn't completed, because we still haven't found their lair. And I suggest that we go about that right now to both keep Taisha busy and so Pirate can become my pet, instead of a member of the Gray Pack. I'm getting tired of him changing color every time you decide to play around with their settings."

Suitor Competition

W E WALKED SINGLE-FILE through the swampy forest, trying to move quietly so as not to attract the attention of any night monsters. It was unusually cold tonight, and a terrible fine mist was raining down from the heavens. Taisha, walking next to me, was wrapped in a black warg fur shivering. Although her thin thief's outfit provided invisibility at night and brought joy to the eye by day, it was not even remotely appropriate for cold weather. We had only taken one wolf with us, Pirate. My sister assured me that her undergrown level-14 forest wolf was able to follow a scent just as well as the adult members of the Gray Pack.

"Hopefully the rain didn't wash out the tracks," I said, slightly worried.

But the wood nymph reassured me, saying that there hadn't really been much rain, and the warg lair must have been somewhere very near the place we'd encountered them yesterday, as the predators had taken less than a minute to get to the road. My sister even said that she thought she knew exactly where the monsters lived. I opened the local map and saw a marker approximately on our path placed by my sister on her first day in-game: "Something's lair, horrible stench." What could I say? It looked very much like this was the lair we were searching for.

"Taisha, tell me about how goblin suitor contests normally go," Valerianna Quickfoot asked unexpectedly.

What I wanted to do was intervene and announce that it was dumb to talk in the forest at night and attract unnecessary attention. But I didn't butt in. The forest around us was empty and the animals were all taking shelter from the rain and cold. Over the last half hour, we had met only a half-sleeping level-26 quillback. We didn't run from it, either. We went on the attack. Its thirty sharp quills made great ammunition for my blowgun, and they were now in my inventory along with a container of quillback blood. I was planning to drink the blood as soon as my companions weren't looking.

The gorgeous redhead bunched up her shoulders, adjusted her fur cloak and said, her teeth chattering:

"I mean, what's there to tell? The suitor competition is an ancient tradition of our race and the rules were established long ago. First, there's the contest to see who's strongest. Young goblins and bachelor veterans lift stones lying near the entrance to the village of Tysh. There are usually many participants gathered, but the most experienced warriors and berserkers always win. Basically, whoever's strength is the highest."

Taisha measured up my bony figure with her gaze and shook her head hopelessly.

"This contest isn't for Amra. Among my admirers, there is a level-seventy warrior from a neighboring village. He's the clear favorite..."

"Is it allowed to use elixirs to increase strength?" the wood nymph inquired, and Taisha confirmed that the rules did not forbid magic, elixirs or magical objects.

"Then all is not lost, and my brother has a chance." Based on that, my sister had just gotten an interesting idea, and the result of the boring, predictable contest to find the strongest suitor could turn out quite unexpected.

"After that follows the contest to determine who is the most agile. The steep hill near the village of Tysh, which has almost no grass growing on it, is slicked down with water to wet the clay and make it slippery. The suitors get into a line at the foot of the hill and, on the shaman's signal, run up it. They fall, slip, grab their rivals by the arms and legs and generally hamper one another as much as they can. It's normally the most fun contest, and the audience laughs their heads off before any of the participants actually manage to get to the top."

I imagined it and couldn't help but smile. Probably, the spectacle of the mud-coated goblins thrashing one another as they tried to run up the hill and slipped back down on their asses was a pretty funny sight. But it wouldn't be very funny to me when I was taking part in all this chaos.

"The third and last contest isn't always necessary. Normally, after two stages, there's already an obvious victor, who then takes a beautiful bride. But if that hasn't happened, the chieftain will declare where he has hidden a valuable object in the neighboring forest, for example a gilded staff or bracelet. The only ones who compete in the last stage are the ones who got the best results in the previous contests. Whoever brings back the trophy is declared the victor."

"We're here, everybody," Val announced, stopping and looking over the wargs' residence.

I saw a dark wide hole going deep into a hill. There was a horrible smell of rotting meat emanating from it. I activated Detect Life, but didn't find anything alive in the burrow, or nearby.

Wincing from the abhorrent stench and covering my face with my hand, I carefully walked into the burrow. The underground path was steep and led into a single room. Under the earth, it was too dark to make anything out, so I had to activate my Night Vision.

I was in a small underground room with a bare soil floor and walls made of crisscrossing poles. In the middle of the room, there was a crudely constructed table, darkened from the damp and marred by many scratches, either from a knife or sharp claws. I didn't manage to see anything else, as I had to close my eyes, blinded by a bright light. It was the wood nymph casting a magic light spell.

"There are so many bones here!" Taisha exclaimed from behind me with hints of disgust and horror in her voice.

Squinting to help myself adjust to the light, I looked in the direction the thief was pointing. In the far corner of the room, there was a birch-wicker box full of old, gnawed bones. That must have been the source of the disgusting rotting smell we noticed up above.

"A locked chest! Just the job for me!" shouted the thief, drawing my attention to a wooden chest next to the box, bound with metal bars. "Mavka, I need some light. I'll try to pick the lock!"

A set of lock picks appeared in Taisha's

hands. The redhead took a seat next to the chest, looked at the large weighty lock and even stuck her finger into the rusty keyhole. Taisha spent a minute contemplating which lock pick would be best, then stuck one of them into the hole and turned it forcefully. Based on the creaking and clanking sound it gave off, the thief hadn't so much opened the rusty lock, as broken it. The girl threw back the heavy lid impatiently and, when she saw what was inside, gasped in disappointment:

"It's just clothes... Dirty villager's clothes..."

Taisha and Valerianna started pulling the dirty, tattered rags out of the chest and throwing them on the floor. If you looked hard, you could tell it was old shirts and pants. A minute later, the chest was empty. There was nothing inside but clothing. My sister rifled through the rags one more time and said her conclusion:

"Eleven sets of men's clothing. Very old, and cheap. Apparently human. And, in that we have killed eleven wargs over the last two days, everything adds up."

Mission completed: Horror of the Gray Pack

Reward received: 8000 Exp., +1 to maximum Gray Pack member limit (up to six)

Level twenty-six!

Racial ability improved: 55% Resistance to Cold

Despite the message confirming that the quest was finished and that I'd reached the next level, I couldn't believe this was really the end. It was just too anticlimactic. All my rich experience in computer games was shouting out that I should have only needed to kill the wargs to finish the quest. There was no reason whatsoever for the developers to add a condition saying we had to find this uninteresting hidden forest lair and dig through the dirty rags and stinking bones... By the way, about the bones...

"Help me get everything out of this box," I asked the girls.

Taisha and Valerianna exchanged glances. Obviously, neither of them wanted to get near the stinking heap.

"I have a lingering suspicion that this isn't the end of the warg story," I said, explaining my strange request. "Based on the sets of clothing, these wargs must have been some kind of shapeshifters. During the day, they looked like normal, inoffensive humans, elves or orcs. But look, there aren't any beds here. Where did these eleven people sleep during the day? This little room looks more like a changing room for the villagers to throw off their sweaty clothes after a hard day's work before they transformed into blood-thirsty nocturnal predators. They must have been spending the day somewhere else. And I want to look for clues that could help us figure out where that might have been."

Taisha looked fastidiously at the pile of bones and cringed:

"Why dig through the trash?! Everything is already clear. Based on the cut, the clothing must be human. And the only human settlement in the whole area is Stonetown. All we have to do is go to Stonetown and ask the locals if they've had any people disappear in the last few days. It's hard to hide the fact that eleven healthy guys disappeared all at once. Their neighbors are sure to have noticed."

Not waiting for help from the overly fastidious girls, I dug into the birchen box and emptied it. First, gnawed-down bones spilled out onto the bare floor, then followed a stinking slurry of putrefaction over top of them. The stench now was utterly unbearable.

Successful check for Poison Resistance
Experience received: 8 Exp.

Taisha was first to rush to run to the surface. I was already preparing to follow her example before suddenly, among the bones and decaying scraps, I saw a spot of color. It was a headband like the kind girls put in their hair.

Overcoming my disgust, I pulled it out with two fingers and showed it to my sister, whose face had turned green, clearly struggling not to dry heave.

"This must have belonged to one of the victims," I supposed, but my sister just shook her head, pressing her hand to her mouth and rushing to follow the thief out into fresh air.

> *Successful check for Poison Resistance*
> *Experience received: 8 Exp.*

I went after the girls and took a deep breath of the fresh night air with delight. Valerianna Quickfoot, doubled over and breathing strenuously, asked me to show her what I'd found. My sister spent a long time looking at the colorful headband, after which she said that she had to get back into the underground lair and check some other observations she'd made. What I wanted to do was go in together with her just in case, but the wood nymph said that she needed literally just thirty seconds. And in fact, my sister was back outside very shortly.

"This headband could not have possibly belonged to a victim of the wargs. First of all, there are no other articles of clothing in the box. Second, I checked, and none of those bones are human. They're the remains of various other kinds of creature: some kind of giant bones, goblin skulls, broken crab shells, and a huge number of fish bones and scales, but nothing human."

Mission received: The Gray Pack's Past
Mission class: Rare, Group
Description: Go to Stonetown and figure out the story of the headband you found in the Warg lair
Reward: 2000 Exp., the ability to include Wargs in the Gray Pack

"That is much less experience than the last stage gave for some reason," I objected. But the wood nymph disagreed:

"I was offered exactly the same amount as for the difficult Horror of the Gray Pack quest. And that is very strange. There are just twenty houses in all of Stonetown. Interviewing all the people there would take thirty minutes at most. I cannot understand why so much experience is promised."

Taisha, who was carefully listening to our conversation, said with dismay in her voice:

"I still don't understand what you're talking about! Undying, can you please be more clear?"

What I wanted to do was explain everything to the beautiful NPC girl, but I was distracted by an incoming message. It was Valentin Wise_Wizard:

"I was just killed by the midnight wraith again. You'll never believe where I found it — in a stream-washed cavern almost directly under your

forest home. This time, I managed to catch a glimpse of the beast. It was just a dark, fast-moving shadow. It was marked with a black skull, so it must be at least level-one-hundred-fifty. It cannot pass through objects. It can fly around them, though, and it moves very, very fast. It used high-level death magic spells again, and broke through all my resists. Amra, you might as well be living on top of a volcano. If that beast can get out, it will slaughter everything alive. I wrote a necromancer friend and invited him to come help. He's a specialist in these issues. I hope we'll manage to eliminate this beast tomorrow night."

While I was digesting the valuable information sent by the illusionist, my sister restated my theory to the beautiful NPC:

"My brother has a firm belief that not all the wargs have been killed. So, Amra suggests we go to Stonetown to look for someone who will recognize this headband. If the owner of the headband is alive, she might be able to tell us a lot about the wargs."

I intervened in the conversation and hurried to add:

"Valerianna is right. But, I'm just not feeling especially up to going to Stonetown right now. We'll figure this all out after the suitor competition. So, let's get back to the Cursed House quickly. The midnight wraith is back and it's up to no good. Let's go inside, lock the gates and get ready for tomorrow."

* * *

The village of Tysh made a very dismal impression on me. The gates were leaning heavily and covered in black ash. The brave Chieftain Ugruem Butcher and the trader Nyle Miser had both met their dooms there, along with many other village defenders. They gave their lives trying to stop the invasion of the undying and even sent eight players to respawn. But the defenders' heroic feat at the main gates ultimately came to naught. The attackers had made it into Tysh regardless, having broken through the wall in two other places. The players had really gone all out on the village, killing more than two hundred peaceful goblins and destroying over half of the buildings.

Now, the corpses had all been taken off the streets, but the ash and charred wood where many of the buildings I'd once known had stood still shocked me. The only thing that remained of Tarek Bigfoot's house, where I had been a guest just two days earlier, were blackened ruins. Taisha's father himself had seriously suffered in the blaze and was temporarily being kept in the house of shaman Kaiak Badgerleg.

"Now you understand, Amra. This is why we need to get revenge!" Taisha got down on her knees near the ash of her family house. "Yesterday, I asked the neighbors and figured out who exactly destroyed all these houses and who was responsible for the deaths of my sisters. It was a necromancer by the name of Larsen Deathless, an elven bowwoman named Dorielle Flexible_Doe, a healer named Antonius Just and a paladin called George Serene_Light_Bearer."

I opened the saved chat of the players discussing the assault on the NPC village. All the figures named by Taisha really had been present. The weakest of them all was the forest elf Dorielle Flexible_Doe, a level-sixty bowwoman. The most dangerous was the level-one-hundred-thirty-seven priest-healer.

Generally, you could only consider healers harmless, if you had no experience in computer games at all. In fact, the 'physicians' of *Boundless Realm* had many very unpleasant spells in their arsenal. They could paralyze, cripple, cause internal bleeding or even stop a heart. And there was one other thing that made you treat healers with respect. Most players preferred to take active part in battle and kill enemies themselves, instead of standing to the side and healing their wounded allies. Yet, in any MMORPG game, the healer class was in demand for raiding and PvP groups, but was always considered the least prestigious. For that reason, it was rarely chosen at random. In *Boundless Realm*, considering that it was impossible to change your class after character creation, healers were all the rarer and were only usually played by capable gamers who truly thought through their strategy in advance. Seeing a level-one-hundred-thirty-seven healer told me unambiguously that he must have been a very great player, indeed.

I noticed that Taisha was silent and was clearly expecting some commentary from me on the list of enemies she'd named.

"Taisha, I already promised you before the very gods of *Boundless Realm* that these undying will not escape unpunished! After the suitor tournament, if I manage to win, I'll try to quickly finish my current business in a day or two and head off with you in search of your sisters' killers."

The redhead looked me from top to bottom without standing up and said in disbelief:

"But where do you plan to search for them, Amra? I mean, the world is huge. You said it yourself!"

"There are various ways. We can talk about that after the tournament. But for now, I've just seen a crowd of goblins with your father at the head. My rivals, I assume?"

The girl quickly shot to her feet and hurriedly brushed the ash and dirt from her clothes. And it was good timing. Tarek Bigfoot, the level-80 goblin warrior stopped two steps from his daughter. I bowed respectfully to the new chieftain of the village of Tysh, but Tarek defiantly refused to acknowledge me. At the same time, he looked with obvious disapproval at the overly erotic form-fitting outfit the thief girl was wearing.

"Beloved daughter, I told you yesterday that you looked unbecoming in those clothes and suggested you dress more modestly."

"Father, I'm an independent adult, so I think I can handle issues of women's fashion without your advice. But I have a question for you. Will I be the only prize for this whole horde of drooling maniacs?" asked the girl, pointing to the male goblins standing nearby, who varied in age from snotty teenagers to bald old men.

Tarek shook his head and said that another three young girls would also be finding themselves a mate today based on the result of the suitor competition. Only after that did the chieftain turn to me, looking skeptically over my bony big-eared character and saying:

"I'm glad to see you showed up, Amra. To be honest, I was afraid you'd take advantage of Taisha's good opinion of you and just run away with her."

I chuckled, as Taisha's father had guessed my thoughts. The idea really had occurred to me and was carefully considered. But in the end, I decided against it due to the potentially devastating complications it could bring.

"Yes, Tarek. I could have easily done without

any competition and convinced Taisha to be my bride. But, as I gave you a promise to take part in the suitor tournament, I intend to compete on even footing with everyone else and earn my right to her fair and square. Nature has not blessed me with powerful muscles, but I am an herbalist and so can cook up all kinds of magical elixirs. You'll all see with your own eyes that I can become very strong indeed, if need be. In order to demonstrate that clearly, I asked all my friends to bring a huge boulder to the square for the competition. It was once lying next to the gates on the road to Tysh. I will be lifting this very boulder, as the other stones will be too light for me."

Reward received: 1440 Exp., +10 to Taisha's opinion of you, +10 to Tarek Bigfoot's opinion of you

So then, I officially agreed to take part in the strongman contest and even received the experience promised for it. There was no way back now. From the crowd of challengers, one huge muscular goblin stood out. His face was disfigured by a crooked, unevenly healed scar across his whole face. The old wound of some sharp weapon had cloven the goblin's nose in twain, which had made the brute, not born a beauty in the first place, look like a downright freak of nature.

~ Dark herbalist Book One ~

Hanry Noseless
Level-70 Goblin Berserker

The tall goblin towered over me by almost two whole heads and loomed threateningly over my big-eared Amra:

"Let's see what your boasting is really worth. All I see now is a puny herbalist spinning fables as he practically pisses himself in fear. Boy, you better get out of here while the going's good. Gather your herbs before the truly strong men kill you on accident. It'd be all too easy to overlook a speck of dust in the road like you."

I smiled a predatory smile and answered the impudent fellow's insults with an insult of my own:

"Look here, Hanry. You must know a thing or two about truly strong men. It seems they decided to take pity on you. Instead of killing you, they just made you a new face. They probably figured it'd make a good profession for you. Someone's gotta play the freak in traveling circuses, after all!"

What I said didn't reach my opponent right away, which only confirmed my supposition that the berserker was so skewed toward strength and constitution that it was to the detriment of his intelligence, a parameter that was already a soft spot for any goblin. Only the crowd laughing a few seconds later, which gradually figured out the meaning of what I'd said, forced Hanry to make a fist.

Tarek Bigfoot got up between us at the exact right time, stopping the imminent conflict from breaking out. The chieftain ordered us all to calm down and get to the village gate, where stones of various sizes had already been set on a sand-covered area to find the strongest contestant.

Here there were already a few hundred spectators gathered. Based on that, the crowd was not only the surviving residents of Tysh, but also many goblins from the neighboring villages. Their attention was laser-focused on the bizarre multiracial foursome of Tamina Fierce, Shrekson Bastard, Max Sochnier and Valerianna Quickfoot who had carried the huge rain-slicked boulder onto the sandy square with obvious strain. My friends were dripping with sweat from the exertion and had to stop for a breather every few steps. But then, finally, they threw the huge boulder next to the other stones, and collapsed right next to it on the sand, totally exhausted. Tamina Fierce, looking for me in the crowd, shouted out loudly so everyone around could hear:

"Amra, if you can't lift this thing, and I dragged it all the way up the hill for no reason, I'll break your arms and legs! Believe that! They don't call me Fierce for nothing!"

It seemed to me that the goblin lady and all my friends were seriously overacting, pretending to be tired from the exorbitant load. I though, understood perfectly that this titanic boulder was just an illusion created by my sister, and that the stone they were actually carrying was no larger than a brick. But the audience believed what they saw with their own eyes, and no one had any doubt that the boulder would be impossible to lift.

The competition began. One after the other, the suitors walked up, chose one of the stones arranged by weight and, with varying levels of success, lifted their chosen weight and stepped back. In that every contestant had only one chance, no one took the risk of approaching the boulder my friends had brought. Even Hanry Noseless decided in favor of the second largest stone, though he lifted it without particular strain. The only participant remaining was me. To the surprised gazes of those gathered, I set about undressing.

"This is so my clothes don't rip when my muscles bulge out," I said, explaining my behavior to the spectators.

Stripped down to my belt and having handed my chainmail and vest to Valerianna Quickfoot, I took out a vial of thick orange fluid from my bag and showed it to everyone. It really was an elixir of strength I'd prepared, but it raised the stat by just fifteen points, and for only four minutes. But the audience didn't have to know that. I popped the cork from the vial and drank the elixir down. The spectators gasped in concert. I do not know who they were seeing now, but it wasn't the small, big-eared herbalist anymore. They were all impressed. When my sister and I had been planning our roles in the show, Valeria said that she'd turn me into some kind of great green "hulk," but I didn't really know much about old movies, so I couldn't picture who she had in mind. It must have been a giant of some kind.

Successful check for Kaiak Badgerleg's reaction
Experience received: 80 Exp.

It seemed the local shaman had started doubting the veracity of what he was seeing, but Kaiak Badgerleg nevertheless decided not to interfere and spoil my display. I stomped my legs resolutely and, demonstrating my muscles, walked up to the boulder. The viewers would have died laughing, if they could have seen the true spectacle instead of the picture created by the mavka. As I expected, the stone wasn't actually all that heavy. Nevertheless, I had to pretend I was making a huge effort. I grunted like a bodybuilder, lifted the object over my head, held it for a few seconds and threw it forcefully back onto the sand. The earth shook. The thundering sound it caused actually scared me a bit. My little illusionist had overdone the special effects. But the spectators liked it. Their elated shrieks and cries were deafening. I spun around a bit more, showing my "powerful" biceps and triceps until I got a private message from my sister:

"That's all. You can put your clothes back on. I removed the illusion. You look normal again."

When the chieftain and shaman declared me the victor of the strongman competition, my advantage was so obvious that even the noseless berserker didn't object. The crowd, discussing what they'd seen animatedly, started snaking over to the other end of the village where the steep clay slope was already being covered with water, preparing it for the second stage of the suitor contest. I hung a bit behind to ask Tamina, Shrekson and Max to drag the "champion boulder" somewhere out of view before the illusion passed and our trick was revealed.

The naiad, wearing a set of shimmering plate armor he had fished out of the lake on the site of the top-clan battle wanted to do it alone, but I insisted all three of them carry the stone off together, even though it wasn't too likely anyone would be following them. The wood nymph, though, I would need for the agility contest. It was her Water Magic skill that would define whether I'd manage to run up the steep wet slope or not. When my sister and I had reached the site of the second stage, everything was ready for the beginning of the competition. There were streams of mud flowing down the washed-out slope, but it probably would have been possible to get to the top just by grabbing the sparse tufts of grass that remained on the hill. The participants were already standing at the bottom waiting for the start signal, and I also took my place.

Reward received: 1440 Exp., +10 to Taisha's opinion of you, +10 to Tarek Bigfoot's opinion of you

Yes, the system now considered me a participant in the second stage of the competition and so I had earned the established reward. But this was the most delicate part of the whole plan. My character had to compete with about twenty other goblins, each of them having a 30% bonus to agility leveling from birth. I'd never manage on my own here, even with a magic potion giving +15 to agility, which was the most I could manage with my Alchemy at level 15.

I took the elixir demonstratively from my pack and froze with the vial in my hand, ready to pop the cork and drink it down at any moment. The competition would start very soon. But where were my helpers?

"Why is Uncle Amra the only one drinking magical potions? That's not fair! Let everyone else have some!" cried Yunna, who had wormed her way into the crowd.

"That's right! They should share so it's fair!"

her sister Hosh chimed in.

"I saw with my own eyes. His bag is full of potions. There's enough for all the suitors!" Irek injected from the other side of the large crowd.

Foreman skill increased to level 5!

Similar exclamations came out from all sides. Tamina's children earned their keep fair and square. The impression formed that the whole crowd was demanding this in unison. Soon, other spectators really did start joining their call to give alchemical elixirs to all participants in the contest so "it would all be fair."

Even shaman Kaiak Badgerleg, who was supposed to give the start command, was at a loss, standing next to the group of suitors. He asked the chieftain's advice. They discussed it for a minute and walked over to me.

"Amra, you see it yourself. The people demand equal conditions for all. So, I have to ask. Do you actually have enough of those elixirs for everyone?"

I sighed quietly. Everything was going exactly the way my sister and I had hoped. It would have been much worse if they had said, to even the playing field, that I couldn't take magical elixirs. Alright. I just needed to act natural now, and not show how happy this made me. I made a sad face and answered the shaman's question:

"I really do have enough elixirs to share, but why should I just give my enemies valuable advantages for free? Although... If the viewers are demanding it... Alright. But I do have one condition: no one drinks any potions until the signal! Let us all have truly equal conditions!"

I laid out twenty visually identical vials of orange-yellow liquid on the ground and offered the participants to come and take one. A few seconds later, there was just one left, which I took for myself.

The shaman walked away and raised his hand, calling all participants to get ready for the beginning of the contest. My arm shot up, and at the same time, I heard the sound of dozens of corks popping in unison. All my competition gulped down the contents of their vials. I though, not hiding my mischievous face, put my unopened vial back in my bag. Technically, I could have drunk the potion of exhaustion that remained for me. I had 55% Resistance to Poison, so the chance of avoiding negative consequences was high, but I didn't want to risk it.

Initially, I had prepared fairly inoffensive potions for my competitors, which would just lower their endurance to zero for a few seconds. Try scrambling up the steep wet slope when you can't even stand! But, due to a banal lack of ingredients, a third of the participants ended up with a potion I had named in my lab journal

"Pickled Herring with Milk," which caused a very intense attack of diarrhea. I don't even know which of the elixirs was more effective in this situation. A few seconds after start, some of my enemies were lying on the ground. The others were running away from the hill as fast as they could toward a thicket of bushes.

"Run straight forward. I'll freeze the earth in a thin strip."

This morning, my sister and I had argued about the best way to make the slippery slope walkable. I had suggested the wood nymph dry it out but, according to her, it was much easier and faster to freeze the water. My concern with that was that a wet clay slope would only get slipperier when frozen. My sister had assured me that it wouldn't, though. We had even done experiments near the Cursed House on whether I could run up frozen clay, and I was left totally satisfied with the result. And so, now I was going up the hill at a fairly steady pace.

> *Successful Agility check*
> *Experience received: 8 Exp.*

It seemed I had almost gone off the path. I had to slightly adjust my direction. And then, I reached the top... But I came in second! Hanry Noseless had made it up the slippery slope a few seconds before I had. Either his poison resistance had come through or... No, it wasn't that. Eew! I frowned in disgust as a breeze carried the unpleasant smell over to me. Nevertheless, in this competition, the noseless berserker had emerged victorious and now, before the last stage, he and I were at a dead heat.

"I heard Hanry just ordered some warriors from his village to set up an ambush on the log road through the swamp," Yunna came up to me and whispered in my ear. "Amra, he's planning to kill you!"

"Don't worry. Killing the undying isn't quite that easy," I replied, reassuring Tamina's oldest daughter and thanked her for the warning.

I had to wait for the other contestants to finish. Finally, Tarek Bigfoot called me and the berserker, along with the other two goblins who'd earned points in both of the last rounds. We were the only ones remaining who had any chance.

Reward received: 1440 Exp., +10 to Taisha's opinion of you, +10 to Tarek Bigfoot's opinion of you

So here was the last stage of the suitor competition. The chieftain began elaborating in detail on where exactly he'd hidden a bronze totem that had to be brought back to him before sunset. Tarek named a few reference points and described a few places. My opponent, wet after a dip in a barrel of water, nodded and listened carefully. It was obvious that Hanry Noseless was quite familiar with the places being described and had no doubt in his ability to find the valuable trophy. For me though, names like "the motley log road," "wolf ravine," and "graveyard of burning skeletons," meant nothing. I had no idea where they were talking about.

The two other participants were whispering to each other and looking sidelong at me. Their sullen glances seemed to promise nasty surprises as soon as I was out of audience view.

Finally, the shaman gave the start signal and the berserker shot off at full speed down the road into the distance. The two other goblins weren't rushing. They picked up two knotted clubs and walked down the road, glancing periodically at me. I though, stayed where I was, watching with a smile as my rivals ran off into the distance.

"Amra, what is going on? Are you refusing to finish the contest?" Tarek Bigfoot asked in surprise and raised an eyebrow wickedly.

"Quite the opposite, chieftain. I've already won," I stated. With these words, I pulled an ancient bronze statuette of a winged woman of an undefined race from my inventory. "Here's the trophy you're waiting for!"

The spectators watching the scene all gasped in unison. Yep. It made a very strong impact. The idea of following Taisha's father this morning when he went to hide the trophy in the forest, had come from the thief girl herself. She was not at all amenable to being given away to some random victor, so Taisha decided this was worth doing as a kind of insurance. I had given her the Gray Pack for protection, the lame Akella excepted, and the gorgeous redhead had followed after her father, picked up the trophy and brought it to me.

Tarek Bigfoot stared vacantly at the statuette, not knowing how to react to what was happening. A second passed, then another, then five more, but the chieftain simply could not make up his mind. I just kept watching the NPC keenly, as he tried to invent a solution to the difficult situation. The conditions of the mission were technically completed, but Tarek understood perfectly that I couldn't have actually finished the contest yet.

SYSTEM ERROR!

Response time for NPC $FF0076-BB0880 has surpassed allowable value

Error code #LOC/ER-000016

This message has been sent to **Boundless Realm** *tech support*

Character automatically reset

We apologize for the possible inconvenience

Oh really! I rubbed my hands together, mentally satisfied. As a tester, any error uncovered was pure gravy. The shaman, rubbing his forehead in contemplation, walked up to the chieftain. Tamina Fierce also drew nearer to our party. The key NPC's of the village of Tysh had a fairly quick discussion, came to an agreement and turned toward me.

Successful check for Tarek Bigfoot's reaction.
Experience received: 80 Exp.
Successful check for Tamina Fierce's reaction.
Experience received: 80 Exp.

Successful check for Kaiak Badgerleg's reaction.
Experience received: 80 Exp.

My good personal relationship with all three of them had led them to decide I could be trusted after all. The shaman took a step forward, calling the spectators to silence and pronounced triumphantly:

"Amra, you have proven your strength, agility and valor! It is with great joy that I declare you the victor of today's suitor competition! You may select the bride of your choosing from among these beauties!"

The crowd made way, and I saw four goblin

ladies. To my surprise, none of them were complete duds. In fact, they were all quite comely. Either that or I had recently grown accustomed to the appearance of goblins from spending so much time with Tamina, Yunna and her little sister. I couldn't say for sure. Either way, beyond all shadow of a doubt, Taisha stood out from the group like a shimmering diamond in a field of gray gravel. I walked up to her, took the pair of golden sapphire earrings I'd bought several days earlier from my inventory and, bending down on one knee, handed the valuable gift ceremoniously to the chieftain's daughter.

Mission completed: Suitors' Games
Reward received: 8000 Exp.

Taisha slowly extended her hand, took the gold earrings and looked them over carefully.

"I'll admit, Amra, I am used to receiving more valuable gifts from you," the gorgeous redhead whispered to me, barely audibly. "Two expensive daggers, a valuable belt, an excellent lock-pick set... those gifts were all bought with me specifically in mind, so when I got them, my heart fluttered in joy. But these earrings are nothing but shiny baubles. I mean, for such an auspicious occasion, you could at least have prepared something more to my taste. Alright then. I guess the real gift must still be coming."

Mission received: A Gift for Taisha
Mission class: Personal, required
Description: Find an object that could only be meant for Taisha
Reward: Variable

I'll confess, when I first heard Taisha's words, I was taken aback. The earrings had cost five hundred coins, which was more money than circulated in the whole village of Tysh! But after I saw the class "required," I calmed down and realized that the reaction of the NPC girl was programmed-in and would have been triggered by whatever gift I gave. Taisha put on the earrings I gave her, winked at me and loudly, so everyone there could hear, said:

"Your gift has gained my favor, Amra, and I agree to become your bride. From this very minute, I only take orders from you. I pledge you my loyalty and promise to be your companion."

"Look! Up there!" Yunna's delighted cry forced Taisha and I to raise our heads and look at the cloudy sky.

I saw a pair of wide wings with bright red membranes flapping up above, and my royal forest wyvern came down to us! On reaching level 15, VIXEN's wings had finally sprouted! The two-meter-long emerald lizard landed at my feet, her wings now rolled into two tight cylinders on her back.

"Awesome!" Max Sochnier got down on his haunches and led his webbed hand over the leathery wings of the wyvern. "When will you be able to fly on her back?"

I shrugged my shoulders indefinitely. Now, VIXEN was still too little to lift anyone into the air. Maybe at level twenty, maybe twenty-five...

Taisha's father walked up, embraced his daughter and prepared to say something festive, appropriate to the occasion, but didn't manage because tears suddenly welled up in his eyes. The wizened warrior grew embarrassed at the display of emotion and turned away. I, though, took advantage of the opportunity and handed the goblin the burn cream which had already done such a good job on Tamina Fierce.

"Amra, what are your plans now? Will you go to Stonetown to find the owner of the headband?" inquired the wood nymph.

"Val, not now. I've been in the game for the last seventeen hours. I'm dead tired. I'm collapsing as I walk. I'm gonna go to shaman Kaiak Badgerleg's house now. I have permission to stay there. After I'm inside, I'll leave *Boundless Realm*."

"Amra, will you be taking me with you to your world? After all, I am now your legal wife and must accompany you everywhere!" Taisha demanded, putting me in a difficult spot.

I turned to the NPC girl and embraced her.

Then, looking her right in the eyes, said:

"Taisha, I don't yet know how to bring you into the land of the undying. Perhaps there is a way, but I don't know it yet. I promise that, if I find a way, I'll show you our world. But for now, go with Valerianna Quickfoot to Stonetown. I'll assign the Gray Pack to protect you. This evening, we'll meet in the Cursed House."

Taisha nodded dejectedly and, looking like a beaten dog, shuffled off to the village gates. I felt extremely uncomfortable, but really did have no way to help the goblin beauty in this matter. When I finished telling my sister what the goblin girl had said, Val got very surprised and thought it over.

"Sometimes, it seems to me that Taisha is being controlled by a real person. Her behavior is just too unlike that of a normal NPC. Tim, do you really not want to give your green-skinned bride a modified Turing test?"

"What do you mean? That wouldn't get us anywhere. A living player could fail that test on purpose, if need be. And machines have already managed to confuse these tests several times, if attached to a sufficient number of libraries and reference guides."

I sat cross-legged on the floor of the shaman's home and chose the menu point "Exit Game." I climbed out of the virtual reality capsule with strain. My arms were shaking like an old man's. I was very tired from the extended game session! I grabbed a towel and headed for the shower. When I opened the door of the game cabin, a white sealed envelope fell down onto the floor without anything written on the outside. I opened it up and discovered an orange plastic card with the words: "Guest Pass" written on it, and a greeting card with a smiling mouse.

"Timothy, this is to remind you that you are invited today to my birthday and will be playing the role of my boyfriend. The festivities will be taking place on the 333rd floor of the northern tower of the Fortress skyscraper. In the envelope, I have placed an electronic pass that will let you through all the turnstiles and doors. It starts at 6:00 PM. Don't be late!

P.S. If you can't figure out what to get me, don't worry about it. Just tell me I can take any object I want from your inventory.

Eagerly looking forward to seeing you,
Kira"

I looked at the clock. It was eleven thirty in the morning. There was just a sliver of time to get ready and get some rest. I didn't even have enough time to take a shower or make a video clip on today's adventures. That would all have to wait! Now, it was much more important to buy myself appropriate clothing and get a gift for Kira. After all that, I could hopefully sleep for a few hours. I had plenty of gift ideas spinning around in my head, but they all had to be ordered.

I certainly wasn't going to let the Queen of the Harpies rifle through my inventory, though. I mean, it was obvious that Kira would hardly be interested in bunches of forest plants or vials of weak alchemical elixirs. She must have been counting on getting the golden wyvern egg, which she must have guessed I'd gotten. Not many knew yet that the wyvern had hatched and even leveled up somewhat. When Kira found out, she would probably be very upset. She might even think she'd been cheated if I offered her an object from my inventory, and it wasn't there. Other than the cursed irremovable Ring of Fenrir, I didn't have anything of value.

It was unusually crowded and noisy on the testing floor. I had already managed to grow accustomed to the quiet and emptiness of night. Now, though, all the couches in the break area were occupied by corporate employees, discussing animatedly and arguing loudly. A big group of people I didn't know were standing by the railing of the long walkway and talking about something. Walking past, I accidentally overheard a fragment of their conversation and couldn't hold back a smile. They were discussing how to remove the chain from your wrist on the slave-traders' galley. It was all clear. Before me was the newly hired group of videogame plotline testers. Just to think, only five days had passed since I was in the very same place as them, but I already felt like a near veteran.

One of the newbies called out to me and asked if I'd managed to get off the pirate galley. When I answered him that I had already passed the trial period and had been a fully-fledged corporate employee since yesterday, I was immediately surrounded and flooded with questions. How had I gotten the chain off? How could they redraw their character's face? How could they handle three level-1 rats at the same time? And basically, what could they do to pass the trial period successfully? I answered only the last question:

"There are three simple rules. If you follow them, you'll be guaranteed to pass the trial period. First: be totally honest with the corporation. Second: don't listen to other people's advice. Cut yourself a new path. Third: spend your time at work in the virtual reality capsule, not with a mug of coffee talking in the break area."

"But it's noon. We're on lunch break!" objected a freckle-faced boy.

I turned to him and, in a calm tone, said:

"Five days ago, there were forty people in our group, just like yours. Now, there are only three. They are the ones who realized that life in *Boundless Realm* doesn't stop for lunch breaks. I just had a seventeen-hour game session. I ran all night from deadly monsters, dug through stinking bones in an underground lair, got soaking wet and frozen in the rain, killed players and was myself killed. I found four rare objects, leveled up three times and earned around five thousand game coins. Yes, I am extremely tired, but that's the big difference between normal players and corporate testers. The former just enjoy the gorgeous, realistic game, but the latter realize they're actually working."

The smiles were immediately wiped off the newbies' faces. Their conversations ceased. No one else had any more questions for me. The employees started going back to their cubicles.

Conclusion

I WAS NEARLY late. I mean, I knew exactly where the Fortress was located. That wasn't the issue. It was the tallest residential skyscraper in the metropolis, stylized to look like a colossal medieval castle with eight towers that rose up two kilometers into the sky. But I had just underestimated the length of the hallways inside gargantuan edifice and the time necessary to catch the four freight elevators I had to use to reach Kira's apartment. They moved at a snail's pace, and for some reason, only went up one hundred floors each. The normal high-speed passenger elevators, whose shafts pierced the whole northern tower right up to the five-hundredth floor had not been big enough. My oversized gift, two by three meters in size, didn't fit into them.

Six minutes before the party was supposed to start, I tumbled out of the elevator on the three hundred thirty-third floor, not having any concept of how to find Kira's apartment from among the sixteen in the hallway. Fortunately, I didn't have to guess. There were colorful arrows stuck to the walls joyously proclaiming "Happy Birthday!!!" and I followed them. Her door was perfectly normal with a cheap lock and didn't stand out in any way. The thin walls allowed me to hear music playing inside. I looked around a bit bewildered. Somehow, I couldn't believe that the owner of a Black Crystal and several sixty-thousand-credit rings could live in a place like this.

But my final doubts were dashed when Kira herself answered the doorbell. My colleague was wearing a chef's apron over her dressing gown and was holding an electric knife for cutting through bones in a roast.

"Hey! It's you, Timothy..." Kira said, freezing in the doorframe and placing the kitchen implement in her apron pocket. "Sorry for greeting you looking like this. I thought it was my old classmate Inga and her date. They called just a minute ago saying they were in the elevator. And just what is that huge thing?"

I wished her a happy birthday, and handed her my gift, sealed and packaged in opaque polyethylene.

"Let me guess. Some kind of painting?" Kira asked with a happy smile. I guess the dimensions of the gift were just too characteristic. She took the vibrating knife back out and carefully made a long slit in the packaging.

The wrapping fell downward, revealing the painting it was hiding. It was a huge black and red harpy with sharp claws, opening her wide wings in front of a high cliff. I used an image of Kirra'ellita, Huntress of the Night from the game as my basis and ordered a workshop to paint the portrait on a mountainous backdrop. I had to pay double because of the urgent nature of my order, so the gift had run me almost eight hundred credits, which was a sum that was in fact quite considerable for my sister and me. I was hoping very much that my effort would be duly appreciated, and that the gift would be to the birthday girl's liking.

But Kira had barely glanced at the image before the smile crawled off her face.

"How dare you!?" the birthday girl shouted, slapping me across the cheek, thankfully, with the hand that didn't have a knife in it.

She instantly got "payback," though I didn't really consciously realize I was striking her. Kira fell to the floor and just sat there, pressing her hand to her burning cheek. The next few seconds we just stared at each other in silence, not believing what had just happened. I was the first to come to my senses.

"Kira, I'm so sorry! That was a complete accident. It was a reflex. It's just that I've been living in a criminal neighborhood for the last few years and, there, you need to be ready to hit back, otherwise they'll never leave you alone."

I extended my hand to help the girl back up. Kira accepted and stood to her feet.

"Think nothing of it. I started it. Harpy Claw is my main attack. It paralyzes and blinds the enemy. It has also become habit for me. It's my natural response," Kira chuckled unhappily, then led her hand over her cheek and winced in pain. "It's turning red, isn't it? I need to put healing cream on it right away or it'll bruise. I guess you could say our date is starting off pretty hot and heavy..."

A bell rang indicating the elevator had arrived, and a beautiful dark-blond woman of twenty-three years stepped out wearing a pink frock. A rugged-looking man with short hair in a naval officer's uniform accompanied her. Kira instantly turned the inauspicious picture to the wall and, only thereafter, adjusted her clothes. After the introductions, Inga noted:

"Kira, Timothy, you look so on edge. Like you've just been fighting."

"Well, he gave me a gift with a double meaning," Kira answered just then without letting me open my mouth. "It depicts me in a fairly piquant pose."

"Come on! Let me see?" The sailor laughed good-heartedly, but Kira refused determinedly.

Kira gave me the key to the neighboring apartment and asked me to bring the gift there for now. When the guests were inside, the birthday girl gave me an unexpected kiss and whispered as she did:

"Timothy, your gift was very nice, but equally unexpected. I appreciate it. We can talk more about it tonight, after the guests are gone. But for now, with the guests here, not a word about the mountain harpy! There won't be very many people at the party. Just three of my girlfriends from school and their dates."

It became clear to me very quickly that Kira was doing everything she could to hide, not only her real job, but also her true income. Though the birthday dress she changed into looked lovely, it didn't even come close to the chic outfits I'd seen Kira wearing in the *Boundless Realm* building. The fancy rings had disappeared from her hands, and been replaced by simpler ones, which were basically cheap imitation jewelry. And also, in conversations with Kira's friends, she complained about high taxes and rent on commercial spaces in the center of the metropolis. She claimed her designer clothing store was barely breaking even because of them.

I told them I worked in a science laboratory for a famous chemical corporation. I was very familiar with the topic since college, so I wasn't afraid of slipping up on trick questions and really was able to easily answer every query they had about my "profession." Basically, I felt comfortable around these people. They were of approximately the same age and social status as me, so I blended in no problem.

As we danced, played games and ate, the time just flew by. I only had second thoughts when the first guests started going back home. At that time, the clock was showing ten thirty. Damn! To be honest, I didn't even think it was ten yet. It was still totally light outside. Only when I walked up to one of the windows did I understand the reason for my mistake. It wasn't transparent glass at all, but a high-resolution screen showing a picture of the city drowning in sunlight and green. I flipped a switch and changed the view to that of an underwater cave with various tropical fish.

"Oh! That's the ticket! Now I'm in my element!" Inga's boyfriend lit up, having served at an underwater base in the Atlantic near the equator.

But the birthday girl unexpectedly asked me to change the view. She took the remote from me and switched the image to a green grove with fairy-tale snow-white rhinoceroses grazing in it.

"I don't like the ocean," Kira stated loudly.

She then added totally quietly and just for me: "The water makes my feathers wet. I almost died like that once."

The party continued. The couples danced, the guests acted foolish and played all kinds of raucous games. Inessa, one of Kira's friends even tried to flirt with me. But, to be honest, I'd lost my appetite for it. I mean, I was still smiling and joking, but I was taking furtive glances at my watch with greater and greater frequency. In *Boundless Realm*, it was already the middle of the night, and I had promised Taisha that I would meet her this evening. Finally, the last of the guests bid us farewell and, giggling pointedly, left me alone with Kira.

"Ugh. The day is finally over!" Kira exclaimed, collapsing into a deep armchair. Exhausted, she threw off her high-heeled shoes. "And you did great, Timothy. You didn't mess up once! The girls even liked you. They were coming up to me all night and whispering about you. Inga, Anna, and Inessa are my only friends and I am very afraid I would lose them, if they found out the truth about me. That is why I meet them all here in a rented apartment, and not in my condo in the elite part of town. Basically, I only use this apartment a few days a year. If you want, you could move in here with your sister. I mean, the place you rented yesterday is uncomfortable and too far from work..."

I shuddered, at Kira's unexpected offer. The girl, watching my reaction, chuckled happily:

"See, you're not the only one who does your homework. It's just that, in my case, it was very easy. After getting such an unexpected gift from you, I ordered my security to find your address in the rental database. This information is normally only available to the police, but money and connections get you a lot of things that aren't available to mere mortals. I got your full name yesterday, when you accepted my money transfer. So, it only took me ten minutes to discover that you finally moved out of the criminal outskirts yesterday together with your younger sister, Valeria. I assume she plays the wood nymph that accompanies you in all your video clips. And now, I'd like to hear just as honestly from you how you were able to connect me with Kirra'ellita, Huntress of the Night."

I had nothing to hide, so I told her my method. I searched my list of those who bought my map of the wyvern island, and found someone connected to her. Kira started thinking and cringed in dismay:

"I'm losing my vigilance, and that is very bad. You see, Timothy, I have many very strong and dangerous enemies in the game. They've made a number of attempts to capture the Land of Gloom or kill its ruler already. Initially, their error was thinking me a mere NPC and just trying simple tricks. But, after a whole series of unsuccessful assassination attempts and attacks deflected by my defenders, they began to suspect something. If you look in the *Boundless Realm* forums, you'll find that the leaders of several strong clans are offering a generous reward to anyone who can tell them the name of the person in control of Kirra'ellita, Huntress of the Night. So, I must know Timothy, what do you want in the game from the ruler of the Land of Gloom or in real life from me to keep you quiet?"

Before I'd even begun to answer, I already knew this was just another test. The apartment owner had been looking on me with suspicion from the very minute the last guests had left. She was holding tightly onto a tiny plastic ring with a button. I couldn't see it clearly, but I suspected it was some kind of alarm. In fact, she was now sitting in an armchair and hiding her left hand behind her thigh.

"It was a pretty stupid gift," I admitted, sitting in the chair opposite Kira. "If I knew you'd react to it like that, I'd have gotten something else. I don't need anything from you at all. I wasn't thinking of revealing your secret to anyone anyway. But in the end, it created mistrust and even fear. And now, you're sitting on guard, convulsively squeezing the remote in your hand that can call your bodyguards, who are probably sitting in one of the neighboring empty apartments ready to burst in here at any second. Yes, Kira, I have been paying attention all night, and your neighbors haven't come home. Terribly thin walls also have certain benefits. I am now sure no one lives in any of the neighboring apartments."

Kira gave a forced smile and showed me the plastic ring with red button she was wearing on her pointer finger. It turned out that I was right about it being an alarm.

"In fact, the whole story with the picture was just an excuse to not let you dig through my inventory. The object you were hoping to find there is long gone. My wyvern hatched and is already level-fifteen. Its wings are out even."

Kira, sitting opposite me, suddenly broke down in joyous laughter, totally throwing me off with her behavior. While she was still laughing, Kira began speaking through fresh tears:

"Oh, Timothy... You seem like such an intelligent and observant person. You were totally right about my guards, for example... I knew absolutely nothing about your wyvern. Think seriously about this for one second. I am one of the few characters in *Boundless Realm* that would have utterly no need for a flying mount! That has to have occurred to you, right?! I mean, I have wings already!"

The girl began cracking up again, and I also found myself overtaken by laughter. It really had been dumb. We had both suspected one another of various stupid things, and we were both wrong. I asked her how she had been able to get such an unusual race, as the rules of *Boundless Realm* didn't allow players to fly. Kira explained readily:

"A very long time ago, when the game was in beta-testing, the corporation was considering adding a 'hero' mode to *Boundless Realm*, with no respawning and just one life. In order to attract players to such a hardcore version of the game, they were given the chance to play rare races: vampires, dragons, harpies, sea serpents, mountain spirits and other such monsters. In the end, the corporation decided against the plan, but some of the original beta-testers are still alive. There aren't many of us at all. Other players consider us nothing more than strong, unusual bots, which create a particular atmosphere in *Boundless Realm*. And your valuable egg didn't interest me at all. The last thing I want is to attract undue attention, after all. I just didn't want to burden you with an expensive gift for my birthday and gave you the opportunity to get out of it with a simple item from your inventory. It was just because I really wanted you to come."

Kira removed the plastic ring with alarm button from her finger, threw it carelessly on the floor. Then, one shoe back on, she crushed it with her high heel. She took her shoe back off and walked around the room, touching various decorations.

"My bodyguards weren't able to hear us before, but now they can't see us either."

The girl walked up to me and, just like the time in the flying car, sat on my lap. Our lips drew together all on their own. I, looking Kira right in the eyes and carefully observing her reaction, plunged my right hand down her deep neckline. The beautiful lady froze and, looking me in the eyes as well, blurted out:

"Timothy, I'm very grateful that you came to my birthday and played a part for me... No, that's not what I wanted to say at all... You've earned my trust. Still not right... I can't find the right words or a good excuse, so I'll just come out and say it. I really want you to stay the night!"

Kira decisively pulled her dress over her head, then unbuttoned and removed her bodice, revealing a flawless figure. After letting me admire the entrancing curves and shapes of her body to my heart's content, the beauty stood and reached for the remote, turning the light down in the room.

* * *

I quietly stood up at two thirty, still not able to fall asleep. Kira was sleeping soundly, her arms outstretched with a happy smile on her face. Her copper red hair was spread out on the pillows like the beams of a bright midday sun. Trying carefully not to wake her, I covered the beautiful woman with a blanket and started getting dressed. I felt unwell in my heart. Though I didn't know exactly why, I felt that something bad had happened. Somewhere, my help was needed. I turned out the light and walked into the hallway, locking the door behind me.

Two tall men of athletic build wearing navy blue security-company uniforms shot up out of their chairs on my appearance.

"Kira is asleep. I need to leave for business," I told them, and they nodded in understanding.

"Just a minute. We'll unblock the elevator now. Otherwise, it won't stop on this floor. Timothy, would you like us to call you a taxi?"

"Yes, please," I agreed, trying not to get surprised at the fact that Kira's bodyguards already knew my name.

The elevator doors opened and I carried myself determinedly downward into the main room on the first floor. The car the bodyguard had promised was already waiting for me near the building entrance. Where should I go? I told the taxi driver the address of the place my sister and I had just moved. My first thought was about my sister, left alone in an apartment she barely knew. Maybe she couldn't sleep either and was worried for me, and that was transferring onto me. Despite the late hour, I decided to call Valeria. An unhappy, sleepy voice answered me:

"Tim, did you even look at the time? It's two thirty in the morning!"

"Yes, I just got out of the party and wanted to call you to make sure you were doing alright."

"I'm doing fine. Or I was. Until you woke me up. Are you coming home now?"

Technically I was, but now I'd had a change of heart and told the taxi driver to go to the corporation.

"Val, I'm going to work first. There's something I need to do in *Boundless Realm* before the sun comes up."

"Oh, well alright. Taisha and I searched Stonetown top to bottom but didn't find the owner of the headband. But I did get an interesting lead. On the far farmstead, they hire cheap day laborers for seasonal work. According to the farmer, some of his workers ran away yesterday before the end of harvest and before getting paid. Around ten guys left, along with a dark-haired pregnant woman and her two young nephews.

I first assumed the headband belonged to the pregnant lady, but all the neighbors agreed that she never wore them, and say her hair was cut short. So, the run-away day laborers are probably the wargs we killed. But our search for information on the headband was a failure.

Afterward, the thief and I went hunting together, fed the wolves and returned to the Cursed House before night. Taisha was eagerly awaiting your return before dark fell, but you never showed up. I tried to explain to her that you might have had business in the realm of the undying, but she didn't want to listen. She said that you'd surely show up, because you promised."

I felt ashamed. It really was too bad that I had to break that promise with Taisha. And though she was just a computer program, I still felt guilty. It was dumb, of course, but what could I do? It was nothing too horrible, though. I'd go into the game now and apologize. I finished my conversation with my younger sister just as the car pulled up to the marble steps of the *Boundless Realm* skyscraper. I asked the driver how much the journey had cost and was answered that it was all paid for in advance. I ran up the stairs for my dear life, as if I was late to something. The night guard tried to stop me, pointing to the importune hour and smelling alcohol on me, but I managed to convince him to let me through.

So, here I was on the tester floor. It was surprising, but there was a whole row of cabins active. It must have been the newbies trying to finish the Surviving the Night quest. What could I say? Best of luck to them! I locked my door from inside and started throwing off my clothes. Ok then, loading game client...

~ Dark herbalist Book One ~

Name	Amra
Race	Goblin Vampire
Class	Herbalist
Experience	127957 of 131000
Character level	26
Hit points	207/207
Endurance points	177/177
Statistics	
Strength (S)	27 (27)
Agility (A)	28 (78.1)
Intelligence (I)	5 (15)
Constitution (C)	28 (34)
Perception (P)	3 (20.5)
Charisma (Ch)	51 (62)
Unused points	**0**
Primary skills (6 of 6 chosen)	
Herbalism (P A)	6
Trading (Ch I)	11
Alchemy (I A)	15
Dodge (A P)	9
Stealth (A C)	13
Exotic Weapons (A P)	6
Secondary skills (5 of 6 chosen)	
Veil	4
Acrobatics	8
Athletics	7
Foreman	5
Riding	4

Yep. My big-eared goblin had grown up, alright. It occurred to me that the monsters living in this area during the day were no longer such a serious threat to me. The night ones, on the other hand...

While I was not in the game, I had received three messages. I began reading them in the order they'd come in. The first message was written at six PM by Max Sochnier:

"I just got back from the director. He praised me for my good work and let me sign a permanent employment contract. Thank you, Timothy! Mr. Tobius said he was expecting me to set up trade routes in the next few days from the undersea settlement and wanted to see material on underwater cities. Now that I'm out of the trial period, this is the very time for you and me to get started on that."

At nine thirty, another message had come from Shrekson Bastard:

"I almost finished Tamina Fierce's house. The goblin villagers helping me were very hard workers, so we're ahead of schedule. Tomorrow, the goblin lady will be able to have a house-warming party. I also got many other orders, so I've got stuff lined up for the next month. And yes, I became a permanent employee of the Boundless Realm corporation! My salary was set at fifteen hundred credits a month. I didn't even make that in my best days as a construction worker! I suggest we celebrate the

occasion somewhere in a restaurant with all the members of our group. It's my treat!"

I was very glad for my friends and went to the third message. It had come in at one in the morning from Valentin Wise_Wizard:

"Amra, there are some strange figures hanging around near your log cabin. I saw five people, though there could have been some invisible ones too. They didn't risk touching me or the high-level necromancer, but they did question us about you. By the looks of it, they were coming after you. Be very careful!"

After reading that letter, my sense of anxiety grew much stronger. The killers were searching for me and had already found the Cursed House. Not good! Not good at all! And though Tamina Fierce, a level-80 warrior, should have been in there, and she would be a threat to many players, there were five attackers, and just one of her. Other than Tamina, there were no serious defenders in the Cursed House. Just the wolves, none of which were over level thirty, the level-twenty-three Taisha and six children. And none of them could use the ballista...

The image loaded. I appeared in *Boundless Realm* sitting on the floor of the shaman's house. Kaiak Badgerleg was sleeping peacefully on his bed. I didn't wake him. I opened the door and went outside. The village of Tysh was asleep. The only sound was the watch calling back and forth to one another from the towers near the main gates. I tried to call the Gray Pack so I could get to the Cursed House faster on wolfback but... nothing happened! The Ring of Fenrir refused to activate!

With the most terrible sensations, I hurried to my forest hut. First, I needed to get out of the goblin village somehow. I knew that the main gates weren't usually opened at night, but I saw a hole in the wall and decided to take advantage of it. I needed just one minute to drag away the logs and boards leaned against it, and there I was, already outside. I placed my map marker on the Cursed House and rushed to the visible arrow. I ran straight through the forest, not giving a damn about my safety, and hoping to just make it. But reason was telling me I was already hopelessly late, as the Gray Pack, which had been guarding the shelter, wasn't answering my call...

Clearly, fortune favors the fool. The night predators had no desire to tangle with a being self-assured enough to scramble loudly through the forest as I was now doing. I saw red monster markers on the map, but they heard me from far away and gave me a wide berth. The surprisingly thoughtless way of moving through the dangerous woods was working for now. Two times on the frantic run, I increased my Athletics skill before I got completely tired and took a more relaxed pace. Already next to the Cursed House I drank down some elixirs to restore my energy and began moving in Stealth.

I saw the enemy from a distance. On the mini-map, right inside my blockhouse, there was a red player triangle, meaning he was hostile. He must have stolen my things or attacked my allies, and his criminal timer had yet to leave him. Why was he alone? That was very suspicious. The illusionist had said there were five killers searching for me. But worst of all was that I couldn't see any markers for NPC allies on the map. Already guessing what I'd see in the Cursed House, I began stealing up to the gates.

The picture that revealed itself to me confirmed my worst suspicions. Next to the chopped-through gates there were dead bodies strewn about. White Fang. Blanca. Irek. On the watchtower, next to the ballista, I saw the shot-through corpses of Yunna and her younger sister. Something got caught in my throat and my hands clenched into fists all on their own. Morally prepared and keeping one eye on the red triangle, I sneaked up to the open gates. The enemy inside still wasn't moving or reacting to my appearance.

One of the gates was breached right through, and the log locking the gates had simply been chopped in two. Right beyond the gates was Tamina Fierce, still holding an old pock-marked blade in her hand. The body of the powerful goblin lady was stuck through with a dense bristling of arrows and covered in countless chops and tears.

This mother had struggled frantically to protect her children, but still hadn't managed to save them. Next to the dead Tamina, I saw the bloodied bodies of Hosh, Shim and Tsak, as well as the body of one of the attackers.

Morrius Heartless
Human
Level-48 Barbarian

In that the body of the dead player had yet to disappear, the bloody events in the Cursed House must have taken place less than an hour ago. The corpse of the second attacker took a bit longer to see. It was buried under the bodies of Akella and Lobo. And by the way, the corpse was quite remarkable:

Lilith Sinner
Succubus
Level-64 Chaos Mage

A succubus?! Demonic races were extremely rare among players. Very few chose them due to their bad relationship with humans and, of course, the fact that they couldn't enter large cities. Despite the tension of the moment, I approached the demon's corpse and opened the loot window. Empty. The friends of the magess had already taken everything of value. But, nevertheless, I was able to fill an alchemy vial with succubus blood.

Achievement unlocked: Taste Tester (12/1000)

I took another careful look at the yard, but still didn't see Taisha's body anywhere. I ordered VIXEN to stay put and began slowly creeping up to the house. By the way... For some reason, my Stealth skill bar wasn't going up, even though I was quite close to the enemy. Very strange.

But then, everything became clear. There were no active enemies near me. After the slaughter in the Cursed House, the players had simply exited *Boundless Realm*. They had killed only NPC's so, according to the game's rules, they only had to wait ten minutes to leave safely. But one of the attackers was still in the game, clearly having committed more serious crimes. He must have killed or robbed a living player recently.

After gathering my bravery, I stood up to my full height and hurried to the house. The entrance door had been burned through with some kind of fire spell. In the entryway, I could smell the acrid odor of smoke. The wooden walls carried the traces of a fairly serious fire. The logs were charred and the floorboards were burned through and broke underfoot. The stairs had also taken serious damage. And there I saw Taisha. I didn't even realize right away that the dark burned rags in the corner were all that remained of my NPC bride. Only a golden sapphire earring gleaming up in the moonlight told me the horrible truth. After a cry of despair and rage, I rushed up to the second floor.

Polichinelle Blind_Mole
Drow Elf
Level-54 Bowman

The dark-skinned elf in obnoxiously bright attire was sitting on the floor in the middle of the room, clearly having already exited the game. Over the bowman's head, there was a bright red ball shining with the criminal marker.

I looked around. The coast was clear. My enemy had been drawn by the luxurious black warg fur on the bed and he had stored it in his inventory. That was precisely why the drow had received a two-hour timer. He had stolen a real player's property, so he couldn't disappear along with the other henchmen. What could I say? It would be a good lesson for him in the future. I walked unhurriedly around the drow elf, activated Veil and bit the enemy calculatingly in the neck, for the first time choosing the option "Infect with Vampirism." After that, I killed him with another Vampire Bite.

Experience received: 3780 Exp.

Racial ability improved: Taste for Blood (Gives +1% to all damage dealt for each unique creature killed with Vampire Bite. Current bonus: 7%)

Achievement unlocked: Player killer (4)

Achievement unlocked: Taste Tester (13/1000)

Quickly, while Veil was still active, I wiped the elf's last game logs, after which I placed a line in I'd copied from my own old logs:

Damage taken: 2757 points (Bite from Cursed Bat)
You have died

Veil skill increased to level 5!

I didn't take any of the drow elf's possessions, not even the warg fur. I didn't touch anything in the room either, even though I had rare herbs drying on strings all around, and they would be very hard to find again. I wanted everything to look like the drow elf had really just been bitten by a cursed bat. It was very rare, but it was infamous in the player-made *Boundless Realm* bestiary for it's extremely unpleasant ability: 25% chance of being infected with vampirism per bite.

Being a vampire myself, I had read through all available materials in the game forum on the topic. Vampirism had to be cured immediately. You just had to drink an Elixir of Cure Disease, a strong anti-venom or apply healing magic soon after infection. But with every hour of delay, the consequences became more and more drastic, and just a day later, the vampirism would become irreversible. If my enemy didn't hurry back into the game now, he could expect another unpleasant surprise. Fifteen hours from now, Thirst for Blood would be turning him into a crazed bloodthirsty monster, unable to control his behavior and throwing himself at everything alive with abandon.

My revenge on one of the attackers secure, I still didn't feel any relief. Apathy and depression rolled over me. The Cursed House, which not too long ago I had considered a safe refuge, had become empty with the deaths of the goblins and wolves, which caused me an internal sense of rejection. Doing anything here or even trying to clean up was entirely meaningless. I knew perfectly well that, in the next few days, more and more killers would be coming around, so there was no reason for me to stay.

I went down to the first floor, preparing to say my last farewell to Taisha, but her body had already disappeared. Then, I discovered something strange. Now, with the floorboards burned through, it became obvious that some of them formed a square hatch. Perhaps, I had found the way down into the basement we had been searching for. A system message jumped in confirming my suspicion:

Mission renewed: Old Cursed House
Description. Go down into the basement built by the Ogre Hunters and kill the night creature
Mission class: Reputation
Reward: Improved relationship with the village of Tysh
ATTENTION: Recommended character level for mission: +50

I probably should have thought it over a hundred times before climbing into the beast's lair, given that it had so easily taken down the high-level wizard and necromancer, but I wasn't feeling any fear. I didn't care at all what happened down there now. Marveling at my own audacity, I activated Night Vision, Detect Life and Apathy of the Undead, after which I cracked open the hatch and started down into the darkness.

The extremely long stairwell, led me down into a damp basement caked with thick mud. As my feet squelched into the floor, I took a look around. There were old rusty hooks in the ceiling, and darkened, crooked shelves on the walls. Based on what I could see, at some point, it had been cold here. Perhaps this even used to be permafrost. This must have been the very icehouse the ogre hunters had stored their meat in. A hole in the collapsed wall led me into the next room. It was a natural cave with a small circular pool. This seemed to be where the hunters had obtained clean water.

My attention was drawn by a strange dark massive object on the other side of the water source and I walked up closer. It was a giant old skeleton with no flesh remaining on the bones whatsoever.Clearly, this was one of the ogre hunters, having died here under the earth. I looked at the old bones and saw a vague movement out of the corner of my left eye. At the same time, a round yellow NPC marker appeared on the mini-map. I turned abruptly and froze, afraid of making a false move and provoking aggression.

Three steps from me, there was a thick dark shadow hanging in the air. Above it, there hovered a red skull.

Midnight Wraith
Level unknown

Level unknown... Clearly, the creature surpassed me by so much that I couldn't even find out any information. Although... wait a minute. The skull over it was red?! That meant it was just twenty-some levels higher than me, but still less than fifty. How could that be? The level-96 illusionist had written that, for him, the midnight wraith was marked with a black skull. It can't have been that the level of the dark monster changed with time, right? Or... was it different for different creatures?

Sensing that I was on the right track, I called VIXEN down. The winged snake tumbled loudly down the stairs, knocking some shelves off the wall with a ghastly thud, and casting bits of mud everywhere. After that, it didn't so much fly into the cave as run, then stopped next to me. With alarm, I looked at the midnight wraith, but the frightening monster remained apathetic, it's interest not at all kindled by the sound. I walked a bit further to the side and left my mount next to the strange monster, then saw an interesting picture. The red skull over the dark ghost disappeared, and the creature itself clearly acquired flesh and fell down to the very earth. Now, it was a thick wisp of darkness, and had a body.

Midnight Wraith
Level-30

It was always twice as strong as it's opponent! That was why the midnight wraith had been nearly level-two-hundred for Valentin Wise_Wizard, fifty-two for me and just thirty for

~ Video Game Plotline Tester ~

VIXEN! Starting from that rule... The solution came instantly. I took the most powerful poison I had from my bag. For thirty seconds, it lowered its target's level by fifteen.

VIXEN flew up obediently to my call and even allowed me to open her toothy maw. She clearly wasn't expecting such maltreatment from her master! A second later, there was a tiny half-meter long snakelet weaving around my legs. I pointed her to the enemy:

"Attack, baby! Hit it with poison!!!"

The now level-2 midnight wraith looked like nothing but a thirty-centimeter-long thick black worm. While my little snake was crawling over to it, I walked further away, making sure I wouldn't accidentally join the baby fight.

VIXEN bit first, instantly draining the enemy's life bar by two thirds. The snake also managed to poison the wraith with the poison that was still on her fangs, lowering the enemy's level to one. The battle was off to an excellent start! Not a trace remained of the wraith's former passivity. The worm instantly took evasive action and sunk its round toothy jaws into the snake's body. VIXEN lost half of her health, and the midnight wraith restored its life back to seventy percent. My little snake shuddered in pain and made another bite. Victory!!!

Experience received: 4 Exp.

What?! Just four experience points? I guess the system had a fairly dim evaluation of how hard it was to fight this creature, which had killed high-level players several times before. And why wasn't the mission completed?

Just then, my wyvern grew abruptly in size, reacquiring her normal dimensions. I walked up to my mount and petted her:

"Good girl. You just killed a nasty brute!" Stop. And just what is that?

On the place where the midnight wraith had died, in a puddle of thick dark blood, there was a wide metal end-piece either from an arrow or a tiny spear. It was flat, the size of my hand, and looked somehow sticky, vile and odious.

Fragment of Dark Rider arrow (cursed item)

I had no idea what a "dark rider" was but, from my computer game experience, I realized that such objects weren't usually just found lying on the roadside. Someone probably wanted this fragment for something, so I started shivering just from looking at it.

Not wanting to touch the unpleasant item with my hands, I wrapped it in a rag and put it in my bag. The dark blood that had spilled was just enough to fill an alchemy vial.

Dark Creature Blood (poison)

All the previous vials of blood I'd gathered had been marked as "alchemy ingredients," but for some reason, this one was "poison." Nevertheless, I decided I would try it and pressed it to my lips.

"I wouldn't do that if I were you!" came a voice from behind me. I turned around abruptly to face it.

In the air, there was a winged silhouette hovering, reminiscent of an angel but transparent. The information I could get on him was quite scant:

Keeper

Simply "Keeper" and nothing more. Nothing saying what he was keeper of, nor his level, nor his skills. Nevertheless, I decided to heed the stranger's words, sealed the vial and put it away.

"That's better. Sure, vampires are supposed to drink blood, but this is a special case. This dark blood will burn any *Boundless Realm* creature from the inside, turning them into wretched monsters like the one you just killed. At one point, that was a normal hunter. After taking an evil arrow to the chest, though, he met his fate at the hands of a dark rider. The dark blood burned the ogre out from the inside and turned it into a dangerous beast."

"Can this blood be used to fight the undying?" I instantly wondered aloud. "Just smear the dark blood on an arrow and shoot it? Can it turn any high-level player into a monster?"

The keeper shook his head:

"The transformation process isn't instantaneous and, also, the arrow has to be cursed so it cannot be removed from the body. Basically, this function has yet to be added to the game. It's still in testing. There are too many factors to take into account. By the way, I don't see the arrowhead here... I guess it must be in your inventory. Amra, I'm afraid I'll have to take it."

I objected totally sincerely:

"Hey, no way, keeper. You've got your job, I've got mine. I'm a tester with the *Boundless Realm* corporation. I found the beginning of an interesting story here. These dark riders, cursed arrows and poisonous blood have caught my interest. So, I need the arrowhead, keeper. Also, do you have a normal name so I don't have to address you so pretentiously? At least some kind of 'support number something?'"

"What?" the glowing angel was thrown off, but then chuckled good-heartedly. "No, you're mistaken, Amra. I'm not from tech support. I'm a tester just like you, but I'm from the Global Simulation Department. We don't actually play. We just test the stability of new global changes before they're introduced into the larger game world. A program trigger was tripped and told me that a dark being had been killed, so I came to see what it was and how. By the way, that was an interesting tactic you used. Taking advantage of the Apathy of the Undead skill to get close, then lowering its level... I mean, in the mission description, it was clearly stated: 'Recommended level for quest: +50.' The dark creature was supposed to have been around level one hundred. Then you'd really have struggled."

"I know," I laughed. "My illusionist friend is level ninety-six and has been killed three times by the midnight wraith."

"Are you talking about Valentin Wise_Wizard? He's actually died five times, and the last time, he also thought to bring a level-one-seventy necromancer with him, which made the midnight wraith far over level-three-hundred. Their bodies are right there in the stream-washed-tunnel," said the glowing figure, pointing somewhere into the pitch-darkness. "Some loot even fell there. Feel free to take it."

I shook my head. The illusionist never did me any wrong and even helped me with advice and warnings, so I would let him get his own dropped items after respawning. The keeper took my refusal with utter calm.

"You know best. But back to the main topic. The dark creature invasion is still only in the planning stages. It's an add-on that will be put into *Boundless Realm* in three weeks. Right now, the mission is to release information on the update piece by piece and only the general outlines, nothing concrete. We definitely cannot go throwing cursed items around willy-nilly. What do you want in exchange for my requisitioning the arrow?"

Mentally crossing my fingers for luck, I made my request:

"One hour ago, on the surface near this place, several NPC characters died: four wolves and eight goblins. All the NPC's killed were in my group, and I worked with them. I had a lot of plans for them. But a stupid random encounter with other players left them all dead. That was actually what attracted me to this dark-creature plotline in the first place. Can you bring these NPC's back to life? I won't need the cursed arrow anymore, if you do that. I'd be happy to give it back to you."

The glowing angel thought for two minutes, then answered:

"Listen, Amra. The wolves are coming back to life just now anyway. In the database, they are considered your pets, so you'll be able to call them an hour after they die no matter what. And another NPC is coming back too. I'll look now to see who..."

My heart missed a beat, then heard the very name I was hoping for: "Taisha." The keeper, though, clearly having familiarized himself with some internal information, whistled in surprise and said excitedly:

"Christ! This is the first time I've seen

anything like this! It's a next-generation NPC with advanced self-teaching intelligence, the rudiments of abstract thought and so on. It's written here that a whole a group of employees led by Alexandro Lavrius were working on the development of her behavior algorithms. I don't know where you found such a companion, but you don't have to worry about her one bit. In the description, it says that, after testing and debugging, such advanced thought algorithms are planned to be implemented for all key NPC characters in *Boundless Realm*. The corporation has spent a bundle of resources on this project, so the directors aren't going to let Taisha just up and die. We need her badly. I'm manually giving her the Indestructible parameter right now even, so your companion will respawn automatically one hour after every death just like living players."

"Yes, please do," I asked, trying to hide the worry in my voice. "And do the same with the two dead wolf riders. I need them for the Gray Pack. The other goblins you can just bring back in five minutes."

I tried to speak confidently, as if this was matter of course but, in my soul, I had certain doubts that he would agree to make Irek and Yunna invincible, or bring the others back to life at all. But no objections followed. This cursed arrowhead was really that valuable? Maybe I should have asked for more. I mentally shook myself. Greed never led to good places.

The keeper froze for a minute, then told me everything was ready. It worked! I gave the angel the dark arrowhead wrapped in cloth, and the glowing figure disappeared, wishing me good luck with my plans before he went.

Mission completed: Old Cursed House
Reward: Improved relationship with the village of Tysh

Attention!!! You have reached maximum average opinion with the residents of Tysh: 100.

Hidden mission completed: Socialization 4/3 (Goblins)
Reward: 8000 Exp., Charisma increased by 2 points, automatic +5 to the opinion of all Goblins, Hobgoblins and Kobolds

Level twenty-seven!
Racial ability improved: 60% Resistance to Poison

I stood up, read the system messages and grew afraid to check if the last few minutes had really happened. I can't seriously have gotten everything I asked for, right? All my NPC's were going to be respawned? Taisha, the Gray Pack,

Tamina and her children... I told my level-16 royal forest wyvern to follow after me, went back through the underground room and began climbing up the stairs.

It was all real! I saw a whole scattering of blue and green circles on the map, indicating NPC's allied and friendly to me.

I had to see this with my own eyes! One after the other, goblins and wolves started materializing. Some with cries of horror and pain, others covering their heads with their hands, and still others continuing the fight. Tamina spent a whole thirty seconds frantically hacking the air with her blade before she stopped and looked around in surprise. The last to appear was Taisha. The girl stood timidly from the charred boards, looked at her arms and legs, then her spottily burned outfit. Finally, the beautiful goblin saw me and threw herself at me with reproaches:

"Amra, where'd you disappear off to for so long?! I almost got killed by undying!" Taisha suddenly stopped sharply, following my gaze and noticing that one of her pert green breasts was poking out of a hole in her shirt. "Hey!"

It was very easy to mend clothing in *Boundless Realm*. You just needed free time, a needle and thread. So, I had no doubt that, soon, Taisha would put her thief's costume all back in order. But, to tide her over, I gave the embarrassed girl my vest and "reassured" her at the same time:

"The undying actually did kill you all. But I had the good fortune of meeting with one of the keepers of *Boundless Realm* and, in exchange for a very valuable object, he agreed to bring you back to life."

After my words, silence came over them all, then Tamina Fierce fell to her knees with a heavy groan. All six of her children followed their mother's example. Taisha hesitated, then decided to express her gratitude simply by kissing me. I filled my lungs and spoke in a stern and powerful voice:

"Tamina, I am taking your two oldest children and, from this point on, they will be under my care. The keeper has given Irek and Yunna immortality so they can accompany me on my journeys."

Yunna and Irek jumped to their feet with joyful cries, but then suddenly reined themselves in and froze, looking to their strict mother and anticipating her answer.

Successful check for Tamina Fierce's reaction
Experience received: 80 Exp.

"This is just a great honor for me, Amra!" said the goblin lady, not raising her head. But then, she added a bit more quietly: "Yunna and Irek have long been grown and have asked me to let them go see the world a number of times. I always refused them but, today, I give my parental permission and blessing."

"You, though, I suggest to return to Tysh when morning comes. Your big spacious house will be ready today. And also..." Here I made a pause, thinking over another option that came to me spontaneously. "The new chieftain, Tarek Bigfoot, doesn't have a roof over his head. He's a widower and will be sure to look in your direction."

Tamina Fierce blushed sheepishly and said in embarrassment:

"I understand, Amra. I'll go have a talk with the chieftain today."

When the joyful cries had died down a bit, and the older children began bidding farewell to their mother, Taisha asked quietly:

"And what are our plans now, Amra? Are we going off to find my sisters' killers?"

I looked at the sky over my head, which was starting to grow just barely light in the east. The thick dark clouds promised a rainy overcast day, but it was still dry now. I had to take advantage of that. There hadn't been any rain yet, so I should try to reach Stonetown and try to pick up the trail of the dark-haired pregnant lady who'd run from the far farmstead. The pregnant woman wouldn't have run without a very good reason to do so. I suspected that the killing of her eleven warg friends and the risk of her being revealed was that very reason. She wouldn't be able to run very fast or far, though. So, with the help of the Gray Pack, I was hoping to track down the runaway.

After that, I would go with Max Sochnier on a big trip through the coastal villages, looking for a good place for a new house on the way. Somewhere cozy and safe, where no killers would be able to threaten us. Only after my royal forest wyvern grew up and became capable of bringing passengers long distances could I really start fulfilling my promise to Taisha, though. I looked at Taisha, who was impatiently waiting for an answer from me.

"Yes, Taisha. We're going on adventures. It's too dangerous to stay in the Cursed House, now. The same undying who attacked tonight might return. And also, other murderers will be sure to come after me. So now, I'm going to call the wood nymph, and we'll start off on a big journey on wolfback. Where that long path will take us, I myself do not know. And what difference would it make? *Boundless Realm* is enormous, and our journey is just beginning!"

End of Book One

About the Author

Michael Atamanov was born in 1975 in Grozny, Chechnia. He excelled at school, winning numerous national science and writing competitions. Having graduated with honors, he entered Moscow University to study material engineering. Soon, however, he had no home to return to: their house was destroyed during the first Chechen campaign. Michael's family fled the war, taking shelter with some relatives in Stavropol Territory in the South of Russia.

Having graduated from the University, Michael was forced to accept whatever work was available. He moonlighted in chemical labs, loaded trucks, translated technical articles, worked as a software installer and scene shifter for local artists and events. At the same time he never stopped writing, even when squatting in some seedy Moscow hostels. Writing became an urgent need for Michael. He submitted articles to science publications, penned news fillers for a variety of web sites and completed a plethora of technical and copywriting gigs.

Then one day unexpectedly for himself he started writing fairy tales and science fiction novels. For several years, his audience consisted of only one person: Michael's elder son. Then, at the end of 2014 he decided to upload one of his manuscripts to a free online writers resource. Readers liked it and demanded a sequel. Michael uploaded another book, and yet another, his audience growing as did his list. It was his readers who helped Michael hone his writing style. He finally had the breakthrough he deserved when the Moscow-based EKSMO - the biggest publishing house in Europe - offered him a contract for his first and consequent books.

Want to be the first to know about our latest LitRPG, sci fi and fantasy titles from your favorite authors?

Subscribe to our NEW RELEASES newsletter: http://eepurl.com/b7niIL

Thank you for reading *Plotline Tester!*
If you like what you've read, check out other LitRPG
novels published by Magic Dome Books.

Reality Benders LitRPG series by Michael Atamanov:
Countdown
External Threat
Game Changer
Web of Worlds
A Jump into the Unknown
Aces High

The Dark Herbalist LitRPG series by Michael Atamanov:
Video Game Plotline Tester
Stay on the Wing
A Trap for the Potentate
Finding a Body

Perimeter Defense LitRPG series by Michael Atamanov:
Sector Eight
Beyond Death
New Contract
A Game with No Rules

League of Losers LitRPG Series by Michael Atamanov:
A Cat and his Human

The Way of the Shaman LitRPG series by Vasily Mahanenko:
Survival Quest
The Kartoss Gambit
The Secret of the Dark Forest
The Phantom Castle
The Karmadont Chess Set
Shaman's Revenge
Clans War

The Alchemist LitRPG series by Vasily Mahanenko:
City of the Dead
Forest of Desire
Tears of Alron

El Diablo by G.Zotov
(a supernatural thriller)

Mirror World LitRPG series by Alexey Osadchuk:
Project Daily Grind
The Citadel
The Way of the Outcast
The Twilight Obelisk

Underdog LitRPG series by Alexey Osadchuk:
Dungeons of the Crooked Mountains
The Wastes
The Dark Continent
The Otherworld

An NPC's Path LitRPG series by Pavel Kornev:
The Dead Rogue
Kingdom of the Dead
Deadman's Retinue

The Sublime Electricity series by Pavel Kornev:
The Illustrious
The Heartless
The Fallen
The Dormant

Citadel World series by Kir Lukovkin:
The URANUS Code
The Secret of Atlantis

You're in Game!
(LitRPG Stories from Bestselling Authors)

You're in Game-2!
(More LitRPG stories set in your favorite worlds)

The Fairy Code by Kaitlyn Weiss:
Captive of the Shadows
Chosen of the Shadows

More books and series are coming out soon!

In order to have new books of the series translated faster, we need your help and support! Please consider leaving a review or spread the word by recommending *Video Game Plotline Tester* to your friends and posting the link on social media. The more people buy the book, the sooner we'll be able to make new translations available.

Thank you!

Till next time!